"The villains in the book are real, both people and prejudice. Yet despite some pushback, Triss and Everlove manage to face their challenges—some of their own making—with support for one another. A tender read, for sure."

—ELISE SCHILLER, author of the memoir *Even If Your Heart Would Listen* and the novel *Watermark*

"*The Tender Silver Stars* is a delightful story of unlikely friendship, women sticking together to raise each other up, a bad decision based on good intentions, power, and greed, that all come together thanks to a wonderful cast of characters. Set in the deep South in the '70s, the dialogue is spot-on (I'm Louisiana born and bred myself), as is the portrayal of women's struggles to be recognized for their abilities and the racial tension and distrust of the time. Highly recommend."

—DENSIE WEBB, award-winning author of *When Robins Appear*

Early Praise for
THE TENDER
SILVER STARS

"In Pamela Stockwell's *The Tender Silver Stars*, Robin Hood's merry band isn't your typical crew—it's a delightful mix of a would-be lawyer turned thief, a runaway bride, and a meddling senior with a penchant for adventure . . . When Mrs. McCabe meddles her way into their lives, the three slowly, beautifully create a new version of family. This is a heartwarming novel where mystery, the search for justice, and the unbreakable bonds of friendship take center stage. An unputdownable read."

—CARLA DAMRON, award-winning author of *Justice Be Done, The Orchid Tattoo,* and *The Stone Necklace*

"Readers who relish whimsical capers about clumsy rule breakers who impulsively get into trouble will delight in reading how Triss Littlefield wreaks havoc with good intentions."

—MARTA LANE, author and creator of
Trust Your Words

"The well-paced story made me turn the pages long after my bedtime because I wanted to know that the girls were okay. The author makes the reader care deeply, and the characters pull us into their tribe, making room for everyone in the bosom of their humble home and their rich lives."

—MICKI BERTHELOT MORENCY, author of
The Island Sisters

"Such a great second book for Pamela Stockwell . . . She worked old characters with new characters that are now in my heart. She dealt with a very tough subject with strength, tenderness, and insight. This subject is not just relevant to the 1970s, but also now . . . I saw myself in Triss and can understand some of her feelings."

—MARY TRAUTNER, retired federal employee

"If you love Southern charm and relish stories centered around women supporting and uplifting others, this feel-good book is for you. A lovely and endearing read."

—MAGGIE SMITH, author of the award-winning *Truth and Other Lies*

"From page one, Pamela Stockwell had me hooked. The writing is brilliant, but more than that, the characters are beautifully crafted and developed."

—MARINA DELVECCHIO, author of *Unsexed: Memoirs of a Prostitute's Wife* and *Dear Jane*

"Stockwell treats each topic with care, creating a sensitive, warm-hearted novel, with just the right touch of mystery that left me wanting to return to the charm of Magnolia Avenue again and again."

—LAINEY CAMERON, award-winning author and host of The Best of Women's Fiction Podcast

"I loved revisiting the era and setting of a simpler time filled with heartwarming characters you'll cheer for living in a neighborhood that reflects the importance of people and kindness over status and wealth."

—JILL HANNAH ANDERSON, award-winning author of *Closer to Home* and *Crazy Little Town Called Love*

THE TENDER
SILVER STARS

Pamela Stockwell

www.ten16press.com

This book is dedicated to my own *Tender Silver Stars*
—the women who held my hand throughout my journey
to motherhood and beyond: Angela Allenbrand, Vicki Baker,
Diana Bennett, Renay Boyes, Karyn Campbell, Sandy Carey,
Susie Conley, Janice Giles, Susan Knupp, Linda O'Connor,
Brenda K. Rice, Ann Rogers, Randi Rosenkrantz, Helen
Snyder, Ann Tembreull, Mary Trautner, Roslyn Weinstein,
Ashley Versluis, Beth Whipple, and Pam Wohlgemuth.

You have been there every step of the way,
and I love each and every one of you.

Prologue

Triss

In 1957, when Triss was six, she snuck some of her birthday cake up to her brother's room where he had been banished as punishment for a long-forgotten infraction. In the hallway near his door, she tripped and dropped the cake onto the Persian carpet. The rug was woven with rich reds and exuberant blues, but her pink frosting landed squarely on a beige patch, leaving a prominent and permanent reminder of her rule-breaking clumsiness.

When she was nine, she answered the telephone one Saturday afternoon. A girl's voice came through the line, asking for her brother, who was outside at the far side of their yard. Rather than walk out to him in the sticky South Carolina heat, she shouted at him. Their yardman, Theodo, was mowing the lawn, and the humming motor swallowed her words. She started down the steps but spotted a rock under a shrub. She could throw it and get her brother's attention and save herself the trip. Although she couldn't have hit the broadside of a barn on a good day, she watched that rock sail through the air in a perfect arc. She gaped in horror as it rose then descended and collided with her brother's head with astounding accuracy. He crumpled to the ground as a startling amount of blood poured from the wound. He got eight stitches. She got sent to her room for what was left of the summer.

When she was twelve, she witnessed a boy picking on a girl who had a limp. He mocked her and dragged his leg as he walked and called her Cathy the Crip. Triss strolled up to the boy, tapped him on the shoulder as he laughed with his gaggle of friends. He turned, and she punched him. Triss had never hit anyone before, but the angry trajectory of her fist combined with the unknowing turn of his head transformed her wild thrust into a jab that broke his nose. He went to the emergency room, and she went to the principal's office and then home for a week.

After that incident, her mother told her she had never seen someone wreak so much havoc with their good intentions, and she hoped Triss would learn to fix the wrongs in the world without wrecking everything else. Perhaps she might think a little more before she acted.

Apparently, in the intervening eleven years, she had not learned a thing. For here she sat at her kitchen table, staring at a pile of cash she had stolen from her boss. With all the best intentions, of course.

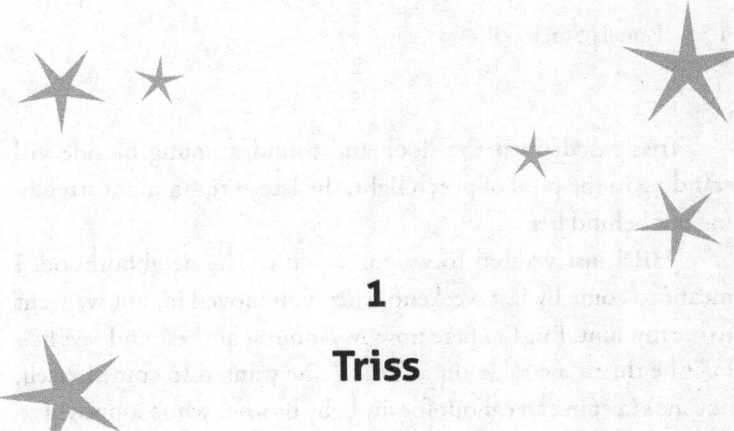

1

Triss

Friday, November 3, 1972

Triss could say she had thought it a good idea to take the money, but it would be more accurate to say she had not thought at all. Like other times when she had gotten into trouble, she had an impulse, she jumped to obey it, and consequently found herself on the wrong side of a bad decision. Like now. Here she was, at her kitchen table, hyperventilating, wondering if Horace Haine had a way of tracing the cash sitting in front of her.

A knock sounded at the door, and Triss jumped so high she momentarily lost contact with her chair. She clutched her chest as if that would slow down her heart's galloping pace. What if it was the police?

She gathered the cash and stuffed it under the kitchen sink, then smoothed her clothes as she walked to the door. After clearing her throat, she called through the door, "Who is it?"

"It's your next-door neighbor, Arabella Fitzgerald." A young girl's clear, fluting voice contrasted with her own tremulous squeak.

Triss eased open the door and found a young blonde girl standing in the pool of porch light, the late autumn night stretching out behind her.

"Hi! I just wanted to welcome you to the neighborhood. I meant to come by last weekend when you moved in, but we went to see my aunt. But I'm here now. My mom sent these and says hello." She thrust a cookie tin at Triss. "She wanted to come herself, but she's keeping an ear out for my baby brother who's supposed to be going to sleep but isn't. She's right over there."

Triss blinked, struggling to switch gears from thinking the police were on her doorstep to instead finding this little girl who talked a mile a minute. She peered around the edge of her door to see a woman standing in her own porch light, turning her blonde hair into a corona. The woman waved and called out, "Hi, there! Welcome to the neighborhood!"

She weakly returned the wave. "That's very kind of you and your mother," she said. "Thanks to both of you."

"You're welcome! I've gotta get back and help. It was good to meet you." She started to turn away, but stopped. "Wait! What was your name?"

"Triss. Triss Littlefield."

"That's a nice name! Hopefully I'll see you soon. Bye!" She jumped down the steps and skipped back to her house.

Triss closed the door and leaned on it, willing her body out of high alert. How on earth had she ended up here, living in a trailer with a stash of stolen money stuffed under her sink, shaking in her socks when little girls came and gave her cookies?

She carried the container to the table as she thought about the path that led her here. Had it started when her parents died when she was fourteen? Would they have been more supportive of her desire to go to law school, unlike her grandfather, who did not think women should work outside the home? Or perhaps when she had argued with her grandfather and taken a job with the one person in town he despised? Or when he had told her that if she was going to defy him so blatantly then she should find somewhere else to live?

She supposed it was all the above.

But what else could she have done? She thought of Mrs. Singleton and Mrs. Doyle, who were both about to be evicted by that greedy old miser Horace Haine. Their problems were far worse than hers. And she was going to help them. She simply had to figure out how.

First, she needed to hide the money. But where? She did an inventory of her house. A closet? The freezer? She had an aunt that stashed her cash in her icebox. Of course, that same aunt talked to her cats like they were people and knitted little sweaters for them. But Triss had just moved in and didn't have enough stuff to conceal the money. Not in a drawer or a cabinet. Not in a closet. She looked at the mobile home's linoleum floor. She didn't even have a board to pry up like they did in movies.

Her stomach rumbled. She would deal with the easier problem of hunger first. She dumped a can of ravioli into a battered saucepan and heated it while she mulled over her situation. Under the mattress seemed too predictable. Buried in her underwear drawer likewise. And she didn't want it staring back at her accusingly every time she opened the drawer.

Triss stopped stirring the pasta. Bury! That's it. She would bury the money under the house.

After gulping down the food, she left the pot to soak and retrieved the cash. She encased it in plastic wrap, then, for good measure, added a layer of aluminum foil. The sheet's metallic rattling echoed in her small kitchen.

She slipped into a jacket before taking a detour out the front door to fetch a flashlight from her car. It was nestled in her trunk, next to a flare, a tire gauge, and a set of jumper cables—all placed there by her grandfather when he gave her the convertible Pontiac for her college graduation. Grandfather was all about preparedness. For once, she was grateful. She shot surreptitious glances at the surrounding trailers. Every window seemed to have a pair of eyes watching her, knowing she was up to no good. She darted back into the shelter of her mobile home, gathered the packet of cash, and headed for the back door, but stopped when she realized she had nothing to dig with. She opened some drawers and found a metal cooking spoon. That should do. After all, she didn't need a very big hole.

Triss stepped gingerly onto the cinder blocks that served as her back steps.

Thinking about spiders and other creepy-crawlies made her hesitate. But it was November— they should be gone, right? She hoped so, for there was no other place. Her backyard was spartan. A slender tree. A clothesline that stretched to where the property ended at a cornfield. And an oil tank that huddled against the back of the trailer as though it was the one needing warmth and not the other way around. That was the spot, she decided. She squared her shoulders, turned on the flashlight, and crawled a little way under the house, slightly behind the oil tank.

A cobweb brushed her cheek, and she turned a loud scream into a quiet yelp. She slapped at her face and shuddered. *Lord, I am paying for my sins now. I promise if you get me out of this, I will behave myself for the rest of my life.* The damp sand was easy to dig. Anxiety made her work quickly, and she soon had a decent hole. She stuffed the foil package into the cavity and shoveled the dirt over it. Just as she was patting the soil down, another light joined hers and a deep voice boomed, "Can I help you?"

She shrieked, jerked her head up, and hit the underside of the trailer. As she tried to back out, her coat sleeve caught on the supports of the oil tank. She was about to clear the mobile home when she remembered she was holding the cooking spoon, so she tossed it under the trailer before she stood. She brushed her hands off and started to smooth her slacks but thought better of it. Though it probably didn't matter. Her knees had to be as dirty as her hands.

"What in the Sam Hill are you doing?" asked a gruff male voice that emanated from a large, hulking shadow.

Triss's brain worked furiously. She should have come up with a cover story for this scenario. Now she improvised.

"Uh, I was fixing a pipe."

The silhouette paused before replying. "You were fixing a pipe?" The voice was less threatening but a lot more doubtful.

"Um, yes. I had a small leak."

The flashlight beam shifted down to the ground. "I don't see any water."

"It was earlier. I was just checking it."

"You live here?" His voice sounded rusty as if he didn't use it much.

"Yes. I moved in a week ago."

"Hmmph. I live across the street. Your next-door neighbor"— he jerked a hand toward the house where the little girl lived— "called me because she saw a flashlight in the backyard."

"Oh! I hope I didn't scare her."

"She was a mite alarmed."

"I'm terribly sorry," Triss said. The man didn't say anything, and she rushed to fill the void. "I'm Triss. Littlefield."

"Maynard Pritchard."

"Nice to meet you. I mean, under the circumstances."

He directed his light toward the spot under the trailer again. "You want me to check that? I'm a handyman by trade."

Triss felt the blood leave her face and was grateful he had trained the beam on the ground. *Please, please don't let him ask any questions about the leak or how I fixed it.* "No, really, it's fine." She wanted to add more about how she tightened the pipe, but she had no idea if that's what one did with pipes. Perhaps the less said, the better.

"All righty then. I'll leave you to it. If you end up needing anything, I'm right across the way. Corner house."

"Thanks, Mr., uh, Pritchard. I appreciate that."

He turned and walked away, and as soon as he rounded the edge of her house, Triss slumped in relief. Once again, she pondered how she got here.

2

Triss
Six Months Earlier

May–September 1972

Triss thanked her lucky stars she was old enough to imbibe a glass of sherry after dinner. She took a healthy gulp and imagined that the warmth spreading through her chest was courage.

Across from her, Grandfather sipped his brandy as he perused the evening paper. She studied him, wondering if now was the right time to ask about continuing her education. Her auburn hair and pale skin came straight from him through her dad. Was it possible for Grandfather to realize their similarities ran deeper than appearances?

"I want to go to law school," she said. The words rushed out, then hung in the air. Her brother, Jay, sat next to her, and out of the corner of her eye, she saw his head turn towards her. But Triss kept her attention trained on Grandfather.

"Absolutely not," Grandfather replied without lifting his gaze.

She plowed on. "But I want more than marriage, tea parties, and charity auctions."

He turned his gaze on her, his blue eyes mild under the shelter of his wild, white eyebrows. He raised one now, a minuscule movement with mammoth power to intimidate. In the courtroom, everyone knew when that one eyebrow shot up, his sharp, oratorical sword was poised to pierce someone's testimony. Panic fluttered just beyond the reach of Triss's sherry.

"There is nothing wrong with any of those," he said.

"No, there's not, but I want to use my brain, expand my horizons, learn new things."

He snapped his newspaper, straightening its sagging middle fold. "The law is no place for a young lady," he said, and turned back to his reading.

"Why not?" she pressed.

He peered over the edge of the paper, his gaze as stony as a statue's. "Patricia, no one is going to hire a female lawyer. A woman may work for a few years, but then she will marry and take care of her husband and home. And the children that come along. It's inevitable."

"You do know there are women who have jobs and a husband?"

"They are generally not well-bred Southern ladies. You should be grateful you do not have to seek employment."

"But I want to work. I want to be challenged."

"Perhaps you can become a teacher or a librarian. Females are too delicate for the exacting and sometimes ugly nature of the law."

"Grandfather, I managed to handle the exacting nature of a college degree with honors."

"You are too tenderhearted for the legal profession. Leave it to your brother to continue the family practice."

Exasperated, she let it go. But over the next few weeks, she brought up the topic, and the only change she noticed was that her grandfather became more adamant and offered up new arguments. What man would ever marry a female lawyer? How would she be able to have and rear children with the long hours a law career required? What would their friends and neighbors think?

She asked him—begged him—to let her try.

"Please, Grandfather! I'll prove to you I can do this."

"It would be a shameful waste of money," he replied.

"Can you at least put in a good word for me to work at a law office as a secretary?" she asked, thinking of a new angle. "Maybe that will get the idea out of my system."

He didn't bother to answer but retreated to his study. Jay, who supported her and sometimes interjected an argument of his own, shrugged.

"Sorry, sis."

So was she. But she was not cowed. *I can do this without him.*

She set aside her application for law school. If he wouldn't pay for it, there was no point in applying. But that didn't mean she couldn't try an alternate path. She took a secretarial course, which still did not please Grandfather, but he didn't object. She learned shorthand and typing over several quick summer courses. Once she earned her certificate, she searched for a job in a law office where she might learn more about the profession.

She thought it an auspicious sign when shortly after she finished her last class, Clayton Durant ran an ad in the paper for a receptionist. He was more a contemporary of her father's than her grandfather's, so she hoped he would be more forward-thinking. She had known him all her life in the way you know people you see at church and social events. He would, of course, think of her as poor Patricia Littlefield, whose parents were killed in that terrible car accident. She usually avoided any mention of her mother, father, or her orphan status, but briefly considered playing that to her advantage before discarding the idea. She dressed in her smartest outfit, marched into the Durant Law Office, and applied. When days passed without a word, she called and asked to speak with him.

"Patricia! How are you?"

"I'm fine, Mr. Durant. I'm checking on my application for the receptionist's job."

Mr. Durant cleared his throat. "Ah, well, it wouldn't be right for me to hire a daughter of the Littlefield family, would it? Your grandfather made it clear you don't need to work."

Triss silently fumed. So the two had talked. She should have known.

She tried a few more places but with the same results. Sometimes she was told the position was filled, or a secretary fended her off, telling her Mr. So-and-So was in a meeting, at lunch, at court, unavailable.

She considered seeking a job in Columbia. Although Grandfather was known all over the state, perhaps she could find someone who might not be so chummy with him.

And then her luck changed.

In early September, she spotted an ad for a secretary with the one person over whom Grandfather had no influence. A man he barely tolerated in public and despised in private. Horace Haine.

She did not know what lay behind the bad blood between Grandfather and Mr. Haine, but she knew Grandfather could not abide him. They inevitably shared space in court and at social events. They were cordial in the way polite people were. But if the two men ended up within a foot of each other, the air frosted around them like rime on a winter window.

The townspeople perceived Haine as a ruthless skinflint. But they also deemed Triss an impetuous troublemaker, and she didn't think she deserved so harsh an assessment. Small towns could be judgmental, and they could shrink you or enlarge you. She was sure that, like hers, his reputation was greatly exaggerated. His appearance certainly contradicted the town's opinion. He was about her grandfather's age—mid to late seventies. His shoulders stooped, his jawline sagged with the weight of his years, his chin receded into his neck, and his blue eyes were weak and watery. He appeared to be a mild-mannered, bland old man worn down by the years.

Her interview went well, and when he offered her the job, she jumped at it. Her grandfather flew off the handle.

"You did *what*?" His words thundered across the room and bounced off the leather-bound books encircling them. He had never before raised his voice to her. She shuddered as a fault line tore through their relationship.

"If you want to remain under my roof, you will quit working for that pettifogger," he said. All her life, Grandfather had been even-keeled. A safe harbor. Even his grief when his only son and daughter-in-law died had been composed and contained. But now, his lips compressed, his eyes hardened, and Triss knew without a doubt he would not be swayed. "And if you choose not to, you may find yourself other accommodations." He hissed the words.

A chill quivered down her spine. This was not the outcome she hoped for. Why couldn't he see she was serious? That her intellect should be put to work?

That night, sleep eluded her. A three-ring circus played out on her bedroom ceiling. Questions in the first ring, what-ifs in the second, and doubts in the third. Should she bow to her grandfather's wishes? Stay true to her own ambitions? What if her parents had not died? Would they have been more supportive? She didn't want to hurt her grandfather. While she had lost her mother and father, he had lost his only son. They only had each other and Jay. The three of them had reknitted their family, and now Triss was unraveling the threads. But why should she give up the one thing she wanted above all else because he was stuck in the last century?

She had wanted to go to law school since she was ten and her dad had taken her to court. He told her to sit quietly, which was not something she excelled at, but her fascination stilled her restless limbs. She loved the stateliness of the courtroom, the structure of the rules and routines, the confidence her father radiated standing before the judge.

She craved it more when, in high school, she was denied a place on the debate team because she was a girl. She had accepted that rejection, and her capitulation shamed her. In an effort to override that experience, she joined the college debate team. And triumphed.

A tide of change was sweeping the world, and she wanted to ride on the crest of it. She could do this. She would do this.

During the next several weeks, Triss grabbed the newspaper as soon as Grandfather left for work and scoured the For Rent ads. She viewed various places: one apartment was so dirty, she didn't want to lean on a wall much less live there; another was cheap and clean but had no furniture. In October, she settled on an affordable, modestly furnished, freshly scrubbed mobile home. It was on a little street with a big name: Magnolia Avenue. Her grandfather would have a conniption fit. A trailer, for goodness' sakes! Her tiny monthly income from her trust fund that would come to her in full when she was twenty-five supplemented her salary. She had thought about biding her time for the next two-and-a-half years but discarded that as a waste of time. Also, she didn't want her grandfather to think she was caving in. She would prove to him she wanted a career in law bad enough to work hard and make sacrifices.

When she told Grandfather, and he wished her luck with a voice so sharp it could cut diamonds, she realized she had held on to the conviction that he would praise her determination and allow her to stay. She informed him she'd move at the end of October when her place (she didn't mention what kind of place) would be ready. The flame of hope flickered out when he turned his back on her and retreated to his study. Triss's mother used to tell her that Triss was like her father: too stubborn for her own good. Apparently, he—and she—had inherited that trait from Grandfather. As Triss dug in her heels, Grandfather dug in his. Georgina, their housekeeper and cook, tiptoed around, wringing her hands, not wanting to see more strife in a family already fractured. Jay tried to lobby on her behalf, but Grandfather didn't listen to him, either. So now she had a job and her own place to live. Her work was mostly menial—filing, typing, answering the telephone—but Triss told herself that by wrapping herself in the language of law she would surely learn some things by osmosis.

The important thing was she was on her way.

3

Triss
Two Months Earlier

September–November 1972

Triss threw herself into being the best secretary this side of the Mississippi. She learned the office routines as well as Mr. Haine's preferences and habits. Unfortunately, she also learned that not only had Haine's reputation not been exaggerated, it may have been underreported. In addition to his law practice, he managed hundreds of rental properties, most of them in the Black sections of town. And he had a penchant for evicting his occupants for the least infraction. Why have rental houses if you didn't want tenants, she wondered. And wasn't there a process? In the interest of learning more about the law, she asked him one day if evictions involved a court hearing or a magistrate. He sat behind his massive mahogany desk, which seemed as weighty and imposing as a small building, and regarded her with a gaze that managed to be both dismissive and steely.

"As an attorney and a landlord, evictions are at my discretion."

His tone ended that line of inquiry but not her churning curiosity.

She got to know the renters who came in, hats in hand either figuratively or quite literally, pleading for another few days to scrape together their rent. Haine seemed to welcome the news that they did not have the money so he could oust them for nonpayment. He would also evict them for failing to maintain their residence or taking in an extra family member or three, and he never showed a scrap of mercy. Of course, he was not the one in the trenches. Instead, Haine was the general, safely back at headquarters—in this case, his office—issuing orders to move the front line forward, no matter what mines or onslaught of enemy fire they—she—encountered.

A handful of the people who came in lived up to Haine's pronouncements that they were lazy liars or shifty spendthrifts. Pete Powell drank his paycheck every Friday but still pleaded for a reprieve. Florrie Kettingham could not resist new clothes, and when she came in begging for more time, she was well-dressed for it.

But most appeared to be honest, sincere, hardworking people whose plights stabbed Triss in the heart. Mrs. Calvin was a widow who barely made ends meet each month. Mrs. Doyle came in with her grandson in tow, a handsome, quiet, big-eyed child she was raising because one parent was an alcoholic and the other dead. Pretty Peach Singleton brought all four of her children and told Triss her husband was out of work with a back injury, and could they please have a couple more days? Triss's new independence had opened her eyes to how hard paying your bills could be. She couldn't afford a phone yet. She ate a lot of canned soup. But she was nowhere close to the desperation of some who came into the office. At first, she pleaded their cases to Haine, but he never wavered.

"You would seriously kick someone named Peach out of their home?" she asked once.

"I kick out—as you so eloquently put it—people who do not pay rent." Mr. Haine slid on his jacket and shot his cuffs. "It's simple. Pay rent; live in my houses. Don't pay rent; find somewhere else. I don't care if their name is Peach or Paul Newman."

"But she's just asking for a few extra days. She has four kids."

"Perhaps she should have thought of the future before she had so many children. And as a footnote, I hired you to file, answer phones, and type. Not to beg on behalf of these freeloading people. If you give these people an inch, they'll take a mile."

He placed his hat on his head and exited the building, leaving her smarting from the sting of his words. This wasn't the first time she had heard people express such stupid, uninformed opinions, so why did it always surprise her?

As the days went by, Triss did not develop thicker skin. In fact, her skin seemed to grow thinner. She found herself worrying about the people at night and toyed with the idea of quitting. She didn't want to, because that would prove her grandfather right, but she didn't think she could take many more tortured people traipsing through her dreams. Or her real life. She didn't want to continue to perpetuate Haine's ruthless removals of poor people who had few resources.

Haine had two other employees, although they didn't work in the office. Sheridan Rudd and Copper Cavanaugh collected rent and handed out eviction notices. She met Sheridan first. With his elaborate cowboy boots, large Stetson hat, and a belt buckle almost as wide as his scrawny waist, he looked like he was from South Dakota rather than South Carolina. He had a pretty face but often wore what her Aunt Amelia called a fish-eating grin. Triss was in college before she discovered another word was normally used in place of fish.

And as for Copper . . . she didn't know if he earned his name because he had the personality of a copperhead snake or because of his dull red hair that bled right into his bright red neck. He had a sneering smile that grated on her. She avoided him as much as possible.

She discovered Copper had an additional job when she came back a little early from lunch one day. Through the open door to Haine's office, she could see Copper standing on one side of Haine's desk and Haine on the other. Between them on the desktop sat a scuffed leather duffel bag. Triss went about her business, stowing her purse and attacking the pile of work.

Soon, Haine emerged from his office and stalked to the file room with his peculiar stooped walk, bag in hand. He returned a few minutes later, still clutching the bag. Within a minute, Copper appeared in the lobby with the duffel and left the building.

All this made Triss a little curious, but she was about to dismiss it when Haine came to his door.

"I hope you remember our conversation about confidentiality," he said to her. "It's imperative that my staff not tell tales outside of the office."

"I do remember, and of course I'll keep everything confidential."

"You should also know there are some business dealings I take care of myself. You needn't concern yourself with that."

She nodded and turned casually back to her typewriter as Haine closed the door.

But Haine might as well have placed a lit match to the wick of Triss's curiosity. She noted that the funny thing about being told there are things that needn't concern you is suddenly they concern you very much. But she pretended she'd forgotten all about it. Whenever Copper came in, Triss kept her eyes on whatever task was at hand, but she watched and listened surreptitiously. If she was typing, her back was to the file room. But if she faced the other part of her L-shaped desk, she could see into it. One day, she was preparing envelopes and letters for Haine's signature and was able to track Haine's trek across the office out of the corner of her eye. She saw him open the safe that was set in the wall. She thought that was odd, because if Copper was giving him rent payments, she kept the ledgers for that.

And thanks to a sticky door latch on Haine's door, she picked up more clues. Copper was bringing in cash for something—cash Haine kept out of the general ledger she maintained for him. She overheard bits like "he was short a hundred" and "he said it was a bad week" from Copper and "tell him the sheriff will be interested to hear that" from Haine. She also caught a couple of names. Weevil (had she heard right?) Carr and Jenny Blazey were the two mentioned most often.

She wondered what was going on. One evening just before she moved out, she knocked on her brother's bedroom door. He was the good grandson who worked in their grandfather's law firm, lived at home to save money, and did what was expected of him. She wanted to resent him, but he was far too agreeable. And also the one responsible for her nickname as "Patricia" proved too complicated for his four-year-old self.

He stood in the doorway now, eyebrows raised.

"If you're here to ask me to talk to Grandfather, you can forget it."

"No, it's not that. I was wondering if you'd heard of Weevil Carr or Jenny Blazey."

His eyebrows shot up further. "Where on earth did you hear those names?" he asked.

"Around." Triss shrugged, trying to act nonchalant.

Jay guffawed. "Carr is a moonshiner. Jenette—not Jenny—Blazey is a madam."

"A madam?"

Jay rolled his eyes. "Sometimes you're so naive. She runs a house of ill repute."

Triss scowled at him. "I know what a madam is. But around here?"

"Yes, around here. Carr also operates a gambling joint in his barn. It looks broken down, but inside it's fixed up a bit. Not the Taj Mahal but nicer than one would think."

Triss narrowed her eyes. "How do you know that?"

"I heard it 'around,'" he said with his cheeky grin. "Who do you know who's talking about them?"

"Just something I overheard," Triss said.

She wouldn't admit it to Jay, but he might be right about her naivete. She had no idea they had a house of ill repute in their little town. Or that a man well-established in polite society would have dealings with it or with a moonshiner. What had she gotten herself into? Was he doing something he shouldn't? What if he was and he got caught? Would she get in trouble, even though she had nothing to do with it?

Between this new knowledge and the parade of petitioning renters, Triss regretted taking the position in Haine's office. She worried the job could derail her life. Not that her life was exactly on the rails. But she was trying, and now she was afraid her current situation might make things worse. A small froth of anger bubbled inside her.

And then the fateful Friday came.

Haine had arrived ahead of her, which was not unusual. When she walked to her desk in front of his door, he called out to her.

"I'm expecting a call from Arthur Benson this morning. Interrupt me when he calls, no matter what I'm doing."

"Yes, sir," Triss said.

Later in the morning, Copper strutted into the office carrying the leather duffel bag. As he walked past her, he swept off his seed cap. "Hi there, purty little lady."

She could not exactly ignore him, so she opted for crisp professionalism. "Hello. Mr. Haine is in his office," she said and fed a sheet of paper into her typewriter platen to indicate she was busy.

Copper moved to Haine's open doorway and knocked on the doorjamb.

"Come in, Copper. How is our friend Mr. Carr today?" Haine asked.

"Friendly as can be." Copper entered the office and closed the door, but the latch did not hold. Triss easily heard a zipper.

"All of it's here?"

"Every red cent," Copper said.

"Wait here."

Haine carried the duffel into the file room. The telephone rang.

"Haine Law Office. How may I help you?" Triss said.

"I have Arthur Benson on the line, calling for Mr. Haine," a female voice drawled.

"Oh, yes. He's expecting him. Please hold."

Triss found herself in a quandary. Haine said he wanted her to alert him when this call came, but did he mean when he was stashing what she was sure was illicit money into his safe? But he had said no matter what. Triss pushed her chair back, rose, and walked to the little room.

"Mr. Benson is on the phone for you, sir."

He turned as he withdrew his hand from the cavity in the wall. "I'll be right there." He closed the thick steel door and carried the now-empty duffel bag back to his office.

He thrust it at Copper. "Well done."

Copper took the bag, gave a little salute to Haine, and placed his cap on his head. He nodded at Triss. "See you later, darling," he said as he rounded the corner heading to the back door. Ten minutes later, Haine came out, carrying his briefcase. "I have lunch and then some meetings. I don't think I'll be back today."

"Yes, sir."

"Be sure to lock up."

"Yes, sir. Here are the letters from earlier."

He set the briefcase on the floor, perused the pages, scrawled his signature on the bottom of each sheet. He then picked up his case and departed without another word.

Triss addressed three envelopes, stuffed the correspondence into them, and laid aside the carbon copies to file. She ate her lunch at her desk and tried to read, but it was the first Friday of the month, so she was interrupted by renters coming in to make their payments. After lunch, the trickle of clients turned into a steady flow. Some brought their rent money. Others pleaded for more time, and she had to tell them Haine never gave extensions, but they did have until the fifth of the month. They left, shoulders slumped, mouths drawn tight with worry.

During a break in visitors, she carried her stack of filing to the file room and placed it on a table. She lifted the first sheet and turned to the line of cabinets, but the sight of the safe door stopped her. It was slightly ajar. She frowned, remembering Mr. Haine when she had interrupted him and how he'd left the room to take the call. He had closed the door, but she had not seen him turn the dial. *I wonder how much money is in there. I could just peek.* She shook her head to clear the thought. She shouldn't. She wouldn't. She opened a drawer, found the appropriate folder, and eased the paper into it. She did that again and again, trying not to look at the safe, but her eyes were drawn to it as if they had been magnetized. *I'll simply look and get it over with. Then I'll close the door and finish my filing.* She walked over to the safe and swung the door open, revealing a few books and stacks and stacks of bills. *Whoa.* There was far more money than she had imagined. She had an irresistible urge to pick up a stack and see what it felt like, but she stopped herself. *Good for you, Triss.* She was cheered by that tiny self-control victory. She nudged the door until it was exactly how she found it. If he didn't come back, she'd close it later.

Haine had provided her a set of office keys, but he had not given her the combination to the safe. But she wouldn't need it. She just needed to spin the dial. But she worried that if he did come back, he would remember he had not locked it, and he would know she had closed it. Would he wonder if she had looked inside? She thought it best if she left it as it was.

A few minutes before five, an elderly woman hobbled in, leaning heavily on a cane. Her carefully styled white hair contrasted with her deeply lined, brown face.

"Mrs. Calvin. How are you today?"

"I'm right as rain, Miss Littlefield. Right as rain."

"I'm pleased to hear that."

"But I'm a little short this month."

Triss's heart compressed. Last month, the old woman had paid the last few dollars she owed in change. It had pained Triss to watch her count it out.

"How short are you?" Triss asked.

"About seven dollars. I'm going to get ahold of that in a day or two." Mrs. Calvin's smile was as optimistic as a sunflower gazing at the sun. Triss sighed.

"Don't worry about it, Mrs. Calvin. Save up for next month." She wrote out a receipt and noted that she had received the full amount.

Mrs. Calvin took the paper Triss proffered and folded it carefully, tucking it into the purse dangling from her free arm. "Thank you, Miss Littlefield. That's so kind. I'll see you next time."

When Mrs. Calvin closed the door behind her, Triss tugged her oversized handbag out of the bottom desk drawer. She plucked some bills from her wallet and added them to Mrs. Calvin's payment. She'd be damned if she would let someone get evicted over a seven-dollar shortfall.

She readied the office for closing: filled out a deposit slip for the cash, tidied her desk, covered her typewriter. She washed the mugs and percolator in the little kitchen, thinking her grandfather would be pleased to see the menial tasks her rebellion had earned her.

She locked the front door and pulled down the blinds, noting the growing dusk. Except for the bank on the corner, the nearby buildings were dark and buttoned up for the weekend. No cars drove down the street, and no pedestrians strolled the sidewalks. Another couple of weeks and she'd be leaving in the dark. She closed Haine's blinds and turned off his lights. She shrugged into her coat, grabbed her handbag, and headed to the back door, stopping by the file room to flick off the light. She stopped, remembering the safe. Should she spin the combination dial or leave it? She decided she would lock it. She walked over to the safe and raised her hand to the dial, but instead of rotating it, she pulled the door open. She looked again at the piles of cash which all but obscured several leather-bound books and a couple of small boxes. She picked up a stack. All twenty-dollar bills, or so it seemed. What if she took some and gave it to people like Mrs. Calvin and Mrs. Singleton?

No. She couldn't do that. She was sure that, like Ebenezer Scrooge, Haine knew down to the penny what was in the safe. But . . . she assumed this was all off the books since they weren't on the ledgers she kept. Did he report it to the IRS? If not, if someone were to break in and find the money, he couldn't report it to the authorities, could he?

She replaced the bills, but before she closed the door, Mrs. Calvin's face appeared before her. The anxiety creasing her features, the relief that washed over them when Triss told her not to worry. She thought of Mrs. Doyle and her too-solemn grandchild. She grabbed a pile of bills. Then another. And another. A definite gap appeared, but there was still plenty left. She hesitated. A thief would take all of it. But she couldn't bring herself to do that. She dropped two stacks on the floor so it would look like a burglary had been interrupted.

She dumped her purse out on the table and stuffed the money in, then piled everything back on top.

She returned to her desk and grabbed a file, holding it upside down. Papers drifted to the floor. She could stop now. Clean this up. Put the cash back. No one would ever know. But the faces entreated her. She emptied another file. Then another. She opened her drawers and rummaged roughly through them, as though looking for things of value. She went to Haine's office and knocked the few files he had on his desk onto the carpet and dug through his drawers and left them open. He had one locked drawer, and she pried at the keyhole with a letter opener until the lock popped— which was surprisingly easy. There were just papers inside, so she left them. She wiped the opener to get rid of prints and dropped it.

Heart hammering, she turned off the last lights and stepped into the unlit back parking lot. Wood smoke and rotted leaves infused the cold air. She locked the door and closed it, then looked around. Near the garbage cans, exactly as she recalled, lay several weather-worn two-by-fours. She picked one up, hefted its damp weight, and decided it was solid enough.

She jammed the board at the door's window and bit back a yelp as the jolt sent shock waves up her arm. The window remained intact. Glass was harder to break than she would've thought. She tried again and almost fell into the door as the wood went right through the pane. The crash and tinkle of the broken fragments echoed in the quiet night, and she froze, listening for a door opening, a car, a halloo from someone, but nothing broke the silence except the wind blowing dried leaves across the pavement.

She knocked out the remaining shards and reached a shaky hand through the empty frame, unlocking the door and opening it. She dropped the wood on the ground.

She slipped into her car and cranked down the window. Despite the chill evening air, sweat poured down her back and dampened her hairline. She started the engine and drove slowly down the block to the bank. She parked and wiped her hands with a tissue as best she could. Her handbag sat accusingly on the seat next to her. She carried it with its new, guilty weight into the bank.

Dismay filled her when she saw that Misti was the only available teller. Misti was her favorite, but she was also the chattiest, and what she needed now was Alice May with her terse, move-it-along attitude. Triss hesitated, but Misti waved her over.

"Miss Littlefield! How are you today?" Misti said. Her infectious dimpled grin that normally cheered Triss made her antsy now.

Triss handed her the deposit. "I'm good," she said.

"Did you dig up this money in your backyard?"

"What?" Triss froze.

"Your hands are dirty. What on earth have you been doing?"

"I, uh, um, there were leaves on my car. On the windshield. I cleaned them off."

"What a mess. Here's a tissue for you."

Misti handed her the small square of paper and rang up the deposit. "Need anything else?"

"No, thanks." Triss tried to smile but wasn't sure she succeeded.

"You have a nice weekend then! Don't do anything I wouldn't do!"

Triss mumbled a goodbye and ducked her head to cover her blush. She was sure she had already done something Misti wouldn't do in a million years.

As she exited the bank, the cold air made her realize how much she had been sweating. She got into her car and tossed her handbag onto the passenger seat as if it were poisonous.

When she got to her trailer, it was all she could do not to sprint from the car to the house. As she climbed her steps, she realized she was hugging her purse like she expected to be mugged in her own front yard.

And that's how she came to be sitting at her kitchen table, contemplating a pile of stolen money and her life choices.

4

Triss

Saturday, November 4, 1972

Triss spent Friday night thinking about her next steps. She felt like one of those cartoon characters with an angel on one shoulder and a devil on the other. The angel said take the money back. She couldn't undo the damage she'd done, but she could leave the cash in a bag in the parking lot or something. Then she wouldn't dig herself deeper into the hole she had created.

But the devil conjured up visions of Mrs. Calvin out on the curb with a battered suitcase next to her and nowhere to go. And what would Mrs. Doyle do? And Peach Singleton with her four children? Or was that the angel creating those images and the devil telling her to turn her back on them? She didn't know which was which.

After her restless night, Triss awoke late. She stretched, looked at the clock, and was surprised it was already eleven. Last evening's escapade flashed into her head, and she moaned. What on earth had possessed her? Whenever she had an impulse to do something, she should do the exact opposite. In this case, that should have been easy. She wasn't a thief. Usually.

She tried to put it out of her head as she dressed. She was going to retrieve more of her belongings from home—from Grandfather's home, she corrected herself. Perhaps if she kept busy, she'd stop thinking so hard, and her brain would work on it subconsciously and hand her a splendid little plan, all wrapped up and tied with a bow.

After a quick breakfast, she tossed her handbag and an empty suitcase into her car and drove to the neighborhood convenience shop which shared a parking lot with a feed store. Before she entered the store, she walked to a pay phone that was bolted to the cinder block wall. She lifted the receiver, fed a dime into the silver slot, and dialed her grandfather's number.

"Miss Patricia!" Georgina's voice came through the line and a pang of longing swept over Triss. Although she had been enjoying her new independence, that didn't mean she didn't miss having someone take care of her, and the person who had done that for the last eight years was Georgina.

"How are you doing? Y'all ready to come to your senses and come back home?"

"I'm afraid not."

"Your granddaddy is lonely."

"He's got Jay."

"Jay's hardly ever home between work and that community center. Your grandfather's been eating alone."

"He wouldn't have to if he was more understanding."

Georgina sighed. "You're both as stubborn as two old mules."

"So I've heard. I want to come by and get more of my clothes. Is he going out today?"

"He has a one o'clock tee time, so he's fixing to leave right now."

"And he'll be gone all afternoon?"

"Yes, indeed."

"Cool! I'll be over in a few."

"Have you had lunch?"

"I had a late breakfast."

"Humph. I bet it wasn't filling or healthy."

"It was cereal."

"I'm making you lunch. How about a BLT?"

"That sounds good, Georgina."

"I'll see you when you get here."

Triss walked into the convenience store. A short man with a round belly and an equally round face was handing a bag to a customer. He reminded Triss of a snowman, one circle on top of another.

"I was wondering if you had some boxes I could have," Triss asked when he finished.

"Sure do. Got 'em in back. I'll go fetch 'em." The man heaved himself off a stool as the customer walked out, setting the little bell attached to the door to tinkling. The man waddled toward the back of the store. As he passed her, she saw his name tag. Earl on one line and Owner on the other. "Are ya moving in or out?" Earl the owner asked.

"In."

"This close to the air base, we always have people coming and going. Lucky for you, no one has picked up boxes in a few days." He disappeared behind a door and reappeared a minute later, bearing four cardboard cartons. "Y'all need more'n this? I got more."

"No, this should do it. Thank you."

"Anytime. Come back if you need more."

"I'll do that."

The bell jingled and four teenage boys came in. Earl's eyes narrowed as he appraised their boisterous entry. She grabbed the boxes and eased around the teens, who had bunched up at the door as if Earl's grim demeanor had thrown up a force field. Triss made her escape and left them to their fate.

She turned into a long circular driveway that hugged an elegantly manicured lawn. Above that rose a white house with black shutters. Six pillars held a roof up over a long porch. A balcony with wrought iron railings ran the length of the upper floor. How odd that one week had turned her childhood home into a place that felt alien to her now. Familiar, yet not.

She headed to the kitchen and found Georgina standing at a high wooden table, slicing tomatoes, and bathed in light from a row of south-facing windows. Her hair was slicked back in a tight bun, her brown skin, as always, glistening from standing over a bubbling pot or hot oven or steaming sink of water.

"Miss Patricia!" Georgina wiped her hands on her apron and hugged Triss as though she hadn't seen her in months instead of a week. Triss breathed in the familiar smell of starch and bacon and cocoa butter and something that was just Georgina. Triss slid onto a stool across the table from the housekeeper.

"Child, it's good to see you! How's the new place?"

"The furniture is dull, but overall it's not bad." She didn't mention the several hideous palmetto bugs that had her running to the nearest store for bug spray.

"You should come and have dinner with your granddaddy one of these days. It would be a nice start in patching things up. And you'd get a home-cooked meal to boot."

She feared eating one of Georgina's dinners might weaken her resolve to stand on her own two feet. Since she didn't have much in the way of culinary skills, she was consuming a lot of macaroni and cheese and sandwiches.

"As soon as he's ready to listen to me," Triss said, but she grinned at Georgina, who just shook her head.

"Like I said, stubborn as two old goats." Georgina placed a plate in front of Triss.

"You said mules earlier."

"You're both more stubborn than mules and goats put together."

Triss bit into the sandwich and almost swooned. This couldn't be that hard to make. Surely she could fry some bacon, slice some tomatoes, tear some lettuce. Couldn't she?

"Where is Jay today?"

"Coaching at the community center."

"He has been spending a lot of time there. Maybe there's a girl involved," Triss said with a grin.

"I don't know about that. He just loves those kids."

"That's true enough. How's Alfred?" Triss asked between bites.

"He's doing all right. Working hard. I'm hoping now that he and Lorraine have settled down, they'll give me some grandbabies."

"I can't believe he's old enough to be married."

"He's the same age as you."

"Exactly. I'm not old enough to be married." But she knew she was. Certainly all her friends were marrying right and left.

"What happened to that boy in college?"

"We still talk. Well, we did when I lived here and had a phone. Plus, he's in his last year of law school, so he's pretty busy." Triss tried not to think how she could be in her first year of law school if her grandfather wasn't so obstinate and old-fashioned.

Georgina asked about some of her local friends, and Triss told her about Merritt's wedding plans, Joan's engagement. It seemed like everyone was on their life path while she was on a terrible detour.

She carried the boxes to her room and began to fill them with things she had missed: a few books, some framed photos, an afghan. She spotted the black bag that contained the Yashica SLR camera Grandfather gave her for high school graduation and grabbed that as well.

Next, she stuffed the empty suitcase with some of her remaining clothes. She inventoried the room to see if there was anything she'd missed. Satisfied, she turned to the last item on her mental list—the reproduction of Van Gogh's *Starry Night Over the Rhône* that she had acquired on a shopping trip with her mother when Triss turned twelve. Triss had been drawn to its serenity. Years later, in a college art history class, she learned that Van Gogh painted it before the mental breakdown that landed him in an asylum. The same breakdown in which he cut off his ear. She felt an odd kinship with him, as she had also experienced tranquility that was soon shattered—in her case, when her parents were killed. Shortly after their car accident, she could hardly bear to look at the glittering stars reflected in the water as she saw her mother superimposed over it, a pentimento of sorts. She almost asked Theodo to take it down, but even her twelve-year-old self recognized that reminders were everywhere, and she could not eradicate them all. And eventually, she didn't want to.

Triss remembered the day they had bought the painting, her mother in her wool suit with pearl buttons marching up her torso in an orderly line, Triss in her green jumper with the hem pulled loose on one side, thread dangling and tickling her scabby leg.

They were transforming Triss's room from childhood playroom to teen haven.

"Pick a painting," her mother had said. "We will use it as a springboard for all the other décor." Triss envisioned herself in her new room, growing up into a future female Atticus Finch. The world blossomed with possibilities.

Once home with the artwork, Theodo hung it on the wall above Triss's bed. Triss and her mother stood back and admired it.

"Only three things are infinite," her mother said, her voice soft as she gazed at the landscape. "The sky in its stars, the sea in its drops of water, and the heart in its tears."

"That's kind of sad," Triss said.

Her mother smiled and kissed the top of Triss's head. "Gustave Flaubert wrote that. May you have more stars than tears in your life."

Just six months later, both her parents were dead, and Triss had far more tears than she thought possible.

When she moved out a week ago, she had left the artwork because she thought the room and painting belonged together. But she had missed it.

Georgina appeared in the doorway. "Need help carrying all this out?" she asked, waving an arm to encompass the suitcase and pile of boxes.

"I wouldn't say no."

Georgina picked up a box and Triss lifted the painting off the wall, and they carried them to Triss's car. After the car was packed, Georgina told her to wait, returning a minute later bearing a foil-covered casserole dish.

"It's my chicken-and-rice casserole," Georgina said.

Triss took the dish and placed it carefully on the passenger seat. She hugged Georgina. Hard. A sudden, desperate yearning to stay swept over her, but she knew the peace she felt with Georgina would not survive contact with her grandfather. She stepped back.

Georgina patted her cheek. "You'll be fine."

Triss cocked her head. "That sounds like a change of tune. A little while ago you were making a case for my coming home."

"I'd love to see you move back, that's for certain. But more than that, I want to see you patch it up with your granddaddy. I know he's the stubbornest old goat of all time, but he is your kin. And it's not his fault times are changing faster than us old folks can keep up with."

"Maybe one of these days."

Georgina pulled her into an embrace. "Now you go on and take care of yourself."

"Thanks, Georgina. You, too."

She started her car and wound around the driveway, glancing back in her rearview mirror at Georgina standing on the steps, waving. She waved back and drove to her trailer.

5

Everlove

Saturday, November 4, 1972

Everlove repressed a flinch as Norma brushed her cheek with one more stroke of blush. Her eyes constantly sought out the white dress hanging in the corner, and, every time, her breath caught in her throat. She told herself the fluttery feeling in her gut was not full-fledged panic but ordinary wedding day butterflies. Every bride felt this way. Right?

Around her a maelstrom whirled. Her bridesmaids—who were also her sisters—flitted about, chattered, and laughed, overseen by her mother, the imperious queen of the Porter clan. Their clamor created a cyclone of sound that made Everlove's temples throb.

"There." Norma stepped back to examine her handiwork. "Pretty good if I do say so myself." Norma was her official bridal beautician. Everlove had wanted to do her own makeup and thought her sisters could do her hair, but they had insisted she hire a professional. Like everything else about her engagement, Everlove had allowed herself to be swept along.

Now she stared at the face in the mirror. Who was the person staring back at her? Was she herself anymore? It was her face, yet it wasn't. Norma now had more claim to it than Everlove did. And then a thought emerged so clear it was like a scarlet banner stretched across a cerulean sky: *That is how I feel about my life.*

"Ladies, I present Everlove! Isn't she something?" Norma said, smiling.

Six heads turned from their own preening and smiled. Well, five of them were preening. Ruby, dear sweet Ruby, was sorting her pebbles, brow furrowed in concentration. But she looked up as well, her wide-spaced eyes focusing on Everlove, and her mouth breaking into her one-thousand-watt grin, tongue peeking through her teeth.

Ruby jumped up and ran to her and hugged her tight. "Evvie! You are so beautiful," she said, her eyes alight with awe. "You look like a princess!" It was hard to believe that people felt sorry for Avenia when Ruby was born, and it was evident things were not right. Ruby had turned out to be a blessing, always full of light and joy.

"She's right, Evvie, you are lovely." Her oldest sister Leola nodded her approval.

"Look at my baby girl," her mother, Avenia, said.

"I feel like Grace Jones," Everlove mumbled.

"Humph. My work is much classier than that," Norma huffed.

"How about an overdressed mannequin at Bennett's Department Store?"

"Oh, honey. Bennett's would never have a mannequin with your skin color," Josephine, another sister, said, and the other sisters laughed.

"You know what I mean," Everlove said.

"It's time to get you into this dress." Leola unzipped the wedding gown and slipped it from the hanger.

Everlove's panic jumped into overdrive. But she allowed Rosie to ease the nylon robe from her shoulders, leaving Everlove exposed in her newly purchased white lingerie. A blue garter, borrowed from Leola, offered a slash of color across her thigh. Leola and Rosie each held a shoulder of the gown, and Everlove had the crazy notion that they were holding up a drunken bride. She bit back a hysterical giggle. She stepped submissively into the dress, and her sisters pulled it up over her hips, past her curving waist, and onto her shoulders. Leola zipped it and clipped the tiny hook at the top. They all stood back and admired her.

"Well, well. Little Everlove is all grown up," her middle sister Jasmine said, beaming.

Everlove regarded the women in the room. Except for Ruby, each was married. Each had experienced the ups and downs of wedding planning and the final flourish of the big day. But had any of them felt sick to their stomach the way she did now?

She closed her eyes but a tug on her arm got her attention. Ruby stared up at her, concerned.

"Are you okay, Evvie?"

She mustered up a thin smile. "I'm fine, Ruby."

"You have a worried face on."

"It's an important day, you know?" She turned to her other sisters. "Can I have a minute alone?" She wanted to rest for a minute without the cheerful cacophony of her sisters' preparations rising around her like a flock of unsettled birds. She thought if she could sit quietly, she might find some serenity.

"Alone? Everlove, it's your wedding day," Avenia said. "We've got to finish getting you ready."

"We still have over thirty minutes," she said. "And except for the veil, I'm ready. I just need a minute. I need . . ." What? She scrambled for something to say that would clear the room for a few blessed moments. "I need to pray," she said.

Avenia studied her with narrowed eyes, but thankfully, she conceded. And her mother didn't concede very often. *The perks of being a bride.*

"All right, Everlove. We'll step out for a minute." Her mother pulled the door open and ushered the sisters and Norma into the hallway. "Come on, girls. There's a room across the hall where we can finish our own beautifying."

She led the way, and the sisters filed out behind her: golden-rod dress followed by rust followed by plum. A cornucopia of fall colors in swishing satin. Jasmine paused and gave Everlove a hug. "Let us know when you're ready."

"Take your time," Josephine said. "But not too much time or you'll miss your own wedding." She left a contrail of laughter in her wake.

Norma was the last out. She pointed a warning finger at Everlove. "Don't mess up my work," she said. But her tone held warmth.

Alone, Everlove turned to the mirror. Far from withering, the panic blossomed. She breathed in. Then out. She closed her eyes and tried to picture herself walking down the aisle, but instead, a vision of her holding up her skirts and running for all she was worth burst into her head. Her eyes popped open. She shook her head to clear the image. She shut her eyes again and forced herself to picture her future with Rodney. Sitting at a kitchen table, twenty years from now. But the handsome figure of the present-day Rodney slid into a Rodney gone soft with middle-age, chewing with his mouth open, wiping greasy fingers on a dirty undershirt.

Where did that come from? Weren't you supposed to look forward to growing older with your husband?

What was wrong with her?

She glanced at the door her attendants had just passed through. *It's only wedding day jitters. In a few minutes, you are going to step through that door with all your bridesmaids and walk down the aisle. Rodney will be standing at the end of it.* His handsome smile, always looking at her so fondly. His little pats on the shoulder. His telling her she wouldn't need to work. Laughing indulgently when she asked, "But what if I want to?"

She spun away from the looming doorway. A tiny whimsical balcony jutted out past a pair of French doors on the opposite side of the room. She drifted toward them and opened them, welcoming the fresh air that cooled her feverish skin. Thick, gnarled wisteria branches climbed up and onto the balcony, twining around the wooden rails. A carpet of November-brown grass unfurled from the base of the vine to a line of trees. To the left lay the graveyard, tombstones large and small dotting the grassy expanse. Including some of her own ancestors.

The crunch of car tires on gravel from the parking lot on the other side of the church echoed through the afternoon. Car doors thunked closed, and voices called to each other, audible but unintelligible. A blue jay landed in a nearby tree, on a branch not twenty feet away from Everlove. It cocked its head at her, and she thought that if she were magic, she would weave a spell and change places with that bird. As if sensing her thoughts, he squawked at her and flew away.

That bird was free, but Everlove was confined, trapped, stuck fast.

Later, she would not remember picking up her handbag. Or walking out onto the tiny balcony. Or swinging her leg over the railing. But she must have done all of that because she found herself clinging to the middle of the wisteria vine, slippered feet balancing on the gnarled branches, her pocketbook dangling from her arm. *What am I doing? I should climb back up.* She put a foot on a higher branch, and a small twig caught the lace overlay of her gown, and the tiny rip decided the matter. Everlove did something she never did—she rebelled. She climbed down the remainder of the way, and when her feet landed on the dead grass, she gathered up her skirts and ran. Away from the church, away from her life, away from everyone telling her what she should do and who she should be. A last fleeting thought of Ruby tugged at her heart, but it was not enough to pull her back.

Everlove darted through the trees and hesitated there, undecided. Now what should she do? How long did she have before they started looking for her? If she tried to walk home, someone would surely find her.

She spotted a car coming down the street and, again, without thinking, ran into the road, waving her arms to stop it.

6

Triss

Saturday, November 4, 1972

Triss steered her Pontiac Bonneville into downtown Edenton, passing Bennett's Department Store, the five-and-dime, the theater. And Haine's law office. Her heart missed a beat when she passed it. She looked for signs of life—or the police—but all was quiet and dark. Her momentary relief did not quell her rush of anxiety.

Seeing the office made her think of the cash under her trailer. What was she going to do with it? She tried to examine her situation logically. "Problem: People need money," she said out loud. "Solution: You have some. Problem: How do I get the money to them? Solution: I could put the cash in envelopes and drop them off anonymously. Problem: Think anyone would notice a white woman sneaking around a Black neighborhood? What if I mail the cash? I would certainly have no problem getting the addresses."

A blur of white hurtled toward her, yanking her back to the present. She screamed and slammed on the brakes. The tires squealed and the car jerked to a stop. A box fell from the back seat to the floor. She realized her hand had shot out and saved the casserole, in the same way her mother used to throw out her arm to hold Triss back. She checked her rearview mirror to make sure someone wasn't about to slam into her, but the road was clear. She turned her attention to the left, and the blur filled the window. On the other side of the glass stood a frantic Black woman in a bridal gown. "What the . . ." Triss said.

The woman made a cranking motion with her hand. Too stunned to think clearly, Triss unrolled the window.

"Can you give me a ride? Please? I'll pay you." The woman glanced over her shoulder and Triss followed her gaze, half hoping someone was running toward them to drag the wayward bride back to her wedding.

"Uh, well, I, uh—" Triss started.

"Please. Just give me a ride. You can let me out anywhere away from here. I need to get away before someone sees me," she pleaded.

Triss's sensible side warred with her impetuous side, which was always an unmatched battle. Practical Triss said this was none of her business. Impulsive Triss wondered why the woman was running away. Maybe her fiancé beat her or something. Once that thought flashed into her head, Triss knew she wasn't leaving this woman on the street. She appeared to be about Triss's age and seemed desperate, but not threatening. "Get in," Triss said.

The woman ran around the car and yanked open the passenger door. Triss managed to lift the casserole before the woman dove inside and sat on it. As Triss clutched the dish, the other woman tried to rein in her voluminous skirt, patting the billowing material into submission.

"Thank you so much!" she said.

Triss held out the container. "Could you hold this?"

The woman eyed it, bewildered.

"It was on the seat where you're sitting. I can't drive while I'm holding it."

"Oh. Yeah. Sure." The woman took the casserole and placed it on her lap.

Triss pressed the accelerator, resisting the urge to floor it. The woman's panic was contagious.

"Where am I going?" Triss asked.

"Oh, Lord. I don't know. I haven't exactly thought this out."

"You don't say," Triss said, dryly.

The woman stared out the window. "I just left my fiancé standing at the altar," she murmured. "In front of all my friends and family." She sank back into the seat as if the gravity of her situation pressed her into it. "Oh, Lord, what have I done?" She abandoned the food on her lap and threw her hands over her face and breathed rapidly.

"Whoa, there," Triss said. "Do you need a paper bag to breathe into? How about I pull over?"

That snapped the woman out of her emotional meltdown. She swiveled her head to peek out the back window as if she expected to see someone chasing them. "No! I'm fine. Really." She swiped at the tears that had squeezed out of her eyes, then gripped the pan again, leaving a smear of mascara on her skirt. Triss noted the bright-white dress already had a small tear and a few green stains.

"All right. But I kind of need to know where I'm going," Triss said.

"Okay. Let me think." The woman turned to Triss. "Can you take me by my house? My suitcases are there. And then maybe you can drop me off at the bus station?"

"Do you have a destination in mind?" Triss wanted to kick herself for asking. *Simply take her where she wants, leave her there, and get back to your own problems, which are plenty big enough without adding someone else's.*

"I don't know, but I'll figure something out."

"Okay. Tell me the way to your house."

As the woman directed her, Triss drove. The church the woman had come from was perched on the edge of downtown Edenton and Willow Creek. The latter had once been a mill village, but once the mill closed, a few Black families had moved in and the white families moved out until not many people remembered that it wasn't always a Black neighborhood. Deep front porches made the compact houses appear bigger than they were. After a turn here and there, the woman pointed at a well-kept yard, and Triss pulled into the driveway behind two other cars.

"Is anyone home?" Triss asked, eyeing the vehicles. She had a vague hope that maybe someone would come and talk sense to her passenger. Would they take her back to the church in her torn gown?

The woman lifted the casserole. "Everyone is at the wedding. Can you hold this?" Triss took it from her. The woman opened the door and gathered her skirts. "I'm just going to grab my suitcases and be right back." A crease appeared between her brows. "You will wait, won't you? I'll pay you for your trouble."

"Look, I'm not a taxicab. You don't have to pay me. And yes, I'll wait. Do you want to change clothes?"

"I'm afraid it will take too long."

She peered up and down the street before stepping out of the car. A few children played in the road several houses down, but they were on the driver's side of the car and not looking in their direction. Triss realized she would probably cause a stir if anyone noticed there was a white woman behind the wheel. Integration had come haltingly and grudgingly to Southern schools but hadn't come at all to neighborhoods and churches. On top of that, a bride in full wedding regalia was slinking up to her house. Might as well have a neon sign on her car saying, "Look at me!" She thought of all the things her school friends said about this section of town. The crime. The loose morals. But all she saw was a neighborhood with rockers on porches and borders of summer flowers going to seed.

Triss turned her attention to her passenger as she clutched her skirts, dipped her head, and ran across the small yard and up the four steps that led to the porch. The scene reminded Triss of soldiers running across battlefields in war movies, crouching down to make smaller targets of themselves. Except this soldier wore a wedding dress.

A minute later, the woman hurried out the door and down the steps, a suitcase in each hand and wearing a plaid coat that clashed with her dress. She used one of the suitcases to push the billowing material of the skirt out of the way. The woman opened the passenger door and nodded her head at the back of the car.

"Is it okay if I throw these back there?" she said, poking her head in.

"Sure," Triss said. She started to add a warning about the painting, but by the time she summoned the words, the woman had tilted the seat forward, stashed the suitcases behind it, and locked the seat back in place. She climbed into the front, slapping the foaming froth of her dress like little fires were breaking out all over it. She reached for the casserole and settled it back on her lap. Triss gently eased a puff of skirt away from the gear shift.

"Now where to?" she asked.

"The bus station, I guess."

The words were weighted with doubt. Triss pictured the woman walking into the station in her current garb. "You can't get on a bus like that."

"I'll change in the restroom."

"And what will you do with the dress?"

"Oh," the woman said, slumping into her seat. "I didn't think of that."

Triss backed the car out of the driveway. As she wove through the little neighborhood, she cleared her throat. "Why don't you come back to my house and at least change?" The bundle of cash flashed into her mind. She was glad she had buried it. What a weekend she was having.

"I couldn't put you out like that," the woman said, and Triss thought she detected both doubt and hope with a large sprinkling of suspicion.

"It's not a big deal. And I promise, I don't bite."

"Are you sure?"

"I haven't bitten anyone since first grade," Triss said with a grin.

"I meant—" the woman started but stopped when she glanced at Triss. "Oh. I seem to have left my sense of humor along with the rest of my life back at the church."

"I can understand that," Triss said. "I guess I should introduce myself. I'm Triss Littlefield."

"I'm Everlove Porter."

"Nice to meet you, Everlove."

"You, too," Everlove said, chewing on her lip.

"So how about it? Shall we go back to my place?"

"I guess I could do that."

"And after that, is there someone you can call? Someone you can stay with?"

"Everybody I know is at the wedding, and about now, I'm sure they're wondering where the heck I got to. And I really can't face them."

"We'll just take one step at a time."

Triss turned onto the highway, and downtown Edenton slid away behind them, along with a bewildered wedding party and a certain miserly old man who, it seemed, did not yet realize his money had been stolen. She pressed the accelerator a little harder.

7

Everlove

Everlove settled into the vinyl car seat and considered the ramifications of her flight. She shuddered at how angry her mother would be. And her heart lurched when she thought of poor, bewildered Rodney. Shame and guilt prodded her with their accusing fingers, but yet . . . she felt lighter, even with the added weight of remorse. Her breath came easier for the first time in months. Maybe years. Maybe her whole life.

As they drove out of town, Everlove stared out at the brown, stubbled fields, the summer growth long gone. Who gets married in late fall anyway, she wondered. The world is dying, turning in on itself, resting before its rejuvenation in the spring. You don't start things in November. You end them. You shelve them. You hibernate. She shouldn't have let Rodney talk her into a November wedding. But she said yes then just as she said yes when he proposed. She had been happy, but she couldn't say she'd been overjoyed. But perhaps people weren't. Perhaps that was in books and movies, and real people got married for more practical reasons. Getting a home, starting a family. The idea of having her own house and not living with her parents had appealed to her. And she liked Rodney. He just didn't make her heart go pitter-patter. But when she thought about the married couples she knew—which was nearly everyone her age and up—she often saw more irritation than adoration. Maybe romance was a myth. In which case, her mistake had been in running away from her wedding, not in agreeing to have one.

She glanced at the white woman next to her. She seemed nice enough. Her auburn hair framed a heart-shaped face with a strong chin that she jutted out as she concentrated on driving. She'd been lucky that she had been picked up by a sympathetic person. Most white people wouldn't have stopped for her at all. And Lord, what if no one had? Everlove quailed at the thought of what her mother would have done had she caught up to her.

"I appreciate you giving me a ride," she said.

Triss jumped as if she had forgotten Everlove was there. "Don't worry about it. I couldn't exactly leave you on the street in your wedding gown."

"You actually could have. But I'm glad you didn't."

"I admit I want to ask what happened."

"Well, if you ask someone and they know, tell me, because I have no idea."

"Seriously?"

"Seriously. One minute I was getting ready to get married, and the next I was climbing out a window."

Triss turned to gawk. "You climbed out a window? Please tell me it was on the first floor."

"Nope. The second. I shimmied down a wisteria vine."

Triss laughed out loud, then clapped a hand over her mouth. "Sorry to laugh, but the image . . ."

Everlove found herself smiling. "Glad no one spotted me. I don't know what I would have done."

"Weren't there people with you? Your mother? Bridesmaids?"

"I asked them all to leave. Told them I needed to pray."

"That was clever."

Triss steered the car into a driveway.

"You live here?" Everlove asked, surprised to see a small, single-wide mobile home that she could tell even in the gathering dusk had seen better days. She had Triss pegged completely wrong, apparently. The girl carried with her an air of prosperity that did not match this humble home. Everlove would bet her car was worth more than the trailer and the lot put together.

"I do." Triss cut the engine. "Home, sweet home."

Triss came around to retrieve the much-handled casserole, and Everlove climbed out, sliding her handbag to the crook of her arm. Everlove pushed the car seat forward and hauled her luggage out of the back.

Triss nodded at the suitcases. "Can I help you with that?"

"I got it. Thank you." Everlove paused. "What about these boxes and stuff?"

"They'll wait," Triss said.

The two women walked up the steps to the small porch, and Triss braced the casserole against her chest as she unlocked her door and held the screen open for Everlove. But with Everlove's voluminous skirt and bulky luggage, she couldn't squeeze by, and they shuffled positions until they both spilled through. Triss flipped on the light.

The living room that lay before Everlove contained no artwork or knickknacks or homey touches—just a nubby, brown sofa, an almost-matching chair, a battered oak coffee table, and a two-tiered maple end table. A gaudy burgundy tasseled lamp sat on the table's top tier. Next to her sat a television on spindly legs that she guessed was at least ten years old. The kitchen lay to her right. Four chairs, without a match among them, clustered around a dinged-up chrome and Formica table. An aqua refrigerator and oven offered up a splash of color along the back wall. The sink sat under a window that presumably commanded a view of the neighbor's yard, but the curtains were drawn tight. To Everlove's left, a narrow, dark hallway led to other rooms.

"It's not much. The furniture came with it and it's all kinds of hideous. But the price was right."

Everlove smiled reassuringly. "It's fine. I'm certainly not one to judge. I still live with my parents and sister."

"There's a spare room you can change in," Triss said. "It's the size of a postage stamp, but I guess it'll do." She placed the dish on the coffee table. Everlove followed her down the small passageway, her suitcases bumping her thighs and the walls. Her skirt filled the hall to overflowing, a tide of pearlescent satin rolling along the brown shag carpet. Triss switched on another light, illuminating a tiny room. A twin bed huddled against one wall while the other held built-in drawers and a closet. Between the two squatted a nightstand and lamp—a tassel-free one, Everlove noted. A pale-green chenille bedspread brightened up the room. Everlove placed her bags on the floor at the foot of the bed.

"Do you need anything?" Triss said. "There are spare towels and washcloths in the bathroom under the sink if you want to wash up."

"No, I'm fine." Everlove peered down at her dress.

"I'll let you change," Triss said and closed the door gently behind her.

Everlove shrugged out of her coat and kicked off her shoes. She sank down on the creaking bed and put her head in her hands and breathed deeply. What was she going to do? She had made a giant mess of her life and all she wanted to do was to have a satisfyingly long cry. But now was not the time and here was not the place. "Buck up, Ev," she told herself. Determined, she stood and reached behind her, contorting her body to unhook and unzip her dress. How different this process would have been had she gone through with the ceremony. Her stomach roiled at the thought, and she pushed it from her mind.

She stepped out of the gown and set it on the floor at the end of the bed, where it stood limply on its own like a slumped old woman, too worn and tired to stand up straight. After a second, the bodice fell over. *Well, doesn't that sum it all up.*

She heaved a suitcase onto the bed and clicked the fasteners open. She dug out a pair of blue slacks and a blue-and-white striped sweater. After she dressed, she sat on the bed, feeling no better.

What was she going to do? For she had not just thrown away one thing in her life. She had burned her whole life to the ground, and she would drag the ashes with her everywhere she went, leaving a blackened trail. *Oh, there's Everlove Porter. She's the bride that left Rodney Phelps at the altar,* people would say. Headshakes and tsks would shadow her for years.

But yet . . . she could not imagine the other path, the one she had abandoned. Could not imagine herself at her reception, happy and laughing like other brides. Going home with Rodney, and all that would have entailed. She closed her eyes. Why had she not acted sooner? Months ago? She winced at the expense of the wedding, at Rodney's humiliation, at her family's embarrassment.

She dug a pair of wedge shoes out of the case and slipped her feet into them. She needed to figure out what to do from here. But when she thought about it, she came up with only one idea. She hoped it would work.

When she emerged from the little room, she found Triss in the kitchen pouring iced tea into two tall glasses.

"How about we sit for a minute," Triss said, indicating a battered chrome chair. Everlove sat, and Triss placed one of the glasses in front of her.

"I've been thinking," Triss said. "It's late; it's dark. Who knows if there are any buses leaving at this hour? So why don't you spend the night?"

Everlove blinked in surprise. "I really couldn't. That would be imposing way too much."

"Not at all. I have a spare bedroom and plenty of food. I'm heating up that casserole you carried all over town. Why don't you have a bite and think it over. You don't have to answer right this minute."

"All right. I'll give it some thought," Everlove said. She realized she was ravenous. She had been so nervous earlier in the day that she had barely eaten. "Can I do anything to help?"

"There's not much to do. I'm going to heat up a can of green beans and set the table and we'll be good to go." Triss turned the crank on the can opener. "Be glad you are here when I have this casserole. Otherwise it would be peanut butter and jelly or something similar. I'm not much of a cook."

Everlove thought about the boxes and artwork in Triss's car. "I'm guessing you moved in recently?" she asked.

Triss laid a setting for two on the Formica tabletop. "Yes. A week ago." Triss pursed her lips. "I had been living with my grandfather and brother."

"Do you like being here alone?" The idea appealed to Everlove, but it also seemed a little frightening.

"Yeah, I do," Triss said. "The first few days, I had a blast going to the secondhand store or Woolworth's and buying things I didn't have. The landlord told me she usually rents this place to GIs, so it has some things here—pots, pans, stuff like that. And I was able to bring a few things with me. But I needed a shower curtain. And a corkscrew." She grinned at Everlove. "You know. The essentials."

Everlove smiled, thinking of her teetotaling parents and straight-as-an-arrow Rodney. None of them would think a corkscrew was a necessity.

"I must confess, though, that at night it's a little creepy. I'll be drifting off to sleep, and I hear a sound and think, 'Oh, that's just my brother or grandfather,' and then I jolt wide awake remembering they aren't here." She leaned closer to Everlove as if divulging state secrets. "I bought a baseball bat."

"I'd be nervous, too," Everlove said, wondering if a baseball bat would be enough protection.

Triss took the casserole out of the oven and placed it on a trivet on the table. "Help yourself," she said, handing Everlove a serving spoon. "I'm glad you're here because I could never eat this whole thing by myself. Our housekeeper must think I'll starve living on my own."

So Everlove's impression of Triss as being well-to-do had not been off base. She had a housekeeper. Or her grandfather did.

They ate in silence for a few minutes, then Triss said, "May I ask you a question?"

"Sure."

"Did you really not have any inkling you were going to fly the coop today?"

Everlove raked the edges of her rice into a tidy pile. "No, I really didn't. I started having this sense of dread a week or so ago, but I blamed it on pre-wedding jitters. I mean, who isn't nervous before their wedding, right? But the closer it got, the more anxious I got."

"What happened? What put you over the edge?"

Everlove pushed a shred of chicken into the mound of rice. "I don't exactly know. I was getting dressed, and I started feeling panicky. I asked to be alone for a minute. I figured I'd collect myself, then I'd be fine. But I went out on this little balcony and there was this—this is going to sound stupid—but there was this bird. And I remember thinking I'd like to trade places and fly away. Then the bird flew away and next thing I know, I am climbing down a wisteria vine." She paused. "I can't imagine what my family must have thought when they finally went back into that room. Lord have mercy. I can't believe I did it." She leaned into the back of her chair. "Rodney's not a bad guy. I thought I loved him. He's handsome. Kind. Works hard. He'd be a good husband and father."

"But?" Triss prompted.

Everlove shook her head. "I feel like he doesn't see me." Her eyes slid away from Triss, from the dinner in front of her, from the little bare-bones kitchen. She hadn't been able to articulate her feelings before, with the chaos of wedding planning swirling around her. But here in the stillness of this little trailer, talking to a stranger, her emotions coalesced into words. "He saw what he wanted to see. A woman who could cook and clean and raise his children, but behind that image, the real me was standing there, waving, 'Hey, I'm here! This is who I really am!' But he couldn't—or wouldn't—hear or see me." Everlove shook herself out of her reverie. "I can't believe I'm telling you all this."

"Sometimes it's easier to talk to someone you don't know rather than those you do."

"I reckon that's true enough. And Rodney aside, there's everybody else always asking, 'Everlove, when are you going to get married? Everlove, when are you going to start a family?' Like I'm forty-three, not twenty-three."

"I hear that stuff all the time. Why do we have to get married on someone else's schedule? Why do we have to get married at all?"

"Apparently that's what we were put on this earth for. At least according to everybody I know."

"Me, too," Triss said. "I don't even have a boyfriend, but friends and family are already asking, 'When are you going to give your grandfather some great-grandchildren he can dote on?' What I want to say—but don't—is that I am not a broodmare."

"So what is it you want to do?" Everlove asked.

Triss wiped a bead of condensation on her glass as if it were a teardrop. "I want to be an attorney. My grandfather is dead set against the idea and won't pay for it. So I took a job as a secretary at a law office, and I'll make my own way. And I moved out of his house. I kind of regret that because that extends my timeline, what with rent and utilities. Not that I had a choice. He offered me an ultimatum. Quit my job and stay with him or keep working and leave. So here I am." She paused. "Does that make him sound terrible? He's not actually. He's just old-fashioned. To borrow your words, I don't think he sees me either."

Everlove nodded.

"So here I am, hiding out in this little neighborhood, which was all I could afford. Hoping my friends will quit trying to fix me up with eligible bachelors."

"Maybe that's why I stayed with Rodney. He was like a decoy. Except somehow, things kept carrying me along."

"I feel a little carried along myself," Triss said.

"What do you mean?" Everlove asked. Triss seemed to know what she wanted and was going after it.

Triss pushed back her chair and carried her plate to the sink. "Oh, you know," she said, but did not elaborate.

Everlove jumped up. "Here, let me. You cooked; I'll wash up."

"I can't let a guest wash my dishes," Triss said.

"I'd be happy to help."

"How about we do it together?" Triss said.

Everlove agreed. As Everlove scraped the food remains into the trash can, she said, "I suppose I should call my family and let them know I'm all right. Can I borrow your phone?"

"I don't have one yet. Maybe we could ask the people next door?"

Everlove felt a flutter of panic at the suggestion. "Uh, I don't think that's such a good idea."

"I'm sure they won't mind."

She hasn't got a clue, Everlove thought. *How do I explain this?* "I assume your neighbors are all white."

Triss shrugged lightly. "I guess." Understanding crossed her face, drawing her eyebrows together. "Oh," she said. "You think they'd have a problem with letting you use their phone because . . ." Triss fidgeted.

"It's okay to say I'm Black. And yeah, I think there's a good chance I would not be as welcome as you would be."

Triss frowned. "Even though it's 1972? The Civil Rights Act was passed almost ten years ago."

And Bloody Sunday was a year after that, and Martin Luther King was assassinated four years after that. And in that same year, three Black boys were killed not too far from here in Orangeburg. Aloud, she said, "Yeah, even though all of that."

Triss frowned. "Crap. I always think we've come further than we have." She stopped, looking at Everlove's raised eyebrows. "And that was a stupid thing to say. How about I shut up and just say there's a pay phone at the One Stop Shop about a half mile from here," Triss said. "Come on. I'll drive you over there."

They finished tidying the kitchen, then shrugged into their coats and stepped into the brisk night air.

When they got to the store, Triss stayed in the car as Everlove trudged to the half booth mounted on the store's wall. She reached out a trembling hand to drop a dime into the coin slot, then took a deep breath and dialed her home number.

Her mother picked up, and, for a moment, Everlove lost her voice. Standing up to her mother always felt like she was jabbing a rattlesnake. But she was not in range of being bitten, so she cleared her throat. "Um, Mama, it's me. Everlove."

"Everlove Porter! Where in the good Lord's name are you?" She heard a crackle of conversation blaze beyond her mother's fierce voice. Her entire family was probably at her house. She knew they had heard her mother say her name and then erupted with a thousand questions. She closed her eyes.

"I'm—" She swallowed. "I'm with a friend." A bit of a stretch, but desperate times and all that. "I'm safe. I'm fine. I just wanted to let you know."

"A friend? All your friends were at the wedding. Well, at what was supposed to be a wedding. What on God's green earth were you thinking?"

Shame and guilt flowed over Everlove. "I'm really sorry, Mama." She thought of how her parents had scrimped and saved for the wedding. She was going to pay them back. Someday. Somehow. She realized she was about to cry. She turned her back to Triss's car, shielding herself from view. She gathered her last shreds of courage. "Really, I am, but I just couldn't go through with it. I have to go. I'll call you soon."

"Everlove!"

Her entire body reacted to the command in her mother's voice. Years of obedience thrummed in her veins and stopped her finger from pressing the hook switch.

"I want you to come back here and come back now. I don't see how we are going to fix this mess, but we'll do something. I don't know if Rodney will still have you, but maybe we can sit down and talk to him and see. But the longer you drag this out—"

"Mama, I—"

"Everlove, I mean it. We don't do things like this."

"Mama, I have to go. I'll call you soon."

Before she could hear her mother's reply or second-guess herself, she pressed the hook switch with a quaking hand and ended the call. Her mother would be furious that on top of everything else, Everlove had hung up on her. She stood a while longer holding the phone to her ear as if she were still talking, swallowing the lump in her throat and allowing the gathered tears to dissipate. If she had burned a bridge earlier, she had now bombed the nearest shore.

She blinked rapidly and brushed away any moisture that escaped her eyes. She thought about her Plan A (aka her only plan), but she didn't have it in her to make another call. And on this one, she would have to explain what she had done. She wondered if Triss had been sincere when she made her offer. Only one way to find out.

"I take it that didn't go so well," Triss said when Everlove opened the door.

"About as well as it could go." Everlove slid into the passenger seat. "They aren't happy with me."

Triss turned to face her. "I'm sorry to hear that. I'm sure it'll pass."

"Maybe." Everlove cleared her throat. "Did you mean it when you said I could stay the night?"

"Of course I meant it. You need a bed, and I have one. Consider that problem solved."

They drove back to Triss's little trailer in silence. When they got out of the car, Everlove ducked her head against a cold, whistling wind that had picked up. As Triss closed the trailer door against the chill, she motioned Everlove to the sofa. "Please, have a seat and relax."

Triss headed to the kitchen, and Everlove leaned her head against the sofa back, imagining her mother seething. The clinking of glasses in front of her was a welcome interruption. She raised her head to see Triss on the other side of the battered coffee table, holding a bottle of wine and two jelly jars.

"I think we could both use a little drink," Triss said. "I'd like something stronger myself, but this is all I have. Care for some?"

Everlove started to say no, as her family did not drink. The church even served grape juice for communion instead of wine. But she had done far worse today than drink a little alcohol. "I don't mind if I do," she said, and the little act of defiance invigorated her. Perhaps she was getting used to rebelling.

"I also don't have proper wine glasses, but oh well," Triss said, pouring generous portions of ruby liquid into the glasses. Everlove wondered what Triss thought her life was like, that she had to make an excuse for using jelly jars for beverages. It almost made her want to laugh.

Triss plunked down on the sofa and put her feet on the coffee table.

"Go ahead and put your feet up. Pretty sure we are not the first, by the look of it."

Everlove paused, then shrugged, then copied Triss. If she could run away from a wedding, hang up on her mother, sit around drinking wine with a white stranger, she could darn well put her feet up on a coffee table. *I am burning it all down today.*

She took a sip of wine and suppressed a shudder at the sharp tang on her tongue, its burning path down her throat. "What a day," Everlove said. "When I woke up this morning, I sure didn't see this coming. Thanks for giving me a ride."

"I still can't believe I picked up a bride in full bridal gear right off the streets of Edenton."

"It wasn't full bridal gear," Everlove said, taking a gulp of wine. It was growing on her. Probably because it was easing the tightness in her chest.

"Begging your pardon?" Triss asked.

"I didn't have my veil or my bouquet."

Triss burst out laughing. "No, I guess you didn't at that."

Everlove surprised herself by laughing along with Triss. And it felt good. Whatever else happened, she felt good at this moment, and that had to mean something.

8

Everlove

Saturday, November 4, and Sunday, November 5, 1972

Everlove sank into the twin bed and pulled the chenille bedspread up to her waist. The wine had relaxed her, easing the knot of anxiety that had become her constant companion.

She pictured Rodney waiting at the altar; guests smiling at a nervous bride who was late, then growing increasingly restless; heads turning and craning, peering at the church doors. Who had discovered she was gone? Her mother? Leola? Who had told Rodney? What did they say to the wedding guests?

She reached for the spiral notebook she had placed on the nightstand and flipped to her last entry. Sometimes she wrote poetry, sometimes an account of her day, sometimes a wish or a prayer. She read what she jotted last night, how she was looking forward to her wedding. Nothing in the passage indicated her level of anxiety. It seemed she had lied even to herself. But now, thoughts tumbled about her head and would give her no peace until she released them. All she could think of at first were two words: "She jumped." But she knew the rest would pour out once she started writing.

> *She jumped from a swamped boat*
> *Into the roiling waters of a storm-tossed ocean*
> *She thought she was saving herself*
> *From drowning*
> *But perhaps she had just needed to bail more*
> *Row harder*
> *Not abandon ship altogether*
>
> *In stinging rain and surging waves*
> *It's hard to see what will save you*
> *And what will take you under*

What had been the right decision? Stay with Rodney and make the best of it? Or act upon her screaming instincts and jump into unknown waters? She closed the notebook, smoothing one of the frayed corners before placing it on the nightstand. She switched off the lamp and waited for sleep, but while it crept close, it kept skittering away as her thoughts banged around her head like the little ball in a pinball game. When she finally slept, she dreamt fitfully of rocking boats and wild bicycle rides and speeding getaway cars.

The next morning, Everlove emerged from groggy sleep and stretched—hitting her arm on a wall that was on the wrong side of the bed. Confused, she opened her eyes, unable to place her surroundings. Yesterday burst into her consciousness—a wave of tumbling visions that took her breath away: her climb out of the second-floor parsonage window, flagging down a stranger, staying with that stranger. A white stranger. Lord have mercy. Her mother, who had no love of white people, would be even further mortified than she already was.

She sat up and swung her legs around, feeling nubby carpet under her feet.

"Did I really do that? Did I leave my fiancé and escape out a window?" she whispered to the room. But there at the end of her bed was proof. A pile of satin and lace, which this morning should have been hanging in a closet, ready to be cleaned and stored for another generation. Perhaps her own daughter. Instead, it sat, discarded in the corner of a stranger's house.

She looked down at her skimpy white nightie that had been meant for her honeymoon. It was a far cry from her usual cotton or flannel sleepwear. What did a single woman need with—she stopped as the words resonated. A single woman. Not someone's wife. Or fiancée. Or girlfriend. *Think about that, Everlove Porter. You are a single woman.* It was an exhilarating and frightening thought.

As she got dressed, she thought about her plan to call her friend Flora to ask if she could stay with her for a while. Flora lived in Georgia and hadn't been able to come to the wedding. And she had been a young, single career woman herself for a while, and in Atlanta, no less, until she had met her husband. Surely she would understand.

The aroma of frying bacon wafted around the edges of her door, and she followed the scent to find Triss at the stove, fork in hand, flipping the slender strips of sizzling meat.

"Good morning," Everlove said, but didn't know what to say after that. She hovered at the edge of the kitchen where the linoleum and carpeting met, joined by a thin seam of metal.

"Good morning!" Triss gave Everlove a bright, welcoming smile, putting her at ease. "Did you sleep well?"

"More or less. Took a while."

"Then you probably need coffee." Triss nodded toward a beat-up-looking percolator that was keeping a mug company on the countertop. "Help yourself."

Everlove poured a cup and spooned sugar into it.

"Milk is in the fridge if you want."

"Black is fine."

"So how are you feeling this morning?" Triss asked.

"Disoriented?" Everlove answered, voice rising as if there was a right or wrong answer.

"I'm not surprised. Do you know what you are going to do?"

"One of my friends lives in Atlanta. I thought maybe I could go stay with her and figure out what to do next. There's no way I can go home right now."

"Would this friend be, um, sympathetic?"

Everlove nodded. "I think she will be. She might not actually approve, although I'm not sure anyone I know would approve of leaving your groom at the altar," she said grimly.

"I approve," Triss said.

"You do?"

"Far better to leave him at the altar than to wake up next to him every day wishing you had."

Everlove regarded her hostess. "You have a point. But maybe I would have been happy. Maybe I just panicked."

"Maybe you did. Maybe you didn't." Triss stabbed a slice of bacon and transferred it to a plate. Everlove resisted the urge to tell her it could have cooked longer. "You have to ask yourself why you were panicking so much that jumping out a window seemed like a better choice," Triss continued. "Would you like some eggs? I'd offer you something else, but that's all I have. Eggs, bacon, and toast."

"All of that sounds good to me."

"Have a seat, and they'll be ready in no time."

Everlove watched as Triss gingerly broke the eggs, then fished bits of shell out of the dish. Everlove looked away, lest she grab the fork and bowl and show her how to break eggs and whip them into a froth. It didn't seem that Triss and kitchens were very well-acquainted.

Minutes later, Triss placed the breakfast on the table. Everlove forced herself to swallow the runny eggs, eat the barely toasted toast, chew on the half-cooked bacon. She smiled and thanked Triss. Her mother would be proud of that at least.

They chatted about their jobs and their families. Everlove told Triss about how she still lived with her parents, about her four older sisters, one younger sister, and one younger brother. She didn't mention that when her youngest sister Ruby had been born, everyone saw right away she was different and advised her parents to place her in an institution and how they had resisted. Triss didn't mention why she had lived with her grandfather and brother. The two women danced around each other, sharing a little, but holding back more.

After they finished eating, Everlove said, "I have another favor to ask."

"Ask away."

"Can you give me one more ride over to the pay phone? Then maybe to the bus stop?"

"Sure, no problem. I'll go get dressed."

Everlove again offered to clean up, and as she filled the basin with water and squirted dishwashing liquid into it, she thought how satisfying doing dishes was. Dirty things go in the sink, clean ones come out. She wished life were as easily dealt with as a dirty kitchen.

She dried her hands and headed to her little room, stuffing her few things into a suitcase, and thought about the strange limbo she was in. Her life had always followed one logical step after the other. But now that she had blown up her life, there was no retreat, and the way ahead was lost in the fog of the unknown.

She shook off her reverie as she made the bed and checked the room. The only thing left was the gown and shoes. The dress would never fit inside her suitcases. She carried her bags into the living room and set them by the door.

Triss came down the hall from her own bedroom, wearing bell-bottom jeans and a striped sweater. "I see you're all ready," she said to Everlove.

"I am. Sort of. I don't know what to do with the wedding dress. Can I leave it here for a few days? I promise I'll send someone to get it when I can."

"Sure. It's not a problem."

"Thanks. I can't exactly cram it into my suitcase, though I thought about it."

"Don't worry about it. I won't even charge it rent." Triss grinned.

Triss carried one of the suitcases to the car. She looked in dismay at the painting and the boxes. "I forgot all about this stuff."

"Does this need to go into your house?"

"Yeah. I've been getting my belongings from my house—my grandfather's, rather—a little at a time." Triss looked sheepish. "I go over when he's not there to avoid yet another argument. Is that cowardly of me?"

"As someone who just ran away to avoid getting married, I might not be the right person to ask. Why don't I help you carry all this in while I'm here?"

They carried in the painting, Triss's suitcase, and the boxes. Triss propped the canvas against the sofa and stacked everything else against the wall.

"Okay. We got me sorted out. Let's get you sorted as well," she said.

When they arrived at the store, Everlove dug out a tiny address book from her purse. Triss removed the key from the ignition. "I'm going to run in and pick up a few things."

Triss went into the building as Everlove walked to the pay phone. She did not have enough change to make a long-distance call, so she would have to call collect. She mentally rehearsed what she was going to say so she could keep the charges down. Not easy to do when you need to explain how you ran away from your wedding. She looked up to the sky and prayed for strength and luck.

9

Triss

Sunday, November 5, 1972

Triss opened the glass door, and the bell hanging above her jingled loudly. Earl was again behind the counter. He smiled and nodded as she entered.

"Morning! You come for more boxes?"

"Not this time. Just picking up a few things."

"Let me know if you need any help."

Triss wandered the aisles of the small shop and picked up a box of cereal, stir-and-serve macaroni and cheese, sandwich bread, a tub of pimento cheese, hot dogs, and buns—things she could fix without too much difficulty. She took her time, allowing Everlove to make her call, but when Earl asked if she was having trouble finding something, she decided it was time to let him ring up her purchases. He made small talk about the weather. Triss offered some noncommittal answers, and finally, when he had bagged everything up, she told him to have a nice day. She stepped outside and found Everlove sitting on the curb.

Triss placed the bag on the sidewalk and sat next to Everlove. "You don't look like someone who just got good news."

"Flora didn't come to my wedding because her baby had measles. Now Flora has measles."

"Oh no! What are you going to do now?"

"Crawl home, I guess."

Triss didn't want to face her grandfather after their argument. How much harder would it be to face your parents if you'd walked out on your wedding? Triss realized how fortunate she was that she had the means to be on her own. And that gave her an idea.

"Why don't you come back to my place?" she said. "You can stay there until you figure out your next step."

"Why are you doing all this? You don't even know me."

Triss shrugged. "You needed help, and I have a good feeling about you." She bumped Everlove's shoulder. "So I have an idea."

The tinkling of the bell interrupted her. She glanced back to see Earl standing in the doorway. His round face had stopped beaming, his mouth had constricted to a hard line, and his eyes had narrowed to malevolent slits. He walked a few steps toward them and waved his hand. "Y'all need to move on out of here. It's bad enough when the teenagers hang around. I don't need her kind keeping my customers away."

Triss gaped at him, unable to reconcile this beady-eyed man with the cheerful one of five minutes ago.

Both women stood.

"How can you say that?" Triss asked. "I just bought stuff from you, and you come out here and yell at me and my friend?"

"I didn't know what kind of friends you keep, did I?"

"You do realize discrimination is illegal, don't you?" Triss shook with anger.

"So's loitering."

Everlove touched Triss's arm. "Come on. There are other stores we can spend our money at," she said.

"That's fine by me," Earl said.

Triss fumed but grabbed her bag and marched to the car. She shoved her purchases into the trunk, then slammed the lid. And for good measure, she slammed her door as she settled herself in her seat.

"God in heaven, that makes me angry." She started the car with a jerk of the key. Earl still stood in front of his door, arms crossed. Triss imagined flooring the accelerator and running him over, flattening him like Wile E. Coyote. "Arrrghh," she growled.

"Better back out before he calls the sheriff," Everlove said.

Triss did, but she gripped the wheel so hard she thought she might break it in two. She stopped at the entrance to the store parking lot. She had wanted to say more to Earl. Much more. But what purpose would it serve? Would Everlove appreciate it or be embarrassed by it? Or would it put her in danger? And as she mulled that over, she realized she had resisted an impulse. Yay for small victories.

Still, Triss seethed all the way home. She wanted to apologize to Everlove. She wanted to find something to say to let her see she wasn't like the store owner. And that she didn't approve of people like him. But the right words didn't come to her, so she stayed quiet. And so did Everlove.

She turned into her driveway and turned off the ignition and decided to move on. Maybe she would find the right thing to say later.

"So back to what I was saying before that bigot interrupted. You staying here last night made me realize I am not overly fond of living by myself, despite what I tell my grandfather. So why don't you move in?"

"But we barely know each other," Everlove said.

"True, but we can give it a trial run for a couple of weeks. No strings attached."

"What about your neighbors?"

Triss shrugged. "What about them?" She thought this was one of her sensible spur-of-the-moment ideas.

"They might not like having a Black person living next door."

"If they say something, my grandfather and brother are both lawyers. I'll sic them on anyone who objects." She didn't want to talk to her grandfather, but if it came to someone talking to Everlove as Earl had, she would do it in a heartbeat.

"It's not that easy," Everlove said.

"You're right, of course." Triss sighed. "Look. I can't guarantee my neighbors won't object. But you're welcome to give it a try. If this doesn't work out, it's okay."

She watched as Everlove considered this. "I feel like I don't have much choice at the moment. So we can give it a try. And of course, I'll pay my own way."

Triss thought about the room Everlove would have and realized she shouldn't have to pay a full half of the rent. "I'm only going to ask for a third of the rent because that room is so tiny."

"I guess we have a deal."

"Cool!" Triss said. "Let's take your suitcases inside, shall we?"

Triss left Everlove to settle in while she tackled the boxes in the living room. She placed a framed photo of her parents on the end table and threw a blue-and-yellow afghan on the chair. She propped the painting on top of the sofa back and stepped away to get a wider view.

"What do you think?" Triss said as Everlove came into the room. "Not that it matches anything."

"It makes the place look kind of fancy."

"I wish! Listen, if you have stuff you want to put in here to make it feel more like home, feel free."

Everlove laughed. "I share a room with my little sister. I don't have much in the way of decorations."

A sudden hammering on the door made both women jump. The image of the foil-covered cash flashed into Triss's head. She had put it out of her mind while dealing with Everlove's predicament. Now her heart pounded at the thought that she had been discovered. She edged over to the front windows and peeked out.

Her heart dropped into her shoes. "Oh crap," she murmured. "Crap, crap, crap." She balled up her fists and jutted out her chin and opened the door.

Sheridan Rudd, Haine's pretty boy employee, stood on the doorstep.

He looked Triss up and down, then peered around her at Everlove. Remembering Earl, Triss narrowed the gap of the door, shielding Everlove from view.

"Howdy, Miss Littlefield. How are you doing?"

"Fine, Sheridan. How are you?"

"Fine as frog's hair. But Mr. Haine, he's about to have a dying duck fit."

Triss swallowed. "Why is that?"

"Someone done broke into the office. He wants you to come talk to the sheriff about if you heard or seen something on Friday."

Okay, that's good news, she thought. *Breathe.* "He wants me to come now?"

"Yeah, 'fraid so. Sorry to interrupt your Sunday." He peered around as if trying to glimpse Everlove, obviously curious.

"Tell him I'll be right over."

"Will do. I'd hurry if I was you." He tipped his hat at her, and she closed the door as he turned away.

"Crap," Triss said again. Although she knew what she had done would be discovered, she still wasn't prepared for the reality. She turned to Everlove. "Guess I'm going to the office. I'll be back when I can."

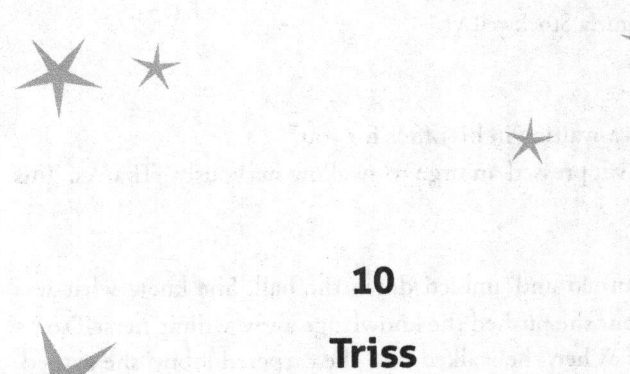

10

Triss

Sunday, November 5, 1972

Triss backed out of her driveway, heart still pounding. She was possibly the stupidest person on the planet. Why in the heck had she stolen that money? Having Everlove around had taken her mind off her own problems, but now here they were, smacking her in the face.

Okay, Triss. Breathe. Just believe you didn't steal the cash. You have no idea what happened. She repeated that all the way into town.

The sight of the sheriff's car in front of Haine's office made her insides turn to ice and transformed her situation from abstraction to actuality. She parked behind the building and tried to gather her wits. She knew nothing about this, she repeated. She was just an innocent employee who left work on Friday with nothing on her mind but the weekend ahead.

The back door was propped open, and as she neared it, broken glass crunched beneath her feet. *You're seeing this for the first time.* She frowned as she stepped through. Sheridan appeared, toothpick sticking out of the corner of his mouth.

"He's a-waiting in his office for you."

Triss suppressed an urge to swallow nervously "Thanks. This is a mess."

"Yep."

He turned and ambled down the hall. She knew what was coming, but she pushed the knowledge away, willing herself to be surprised. When she walked into the carpeted lobby, she gasped. It wasn't hard to sound convincing. The place looked worse in daylight than it had in the Friday night gloom. Her desk sat at one end, a credenza on the other. And in between, papers and file folders were strewn about like autumn leaves. Sheridan delicately stepped around the detritus and plopped onto a chair, leaned his head back against the wall, and crossed his legs out in front of him.

"Oh, my word!" she said. She strode to Haine's door and peered in hesitantly. He sat at his desk. He motioned her in.

"Patricia," Haine drawled. His accent was Southern and white and rich, and images of the Confederate flag, General Lee, and Scarlett O'Hara floated like ghosts on the softened vowels and smothered consonants.

"Sheridan said someone broke in?" She knit her brow, full of innocent concern.

"Indeed, someone did. Sometime between Friday night and this morning. A passerby saw the broken window in the door and called the good sheriff here. He has a few questions for you."

"Sure. Of course," Triss said, struggling to maintain a calm demeanor. Inside, her heart was hammering. *How can it not be audible?* she wondered.

"How y'all doing, Miss Littlefield?" Sheriff Quincy Durant had been leaning against the wall and now straightened. He was tall and broad and had deep lines on each side of his mouth. Triss watched him to see if she caught any glint of suspicion in his eyes.

"I'm fine, thank you," she said.

"And your granddaddy? How's he doing?"

"He's doing well." She knew there was no point in trying to hurry him along. He'd get there eventually. Plus, she needed to maintain the appearance of a polite young lady. Polite and young and, above all, innocent.

"Good to hear." The sheriff cleared his throat. "I understand you were the last one here on Friday night."

"That's right."

"And did you notice anything out of the ordinary when you left?"

She pretended to think for a minute. "No. Everything was like it always is."

"And you locked up as usual?"

"Yes."

"Can you explain what you did?"

"Well, just like I do every time I am the last one here, I turned off my typewriter and covered it. I locked the front door, pulled the shades in the windows. Then I turned off the lights as I closed up each room."

"Okay. Anything else?"

"I checked the kitchen and made sure everything was cleaned up."

"And you locked the back door?"

Triss wanted to roll her eyes. The window was broken, wasn't it? "Yes. And turned off the hall light."

"You didn't see anyone lurking about? A strange car, maybe?"

"No. It was quiet here once the tenants stopped coming by. And even though it was dark when I left, I think I would have noticed. I was taking the deposit to the bank."

His gaze sharpened. "Do you always do that?"

"Yes, I do."

"We may need to get you an escort for the time being."

"Oh my goodness," Triss said, summoning all her acting abilities. "You don't think someone would—" She clapped her hand over her mouth as if the thought were too awful to shape into actual words, then worried she'd gone overboard.

"Now, don't worry, little lady. Most burglars break in at night because they don't want to run into anyone." The sheriff hitched up his khaki pants. "All right. I guess that'll be it."

"Did they take anything?"

Haine answered. "They got into the safe and stole some petty cash."

Triss wanted to snort. Petty cash, her foot. "The safe? Did they crack it open or something? How would they get into that?" She feigned astonishment.

"I don't know." His voice was hard. One of Haine's talents was maintaining the demeanor of a mild-mannered old man. He did not get angry or blush or flush. He might draw his eyebrows together, or purse his lips when perturbed, which made them all but disappear. And he sometimes got a twitch under his right eye when he was frustrated. Triss had never seen all three happen at once. Until now.

"No one knows that combination but me," he continued, the words squeezing out between his vanished lips. He waved a hand at her. "You may go."

Triss rose. "Should I clean up the papers in the reception area?"

"Yes, that would be helpful. Close the door on your way out."

She did as he ordered then studied the mess in front of her. Sheridan still slumped lazily in his chair, watching her through half-closed eyes. She wished he would leave. She had no love for him or Copper. Though of the two, she'd take Sheridan, but that was a low bar.

"Need help?"

"No, thank you." She bent and scooped up the folders first and laid them out on her desk. Then she began picking up papers and sticking them into the appropriate file, putting to rights the mess she had made less than forty-eight hours before. By the time she finished, the sheriff had left with a tip of his hat and—to her immense relief—Haine dispatched Sheridan on some errand. After she slid the last file into her drawer, she paused as she raised her hand to knock on the doorframe of Haine's office, noting that he sat with his chair turned to one side, staring out the window, face set, fingers of one hand drumming on the leather desk pad. She had never seen him simply gaze at nothing. This had rattled him, she thought. But what bothered him more? Was it the violation of his domain or the loss of his money?

He turned as Triss rapped on the wood. "Yes, Patricia?"

"I finished cleaning up out here. Is there anything else I can do?"

"No, that's fine, but I have a question. Have you ever told anyone about the safe in here?"

She learned then that you cannot keep yourself from blanching at will. It either happened or it didn't. She hoped the sunshine from the front windows back-lit her enough that his still-sharp beady eyes couldn't detect the change in her skin color.

"No, sir. I don't know why I would want to." Which was true enough.

He regarded her for a long moment. "Interesting fact about Old Man Haine? Bragging? I have been around long enough to know that people do things for some very strange reasons."

"Honestly, Mr. Haine. I don't think I know anyone who would be interested." This was perhaps the most honest thing she'd said since entering the building this morning. Her friends were largely the children of other affluent Edenton movers and shakers. They were all wealthy enough to not care that Haine stashed away sizable sums of cash in his office. But her heart still hammered as much now as when she had told the bald-faced lies earlier.

He seemed to do a mental inventory of who she probably knew. Then pointed his nonexistent chin at the door. "You may go."

She was used to his royal dismissals and didn't usually appreciate them, but this time, she did. She walked as quickly out of his office as decorum would allow.

Minutes later, Triss stood in front of the meat case in H&L Groceries. Her knees wanted to give out from the released tension. Who knew a life of crime would be so nerve-wracking?

She pushed away those thoughts and perused her food choices. Maybe she could ask Georgina to give her some cooking lessons. She lifted a pack of pork chops. You fried them, right? How hard could that be? She scanned the other meats. She spotted ground beef and remembered a commercial she had seen. "One pound. One pan. One happy family." Best of all, instructions. She added several pounds of ground beef to her cart before going in search of boxes of Hamburger Helper. Next, she added potatoes, canned vegetables, milk, eggs, and soda to her cart. She didn't think she had bought much, but she watched in dismay as the numbers on the cash register ratcheted up. The thought of the money sitting under her trailer flashed into her mind, but she squelched it. She hadn't taken the money to spend on herself. She stiffened her spine and paid. There went the phone line she had been planning to get.

When she got home, Everlove greeted her. "Is everything okay at your office?"

Triss hadn't thought about how she would have to explain the fictional version of events to Everlove. She bit her lip. "Yes, everything is fine. I answered some questions and cleaned up. Whoever broke in left a mess of papers everywhere."

"Was anything missing?"

"Not really." She decided not to mention the so-called petty cash. She was afraid the more she talked about it, the more she might reveal. She placed the grocery bag on the counter. "I went to the grocery store."

"You have any more bags in the car?"

"Yeah, a few."

Everlove nodded. "I'll go get them."

Everlove returned with more sacks. As she began unpacking them, she held up a box of Hamburger Helper. Although she didn't say anything, Triss saw the doubt on her face.

"I told you I wasn't much of a chef," Triss said, a trifle defensively.

"I can help out with the cooking." Everlove pulled out a pack of pork chops. "I can fry these up tonight."

"Sounds good. And speaking of food, have you eaten lunch yet?"

"No, and my stomach is starting to think my throat's been cut."

Triss pulled out the pimento cheese. "How about this?"

"Fine by me."

After lunch, Triss walked into the living room and studied the painting propped against the sofa.

"You want to hang that?" Everlove asked.

"Yes, but . . . I don't have a hammer. Or a nail." Triss sighed and sank down onto the love seat and rested her head against the back. She stared at the ceiling. "I'm really not good at this living-on-my-own thing."

"You seem to be doing okay."

"I had no idea that I couldn't live within my means. Every time I turn around, I need something. Roach spray one day. A can opener the next. And now a hammer."

"You don't have to buy one."

"What do you mean?"

Everlove sat down on the sofa near the painting. "You can just borrow a hammer from someone."

Triss envisioned herself asking her friends Merritt or Joan for a tool and almost smiled. She opened her mouth to tell Everlove she didn't know anyone who could lend her a hammer, but then remembered the man across the street.

"I met one of my neighbors the other day. He said he was a handyman," Triss said, omitting what she had been doing when she encountered him. "I could ask him, I guess."

"There you go," Everlove said.

"Okay. I'll do it. I can do this, right? Living on my own?"

"Of course you can," Everlove said.

Triss stood and straightened her shirt. She grabbed a jacket and slid into it as she stepped out onto her little porch. The sun shone without warmth and a breeze ruffled her hair, making her shiver. Her shoes crunched on the prickly, brown centipede grass as she crossed her yard.

At Mr. Pritchard's front door, she took a deep breath and knocked. A rustle of movement preceded the door opening. The man she had met Friday night stood behind the screen. In the light of day, she could make out his features—hair and beard of a nondescript color, his half-lidded eyes under frowning brows and his unsmiling mouth giving no hint to his age. Triss swallowed at his imposing and hostile demeanor.

"Need help with your plumbing?"

A blush heated Triss's cheeks. "Uh, no, that's all good. But I was wondering if I could borrow a hammer. And a nail."

His frown deepened. "Fixing something else now?"

"Just hanging a picture."

"With a nail?"

"Um, yes?"

"Hang on," he said to Triss, then turned and looked behind him. "Stay." He disappeared from the doorway and left Triss staring at a wiry-haired dog who stood on the linoleum entryway, head down but eyes peering up at her. "Hey, doggy," Triss said, her voice taking on a singsong quality.

The canine wagged its tail tentatively. Mr. Pritchard reappeared with a toolbox in one hand. With the other he reached down with startling tenderness and patted the dog on the head. "I'll be right back," he said to the dog.

Triss started to say something, but he drew his brows into a deeper frown that chased her words away. He pushed open the screen with his free hand, and Triss scrambled down the steps to get out of the way. He stepped past her and began striding toward her trailer.

"Whoa, wait! Where are you going?" she said, breaking into a trot to catch up to him.

"Your house. You apparently don't know how to hang a picture."

Triss thought of Everlove sitting in her house. She thought of Earl. Alarm set her heart pounding. What if Mr. Pritchard was cut from the same cloth? "No, no, it's fine. I don't want you to go to any trouble."

"It's no trouble." Mr. Pritchard did not break stride.

"Um, I, you––" She groped for words that would stop his forward momentum.

"Very well put."

Her face reddened more than it had a minute before, but since she was behind him, Mr. Pritchard didn't see it. They reached her porch, and she rushed in front of him, blocking his way. "Honestly, I can do this myself."

"I'm here. Might as well let me handle it. No charge."

She fumbled for excuses: her house was a mess, her roommate had the plague, she had an attack dog. He wouldn't care about the first, and wouldn't believe the second, and there was no evidence of the third. She wished she had a way to warn Everlove.

"I'm an independent young woman," she finally said, attempting to channel Helen Reddy's famous anthem "I Am Woman."

Her door opened, and Everlove stuck her head out. "Everything okay out here?" she asked.

Mr. Pritchard did not flinch or bat an eye. "I'm here to hang her picture. Apparently, she only knows plumbing."

"What?" Everlove said, frowning.

"Never mind," Triss said hurriedly.

Everlove blinked at the man, then at Triss. "I thought you went to borrow a hammer."

"Looks like I also got the handyman who owns it," Triss said. "He was rather adamant."

"Could be done by now if you'd just let me in."

Triss evaluated the situation. She did not sense a hostile vibe emanating from the man, nor did she see any tension in Everlove. She shrugged her acquiescence.

"Fine."

Everlove stepped back, and Triss followed Mr. Pritchard into the house.

He was a large man, and the trailer was small. He filled the room in a way Everlove and Triss did not, even when they were in it together. He nodded at the painting.

"That it?"

"Yes, I know it's a bit much for this roo––"

"Where do you want it?"

"Pardon?" Triss felt flustered at being cut off.

"Where should I hang it?"

"Oh. Over the sofa?" Her voice rose at the end, turning the statement into a question.

He set his toolbox down and rummaged around, pulling out a piece of hardware. He stood back and stared hard at the wall, holding the painting up. Triss and Everlove watched as he worked. He was brusque and systematic, and his demeanor invited no small talk.

In short order, the picture hung secure and straight on the wall. Triss thought it looked like pearls on a pig, but she still liked it. Mr. Pritchard stashed his tools with the same quiet efficiency he used to get them out. He stood and headed to the door.

"Uh, thanks?" Why was everything coming out a question?

"If you need anything else, I'm right across the street," he answered without turning around. A second later, the screen banged close.

Triss turned to Everlove. "I'm not sure if I feel helped or abused."

Everlove laughed. "That was certainly strange. But he's handy if you don't want someone hanging around until dinner. I have a cousin who comes over to 'fix' things, and next thing you know, he's sitting next to you at the supper table, asking for seconds."

That evening, Everlove made a delicious meal of pork chops, potatoes, and canned green beans. Triss was glad she had invited Everlove to be her roommate before she tasted her cooking, or she would be questioning her own motives.

After dinner, Triss poured some wine and they sat on the sofa, the gaudy lamp adding its glow to the lamplight and starlight in the painting above their heads. She allowed her shoulders to relax. The anxiety still swirled around her, but it was tamped down, held at bay. She felt strangely adult, sitting in her own living room with her new roommate, sipping wine. It was different from the independence she had had at college. There, she had felt like a horse on a long lead. She had a sense of freedom, but she wasn't going too far. Now, no reins or halter restrained her. The freedom was a little scary, but it was also . . . exhilarating. She took another drink and silently saluted her new life. She'd deal with the problems soon enough. Now, she just wanted to enjoy this moment.

"That was a delicious dinner," she said, breaking the silence that had descended. "Thanks for cooking."

"Not a problem," Everlove said.

"Perhaps we can take turns?"

"We could do that. Someone's gotta cook that Hamburger Helper, and it isn't going to be me." Everlove smiled at Triss

"What's wrong with Hamburger Helper?"

"I just think there are tastier meals out there. Next, you'll be heating up TV dinners."

"You missed that by one night," Triss said.

Everlove groaned. "You really eat those?"

"They aren't that bad. Although I do hate when my corn ends up in my chocolate pudding. Did your mother teach you to cook?"

"My mother and my older sisters."

"I have a confession. I don't cook because my grandfather has a housekeeper." She was glad the room was dim because her face flushed thinking how that must sound to Everlove.

"That must be nice."

"I guess it is, but I think I've missed out on some life skills."

Everlove snorted. "Cleaning bathtubs and doing laundry aren't exactly rocket science. I think you can get the hang of them."

"Yeah, I guess you're right about that." Triss took a sip of wine. "Everlove, I'm glad you're here. I don't think I realized how lonely I felt in the evenings."

"I am, too. This has been a strange turn of events, but a good one."

"I agree." Triss clinked her glass with Everlove's. "Here's to us: two strong, independent young women, ready to take on the world."

11

Everlove

Monday morning, November 6, 1972

Everlove stirred sugar into her coffee as Triss made toast. She knew it had only been two nights—and only one since she had accepted Triss's offer—but she felt like she was playing house. It was a bit like wearing someone else's clothes. They might fit, but that didn't mean they didn't feel a little strange.

Speaking of clothes, she needed to go back to her parents' house for more of her belongings. She would go when her parents were at work and leave a note. She mentally listed and then discarded people who could give her a lift. There was no one she was ready to see. She was going to have to ask Triss again, but all she needed was one ride. Her car should be back at her parents' house after her cousin fixed the water pump as a wedding gift. She made another mental note to pay him back for that.

A knock sounded at the door. Triss jumped, and Everlove thought she seemed jittery. Maybe she was afraid it was that cowboy wannabe again. She hadn't seemed very pleased to see him yesterday. Triss blew out a breath and strode to the door.

Everlove watched from the kitchen as Triss opened it, but instead of seeing yesterday's messenger, she caught a glimpse of a petite elderly lady with a nimbus of white hair.

"Good morning!" the woman said, way too cheery for the early hour. "I'm your across-the-street neighbor."

"Oh. Um, hi," Triss said. "Can I help you with something?"

"For one thing, you could let me in. It's too cold for an old woman like me to stand on the porch. I might contract pneumonia." She did not wait for an answer, but instead marched past Triss and into the living room.

"Well, hello," Mrs. McCabe said to Everlove. "So, there are two of you. I thought there was only one."

Triss still stood in the doorway, nonplussed. "Please come in," she said, her voice waffling between bewilderment and sarcasm, though Everlove thought the bewilderment was winning.

"You should probably close the door. Doesn't do any good for me to step inside if you're going to let the wind blow in. Also, you could offer me some coffee or tea. They sure don't teach manners like they used to."

Triss closed the door. "You do speak your mind, don't you?"

"I am eighty-three years old. I don't know how many years I have on this earth, so I don't feel much like wasting them. I'm Agnes McCabe, by the way."

"I'm Triss Littlefield. Would you like some coffee?"

"I would love some!" she said, as if the offer were a delightful surprise and not her own idea.

"Coming right up," Triss said, shooting a bemused look at Everlove.

"And who is this?" Mrs. McCabe asked, peering at Everlove.

"This is my roommate, Everlove Porter."

Mrs. McCabe frowned. *Uh oh. Here it comes,* Everlove thought. *She doesn't approve of whites and Black people living under the same roof.*

"What's with names these days?" Mrs. McCabe said. "Why isn't anyone just called Mary or Betty?"

Everlove blinked.

"My real name is Patricia," Triss said brightly. "Triss is how my brother pronounced my name when I was little, and it stuck."

Everlove didn't volunteer information about her name. It was a long story. But Mrs. McCabe, thankfully, didn't ask. She settled herself in a seat at the table. Triss placed a cup of steaming coffee and the sugar bowl in front of the older woman.

"So, what brings you here so bright and early, Mrs. McCabe?" Triss asked as she got the jug of milk out of the refrigerator.

"I'm just here to welcome you to the neighborhood. I would have come by over the weekend, but every time I thought about it, your car was gone, or it was after five o'clock when I'm settled in for the night."

"Well, here we are. Although I do have to go to work soon."

Mrs. McCabe sipped her drink. "I'll be out of your hair in a minute. This is good coffee, by the way. Hitting the spot."

"Thank you."

"So, what's the story with you two?"

Triss blinked at the sudden change of subject. "Pardon?"

"I mean it's not every day you see a white person and a Black person living together. I don't care, but so many people do. Which is stupid because what does the color of one's skin have to do with anything? Anyhow, I'm curious. I was always a bit of a rebel myself. But only a smidgen. I look back and wish I'd rebelled a little more."

"Well, uh . . ." Triss stammered, trying to think of how to explain.

Everlove briefly considered making up a story. But she didn't want to live a lie. She had been living one her whole life, it seemed. Always doing what people expected whether it was what she wanted or not. Perhaps it was time to conduct her life in a new way. Being honest with others. Being honest with herself. "Triss picked me up on the road," she said, rescuing Triss from her awkward mumbling.

"Were you hitchhiking? That's dangerous! You never know who is going to pick you up. It might have been one of those serial killers you hear about."

"No, nothing like that. I kind of, um, left my fiancé at the altar."

"You didn't!" Surprisingly, it wasn't shock on the older woman's face, but delight.

The bright beam of Mrs. McCabe's appreciation pushed Everlove to tell her more. "I'm afraid I did. I climbed out of a window and ran away."

"And I happened to be driving by," Triss said. "Turned out that while I thought I was helping her, she was actually helping me. I didn't know I needed a friend and roommate until Everlove stayed the night."

"That's some story. Quite exciting."

"Exciting is definitely not the word my family and friends would use," Everlove said.

"No, I guess not. But what a brave woman you are. Not many would have the courage to realize they were making a mistake, and fewer would have the courage to get the heck out of Dodge." She took a long sip. "It's funny, but I met my husband when I was running away."

"You did?" Everlove asked.

"Yes. My mother was trying to marry me off, and I was sick to death of meeting the long parade of men she lined up at one soiree after another. They were either namby-pamby limp biscuits or bossy kings of their own tiny hills. So one day, I snuck out of a party and thought I'd go back home and hide out, and I literally ran into this fellow. I almost knocked him down. Flynn had a bad leg and a cane, and we had to grab each other to make sure he didn't go crashing to the ground. I was a bit of a wild thing back in the day, but not so wild that I went around knocking men with canes over. It turns out he was the nicest man I've ever met. And he adored me, which went a long way to making him even more enchanting."

"You have your own interesting story," Everlove said.

"You live as long as me, you acquire quite a few," Mrs. McCabe said.

Triss looked at the clock and stood. "I would love to continue this coffee klatch, but I have to get to the office."

Mrs. McCabe set her mug down. "Thank you for the coffee." She slowly pushed herself up out of her chair. "And what about you?" she said to Everlove. "Do you have to go to work, too?"

"I am supposed to be on my honeymoon."

"Of course. Silly me. What are you going to do all day?"

"I'm going to walk to the store—" She glanced at Triss. "The other one you mentioned, if you could point me in the right direction. I'll call someone to take me by my house to pick up more of my things. And my car."

"I can drive you," Mrs. McCabe offered.

"I wouldn't want to put you out," Everlove said, not exactly eager to ride in a car with an elderly driver. She thought of her own grandmother, who drove her car as if it wanted to run off the road of its own volition and she had to fight the steering wheel to keep it straight. Everlove always got carsick from all the weaving she did.

"Put me out? It would be an adventure for me." Mrs. McCabe's eyes twinkled. "When shall we leave?"

Everlove met Triss's eyes and saw she was suppressing a grin. Saying no would be stupid. The first store was a half mile away, and, according to Triss, that was the close one. It would be a long-ish walk, but a short drive. And surely the woman could take her that far. "I need to wait until my friend's kids go to school before I can call her."

"Call her? Oh! You thought I was going to drive you to the pay phone? Heck, if you just need a telephone, you can use mine. But wouldn't it be easier if I just take you wherever you need to go? Why bother with a middleman? So, shall we go now?"

Everlove had to admit it made sense—except for her worries about Mrs. McCabe's driving skills. But maybe she would be killed in a fiery crash and she wouldn't have to worry about facing her life anymore. Though she thought slowly drifting into a ditch and getting stuck was a more likely scenario.

"I guess we could."

"Let's get cracking!" Mrs. McCabe made her way to the door. "I'll go fetch my pocketbook and meet you at my car."

Everlove did not see how she could avoid this. And she also didn't see that she had a better option. "Which house is yours?" she asked.

"Across the street. My car is the green Chrysler."

"Okay. Thanks."

Mrs. McCabe shuffled out.

"You think she can drive all right?" Everlove said, peering through the window as the old woman made her way across the road.

"She seems fairly sharp."

"I guess you're right. Wish me luck though. With the drive, with getting my belongings. Pretty much everything."

"I'll wish you luck, but I am sure you'll be fine."

Everlove snorted doubtfully.

12

Mrs. McCabe

Monday, November 6, 1972

Mrs. McCabe settled into her beloved car—a 1950 Imperial that reminded her of better days. As she checked her right mirror, she caught a glimpse of Everlove's tight, anxious face. "You don't have to look so worried," Mrs. McCabe said. "I'm a pretty good driver, if I do say so myself."

"Doesn't everyone say that?" Everlove asked.

"You may have a point there. Where am I going?"

"Willow Mills," Everlove said. "Is that okay with you?"

"Of course it is. But back to my driving. I haven't had a ticket in decades. I used to get them all the time."

"That's not reassuring."

"I got them for speeding."

"Still not reassuring."

"I used to love to drive fast." She caught Everlove's nervous glance at her speedometer. "Used to. Past tense. Police would pull me over, and I would bat my eyes at them. I might have loosened a button on my blouse." She sighed wistfully as she leaned forward to peer through the windshield, both hands gripping the steering wheel. "I always talked my way out of it. And if I didn't right then and there, I could usually talk the judge into letting me off. But time caught up to me. When I got to be about forty-five, I realized I'd gone from beauty queen to old crone." She felt Everlove's eyes on her and turned to see her amused smile and raised eyebrows. "I know it's hard to believe, but I was once quite the bee's knees."

"I believe you."

"You don't look like you do. But I used my good looks until I couldn't. For about twenty years, I had to behave myself. No more speeding. But when I hit sixty-five, I discovered I could work the old lady angle." She glanced at Everlove. "Don't worry. I still don't speed. I guess twenty years broke my bad habit."

They drove into town, and as they passed a trim white church next to a matching parsonage, Everlove suddenly found her lap quite interesting, picking at nonexistent lint. Mrs. McCabe surmised this was the scene of Everlove's crime. Mrs. McCabe smiled to think of it. She had always wanted to flout traditions. Had, in fact, flouted them until she was sixteen when her mother had put her foot down. She had a certain admiration for this young woman. She glanced in the rearview mirror as the church slid behind them, then she turned her attention to the neighborhood in front of them, with its small, nearly identical houses laid out in neat rows.

"Didn't this used to be a mill village?" Mrs. McCabe asked.

"Yes, it was, until a corporation bought the mill in the 1930s. And once they did that, they moved everything to another town."

"Yes, this little burg would have withered up and died if it weren't for the Air Force base. That was before my husband and I retired here."

Somewhere along the line, the neighborhood had changed from an all-white one to an all-Black one. Mrs. McCabe had seen it happen before in other towns. One Black family moved in, and the white ones fled like a pride of lions had taken up residence. If there's one thing she'd learned over her many years, it was that people could be really stupid.

Everlove directed her up one street and down another until they arrived at a small, neat house.

"This is your place?"

"Yes. Well, it's my parents' place."

Mrs. McCabe peered at the house. "Is anyone home?"

"No. My mother and father are working. My younger sister and brother live here, but one's at school and the other is at work." She paused. "Which is a good thing. I'm not ready to face them."

"I'm sure your mother and father would love to have you back."

"I don't know. They're fairly angry. At least my mother is." She stopped. "And I'm not even sure I did the right thing. I mean, one minute I think I did, but the next I think I made a horrible mistake."

Mrs. McCabe smiled at her and patted her hand. "Oh, pish. And as Lao Tsu once said, 'If you don't change direction, you may end up where you are heading.'"

Everlove cocked her head. "Who?"

"Never mind. Just something I learned in China. Do you need any help?"

"Thanks, but I can manage. Thanks for the ride. That's my car right there, so you don't have to stick around." Mrs. McCabe noticed the old Rambler in the driveway. Rust splotched the baby-blue paint. The thing looked as old as she felt.

"I think I'll wait right here just in case," Mrs. McCabe said as she turned off the ignition.

"In case of what?"

"A fast getaway? An alibi? Someone to defend you?"

"I think you've been watching too many movies," Everlove said as she opened the door and climbed out. "I'm sure I'll be fine."

Mrs. McCabe shrugged. "It's not like my calendar is packed with events today." She inspected the surrounding houses as Everlove entered hers. She stepped out of her car gingerly, testing her joints to make sure they all worked. They were not the most reliable things in the world of late. The weak sun was strong enough to chase some of the chill away. And even though November had stolen most of the color from the yards, the neighborhood had—what did young people say these days? A good vibe. Most houses appeared worn but well-loved. A few were falling into disrepair. But then she had allowed her own house to get that way a few years ago. It happened.

She heard a voice behind her.

"You're white."

A little girl on a tricycle had stopped at the edge of the driveway and gaped at her.

"I am indeed," Mrs. McCabe said. "Been that way my whole life."

"I never seen white people on our street before."

"That is their loss because it's a nice street. Don't you think so?"

The girl bobbed her head. She looked to be about four or five. Possibly three. It had been so long since Mrs. McCabe had been around children except Arabella and Baby Allen, she had trouble gauging. But any older and she would have been at school, she guessed. Any younger, she wouldn't be riding a tricycle and talking in complete sentences.

"Sha'ree, don't you go bothering people, now," someone called out. Another unusual name. When she was coming along, she knew five Marys, three Elizabeths, and several Claras. Every other boy had been named John and the others were named William or George. Young people these days were called all sorts of things. At least they wouldn't be getting mixed up with other people who had their names. So perhaps it was a useful thing.

Mrs. McCabe looked over the trunk of her car. "Oh, she's fine," she called to an elderly woman in a faded housedress and cardigan making her way across the yard next door.

"Girl will talk your ears off," the woman said.

"I have a little neighbor like that. Bigger than this one, but that hasn't slowed her down."

"This is my grandbaby, and she takes after her momma. Now you would think because I raised her up, I'd be used to the chatter, but I think I am too darned old for it now." The little girl turned her trike away from them and pedaled for all she was worth. When she reached a barrier invisible to Mrs. McCabe, she executed a masterful U-turn and headed back.

"I hear you," Mrs. McCabe said.

"Are you calling on the Porters?" The woman nodded toward Everlove's house.

Mrs. McCabe didn't know where Everlove stood with everyone, so she gave an evasive answer. "In a manner of speaking. Do you live next door?"

"Yes'm."

"You have a lovely garden," Mrs. McCabe said, admiring the neat borders of flowers now displaying seeds rather than bright petals. At the corners of the house, canna lilies still offered a bright splash of color, as did a cotton rosebush that still had some bedraggled blossoms clinging to it.

The woman considered her house as if seeing it for the first time in a long while. "My flowers keep me moving since I don't clean houses no more. Well, the garden and my grandbabies." As if she had been summoned, the little girl pedaled madly by, making zoom noises as she went. "If I don't move, I stiffen right up."

"I know how that feels."

Everlove came out of the house carrying a suitcase in each hand.

"Evvie, honey, are you okay?"

"Hi, Mrs. Johnson." Everlove's shoulders slumped when she spotted her neighbor. "I'm fine."

The woman frowned at Everlove, but Mrs. McCabe thought her expression held more concern than disapproval.

"Are you moving out?"

"Yes, ma'am. For now, at least. I have a, uh, friend I'm staying with."

"Did you tell your mama? She's been worried about you."

"I've called her, and I left a note just now."

"I know your mama has a powerful temper, but she also loves you. And Ruby is missing you something fierce. You don't have to go moving out."

"This will give all the old busybodies a chance to move on to something else."

Mrs. Johnson chuckled. "And they will. Something'll come along and turn their heads for sure. You talk to Rodney?"

Everlove winced. "No, I haven't."

"You should give him a call and put his mind to rest. He's got to be fretting."

"I know. I shouldn't have stood him up."

"Maybe, maybe not. But what's done is done. You have to finish this by facing him. If you got enough gumption to say no on your wedding day, you should have enough gumption to talk to him."

"I will. I promise," Everlove said.

Sha'ree rocketed by again. *I'd have to take a nap for each lap I made if I were her,* Mrs. McCabe thought.

"I wish that child could give me a spoonful of her energy," Mrs. Johnson said as if she heard Mrs. McCabe's thoughts. "I've got to go stir the beans I got on the stove. Call that young man and get it over with. Waiting will only make it grow bigger."

"Yes, ma'am," Everlove said.

"You take care of yourself, you hear? And it was a pleasure to meet you." Mrs. Johnson nodded to Mrs. McCabe.

"Likewise," Mrs. McCabe said.

Mrs. Johnson walked slowly to her porch and disappeared into her little house, and Mrs. McCabe made her way around the car at about the same pace.

Everlove opened the trunk of her own car and stashed her bags inside.

"I'm going to drive to the Sun Vine and tell them I can work this week," Everlove said.

"I guess my job here is done." Mrs. McCabe hesitated as Everlove opened the passenger-side door and started to slide in. "Um, Everlove?"

"Yes?"

"The steering wheel is on the other side."

"That door doesn't open."

"Ah. Well, I'll see you back in the neighborhood."

"Mrs. McCabe?"

"Yes?"

"Thank you for the ride."

"To tell you the truth, I was hoping for some fireworks, so I'm a little let down." But she smiled as she eased herself into her own car.

When she got back home, Mrs. Fontaine had arrived to do her weekly cleaning. This service had been a gift from Mrs. McCabe's neighbor, Violet, last Christmas. Mrs. McCabe had said thank you to Violet, not wanting Violet to have any reason to tell her things like "more flies with honey" or other nonsense about being polite. She knew how to be polite. She just didn't think it was always necessary. And sometimes not deserved. She wasn't sure then if Violet deserved it or not. Did she think Mrs. McCabe was getting too old to take care of herself? But Violet said it was simply a gift and that it was also a gift to the woman she had hired. Violet explained the woman had a bad leg and had trouble finding work but was a hard worker. One of Violet's co-workers had recommended her and said she was looking to take on more houses. That had inspired Violet to give Mrs. McCabe the gift of housecleaning for a year.

Mrs. McCabe had serious doubts about whether she would like having someone in her house. The first time Mrs. Fontaine arrived, Mrs. McCabe took in her appearance: a woman twenty years younger than she was, with a slender build and thinning salt-and-pepper hair. No hint of a welcoming smile played around her tightly closed mouth. Her most prominent feature was her noticeably shriveled leg peeking out beneath her dress. It was buttressed by a brace, and she used a forearm crutch with one arm, leaving the other free.

Once she showed the woman around—in her small trailer the tour took about sixty seconds—Mrs. McCabe mentioned her doubts to the woman. Not about her abilities, as even to Mrs. McCabe that seemed rude, but about whether Mrs. McCabe needed a cleaning lady at all.

"Isn't your friend paying for me to come do for you?"

"Yes."

"I don't believe I'd be looking a gift horse in the mouth."

"But what if she thinks I'm incompetent?"

"Are you?"

"No."

"I'd sure enough spend my time enjoying having my house cleaned and not worrying about what people think."

This philosophy aligned with Mrs. McCabe's usual outlook, so she decided she liked the woman. She convinced her to sit down after her cleaning was done and have an iced tea with her. And that had become a ritual they stuck to for the last eleven months. At first, their conversations were light—they talked of the weather, of TV shows, of what the world was coming to what with people wearing such crazy colors and patterns. Eventually they talked about more personal things, and Mrs. McCabe learned they had a lot in common—mostly loss. Mrs. Fontaine had been married but was now widowed. She had three children, though one had passed away in childhood. Mrs. McCabe was also a widow, and she had lost both her children. They had been adults, but that didn't mean her pain was any less. After several weeks, Mrs. McCabe asked about Mrs. Fontaine's leg.

"If you don't mind my asking, do you use that crutch because you had polio?" Mrs. Fontaine stiffened, and Mrs. McCabe rushed ahead. "I only ask because my dear Flynn had polio as a young man. Before I met him. Only affected the one leg, thank goodness, but he had to use a cane."

"I had polio when I was seventeen."

"Terrible disease. I'm so glad there's a vaccine now." She paused. "Oh, maybe I shouldn't have said that?"

"No, it's all right. I wouldn't wish this on anybody." Mrs. Fontaine hesitated before offering a tiny upturn of her mouth. "Well, not decent folk anyway."

All in all, she got the gift of a clean house and someone to talk to. Whether she would admit this to Violet remained to be seen.

When she returned home, and Mrs. Fontaine finished her chores, Mrs. McCabe asked her to sit. Although they had been chatting after every cleaning session, Mrs. Fontaine made no assumptions. She never sat until Mrs. McCabe invited her. Mrs. McCabe poured the iced tea and put out a plate of shortbread cookies.

"I have new neighbors," she announced. "Two young women. And one is white and the other is Black. Now did you ever think you would see the day when that would happen?"

Mrs. Fontaine looked skeptical. "Not unless the one was doing the cleaning up for the other."

That made Mrs. McCabe think maybe she should invite Mrs. Fontaine over on a day when she wasn't working, just to show they could be friends. Mrs. McCabe thought they were, but perhaps Mrs. Fontaine saw it differently.

"Triss—she's the white girl—definitely introduced Everlove—she's the Black girl—as her roommate."

"Everlove? Everlove Porter?"

"I believe that is her last name. Do you know her?"

"I do. I know her whole family. So this is where she's ended up."

"She did, indeed. Small world," Mrs. McCabe said.

"Seems to get smaller all the time," Mrs. Fontaine said.

13

Everlove

Monday, November 6, 1972

Everlove scooted across the bench seat of her car a few inches at a time. She wished she could get the driver's-side door fixed, but her bank account was never where she needed it to be. She turned the ignition, and the car sputtered to life. She watched Mrs. McCabe's car cruise off and smiled. She could barely see Mrs. McCabe's head above the steering wheel, but Everlove had to admit she was a better driver than she had expected.

She checked for Sha'ree's whereabouts and spotted the little girl a couple of houses away, legs pumping so fast they blurred. Everlove reversed and drove cautiously, and when she reached Sha'ree, the girl took one hand off her handlebars and waved without slowing. Everlove gave her a thumbs-up. Everlove wished she had half of Sha'ree's focus and confidence. As she drove west, skirting the edge of town, she shook her head. *I'm comparing myself to a four-year-old. And coming up short. Lord have mercy.*

She arrived at Sun Vine, the recently opened supermarket that anchored a strip mall outside of Edenton. The supermarket rose from what had once been a cornfield, and the line of pines that had served as a windbreak now stood as a backdrop to the new, gleaming store. Glittering glass windows overlooked a parking lot dotted by sapling crepe myrtles. Across the road stood the wealthy white neighborhood of Cypress Woods with its gracefully curved brick gateway. On the other side of the store, loading docks led to dark, gaping maws that stared blankly at the poor Black homes of Cumbee Creek. Streams of rumbling, exhaust-belching semi-trucks lumbered past the dispirited old community, oblivious to the torn screens, peeling paint, and sagging porches. Dry rot, termites, mold, vines—whatever could attack a house did so in Cumbee Creek with abandon as if the elements knew the residents were too tired to stand against them.

Everlove had come here from old, musty Grant's Food Store in Willow Mills with its warped floorboards and squeaking door. She enjoyed the cleanliness of her new environs. Cans and boxed goods marched across the shelves in spotless, orderly rows, no dust or rust to be seen. Produce glistened, plump and ripe. She swore none of it dared wilt in this rarefied atmosphere. And the supermarket was climate-controlled. Warm in the winter and so cold in the summer she sometimes welcomed going out in the scorching heat after her shift. What a change from Grant's with its single fan fighting a losing battle with the breathless swelter.

Everlove turned off her car and slid out the passenger-side door. Now that she didn't have a wedding to plan or a husband to take care of, maybe she could take extra shifts and earn enough money to fix the darn door. She could manage the winter, but she did not want to spend another summer sliding over the hot plastic of the seat, searing her thighs and running her pantyhose. Why had skirt hemlines decided now was the time to creep all the way up one's legs?

The store shone under dazzling fluorescent lights. Everlove craned her neck until she spotted Mr. Chesley's crew cut and black-framed glasses at the customer service counter. He wore his usual white short-sleeved shirt, its chest pocket filled with pens. She headed toward him but hung back as he soothed a patron and issued a refund for some not-as-crisp-as-it-should-be lettuce. Everlove imagined what would happen if she raised a ruckus at Grant's over limp greens. She almost laughed, because unless a farm truck had come in that morning, they were pretty much always limp. But the remedy for that was to pour hot fatback grease over it and make a wilted lettuce salad.

When Mr. Chesley spotted her, his eyes widened. A few other employees were friends and neighbors of Everlove's, but she gathered they had not enlightened him about her . . . weekend.

"Everlove. Aren't you supposed to be on your honeymoon?"

"I had a slight change of plans."

Mr. Chesley had lines across his forehead that always made him appear on the verge of a question. The lines deepened. "You did?"

"Uh, we called it off," she said, then rushed forward to fend off any other questions. "So since I'm not going on a honeymoon, I'm available to work if you have any shifts that need covering. And I'd welcome as many as I can get."

"Let me get the schedule." He disappeared into the office behind the customer service desk and returned carrying a clipboard. He studied the sheet on top and then flipped it back to see the one under it. "Yes, I do have two open shifts. One tomorrow evening and one Thursday morning. And I can also put you on Saturday morning."

"Thank you, Mr. Chesley. Also, I'm not living at my parents' house. I don't have a phone right now, but I can call every morning and see if you need someone."

He looked at her skeptically over his glasses. "You can call by 8:00 a.m.? I might need someone here for the morning shoppers."

"Yes, I can. There's a pay phone not too far away. It won't be a problem." She meant to make herself invaluable. She now needed money for rent, utilities, food. Car upkeep and repairs. "I can also stock. Mop. Whatever you need."

"I'll keep that in mind."

Before she left, she bought some groceries to contribute her part to the household. After she shopped, she climbed into her car and sat for a long moment, hands on the steering wheel, staring but not seeing the parking lot, the store, the people coming and going. She pondered once again whether she had done the right thing. Buried deep inside her, so far down and under so many layers of daily life that she barely could see it, was the hope of one day getting a college degree. The dream had never been close enough for her to grasp—or even touch—but making her own way would push it further away. Any money she made would have to go to living expenses, and not to savings. *But face it, Ev. Would you be able to go to classes as Mrs. Rodney Phelps?* She'd graduated from high school four years ago and hadn't managed to take a single college class. When she brought it up to her mother, Avenia had told her they needed her to contribute to the household, watch Ruby, help with chores. And why did she want to take college courses anyway? A high school diploma was good enough and better than what her parents had achieved. She should be happy with that. It was different for Franklin, her mother said when he started classes at Orangeburg State University. He was expected to be the breadwinner. Thus he became the first college student in the Porter family, while Everlove rang up bloody packages of ground beef and stocked endless cans of soup on metal shelves.

How had running away made her life any better? She was relieved at not being married, but she couldn't say she was happy now. But what about a year from now? She certainly would have been more economically stable with her income combined with Rodney's. Alternate-future Everlove might even be pregnant. The daydream frosted over, froze, cracked. The thought of being a wife and mother made her feel trapped. She knew her family would chide her for having her head in the clouds. But what was wrong with wanting something more? Or maybe not more, just *else*?

If only she had the vaguest idea what the something else might be and how she could achieve it. She realized that running away from what you didn't want did not put you on a path toward what you did want if you had no clue what that was. It merely left you spinning your wheels.

Or sitting in a grocery store parking lot, mulling over your life. She started her car and headed to Triss's house.

That evening, Everlove stood at the stove, stirring a pot of lima beans, when Triss came home. She thought it ironic that she had fled the idea of cooking for Rodney but here she was making dinner for someone else coming home from work. But somehow, she didn't mind. No one was *expecting* her to do this.

Triss closed the door against the already dark evening and dropped her purse on a nearby table. "It smells delicious in here!" she said as she shrugged out of her coat and hung it in the closet.

"Don't get too excited. It's just meatloaf, lima beans, and biscuits."

"Sounds good to me."

"It'll be ready in a few minutes."

"Anything I can do to help?"

"Nope, I got this."

"I see you survived your trip with Mrs. McCabe."

Everlove grinned. "She's actually not a bad driver."

"Really?" Triss said, eyebrows raised.

"Really. I'm as surprised as you are."

"No trouble at your house?"

"No one was home, thank goodness. And I went by work and picked up a few shifts for this week." She peeked into the oven. "I need to go see Rodney, although I am dreading it." Her stomach churned at the thought. "I wish I'd handled this better. Like broken it off with him about six months ago."

Triss nodded. "Well, as my grandfather in his infinite wisdom says, 'What's done is done.'"

Everlove shot her a quizzical look. "That's about as helpful as soap on a pig."

Triss burst out laughing. "My grandfather is very good at cross-examining, but not so good at comforting."

"If you don't mind my asking, what happened to your parents? You don't have to talk about it if you don't want to, though."

"They were killed in a car accident when I was twelve." Triss said it lightly, but her eyes slipped away from Everlove's.

Everlove's heart contracted. She would never have guessed that this seemingly carefree girl with her sparkling brown eyes and easy smile had suffered such a tragedy.

"Now I feel bad, complaining about living with mine."

"When you're in your twenties, you're supposed to want to leave the nest." Triss paused. "I just think it's grossly unfair that we women are expected to jump from one nest into another."

Everlove placed the meatloaf pan on a cloth on the table. "Fair or unfair, dinner is ready in our little nest."

As they dished out the food, Triss pursed her lips. "I feel bad that you're cooking for me. Kind of ironic that you ran away from marriage, but here you are, making meals for someone after all."

"I had the same thought. But we still have to eat and shop and clean. I'm just doing it on my own terms now." As Everlove said the words, the truth of them washed over her. That was it, wasn't it? She was living on her own terms. And if the future was a bit foggy, well, she would make her way through the haze. She had taken the reins of her life, even if she had driven it off the road first. But she had done it. A little glow grew in her chest, a tiny, warm flame she hoped would grow.

14
Triss

Triss was surprised at how quickly she and Everlove fell into a routine. Everlove made dinner every night except Tuesday when she had an evening shift. Triss cleaned up the kitchen afterwards and successfully made Hamburger Helper the night Everlove worked. She had to admit Everlove's meals were tastier than the boxed meal she made.

During her first few days at work that week, Triss startled at every sudden and not-so-sudden sound. When she delivered some letters to Haine's office and he shut a drawer a little loudly, she jumped, and Haine noticed. "Are you all right, Patricia?"

"I'm fine, Mr. Haine." She cast about for a reasonable explanation. "But knowing someone broke in here . . . makes me nervous."

"I am sure we will not have a repeat of that. I've added that deadbolt to the back door, fixed the window, and the sheriff is increasing patrols in the area."

"That's good to hear."

"Copper is also looking into it. And when he finds the culprit . . . well, let's just say he will make it clear we will not put up with someone violating my property. Now if you would bring me the Wilson file."

She swallowed hard at his words and mumbled a "Yes, sir." But there was some good news in what he said: he did not appear to suspect her at all. He seemed confident, though, that Copper would find the person responsible. But then he always sounded confident. And why shouldn't he? He moved through the world as if he owned it. Had anyone ever gotten away with committing some offense against him, however slight? Did she stand a chance against him?

As much as that question nagged at her, business carried on as usual and she did not sense the bright beam of suspicion turned on her. As Sheriff Durant had promised, deputies drove by and sometimes parked and watched. She began to relax. Until Thursday.

On her drive home from work, she stopped at an intersection, and the headlights of a turning vehicle swept over her car and the pickup behind her. She caught a glimpse of flashy red paint. As she accelerated, the truck stayed uncomfortably close to her. *What a jerk*. It took the same turn she did. Then the next one. She wondered if it was following her, but quickly dismissed the thought as ridiculous. It was probably a GI heading back to the base. The idea became harder to shake when she turned onto Air Force Highway and it stayed right behind her, even though the road widened to four lanes and it could easily have passed her. She kept her speed slightly below the limit as they left the town behind, hoping the truck would pass her and go on his merry way. But it didn't. She began to get annoyed, and she slowed down more. And still the pickup stayed with her. She approached the turn into her neighborhood, keeping her eyes on her rearview mirror.

"Crap," she said aloud as the truck also turned. The hair on the back of her neck prickled. When the road forked near the convenience store and its bigoted manager, she turned into the parking lot. She had vowed she would never come back here, but she wasn't here to spend money, only to see what the truck would do. Relief flooded through her as it continued down the road, but she thought she saw the driver's head turn in her direction. It was hard to tell through the mirror's narrow rectangle. And in the dark. He was probably simply annoyed with her for going so slow. Yet . . . he could have passed her. She headed home, chiding herself for her paranoia. But still checked her mirrors.

The lights in the windows of her trailer cheered her when she pulled into the driveway, and she was more grateful than ever that Everlove was there. Not only did having her around take her mind off her own problems, but tonight, particularly, Triss was glad to not be walking into a dark, empty house.

Over dinner, Triss had an idea, budget be damned. "Everlove?"

Everlove didn't respond. Instead, she pushed a green bean around her plate with her fork.

"Yoo-hoo! Earth to Everlove."

Everlove startled. "Oh, sorry. What is it?"

"I'm thinking of putting in a phone. I hate that you have to wake up early to go call your boss. Plus, you can check in with your family easier." *And I'd feel safer with a phone here.*

"You don't have to do that for me," Everlove said.

"It would be for me, too. I'm not used to not having one."

"Sure then. I'll chip in, of course."

"I'll drop by the phone company tomorrow at lunch." Triss paused and studied Everlove. "You seem kind of distracted. Is everything okay here? You have everything you need?"

"Everything is fine." Everlove ate the green bean as if to prove her statement.

Triss raised her eyebrows.

"Everything here is fine," Everlove amended. "But the rest of my life is still a train wreck." She sighed. "You ever have something you have to do, and you know you'll feel better if you do it, but you keep putting it off anyway?" She pushed back her chair and carried her plate to the garbage can, scraping the remainder of her food into it.

"Sure," Triss said. "I think everyone does that." Triss thought of the money lying practically under their feet. She was going to have to deal with that one of these days, but she had no idea how. Like Everlove, she kept putting it off.

"I don't know how I am ever going to mend my fences." Everlove sighed.

Everlove looked so forlorn that Triss thought of confessing, thinking that perhaps hearing about someone else's colossal mistake would put her own situation in a different light. But stealing money was not in the same category as jilting your boyfriend, and she didn't want Everlove to think she'd moved in with someone with no morals whatsoever. But it was tempting to share her burden with someone.

"I need to go talk to Rodney. Talk to my parents in person. Apologize to the minister. But the thought of it makes my stomach feel like a bag of fighting cats."

"I'm really sorry. I know none of this will be easy, but you're a strong person and you can get through this," Triss said.

"I think you have me confused with someone else."

"Listen. It takes a strong person to walk away from their wedding. Most people would just go through with it. So the strength is there."

Everlove still seemed doubtful. Triss again toyed with the idea of telling Everlove about her own problems but didn't want to make this moment about her. And she was still afraid of telling Everlove because . . . why? She realized she didn't want Everlove to think badly about her.

"I wish it was behind me already," Everlove was saying as she set her plate in the sink. "Too bad we can't switch places. You go tell Rodney I'm sorry, and I'll tell your grandfather women should be seen and heard."

Triss smiled weakly. *If that were my only problem.* Of course, a week ago, it had been, but she had to go and make things infinitely worse.

"Here, I'll wash." Triss stood and gathered dishes from the table. "Let me ask you this: What's the worst that can happen?"

Everlove pondered the question. "Rodney will be hurt and angry, and I owe him the opportunity to tell me that to my face. As for my parents . . . my mother might disown me. She's got a firm idea of what's right and what's wrong. I've never tested her this much before."

Triss wiped the inside of a pot with a soapy cloth. "That wouldn't be ideal, but you can stand on your own two feet. You're proving it right now. Also, whenever I have something I dread, I always think about how long it will take and how I'll feel when it's over. Like if I had a big exam, I'd think how it would only take an hour and then I'd be done."

Everlove wiped the table and placed the mismatched salt and pepper shakers in the center. "You make a good point. Although I'd still rather walk over hot coals with my bare feet."

A knock on the door made both women jump. They exchanged glances as Triss's heart hammered in her chest. "Shoot. Who could that be?" she asked, hoping it was Mrs. McCabe, but she didn't believe Mrs. McCabe would walk over this late.

She marched to the door, resolved to face whoever was out there. She wanted to be independent, so she needed to act like she was. When she opened the door, she gaped in astonishment.

"Jay? What on earth are you doing here?"

"What? A guy can't drop in on his little sister?"

"It's just a surprise. How did you find out where I was?"

"I would love to answer your questions, but can I come in first? It's freezing out here."

"Oh, sure. Sorry."

He stepped into the trailer. As he shrugged out of his coat, Triss studied him. She knew girls thought he was cute. Both he and Triss had inherited their mother's doe eyes, but his came with the long lashes women strove for but only seemed to be bestowed on men. Maybe it was like bird plumage, she thought. The males were showier. But Jay also had a gangly look, like a large-breed puppy that hadn't attained its full size. It was kind of endearing.

"Well, this isn't horrible," he said after giving her living space the once-over.

She swatted his shoulder, a gesture he anticipated and dodged so her hand merely brushed his sleeve.

He nodded at Everlove in the kitchen. "I see you have company. Sorry to barge in."

"Jay, this is my roommate, Everlove. Everlove, meet my big brother, Jay."

"Roommate? I didn't know you had a roommate."

"She just moved in."

"Nice to meet you. I'm Triss's most beloved and only sibling."

Everlove laughed. "Pleased to meet you, too, Jay. I'll leave you two alone."

"Don't go," Jay said. "I would love to get to know someone who lives with my sister by choice. You should understand I am questioning your sanity even as I make polite conversation."

"Oh, stop," Triss said. "But yes, Everlove, please sit. Jay thinks he's very entertaining, so after he leaves you can tell me the truth about what an awful bore he is." She sat down on the sofa, and Jay joined her. "To repeat my question, how did you find out where I was?"

"I am an excellent investigator."

"No, really."

"I asked Georgina. I said, 'Georgina, do you have Triss's address?' And she said, 'Yes, but I can't give it to you.' And I said, 'I want to check on her,' and she said, 'Here ya go.'" He grinned.

"What the heck?" Triss said. "I told her to only share it with someone in case of an emergency."

"Don't be too hard on her. She wants to make sure you're all right. Which leads me to a question of my own: does Grandfather know you are living in a trailer?"

"I haven't specifically mentioned it, so probably not."

"What I wouldn't give to see his face when he finds out."

"I'm sure that would be great fun, but I bet you don't want to be the messenger."

"You got that right."

"So are you really checking on me, or is there another reason for your visit?"

"No ulterior motive here," he said, holding up his hands, palms out. "I finished basketball a while ago and thought I'd drop by. I didn't think you'd mind."

Everlove had been studying him, and now she spoke up. "Wait. Are you the coach at the community center?"

"I am."

"I thought you looked familiar. My sister goes there. You've coached her."

Jay raised his eyebrows. "Who's your sister?"

"Her name is Ruby. Ruby Porter. She's on the, uh, special team."

"Pebbles! That's your sister?"

Everlove laughed. "Yes. And what a fitting name for her. She does love her rocks."

"She's given me several. I have them lined up on my windowsill."

"Do you?" Everlove asked, as if she wasn't sure he meant it.

"Scout's honor. Every time she brings me one, she tells me to close my eyes and hold my hands out. Then she places the rock in my hand like it's the greatest gift in the world."

"That sounds like her," Everlove said. Triss saw the words soften something in Everlove, and she was struck not for the first time by her brother's ability to move people. She had seen him do this with children and parents alike. She would probably have insulted them. *How are we even related?* It wasn't the first time she had asked that question.

"Do you work at the community center?" Everlove asked.

"I volunteer nights and weekends. I enjoy spending time with kids."

They chatted some more, and finally Jay said, "I've got an early day tomorrow, so I better be off. Mind if I stop by from time to time?"

Triss stared at him. "Are you wanting to see me or avoid Grandfather?"

"Can't it be both?" he said as he slid into his coat. "Everlove, it was very nice to meet you. Any sister of Ruby's has got to be a-okay. Makes up for your choosing my sister as a roommate."

"You just miss me," Triss said as she walked Jay to the door.

He grinned at her. "I will never admit that." He gave them a two-fingered salute as he stepped into the cold night air.

15

Triss

Friday, November 10, 1972

Triss had managed to put the red truck out of her mind until she headed to work in the morning. She kept an eye on her rearview mirror but saw nothing. At lunch, she drove to the phone company and ordered a telephone line, and still nothing. She began to relax. She walked out of the phone company office with a pale-blue princess phone, an appointment for Tuesday for the phone jack installation, and a copy of the order with her new number on it. She ate her sandwich in the car, then drove back to the office, smiling at the sense of accomplishment and independence this task had given her. Her mood shattered when she neared the office and spotted a truck in the back parking lot. A bright-red truck.

Every vein and artery and capillary in her body seemed to fill with ice water. *Just act normal. It's probably a coincidence.* But she didn't believe that.

She pulled into her usual place and forced herself to walk slowly and casually into the building. She went to her desk, and, as she stuck her handbag in the bottom drawer, Copper's voice filtered through the closed door of Haine's office.

As there didn't seem to be anyone else, Triss assumed the red truck was Copper's. But he drove a blue truck. She had seen it dozens of times.

He strode out of Haine's office, placing his seed cap on his head.

"How are you on this fine Friday?" he said as she slid into her seat.

"Running a bit late, thank you." She turned to her typewriter and switched it on.

"Seems like you might need to drive a little faster. Me? I've got a brand-new truck I dropped a 402 big block V8 into, and now that baby will scat!"

Triss was thankful her back was now to him. She had paled before, but what he said now drained her of any color that might have lingered. She slowly reached for a sheet of typing paper, relying on muscle memory to roll it into her typewriter.

Was he saying what she thought he was? She hadn't given him much credit for being . . . clever. But perhaps she had misjudged him. And what did that mean then? If he had been the one following her, why? Did he suspect she was the one behind the break-in?

His booted feet clomped to the back door.

"Y'all have a good weekend, now, you hear? I'll see you around." The door closed behind him.

Triss's shoulders slumped in relief. Was she reading too much into his words? But she didn't think so. Her gut was waving frantic red flags and setting off screaming sirens.

When Haine came out later, she monitored him for signs that he suspected her, but he seemed his normal, brusque self. No pinched brow or pursed lips or pulsing twitch. Which made her wonder: if Copper knew about her, wouldn't he have told Haine? And wouldn't Haine then be angry? So what was going on?

Haine stayed at the office later than she did, and when she exited the building with the weekly deposit, a sedan from the sheriff's office idled near her car. He followed her to the bank, waited until she went in, made the deposit, and returned to her car. She made her usual chitchat with Misti, all the while thinking she felt oddly safer even though she was the reason for the extra protection. But after the deputy gave her a little salute and went on his way, she drove home with her eyes trained on her mirrors. A pickup truck pulled behind her once and her heart nearly stopped, but the truck roared around her, and she saw in the headlights of oncoming cars that it was white and blue.

Everlove had picked up a shift that night, so Triss stuck a TV dinner in the oven and, despite her anxiety, smiled when she thought of Everlove's expression if she could see her. She changed clothes, went through the mail, unpacked another box of belongings. When her food was ready, she ate without tasting it, her mind whirring, trying to work a way out of her predicament. When she'd grabbed the money, she'd thought she would disperse it to the people who needed it. The honest, hardworking people who tried but couldn't quite make their rent. But she had not thought of how she would do that. She couldn't exactly drop in on people and hand them cash in case Copper followed her again. Plus, she didn't want word getting around that Haine's secretary was calling on his tenants. And she didn't like the idea of using the mail. She would hate for someone to get evicted because an envelope got lost. So what was she to do?

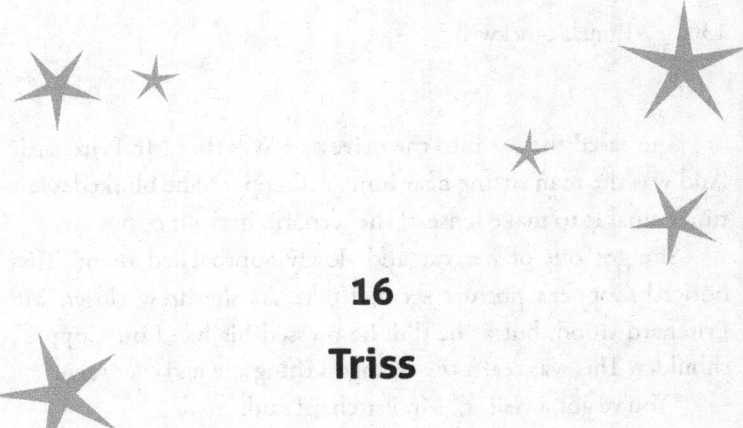

16

Triss

Saturday, November 11, 1972

Triss sat at the white-draped table amidst the glittering cutlery and crystal glasses wishing she were somewhere else. Her friends chatted about weddings past and future, and she was so bored she was afraid she would slide onto the floor. She had no interest in what the current trends were in wedding dresses or if hats were still in à la Bianca Jagger. She ate her eggs Benedict, smiling stiffly in between bites. When her friend Merritt stood, signaling the end of the brunch, Triss almost knocked her chair over in her haste to leave. She hugged and air-kissed her old friends and felt guilty for hoping she wouldn't have to see them too soon. Had she ever shared similar interests with them? She must have, but she had little in common with them now.

She looked forward to going home and curling up on the sofa with a book.

As she approached her house, she did a double take. Two men were on the porch—one sitting on the steps and the other standing. "What on earth . . ." she said.

She eased the car into the driveway. Was that Mr. Pritchard? And was the man sitting near him . . . Copper? She blinked a few times, unable to make sense of the scenario in front of her.

She got out of her car and slowly approached them. Triss noticed Copper's posture seemed odd. As she drew closer, Mr. Pritchard stood, but as he did, he pressed his hand on Copper's shoulder. This was really the strangest thing she had ever seen.

"You've got a visitor," Mr. Pritchard said.

"I see two," Triss said, eyeing them both cautiously.

"He seems a mite more interested in visiting your house than visiting you, which I find suspicious."

Triss looked at Copper. He had not moved, and he kept his hands behind his back. Was he hiding something?

"Care to explain?" Mr. Pritchard said, giving Copper a hard nudge that almost knocked him over. He did nothing to stop himself and nearly toppled off the porch.

Triss leaned forward. "Are his hands tied behind his back?"

Mr. Pritchard shrugged. "Duct-taped. That's gonna hurt coming off."

"I got nothing to explain," Copper said.

"You always hang about in people's homes when they aren't there?"

"I came to ask her"—he jerked his head at Triss—"about some work stuff. Trailer door wasn't closed all the way, so I stepped in."

"That's not true," Triss said. "I always lock the door behind me."

"And why were you looking through her kitchen drawers?" Mr. Pritchard asked.

Crap, crap, crap! Thank goodness she had buried the money.

Mr. Pritchard nudged Copper again. "I asked you a question."

Copper shrugged indifferently. "I was looking for a pen and paper to leave a note."

Mr. Pritchard turned to Triss. "He was also knocking on doors and asking about you yesterday. Want me to call the sheriff?"

Triss thought the sheriff was more likely to take Copper out for a beer than arrest him. She shook her head. "No." So Copper had been following her, and now he had broken into her home. Did he think he would find the stolen money in her house? Why would he think that? Never mind for a minute that he was onto something—what made him think she'd had anything to do with the missing cash? "You can let him go."

Mr. Pritchard widened his eyes. "Pardon?"

"Let him go. He works with me. He's harmless," she said—a deliberate dig. "He just doesn't understand manners all that well." She looked at Copper steadily. Better to look into his hardened eyes than to meet Mr. Pritchard's penetrating ones.

Mr. Pritchard turned his gaze to Copper. "Why are you so interested in her?"

"Background check," Copper said.

"Humph," Mr. Pritchard grunted. "Got any scissors?" he asked Triss.

"Yes. Can you move him out of the way so I can get them?"

Mr. Pritchard pulled Copper up by one arm and steered him down the steps. Triss slipped by them and returned seconds later with a pair of kitchen scissors that she handed to Mr. Pritchard. He turned Copper around and cut through the tape. The silver fabric went pretty far up his forearms, and Triss wondered if that had been accidental or intentional. Whichever it was, Mr. Pritchard ripped the adhesive off, and Copper yelped.

"Ow," he said, rubbing his wrists. Mr. Pritchard reached down and pinched the bill of a seed cap that had been lying on the porch. He handed it to Copper, who placed it on his head.

"I'll be seeing you, I'm sure," Copper said, tipping his chin toward Triss. But having witnessed him trussed up detracted from his threatening demeanor.

"Not around here you won't," Mr. Pritchard said.

Copper rolled his shoulders in what might have been a shrug or an easing of discomfort. He sauntered out of her yard and headed around the corner, where she presumed his truck was.

"Thank you, Mr. Pritchard. I appreciate you looking out for us."

"Anything you want to tell me?"

"Not really."

"I'd lend you my dog, but the only thing she'd do is freeze up and tremble and maybe trip him."

"It's fine. I have a baseball bat."

He drew his eyebrows together. "Having one and using one are two different things."

"I know I don't look it, but I actually got detention more than once for blackening a boy's eye."

One eyebrow shot up. "Wouldn't have figured that. If you think you'll be okay, I'll be going."

"I'm fine. But before you go, can I ask you a question?"

"I'd like to say no, but I won't."

"How did you manage to, uh, tape him up?"

"I learned a few things in the military."

"That's all you're going to tell me?"

"Yep."

"All righty then."

"You know where to find me if you need anything."

He lumbered off, and Triss breathed a sigh of relief.

17

Everlove

Saturday evening found Everlove parked across the street from Jamison's Barber Shop as evening put all the colors of the world to sleep. Rodney usually closed on Saturday nights, so she was hoping she would catch him alone as he cleaned up. She spotted him through the plate glass window, sweeping the floor, his white coat glowing in the shop's bright lights. Nearby, the pack of corner regulars lounged against a wall under the swirling barber pole. The end of their cigarettes flared and flickered like lightning bugs. A man in a long coat and fedora walked past them, tipping his hat. A few of the loungers peeled themselves off the wall, and good-byes bounced back and forth between the men and echoed down the street. Everlove glanced at her watch, tilting its face toward the dashboard lights. It was time.

She circled to the back of the block and parked behind a dumpster. As she slid out the passenger door, she felt queasy and lightheaded. *You can do this*, she told herself. She moved one foot forward, then the other. She remembered Triss's advice. *This will be over in just a few minutes. And it will be behind me.*

She pulled the screen door toward her and jumped as Junior Jamison put his hand out to push it and almost punched her in the nose.

"Who's out there?" he said, squinting into the dark.

"It's me, Junior. Everlove."

"Oh, Lordy," he said, shooting a look over his shoulder. "Lordy," he said again. "Does he know you're coming?"

"No, he doesn't."

"I don't know about this." He'd been about to put his hat on, but instead he scratched his head with the same hand holding the hat so that it flapped above him like a confused and hapless bird.

"I've come to apologize."

He pursed his lips for a minute. Junior was the owner of the shop, which he took over after his father, John Jamison Senior, had died. Even though twenty years had passed, and Junior had to be over seventy years old, he was, and always would be, Junior.

"You be nice to that boy, y'all hear? You put him through the wringer."

"Yes, sir. I know." She winced. She liked Junior. He was a kind, jovial man, and she hated that she had earned his disapproval.

He walked past her, grumbling. "Young people these days. Too many grand ideas or something. Gotta wonder what gets into 'em." She could hear him muttering all the way to his car until the door cut the words off with a solid clunk.

She stepped into the narrow back hallway of the barbershop, then into the brightly lit customer area just as Rodney locked the front door. He did not hear her—a miracle, she thought, as her heart was hammering so hard she could barely hear herself think. "Rodney," she started to say, but it came out as a croak. She tried again. "Rodney."

He jerked his head up and turned. "Evvie. What the hell?" She heard the ghost of other words trailing after those first four: *what the hell are you doing here, what the hell were you thinking, what the hell is wrong with you?*

"Rodney," she said, and the sight of his round face softened her. Made her forget why she had jilted him. She cast about for the other memories, of feeling trapped, unseen, unheard. Should she have tried harder to make him understand? Was this all in her head? Had she wrecked her life—and his—because she was afraid to talk to him? She reached out to him. He took a step back, holding the broom in one hand. She had a brief vision of her ancestors, jumping the broom. Those had been held horizontal. Rodney's was vertical. A visual reminder of how she had upended their relationship. "I came to apologize."

He stared at her for a very long moment, the silence drawing out, thickening, threatening to choke her.

"Go ahead then. I'm waiting."

She drew in a breath. "Rodney, I'm very sorry about what I did. I really am." The words came out more rushed than she had intended.

He walked toward her, and she thought he was going to hug her. He would forgive her. But he brushed by her in the narrow space between chairs. "Not sure I can accept that just yet."

She felt like he'd slapped her. But she couldn't deny that she deserved it. "I guess that's fair enough," she said.

He turned toward her. "I don't think it's fair at all. You humiliated me, Ev. In front of everyone we know."

"I know," she said, quietly.

"What the hell happened? Am I so awful you couldn't go through with it?"

"No, of course not! I just panicked. I started thinking we weren't entirely right for each other. All those months before . . . I kind of got swept up in the planning and everyone's expectations. And then, the day of the wedding . . . something came over me." How could she clarify what she didn't understand? How could she tell him that his dream—to make enough money so she didn't have to work—felt like a pillow over her face? She couldn't. Instead, she said, "You deserve someone better than me, Rodney. Someone who wants the same life you do."

"You're damn right I do." He turned off the lights in the barbershop, leaving Everlove in the dark. She followed him into the back room. He unbuttoned his white smock, tugged it off, and threw it into a laundry bin. He grabbed a tan suede coat from a hook on the wall. "I also deserve someone who thinks before they say yes to something and someone who makes sure they want to actually get married before their wedding day comes."

He practically spit out the last syllables, and she forced herself to not visibly flinch. The words hurt, but he was right. She owed him the courtesy of letting him express his anger. But tears prickled her eyes. She tried to will them away. *Don't cry, don't cry, don't cry.*

"Yes, you do deserve that," Everlove said. "And you'll find someone. I am sure of it. You're a good man, Rodney."

He shook his head. "I've got to lock up now," he said.

"Okay. I'll get out of your way." She wanted to say something meaningful. Something kind. Something that would make all this better. And, if she were honest, something to make her feel better. But she came up empty. She simply told him good night instead.

"Good night, Ev," he said. The words held a bite she was unused to hearing from mild-mannered Rodney. She felt sad that she may have changed him, hardened him. She walked to her car, dejected and defeated.

18

Triss

Sunday morning, November 12, 1972

On Sunday—after a bad night's sleep—Triss was groggily pouring her coffee when a knock sounded at the door, and she jumped, banging the pot against her mug and spilling coffee on the countertop. She was clearly not cut out for a life of crime.

"Want me to answer that?" Everlove asked. She was sitting at the table, dressed for church, finishing her breakfast.

Triss swiped at the spill with a dishcloth. "No, I'm up. I'll get it."

She walked to the door filled with dread, but when she opened it, she found a smiling Mrs. McCabe and not a leering Copper. Relief washed over her.

"You're here bright and early, Mrs. McCabe," Triss said.

Mrs. McCabe raised her eyebrows at Triss, and Triss frowned, puzzled, before realizing what the problem was.

"Would you like to come in, Mrs. McCabe?"

"Don't mind if I do."

"Hi, Mrs. McCabe. Would you like some coffee?" Everlove called from the kitchen.

"I would love a cup, thank you." She peered at Triss. "You're still in your nightclothes."

"It's Sunday. I slept in a bit."

"Pshaw. You young people. Look at Everlove there. She's all dressed."

"I'm going to church," Everlove said over her shoulder. She brought a cup of coffee over to Mrs. McCabe, who had made herself at home at the kitchen table.

Mrs. McCabe spooned sugar into her mug and stirred. "Although I do enjoy your company, this isn't strictly a social call. Someone's been around asking about you." She looked pointedly—and curiously—at Triss.

"Let me guess," Triss said. "A tall, lanky fellow with red hair?"

"That's him. He asked if any suspicious people had been around. I said, besides him? He didn't seem to think that was funny. Then he asked if I noticed you behaving strangely. I told him we only recently met, so I wouldn't know what was strange for you and what wasn't. I also told him I'm eighty-three years old and my vision and my hearing aren't what they used to be. Which is a little white lie. He told me if I noticed any shady characters, particularly hanging around this house"—Mrs. McCabe pointed to the floor—"to call him. And he gave me his name and number." She dug a piece of paper out of her cardigan pocket. "Copper Cavanaugh. Young people and their names these days." She shook her head.

Triss put her hands over her eyes. She was doomed. But, she thought, Haine had not acted any differently toward her all week.

Also, he had a deadbolt installed and had changed the combination to the safe—so he seemed to think someone outside the office had broken in. Also, Copper was trying to determine if suspicious people were hanging around her, so perhaps he didn't suspect her, but thought she knew something. Or had helped.

"Triss?" Everlove asked, concern coloring her voice. "Are you all right?"

"I'm fine," she said, without conviction.

"Yes, you look just fine with your head in your hands like that," Mrs. McCabe said. "Confession is good for the soul, so why don't you spill the beans?"

Triss raised her head. "Who says I have anything to confess?"

"Look me in the eye and tell me there is nothing going on here with a man asking about you and you being upset about it." Mrs. McCabe paused. "Is he your jilted lover?"

"Ew. God, no."

"Well, what is it?" A rhythmic thumping at the door saved Triss from answering. But who was knocking now?

Mrs. McCabe cocked her head. "That's Arabella from next door. She always does that shave-and-a-haircut."

Triss's shoulders slumped in relief. "I met her last week."

"She's quite the socializer," Mrs. McCabe said.

Triss opened the door to reveal Arabella standing on the porch, holding a square cookie tin.

"Hi, Miss Triss." She grinned. "That sounds funny. Oh, hi, Mrs. McCabe! And hi, other person!"

The little girl with the blonde pigtails had a contagious enthusiasm that broke through the tension in the room like the sun breaking through thick clouds.

"My mom made banana nut bread and asked me to bring it over," Arabella said. "She bakes and cleans a lot since my dad is overseas. But we can't eat it all, so she sends me to all the neighbors to give them stuff. So here you go."

Mrs. McCabe nodded. "I loved the oatmeal cookies you dropped off yesterday. But she's going to fatten us all up so we can't fit in our clothes. Maybe she needs a new hobby."

"I'll tell her that," Arabella said.

Mrs. McCabe colored slightly. "Oh, maybe don't mention it after all. Maybe I can come up with something."

Arabella shrugged and handed the tin to Triss. "Here you go. Can I meet your friend?"

"Sure. Sorry. Everlove, this is my—our neighbor, Arabella. Arabella, this is my roommate, Everlove."

Arabella crossed the room, thrusting her hand out. Everlove raised her eyebrows but shook it. "It's nice to meet you," Arabella said, shaking her hand. "I hope my handshake is okay. My dad taught me. He said no one should have to shake hands with a limp fish."

Everlove laughed. "You definitely don't have a limp fish handshake."

Arabella looked at them and rocked back and forth on her heels. "Is something going on?"

"Just coffee among friends," Mrs. McCabe said, lifting her mug and taking a small sip.

"You have that look on your face."

Mrs. McCabe frowned. "What look?"

"Like when we went to the pound and got Sadie for Mr. Pritchard."

"You are imagining things. And, by the way, that was your idea."

"Humph," Arabella said, crossing her arms.

"You sound like Violet," Mrs. McCabe told her.

Arabella grinned. "Is it anything I can help with?"

"We're all fine here," Mrs. McCabe said. "But it's nice of you to offer."

"I'll take your word for it," Arabella said with a little salute. "But remember, when you share your problems with friends, you cut them in half."

"Aren't you a little wise one," Mrs. McCabe said.

"I am." Arabella nodded enthusiastically. "Now I'm off to ride my bike. It was nice meeting you, Miss Everlove. And by the way, you have a cool name! Bye, Miss Triss! Bye, Mrs. McCabe!"

And off she went, sailing across the room and out the door, leaving the air humming with vibrant optimism.

"Now where were we?" Mrs. McCabe asked. "Oh yes, trying to pry Triss's deep, dark secret out of her. So come on. What have you done?"

"I can't tell you."

"Did you kill someone?" Mrs. McCabe said, leaning toward Triss, eyes dancing with delight.

"No!"

"Hurt someone?"

"No."

"Break a law?"

"Well, that, maybe."

"Oh!" Mrs. McCabe exclaimed. "What law?"

"I can't tell you."

"Why ever not? Do you think I will think badly of you?"

"Possibly. Also, I don't want to involve you. Or Everlove." She rested her forehead on the table. "Oh, God. What am I going to do?"

"Perhaps if you tell us, we can help. You heard Arabella. Sharing your problems with friends cuts them in half."

"So you're suggesting I take advice from a child?"

"You could do worse than taking advice from Arabella," Mrs. McCabe said. "Also, since I already have unsavory types coming to my door, I'm think I'm involved."

Triss wavered. She had a deep yearning to share the burden she was carrying, but she also felt ashamed. The two emotions warred with each other.

"I can't."

"Oh, pshaw. You can. And you should."

"Can it be worse than leaving your fiancé at the altar?" Everlove added.

"Yes. Yes, it can."

"Look." Mrs. McCabe leaned across the table. "I think you need a friend to help you muddle through whatever this is. And you have one here in front of you."

"Make that two," Everlove said. "It can't be all that bad. Sometimes telling people can make things less overwhelming."

Triss's eyes unexpectedly filled with tears, and she stared up at the ceiling, eyes wide, hoping none would spill out. She hated crying in front of people. When she felt more in control, she dropped her gaze down to the scarred Formica tabletop and ran a nail along a deep dent. The knowledge of what she had done was swelling, about to burst. She glanced up at the two women and thought how they weren't part of her real life. It was like telling strangers on a street corner. It could possibly help her put things in perspective if she stopped bottling it up. "I stole some money," she whispered.

"You what?" Surprise sent Mrs. McCabe's voice several notes higher.

"I knew I shouldn't have told you," Triss groaned.

"No, no, it's fine. I'm just surprised."

"You asked me if I had killed someone a minute ago, and now this surprises you?"

Mrs. McCabe waved her hand dismissively. "That was to shock you into telling us what you did."

"What did you think it was?"

"An affair with a married man," Mrs. McCabe said. "Maybe your boss."

Triss recoiled. "Ew." A mental picture popped into her head, and she hurriedly erased it. "I work for Horace Haine."

"Ew," agreed Mrs. McCabe. "You work for that greedy old man?"

"Yes. Long story."

"So, you needed money and . . ." Mrs. McCabe prompted.

"No, I didn't need the money. I mean, I could always use more, but I didn't steal it because I needed it."

"I'm not following," Everlove said.

"I'm not following right along with her," Mrs. McCabe said, jerking her thumb at Everlove.

"It's like this. Mr. Haine owns all these properties, and he keeps raising the tenants' rents and evicting people. Last week, this woman, Mrs. Calvin, came in and asked for more time. She's a little old lady—" Triss cut her eyes at Mrs. McCabe. "Begging your pardon. I mean elderly woman. Older person. Anyway, she asks for an extension, and Haine never gives extensions. And she seems so nice."

"I know her," Everlove said. "And she is nice."

"And there are others. I had heard about Mr. Haine's reputation as a miser, but I had no idea he was so heartless. I felt so frustrated and sad for all these people, and then a week ago, I saw that Mr. Haine had not closed the safe door. He got called away, and the door looked shut, but it wasn't. All afternoon, I ignored it, thinking he'd come back and take care of it. At the end of the day, as I was closing up, I remembered the safe. I decided to have a quick peek to satisfy my curiosity." Her cheeks grew warm, and she cursed her Scots-Irish skin that she was sure was flaming now. She continued, "The next thing I know, I'm shoving cash in my purse thinking I can use it to help people. And now Copper is suspicious. He works for Mr. Haine, too. I'm in a huge mess, and I don't know how to fix it."

"Can't you give it back? Like, anonymously?" Everlove asked.

"I suppose I could. Except I kind of trashed the office to make it look like a break-in."

"Ohhhh," Everlove said. "So when that cowboy came by last week about a break-in, that was . . ."

"Yes. Me," Triss said miserably.

"You don't do things by halves, do you?" Mrs. McCabe said. "This is a quandary. But I love a good puzzle."

"It's not a puzzle. It's my life. And I've ruined it."

"I think most problems have solutions if we search hard enough for them," Mrs. McCabe said. "So why is the old skinflint using a safe instead of a bank? I think it kind of serves him right. I mean, if you're going to leave money lying around . . ."

"That's the other part of why I took it." Triss looked up at Everlove and Mrs. McCabe, wondering if she should tell the rest. But why shouldn't she? They already knew the worst about her now. What did she care if they knew the worst about Haine? "I don't think the money from the safe is exactly legal. From what I gather, he gets money from people like Weevil Carr."

"Who is that?" Mrs. McCabe asked.

"He's a moonshiner who has an old broken-down farm on Red Bud Road," Everlove said.

Mrs. McCabe looked Everlove up and down as if searching for evidence of her profligate ways. "Do I want to know how you know that?"

"People talk," Everlove said.

"That's him," Triss said. "My brother told me he also runs a gambling operation out of his barn. Copper collects money from him and others. Since I've been working there, I've put two and two together. I think Mr. Haine keeps most of the cash, but he pays Copper and another guy from what he takes in. They earn regular paychecks. I know because I keep the books. But the money Copper brings in isn't recorded in the ledgers I keep. I also think Mr. Haine pays the sheriff to look the other way."

Mrs. McCabe snorted. "Sounds illegal to me."

"That's why I didn't feel too bad about taking some of it."

"This explains why Mr. Haine sent a hired thug after you instead of going to the sheriff with his suspicions."

"Here's the thing. I don't think Mr. Haine suspects me, but for some reason, Copper does. But I don't think he's voiced his thoughts to the boss."

"We'll just have to get you out of this," Mrs. McCabe said. "You still want to help Haine's tenants?"

"Yes, but I don't know how to get the money to them with Copper watching me all the time."

"First, act like nothing's wrong," Mrs. McCabe said. "Or better yet, tell Haine you're worried about staying late in the office or being by yourself. Maybe say it in a way that makes it sound like you hate to admit it."

Triss had already done that earlier in the week while covering up her nervous guilt. But she had no idea what Mrs. McCabe had in mind. "What will that accomplish?"

"You are a young woman working in a small office. Are you alone sometimes?"

"Yes."

"If you weren't a little anxious after a break-in, that would be suspicious. But if you make too big a deal about it, that might also be suspicious. Act like you are embarrassed to admit it, but your fear drives you to say something."

"Okay, I can understand that," Triss said.

Mrs. McCabe plowed on. "Step two: try and get some proof that Haine is doing something illegal so you can use it against him."

Triss frowned. "Are you saying I should blackmail him?"

"I think blackmail involves some sort of payment, doesn't it? I just mean you will have something to protect you if he begins to suspect you. Knowledge is power, after all. Hopefully you will never have to use it."

"And how would I get this proof?"

"By keeping your eyes open. And maybe talking to people who have worked for him in the past."

"You mean like his last secretary or someone like that?"

"Secretaries, housekeepers. Whoever might be privy to his secrets."

Triss sat back in her chair. She knew his old secretary—a sourpuss if ever there was one. She had retired earlier this year and had taken pride in her job and being privy to some secrets of her fellow townspeople. Triss knew she wouldn't get anything out of her. She also was on the committee that tried to stop desegregation of Edenton's schools. But maybe a housekeeper . . . she thought of Georgina and realized Georgina saw everything. She had witnessed sorrow and celebrations, love and loss. Family fights and slammed doors and the contrition after. It had never occurred to her before that Georgina probably knew everything about them—the good, the bad, and the ugly.

"And how do I do that?" Triss asked.

"Ask around," Mrs. McCabe said then brightened. "I know someone I can ask! I'll check with her. Everlove, perhaps you could ask that nice Mrs. Johnson who lives next door to your parents. She mentioned she used to clean houses."

Everlove shot Mrs. McCabe a wild glance. Triss was getting the distinct impression Everlove did not want to be involved in this. Especially if it meant going near her parents' house. *She's going to hate me.*

"Maybe Everlove shouldn't get involved. I mean, this is kind of risky, and being a Black woman . . . you and me going against Haine is one thing. But Everlove is another."

"Oh. I see your point. Sorry, Everlove."

Everlove nodded, but Triss thought she looked relieved.

"I will see my person tomorrow." Mrs. McCabe patted Triss's hand. "Don't worry. We will help you get through this."

Triss didn't really believe that. Everything was snowballing. Next, she'd be stabbing Mr. Haine with a letter opener and throwing his body in the swamp.

But without another plan, doing a little digging seemed better than doing nothing. Maybe.

19

Everlove

Sunday, November 12, 1972

Everlove composed her face. She liked Triss, but this was too much. Is this what happened when you broke the rules—you fractured one and all the walls that kept you safe started crumbling? Maybe rules were guardrails that prevented you from toppling into the abyss. And a Black woman breaking the rules? She would get into far more trouble than Triss would. Everlove needed to extract herself from Triss's problems. But where would she go? The thought of crawling home to her mother filled her with more dread than staying with Triss. And would that mean her mother was right all those times she said that messing with white people would bring nothing but trouble? What should she do?

Mrs. McCabe left, and Everlove finished getting ready for church. She couldn't stop thinking that she might have jumped out of the frying pan into the fire. But Triss had helped her when she was a total stranger. Now they had become tentative friends. Shouldn't Everlove help her now? Not that she had a clue what she could do. Triss had gotten herself into a bigger tangle than Everlove had.

She pushed Triss's problems out of her head. She first needed to face everyone at church. Let everyone see the runaway bride. Let them gossip about her shamelessness, her audacity, her thoughtlessness. And then maybe the incident would slide into the past. Would she be given a nickname like Pie-Eyed Pete, who was always drunk, or Crazy Betty, who talked to herself? She tried some on for size: Runaway Ev? Neverlove? Everleave? Oh, please don't let anyone think of those. Perhaps, instead, her notoriety would fade with time and become an accepted thread in the fabric of their lives.

She set her hat upon her head and studied her reflection. Here she was, once again clinging to Triss's advice. In a couple of hours, this difficult hurdle would be behind her.

She timed her arrival to a minute or two before the start of the service so she could slip into a pew with little fanfare. She climbed out of her car and stood, adjusting her dress which had twisted around from its trip across the car seat. She straightened her spine, held her head high, and strode through the doors and down the aisle of the church she should have gotten married in a week earlier.

Everlove spied a space seven pews back from the pulpit and headed for it. Heads turned, and she nodded left and right as though this were just any other Sunday. When she stopped at her chosen bench, the other churchgoers scooted down to make room, but before she could sit, the choir director signaled his singers to rise, then turned to the sanctuary and beckoned the congregation to do likewise. Throats clearing, benches creaking, and feet shuffling offered a prelude to the lively opening notes of "I'm So Glad

Jesus Lifted Me." Everlove kept her eyes on the front of the church, but she could tell when word of her presence spread to the seats in front of her by the turning of heads, one row after another. *In a couple of hours, this will be behind me,* she told herself again. She lifted her chin and sang. Her family sat in the second and third rows, and they turned, singing mouths halting in surprise. Except Ruby, who smiled and waved eagerly and might have run to Everlove if their mother hadn't laid a staying hand on Ruby's shoulder. In the choir, her friend Peach's soaring soprano broke free, riffing the lyrics and pulling the congregation's attention back to the worship. Everlove swore Peach winked at her.

By the time the hymn ended, most people had realized Everlove had not sprouted devil horns or worn a scandalously low-cut, high-hemmed dress to church, and so turned their attention to the songs and the sermon. She wasn't there for spiritual redemption as much as she was for secular acceptance. What better place to do that than in a church as the preacher talks about sin and forgiveness, of not casting stones, of being a good Samaritan.

Her eyes drifted to the back of her mother's head and the black hat perched on top, with a fan of netting that looked like a peacock crest in mourning. Everlove did not think it was an accident that her mother had worn black. She dreaded seeing her face-to-face and remembered when her younger brother Franklin had chosen to be among the first Black students to attend the white high school. Avenia had been so furious; she had not spoken to him for days. And so Franklin never told her what his days were like. How the white boys put tacks on his chair at every opportunity. How they would leave bananas on his desk. How he ate his midday meal with his friend Lester every single day for one year and Joe the next, because they were the only Black students who shared his lunch period. These were the kinds of day-to-day degradations her mother had feared for him, and she'd been right. But when Franklin told Everlove about the incidents, he lifted his chin and said someone had to be the one to break the barrier, and he was proud to do it. The only thing their mother knew was how the teachers gave him Cs and Ds, even on some of his best work. He could conceal many things, but he couldn't hide his report card. Fortunately, two Black colleges said they would accept the students despite their grades, knowing they sprouted from the poisoned soil of racism. But still. It seemed their mother spent his whole four years of high school with her lips drawn tight. If Franklin could put up with that while living under her roof, surely Everlove could weather the cold front of her mother for shorter time periods.

When the service was over, she realized she had to file out past Reverend Willis, who should have married her. She wished she could sneak out the back way. But no. She wasn't doing that again. She waited in line with the other worshippers as they shook the preacher's hand, then his wife's. Watching them made her think of Arabella, and when it was her turn, she tightened her grip so she wouldn't have a limp fish handshake. The preacher raised his eyebrows, and his wife sniffed, and the column of people pushed her past them and out into the bright November day. The sun lay like a warm shawl on her shoulders. She found a sunny spot near the road and waited for her family to come out. She kept her back to the parsonage, banishing all thoughts of the last time she was there.

Avenia exited the church and moved toward the sprawling live oak tree that took up most of the front churchyard, her children and their spouses following like obedient ducklings. Ruby spotted her and moved toward her, but Avenia clamped her hand onto hers. Everlove's heart sank at the small gesture, but she gathered up her courage and marched over to her family. She was unsure how to play this. Smile and pretend nothing had happened? Grovel for their forgiveness? Hold her head high as though she were certain she had done the right thing? As she flicked through the options, she studied her sisters' faces, her mother's profile, her father's tall but bent frame. He strolled toward her and patted her shoulder.

"I can't help you with this, baby girl. You know how your mama is." And he walked away to talk with the other men as he always did. She hadn't realized how much she had hoped for some support from him. She shouldn't have. He always said his job was to earn the money, and Avenia's job was to care for the home and children. Never mind that her mother also brought home a paycheck. It would still be Avenia's job to sort her out.

Her sisters looked down at the hard-packed earth, eyes darting up to her. Their husbands peeled away to chat and to get away from the cold war brewing within the family. Everlove had once overheard Leona's husband whisper to Jasmine's husband, "Being a Porter in-law sometimes feels like being an outlaw." Her mother scanned the crowd around them—or pretended to. She did not look at Everlove.

As she stood at the edge of the circle they made, only Franklin and Ruby met her eyes. Franklin winked at her—after a quick glance at their mother to make sure she wasn't looking. Poor Ruby just appeared confused, glancing from Everlove to their mother, not understanding the weather system swirling around them.

"I am glad to see you are coming to church." Everlove jumped at her mother's glacial voice. "Maybe you can make peace with

God. But with the rest of us, it will take more than showing your face here."

"I'm really sorry, Mama."

"Sorry!" her mother said, turning her hard gaze to Everlove. "Who do you think you are to think you can walk away from your promises? From your responsibilities? What got into you?"

Everlove attempted to swallow, but her mouth had gone dry as a desert. "I-I just couldn't go through with it. I don't think I love Rodney enough. Not in that way."

"Not in that way!" her mother scoffed. "Do you think you're a princess living in a fairy tale? Do you think any of us have the luxury of saying 'Oh, I don't want to live up to my obligations to-day, so I will just run off and leave everybody and everything'? No, we don't. We don't let the people around us down. I'm disgusted with you. I'm ashamed you are my daughter."

The pronouncement shook the ground under Everlove's feet. Ruby looked from one to the other, brows drawn together, caught in the shrapnel field of the explosive words. Even in the midst of her own misery, Everlove wanted to pull Ruby against her, comfort her, feel her warm, soft body, her arms tight around her waist.

Everlove groped for something to say that would rebuild the bridge she herself had blown up. She found nothing. Instead, she backed away, tears blurring her family, obscuring them.

She became aware of the gazes of those around her. Some stared, but most darted looks at her—small, furtive glimpses but enough to witness her devastation. To think she had imagined having dinner with her family. What a fool she had been. She walked to her car, thinking how stupid she was not to listen to the tiny voice that had been whispering to her all along. If she had broken up with Rodney sooner, her mother would have been angry but not this furious. The situation would have been fraught, but not beyond repair. Now what was she to do?

She reached her car and glanced regretfully back at the church, but an idea burst into being when she spotted Mrs. Johnson walking with her family. Maybe she could salvage the day. It would be good to help someone after she had let so many people down.

Sha'ree ran ahead, skipping along the gravel, flounces of her purple dress bouncing with each step. Mrs. Johnson followed, clutching her oldest daughter's arm as they maneuvered across the uneven ground. Her son-in-law trailed behind. Before she could second-guess herself, Everlove stepped toward them.

"Mrs. Johnson!"

"Why, Everlove, good to see you."

"Come on, Mama. We've got to get home." Miriam, her daughter, did not look at Everlove.

"Miriam, honey, we aren't in no hurry," Mrs. Johnson chided. "Everlove, what can I do for you?"

"May I speak to you for a minute?" Everlove didn't add 'alone' as she didn't want to call too much attention to her request.

"Miriam, you might want to check on Sha'ree. I don't see where she went. Everlove will help me to the car."

Bless Mrs. Johnson's heart.

Miriam swiveled her head to find her daughter, but not in time for Everlove to miss the narrowing of her eyes. Everlove's best friend in high school was Miriam's younger sister Peach. She had not approved of their friendship then, and it didn't seem like she approved of Everlove now.

Miriam headed toward the far end of the lot, calling Sha'ree's name, and Mrs. Johnson took hold of Everlove's arm.

"So, Evvie, sugar. You doing okay?"

"My mother's pretty angry with me."

Mrs. Johnson gave a little huff. "I love Avenia, but she can be hard as stone."

"You don't have to tell me that."

"She has reasons to be. What she witnessed as a child toughened her up like an old oak tree. But that doesn't mean she don't bend. Give her time."

Everlove nodded. Everyone knew Avenia had witnessed her father being dragged from their home in the middle of the night, accused of arguing with a white man over the price offered for his cotton. In the flickering light of a dozen torches, his wife and children—Avenia the youngest of them—watched as the white men beat him and, when they were done, strung him up in a tree, a dangling signpost of what was acceptable in their Black-and-white world and what wasn't. What does it do to a child to see the family protector and breadwinner stripped of all power and humanity and reduced to less than an animal that was then whipped and discarded? Avenia never talked about that horrific time. Everlove had learned of it from her aunts. She understood that this was the bedrock of Avenia's disapproval of Franklin's attending the white high school—she didn't want him to be another victim of white bigotry. But Everlove wasn't trying to change the world by confronting the status quo. She was just attempting to carve out her own life. She thought about all the times she followed the straight and narrow out of fear of angering her mother. And now, with one act, it was like she had saved up all the things she might have done like individual little matches, then lit them on fire all at once into a spectacular conflagration.

"I'm afraid I've made a lot of people mad." Her eyes slid over to Miriam who, thankfully, had found Sha'ree as well as someone to talk to.

"Don't worry about them. They'll all get over it. Rodney'll find a nice girl, and he'll be just fine. Why I saw one flitting around him at the reception."

Everlove's eyes widened. "Are you serious? Who?"

Mrs. Johnson smiled. "I hate to tell tales, but let's just say one of the Keeler girls saw her chance and didn't wanna let loose of it."

"I bet that was Lynette. I always thought she had a crush on him. When we started dating, she was too young for him. But she'd be what, eighteen now?"

"Plenty old enough to be stepping out, that's for sure. Now what can I do for you, sugar?"

"I was wondering if you could tell me who works for Mr. Haine. Or who has worked for him in the past."

"Lord, don't go poking a stick in that hornet's nest."

"Why not?"

Mrs. Johnson's smile had disappeared. "You listen to me, Everlove Porter. That man is evil. I'm a good, God-fearing woman, and I don't say things like that lightly, but he is a wicked man. I've known a few people who've worked for him, and not a one of 'em has anything good to say. Pearline Galliford. Bessie Fontaine. Willa Moore. I know Bessie the best. She used to clean for him, home and office. She said he hardly paid her anything but expected her to do everything. And she was miserable. She couldn't wait to find a new job. And you know what he does with his rentals. I ain't never seen anyone so apt to kick a body out of their house as that hateful man. Most people are good for their rents even if they fall a little behind. But he don't care. And I don't get it. He has empty houses, so it seems to me he's losing money when he could be making it. Why not just let people stay in their own homes and scrape up the rent? He almost kicked Peach out last month, but I lent her the money she needed. But I can't always do that. Next time she falls behind, I'm afraid he's going to throw her and her babies out on the street. It ain't nobody's fault her man was in an accident and can't work right now."

Everlove had not known Peach had been about to be evicted. Peach was her old school friend from way back. She had been a gorgeous child and breathtaking teen with lips that curved up to playful dimples no one seemed able to resist. But what had that gotten her? Pregnant at fifteen and four children by the age of twenty-two. But Peach seemed happy enough. Tired, but fairly content. And she was a good person. A little spark of anger flickered to life as Everlove thought about Haine putting Peach and her family out. Would he even give them a second thought when he issued the notice? He would have no idea how kind Peach was. How her oldest Serena was reading chapter books. How five-year-old Everett thought he was a world-class athlete. To Mr. Haine, they were simply commodities. She thought of the money Triss had stolen. How much had she taken? Was it enough to help Peach?

"You hear me, Everlove?"

Everlove snapped back to the present and said, "Yes, ma'am, I hear you."

"Messing with that man will land you in a heap of trouble."

"Yes, Mrs. Johnson."

"You should come back to the house for a bite to eat."

"Thanks, but I can't," Everlove said, suppressing a shudder at the thought of sitting across the table from Miriam's scowl and next door to her angry mother. "I promised someone I'd meet them for lunch." Everlove wondered if lying in the church yard was worse than lying in any other place.

Mrs. Johnson patted her arm. "All right. You take care now, Evvie. Give your mother a week or two, then pay her a visit. She'll come around."

"I'll do that," Everlove said, but with none of the certainty Mrs. Johnson exhibited. She left the older woman at Miriam's car and headed to her own while she went over the list of names Mrs. Johnson had given her. She knew them the way one knows people who live in the neighborhood where you grew up and lived your whole life. You know the framework of their lives, the outer trappings, the descriptors. Old Mrs. This. Young Mr. That. Crazy, miserly, homely, fast, snippy. Mrs. Galliford was Little Mrs. Galliford because she was hardly over five feet tall. Mrs. Fontaine was Poor Mrs. Fontaine because she had had polio as a young woman and walked with a crutch. Despite this, she had labored all her life, raised two children to adulthood and lost one in childhood. She now worked at the white laundromat and cleaned houses on her days off. Everlove thought she should have been called Fearless Mrs. Fontaine or Steadfast Mrs. Fontaine. For the first time, Everlove considered how limiting or even unjust some of these tags might be. She had always accepted them at face value, but now she wondered.

And then there was Willa Moore. She was well-established as the Mouth of Willow Mills. Everlove dismissed her immediately. But the other two . . . Everlove had some names to give to Triss and Mrs. McCabe.

At least today had not been a complete waste.

20

Triss

Sunday, November 12, 1972

"How did it go?" Triss asked when Everlove walked in the door. She and Mrs. McCabe were sitting at the kitchen table, nursing cups of hot tea.

"As bad as expected," Everlove said, easing out of her coat and hanging it in the closet.

"Oh, no!" Triss exclaimed. "I was hoping your worries would be overblown."

"You don't know my mother," Everlove said. "She is a force to be reckoned with. I love her, but I'm also afraid of her. Her word is law around our house."

Triss thought about her grandfather and how he was sticking to his guns with her. But he was a man in a man's world. "Your mother must be a strong person," she said, and then wished she hadn't. She should be supporting Everlove, not praising her mother. She tried to make amends. "I mean, that must be hard to live with."

"You're right on both counts."

"I'm sure she'll forgive you soon. She just needs time," Mrs. McCabe said.

"I'm not so sure. She told me it was going to take more than showing my face at church for the family—meaning my mother—to forgive me," Everlove said, shoulders slumping.

"Sorry about that," Triss said. "Guess we're kind of in the same boat."

"Speaking of your boat, I saw Mrs. Johnson." Everlove seemed happy to change the subject. "I asked her if she knew who worked for Mr. Haine now or in the past. She warned me off asking about him, but she did give me three names."

Triss perked up. "That's good, right?"

"Mostly. One woman, Willa Moore, is a terrible gossip. There's a saying in our neighborhood: bad news travels fast, but Willa's news travels faster."

"What about the other two?" Mrs. McCabe said.

"They would both be okay. Mrs. Galliford is retired and lives with her daughter. And Mrs. Fontaine works at the laundromat."

"Bessie Fontaine?" Mrs. McCabe asked.

"Yes. You know her?"

"She's the one I was going to talk to. She cleans my house. I had no idea she once worked for Haine!" Mrs. McCabe rubbed her hands together in obvious glee. "I will speak to her. Can you call on Mrs. Galliford?"

"How about I meet with Mrs. Galliford," Triss said, noting Everlove's drawn eyebrows. "Everlove has enough to deal with without adding my problems."

"It's fine. I can go see her. I don't mind."

"You really don't have to. This is my mess, and I will clean it up myself."

"One thing I've learned living on this street is that friends help each other," Mrs. McCabe said. "My neighbor saved my life just a few years ago. We'll help you, right, Everlove?"

"Um, yes," Everlove said.

Triss wanted to ask about which neighbor saved Mrs. Mc-Cabe's life and when but decided to stick to the topic at hand. She had to admit she was glad for the support. Her determination to be independent warred with a desire to have some compatriots in her quest to straighten out her life. "Maybe I could use a little assistance," Triss said.

"So do we have a plan?" Mrs. McCabe asked.

"I guess we do," Triss said.

Later that evening, Triss and Everlove talked.

"I don't want you to feel like you have to do anything you don't want to. Just say the word. No hard feelings," Triss said.

"I can at least talk to Mrs. Galliford."

"I appreciate that."

"What a mess we have gotten ourselves into."

"My mess is even bigger than yours. And I don't know how I got here, honestly. I was just trying to help when I took the money." Triss paused. "My mother used to say she never knew someone who could create so much havoc with their good intentions. Now I see what she meant."

"I wonder why that is," Everlove said, thoughtfully.

"I don't think before I plunge in. I just don't know how to fix that."

"I apparently do the same. At least this one time. But look, I think if you dig around, you should be able to find some proof about what Haine does."

"I suppose. I just don't know what I am looking for. Or where."

"I guess we should do as Mrs. McCabe suggested and take it one step at a time."

"That's not exactly my forte," Triss said.

"Apparently not mine either."

Triss raised her glass of tea. "Here's to those of us who rush in."

"Wasn't it the fools who rushed in?" Everlove asked as she lifted her own tea.

"Look where we both are."

"Touché," Everlove said and clinked her glass to Triss's.

21

Mrs. McCabe

Monday, November 13, 1972

Mrs. McCabe winced at her creaking knees as she descended the steps to retrieve her mail. When she reached the mailbox and raised her hand to open the little door, her elbow popped loudly. Getting old was no picnic. You would think if God was going to inflict all the miseries of an aging body on a person, he would at least offer a little solace like being able to get a decent night's sleep, but even that had flown out the proverbial window.

As she walked to her house, a car stopped at the end of her driveway. Mrs. Fontaine opened the passenger door of the car and planted her crutch on the ground. She eased herself up smoothly and turned to the driver.

"Thank you, Freeman. I'll see you at four, you hear?"

Mrs. McCabe couldn't hear the reply, but Mrs. Fontaine seemed satisfied with it. She closed the car door and made her way up the drive.

"Good morning, Mrs. McCabe."

"Good morning to you. You know I can pick you up and take you home," Mrs. McCabe said as the two women trudged up the driveway. Despite the twenty-year age difference, they were a matched pair, each making slow progress for different reasons.

"Mrs. Wentworth hired me to be a help, not a hindrance."

"Oh, pshaw. Giving you a ride is not much of a burden."

"I manage just fine."

Mrs. McCabe went first up the steps and opened her screen door. "After you," she said, but she had a devilish grin on her face.

"Oh, no you don't. After you."

"You are a stubborn old mule."

"Looks like we're two peas in a pod," Mrs. Fontaine said as she entered the house and pulled the door closed behind her.

Mrs. Fontaine took off her scarf and jacket and hung them on a coat tree near the door. She headed to the laundry room and slipped into an apron and grabbed a caddy of cleaning supplies. She started work in the kitchen, scrubbing the countertops, while Mrs. McCabe sorted her mail then went off to her spare bedroom to the small writing desk she kept there. She paid some bills and balanced her checkbook. An hour passed in surprisingly companionable silence. Mrs. McCabe had thought she wouldn't like having someone underfoot, and she hadn't at the beginning. She had been grumbly and out of sorts, feeling she was in the way in her own home. But she soon learned to use the time to do her own work. So having Mrs. Fontaine there made her more productive. It gave some structure to her. And she did enjoy her talks with her after the work was done. Today there was more to talk about than usual.

Mrs. Fontaine finished soon enough and put away the cleaning supplies. Mrs. McCabe laid out a pitcher of iced tea and her favorite buttery crackers.

"Care to join me for a snack?"

"I should probably be getting on," Mrs. Fontaine said, shooting a glance at the clock.

"You have a few minutes. Have a seat, and let's chat for a bit." Mrs. Fontaine sat, and Mrs. McCabe poured her some tea. "I've got a question for you."

"Go right ahead."

"I heard you once worked for Horace Haine. I was wondering if he's as awful at home as he is reported to be at work."

Mrs. Fontaine had been lifting her glass to her lips, but that statement stilled her hand. A shadow passed over her face. "Why on God's green earth would you be asking about him?"

"Let's say I have a sort of business opportunity, and I want to learn more about him. But I've heard some things. Like he forecloses on people right and left."

"That's sure enough no secret." Mrs. Fontaine nibbled on a cracker. "My advice would be to stay as far away from him as possible."

"But why does he foreclose so much? It seems like it would be smarter to keep people in his houses instead of having them sit empty."

"There's a lot of people who would love to know that."

"In the time you worked for him, you didn't learn why? Has anyone ever tried to stop him?"

"Now who would do that? He's kicking out poor Black people, and ain't nobody care about them except themselves." Mrs. Fontaine glanced at the clock, and Mrs. McCabe thought she might be trying to urge the hands to move a little faster. "I feel like you have something you want to ask, so why don't you just get on with it, and I'll decide whether to answer it or not."

"That's what I like about you. You are a no-nonsense kind of person. But I don't know the question to ask. I guess I'm on a fishing expedition and looking for anything you can tell me."

"That's easy enough. Nothing. I only worked for Mr. Haine for a couple of years, and he sure didn't confide his deepest, darkest secrets in me. Everyone already knows he is paid by the likes of Weevil Carr. Ain't nobody going to care about that. They never have. There was that business with that poor white girl, but everyone knows about that, too. Nothing is going to stick to Mr. Haine. He's got green money and white skin. That's all that matters."

"Hold on. What girl?" Mrs. McCabe leaned forward.

"Back when he was a young man, there was a girl who died, and people said she was with him when she did."

"When did this happen?" Mrs. McCabe said.

"Early 1920s, I believe. I was born in 1925, and it was before that. When I was coming up, people were still talking about it."

"Who was the girl?"

"She was a poor girl from the mill village, back when the mill was still open, and she had somehow started running with his crowd. Then one day, she disappeared. A few weeks later, they found her body downriver. There were rumors she was alone with Mr. Haine. People say he killed her. It would come up when some white man or other would get in trouble over something. If he got off scot-free, people would say it's just like that Haine business. We all know if a white man does anything against a Black person, the white man's going to win. But some white men can even get away with killing a white girl. Black people ain't got no chance against a world like that." She clamped her mouth shut and looked chagrined, as if realizing just how much had poured out.

"Do you think he murdered this girl?"

"I couldn't say one way or the other."

"What if I wanted to find out more about this?" Mrs. Mc-Cabe asked.

"Then you might want to talk to Haskell Moon. He worked for Mr. Haine's daddy back in the day."

Mrs. McCabe nodded, making a mental note of the name. "Pardon my asking, but if you thought he might have killed someone, why'd you work for him?"

"First, I've got to take what I can get. Second, I didn't know what the truth of the matter was. I've found that gossip may carry a grain of truth, but it doesn't usually hold the whole of it. I figured the business with the girl was probably an exaggeration." She positioned her cane so she could lean on it as she rose out of her seat. "Freeman ought to be here any minute."

"Thank you for telling me what you know."

"If I were you, I'd keep as far away from Mr. Haine as I could."

"I'll keep that in mind," Mrs. McCabe said.

22

Everlove

Monday, November 13, 1972

As soon as Everlove punched out, she stopped by the phone booth that stood sentry near the doors. She opened the phone book that hung by a metal cord. She knew Mrs. Galliford was retired and lived with her daughter, Dorothy. She should be easy to reach. She flipped through the pages, found Dorothy Durant's address. Once there, she parked on the road in front of the once-white house and slid out the passenger-side door, appraising the house. The most solid thing about it was the concrete steps that led up to the sagging porch. The rest of the house looked as though a strong wind might blow bits of it away. Kudzu snaked across the floorboards, as if it wanted to help anchor the structure.

She knocked, and the door creaked open. Mrs. Galliford squinted through the screen door.

"Mrs. Galliford?" Everlove asked.

"Yes? Who's that out there?"

"It's Everlove Porter."

"Everlove Porter?" She pushed open the door and eyed Everlove from head to toe. "Why, I remember you when you was a little bitty thing. Look at you!"

"I was wondering if I might ask you a few questions. I'm doing an article about people who have worked in service for a long time and how they have seen things change." This was the cover story she had invented to get her foot in the door. It was laughable, but she was afraid coming right out and saying what she wanted would earn her a slammed door.

"You're writing an article? Like for the newspaper? Well, isn't that nice. Come on in. Did you bring some cake?" Mrs. Galliford asked, holding the screen open so Everlove could slip in.

"Uh, no, I didn't," Everlove answered. As her eyes adjusted to the dim interior, she spotted a child of around five sitting on the floor, cutting pictures out of magazines. The little girl glanced up as Everlove came in.

"She ain't gonna be able to answer no questions," the child said.

"What do you mean?"

"My mama says her mind's gone. She don't remember nothing except when she was little herself."

Everlove observed Mrs. Galliford to see how she received this pronouncement, but she simply beamed benignly.

"Who's that there?" she asked, leaning forward, inspecting Everlove's face.

"It's Everlove, ma'am."

"Everlove Porter? Why, I remember you when you was a little bitty thing. Look at you!"

Everlove blinked.

"Told ya," the child said. She held up a cutout of an evening dress, nodded at it, and placed it in the small pile next to her.

"Yes, you did." Everlove sighed. She tried anyway. "Mrs. Galliford, do you remember when you used to clean houses?"

Mrs. Galliford smiled. "Of course I recollect that." *Ah, excellent,* Everlove thought. "Like the time I told my mother I had done my chores, but I ran out and played. Lordy, did I ever get my hide tanned for that one."

Everlove's little frisson of hope turned to a pile of ash.

"Do you have any cake?" Mrs. Galliford asked, studying Everlove's hands.

"No, I'm afraid I don't."

"I would sure like me a slice of chocolate cake. Wouldn't that be good right now?"

"It sure would be. I'll let myself out," Everlove said, giving up. "Tell your mama I just stopped by to say hi."

The little girl shrugged and continued cutting. Mrs. Galliford waved goodbye.

Everlove drove home, feeling more let down than she thought she would have. She had only wanted to do the minimum anyway. To help, but not get too involved. This was actually the best outcome: she had done her best but hit a dead end. So why did she feel like a failure?

When she got close to Triss's house—she didn't quite think of it as hers yet—she noticed Triss's car was not in the driveway. But Mrs. McCabe was home. Perhaps she had fared better. Everlove stepped into the house to drop off her purse and scribble a note to Triss, then walked across to Mrs. McCabe's.

"Everlove! What a surprise!" Mrs. McCabe said as she opened the door. "Did you have your meeting?"

"I did. I kind of wanted to wait for Triss to get off work so I could tell you both, but it's not great news, and I didn't want to sit with it on my own."

"Come on in."

Something darted past Everlove, and she jumped.

"Don't mind Clyde. He's shy."

"Clyde?" Everlove asked.

"My cat. Well, maybe it's more like I'm his human."

Everlove regarded the small trailer with interest. While Triss's was spartan, Mrs. McCabe's was packed to overflowing. Doilies, knickknacks on doilies, knickknacks not on doilies. It was hard to focus on one thing. Mrs. McCabe motioned her to sit at the table that was near the door.

"I was just having a snack." Mrs. McCabe gestured to a small plate of cheese and crackers. "Help yourself while I pour a glass of tea." While she went about her task, she talked about how Thanksgiving was just ten days away. "You and Triss should come to our neighborhood feast. Yes, that's quite a brilliant idea."

Everlove wanted to laugh. Her, at Thanksgiving dinner with a bunch of white folks. Her mama would have a conniption fit.

Mrs. McCabe set two glasses of tea on the table and sat down. "So what happened?"

Everlove filled her in on her visit with Mrs. Galliford.

"That poor thing," Mrs. McCabe said, with genuine concern. "And you, too." She sipped her tea. "I don't know if it will make you feel better or worse, but I did get some information from Mrs. Fontaine."

"You did?"

"Why do you look so surprised?"

"Because Mrs. Fontaine is known to be as chatty as a clam."

Mrs. McCabe chuckled. "That describes her pretty well. And she couldn't tell me much, but she did tell me an old story that circulated about Horace Haine."

Before she could say more, a knock sounded at the door.

"Must be my day for visitors." Mrs. McCabe pushed her chair back and walked the few steps to the door. "Violet!" she said as she opened the door.

"Just thought I'd pop over and see how you were doing. I haven't seen you much lately." The soft tones of a woman's voice floated in on a draft of cold air.

"I have company right now, but you're welcome to come in," Mrs. McCabe said.

"You have company?"

A young white woman with deep brown hair and dark eyes stepped into the trailer.

"Hi," she said, eyebrows raised in obvious surprise. "I'm Violet Wentworth. I live next door." She pointed to her left.

"Hello. I'm Everlove Porter. I just moved in across the street."

"Pleased to meet you," Violet said. "I should have come by and welcomed you."

"It's okay. Mrs. McCabe has given us a warm welcome." Everlove waved away Violet's comment.

"Has she now? That seems a bit out of character."

"Oh, pshaw. I'm quite welcoming." Mrs. McCabe said.

Everlove's gaze swung from the older woman to the younger, not knowing what to make of their banter.

"She's not trying to talk you into anything, is she?" Violet asked, cocking her head.

Before Everlove could frame a reply, Mrs. McCabe answered for her. "Talk people into things? I'm shocked you would say that."

"You should come with a warning sign," Violet said, but she was smiling.

"Humph. I was going to ask if you wanted to sit and have a snack, but I am not so sure now."

"How about if I get you more iced tea? May I sit then?"

"I guess so," Mrs. McCabe said. She leaned toward Everlove. "She thinks I'm too old to look after myself. She did take care of me once. And ever since, I can't get rid of her."

Violet had her head in the fridge, but that did nothing to muffle her snort. She emerged with the pitcher of iced tea and said, "I think you got the wrong end of that stick."

"You don't see me making myself at home in your kitchen, do you?"

"I have. Plenty of times." Violet sat. "So Everlove. What do you do?"

"I work at Sun Vine."

"I hear it's rather chic."

"It is. Very modern."

"I want to check it out, but I keep going to H&L out of habit."

"To be honest, and don't tell anyone I told you, the prices are better there."

"Good to know. Thanks."

"So what do you do?" Everlove asked.

"I'm working on my teaching degree, but I also work at Turner's T-Bones."

"Perhaps you can quit the job in June and concentrate on your studies," Mrs. McCabe said.

"That's something we've talked about," Violet said. "I'm getting married in June," she explained to Everlove.

Everlove's breath caught in her throat at this casual, unexpected collision of where she was and where she might have been.

Mrs. McCabe continued. "She's a lucky young woman. Nick's an excellent cook, and he supports her going to school." Everlove placed her hands in her lap and gripped them tightly, forcing herself to smile pleasantly. "But," Mrs. McCabe added, dabbing at her mouth with a napkin. "Violet has been through tough times. Now here she is on the other side."

"I'm sure Everlove doesn't want to hear about all that."

"I'm simply pointing out that rough roads smooth out. You just have to keep walking them long enough."

Violet was now the one staring at Mrs. McCabe, her brow furrowed. Mrs. McCabe took another bite of cracker. But while Violet didn't understand the not-so-subtle message Mrs. McCabe was relaying, Everlove did, and the little knot in her chest eased.

"Mrs. McCabe, I don't know what you're up to, but I am sure it's something." Violet shook her head. "Don't trust her as far as you can throw her. She's always scheming."

"Violet! I am offended! I don't scheme all the time."

"Maybe not all the time, but you do a lot of it." Violet turned to Everlove. "My fiancé calls her the tiniest bulldozer ever."

"What? Nick said that about me?" Mrs. McCabe placed her hand to her chest. "Well, I'm sure he meant that as a compliment."

Another knock interrupted them.

"Goodness. It's like Grand Central around here," Mrs. McCabe said as she headed to the door.

"Triss! Come on in and join the party!" Mrs. McCabe exclaimed.

"I saw Everlove's note that she was here. Hope I'm not interrupting anything."

"Not at all! Come in and meet my neighbor, Violet." Mrs. McCabe pulled Triss in.

"I'm glad I dropped by so I could meet you both," Violet said after introductions were made. "I was telling Everlove I should have come by earlier." She glanced at the clock. "I wish I could stay longer and chat, but I better get back. I'm making dinner tonight."

"Oh, dear," Mrs. McCabe said.

"I'll have you know my cooking is fine."

"I'm sure it is, but not when stacked up against Nick's."

Violet ignored that and turned to Everlove and Triss in turn. "It was nice to meet you. I hope to see you again soon. But a word of warning: She can talk a zebra out of its stripes."

Once the door closed, Mrs. McCabe said, "Don't listen to her. She should be grateful to me. She and Nick split up once, and it was thanks to me they got back together." She pressed an index finger into the buttery cracker crumbs on her plate and licked her finger.

"Maybe Nick should have called you Cupid instead of a bulldozer," Everlove said.

"I think I like you, Everlove," Mrs. McCabe said with a luminous smile. "Now about what I found out . . ." She related the story of the girl who died, about how there were rumors of something amiss but nothing tangible.

"Do you know this Haskell Moon?" Mrs. McCabe asked Everlove.

"Everybody knows Mr. Moon. Lives in Cumbee Creek with one of his children. Or a grandchild. I can't remember."

"We should go talk to him."

"We can do that, but I bet there would have been something in the newspapers back then. We could check at the library," Everlove said.

"Would they have papers that are fifty years old?"

"They should." She looked thoughtful. "If they don't have the actual paper copies, they might have them on microfilm."

"I don't know what that is, but we should definitely go have a look-see." Mrs. McCabe glanced at her watch. "It's a bit late today. How about tomorrow?"

"I can go after I finish my shift at three."

"Shall we say four, then? I'll drive because I hate to see you scooting across your car seat."

"It's a date."

"I appreciate y'all doing this for me," Triss said.

"Who's to say I'm not just doing it for me," Mrs. McCabe said. "This is the most fun I've had since I met Little Richard when he was with Buster Brown's orchestra. But that's a story for another time."

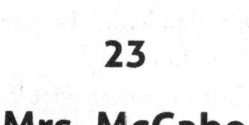

23

Mrs. McCabe

Tuesday, November 14, 1972

The next day, Mrs. McCabe and Everlove stood in front of the library reference desk where a woman with short dark hair and cat-eye glasses was typing an index card.

"Hello! Where can we find your newspapers?" Mrs. McCabe said.

The woman glanced up. "The daily papers are over there," she said, her words brusque and clipped.

"I need something older." Mrs. McCabe noticed that when the librarian's eyes drifted to Everlove, they narrowed. Mrs. McCabe stepped up the charm, thinking of Violet's "more flies with honey" mantra.

"How much older?" No change in the woman's demeanor.

"Between 1920 and 1925."

"That's a rather large timeframe."

Mrs. McCabe stared off into space, trying to decide where to start.

"Ma'am?" the librarian prompted.

"I'm thinking. Hold on." Then Mrs. McCabe spotted a woman behind the checkout desk. She was about the right age. "I'll be right back," she told the librarian in front of her and motioned Everlove to follow.

At the other counter, the woman looked up at them expectantly. "Ready to check out?" She frowned as she noticed neither one was carrying books.

Mrs. McCabe peered at her name tag. "Actually, Mary, I have some questions. Are you from Edenton?"

"Born and raised on Juniper Spring Road." She was much friendlier than the reference desk woman.

"I haven't lived here all that long, and I have a ticklish business situation. I am trying to find out more about the person on the other end of it." She was counting on librarians being the sort who liked to help people. Especially little old ladies who might be taken advantage of by ruthless businessmen. "Do you know Horace Haine?"

"Who doesn't? We went to high school together, although he was older than me."

Mrs. McCabe leaned toward Mary conspiratorially, though her lower back creaked in protest. "I was getting ready to let him handle a property sale, but I caught wind of something that is bothering me." She stopped, looked around, and bent further across the counter. Mary mirrored her action. "I heard he was involved in a terrible scandal. It was from when he was young, but it was dreadful."

"Oh." Mary's face grew somber. "You must mean the business with the Sadler girl." She shook her head.

"Sadler, did you say?" Mrs. McCabe asked.

"Yes. What was her first name? Marjorie? Margaret? I never thought I'd forget that."

"So what happened to Marjorie, exactly?"

"I don't think the name is right. It was something like that."

Mrs. McCabe repressed an urge to glare and, instead, smiled graciously.

"I'm sure it will come to me, probably at dinner tonight, right?" Mary laughed, a little whispery, library laugh. "Anyway. She was part of a crowd of young people that ran around together. Well, sort of. All of them but her were from the ritzy families. She was more of a palooka."

Mrs. McCabe smiled. She hadn't heard that term for an outsider since she had finger waves and pretty calves.

"I'd see the lot of them at the soda shop or the nickelodeon," Mary said. "Marjorie, or whatever her name was, was quite lovely, although she was not at all the type who usually ran around with the Haines and the Baxleys and their like, as she came from the mill village. But it was after the Great War and that appalling flu, and the world was a bit giddy. My mother was horrified by the shorter skirts and bobbed hair." Mary paused, a small smile curling her lips, and Mrs. McCabe wondered if she had enjoyed the scandalous clothes. Mary continued, "Change was in the air. Maybe Marjorie thought she could be swept up in the changes, and one of the boys in the group would fall in love with her, marry her, and save her from the mill village."

Mrs. McCabe thought Mary might be projecting her own past dreams on poor Marjorie, but she said nothing, keeping her slightly frozen smile in place.

"One night, all six of them went out on the town, but only five came back. It was quite shocking in our little town, to have a young person disappear. Days went by, and rumors flew that she had run away, been kidnapped by white slavers, or maybe died. And then her body was found downriver several weeks later." The librarian leaned closer. "Her death was ruled an accident, but there were a lot of rumors. But nothing ever came out officially."

"What were the rumors?"

"That she'd been alone with Horace Haine, though the official story was she met up with a stranger. But no one else was ever found or questioned. And then her family moved away, and people said they left in a Tin Lizzie they hadn't had before." She gave Mrs. McCabe a meaningful look.

"That is quite a story."

"It was a dreadful scandal back in the day. That poor girl. She was only a year or so older than me. And while my family was a little better off than hers, we were by no means in the country club set. I felt a kinship with her. When I graduated from high school, I stayed away from parties. The paper painted her as a young woman with loose morals, out drinking and carousing with young men. Kept me on the straight and narrow, I'll tell you."

"Is that what you thought? That she was a loose woman?"

"I didn't know what to believe. Sometimes I thought she was, sometimes I thought she was in the wrong place at the wrong time." She shook her head. "Marjanne!" Mary said suddenly, then looked around, chagrined as she realized she'd raised her voice in her own library. She turned back to Mrs. McCabe. "That was her name. It was Marjanne Sadler."

"Marjanne, huh?" Mrs. McCabe said. "One more question. Do you remember when all this took place?"

"It's seared in my brain. It was the summer of 1921, the year I graduated from high school. Pretty sure it was August when she disappeared because it was right before college started." Mary's brow creased. "I don't know how this has any bearing on his life today. It was an awfully long time ago."

"I like to look at the whole picture. And you've been most obliging. I appreciate your time. Have a good day."

"Glad I could help."

Mrs. McCabe and Everlove headed back to the reference desk. The woman looked up at Mrs. McCabe's approach. "Ah. Have you remembered the year, dear?"

The patronizing tone and the frown at Everlove's presence got Mrs. McCabe's hackles up. Silently, she repeated, *Flies and honey, flies and honey*.

"Why, yes," Mrs. McCabe said sweetly. "I need to see the August 1921 issues of the *Edenton Register*."

The woman looked concerned. "Oh, sweetie, those are on microfilm."

"Is that a problem?"

"It's modern technology, you see. A little tricky to use."

The mantra exploded into a thousand tiny shards of irritability. If there was one thing that set Mrs. McCabe's teeth on edge, it was suffering fools. The only thing worse than that was being treated as one herself. She leaned over the counter.

"I may be old, but I'm not senile. I believe that if you show my friend and me what to do, we can grasp the general principle."

The librarian—Eunice, Mrs. McCabe noted—straightened her spine and pursed her lips. She pushed back her chair and stood, peering over her glasses at Mrs. McCabe and Everlove. "Well, I'll go get the reels."

Eunice returned, bearing several small cardboard boxes. She curtly told Mrs. McCabe to follow her to the microfilm reader and ignored Everlove entirely. Mrs. McCabe thought the contraption looked like the space capsule the astronauts used in their splash-downs. Eunice showed Mrs. McCabe how to slip the reel on one little spindle and feed it to another. The image was projected down onto the bottom of the space capsule. A crank on the right-hand side allowed Mrs. McCabe to advance or rewind the film. Eunice told her that when she was done and if she needed another reel to come get her as they didn't allow "just anyone" to touch and handle the film and the state-of-the-art machinery.

As she left, Mrs. McCabe glared at her. "If I knew voodoo, I'd stick a pin in that woman's foot." She turned to Everlove. "Let's get cracking. You want to do this? Did you follow her instructions?"

"I know how to work this," Everlove said.

"Why didn't you say so?"

"If she didn't want an old lady—pardon the expression—to handle her precious microfilm, how do you think she'd feel about a Black woman?"

"Ohhh, people are so aggravating. I don't understand how humans managed to move up to the top of the food chain." Mrs. McCabe scooted her chair over. "Take a seat and have at it."

Everlove did. She fed the film through, stopping periodically to scan the page in front of them, searching for the mention of a death of a young woman, or her disappearance. Or the name Marjanne Sadler.

"I had no idea they had such things," Mrs. McCabe said.

"I had a teacher in high school who was all excited about this. She said it was a great way to save space and preserve written records. She took us to Columbia on a field trip, and we were shown how to use it, though we had to go after hours because they didn't allow Black people during regular hours." As she talked, Everlove continued skimming the microfilm, turning the crank. The machine whirred and stopped, whirred and stopped. Mrs. McCabe, looking over Everlove's shoulder, hadn't realized how much newspapers had changed, but they were much more readable now. These old papers had columns of tiny, smudged type barely broken by headlines. Her eyes began to dry out. She was glad Everlove was doing the search.

A couple of stops and starts later, Everlove yelped and pointed to a newspaper dated August 8.

Police Seek Information on Missing Woman

Police have been notified of the disappearance of Marjanne Sadler, age 19, of Willow Mills Village. She has been reported missing by her parents when she did not come home after an evening out on Saturday. Friends Edith Bailey and Paul Sullivan left her in the company of Horace Haine, and she has not been seen since. Her parents described her as being five feet and two inches and weighing 105 pounds. She has blue eyes and blonde hair and was last seen wearing a pink dress with a white collar.

Everlove scrolled some more, stopping on August 12.

Body Found in Supplejack River

The body of a young woman, possibly between the ages of 18 and 25, was found in Supplejack River yesterday by a fisherman out for an early-morning fishing expedition. Mr. Charles Blakely was rowing his boat to a small cove when he spotted what he thought was clothing caught on some branches near the shore. Upon further investigation, he found the clothes were on the body of the unfortunate young woman. The coroner's office is holding the body pending identification.

Well, Mrs. McCabe thought. *Well.*

Everlove scrolled to the next day and found a follow-up article.

Body Found in River Identified as Missing Willow Mills Woman

The body of a young woman found in the Supplejack River on August 12 has sadly been identified as Marjanne Sadler, age 19. The body was identified by her father, Jared Sadler, at the county morgue. Miss Sadler was last seen in the company of several young people, but left them to meet someone else, and they assumed she was safe when they parted company. Miss Sadler was reported missing on August 7 by her parents. The police believe she died from accidental drowning and no foul play is suspected.

Another article appeared the next day but contained no new information except for the funeral arrangements and a photograph of Marjanne. A wave of sadness washed over Mrs. McCabe as the name turned into a person.

The photo showed a slender young woman, hand on her hip, bobbed hair ending in bouncing curls just below her ears. Three little pin curls graced her forehead. Marjanne stared directly at the camera, her expression confident and hopeful.

"This is the saddest thing," Everlove said, staring at the grainy black-and-white image.

"It is." Mrs. McCabe sat back in her chair. "She looks ready to take on the world in that photo, but the world chewed her up instead."

Everlove jotted down Marjanne's full name, age, and family. Date of her disappearance. The names of the two friends who had been mentioned in the article as being with her.

After she wrote everything she could, Everlove turned the crank to find more stories, but Marjanne had disappeared.

24

Mrs. McCabe

Tuesday, November 14, 1972

When Mrs. McCabe and Everlove left the library, rain had begun to patter down, starting slowly then working up to a downpour. Mrs. McCabe parked at Everlove and Triss's house and grabbed her umbrella—which she had thankfully remembered to put in her car—and hurried to the shelter of their trailer. Her eighty-three-year-old version of hurrying, at least. Everlove, being young and agile and blessed with joints she took for granted, threw a clear plastic headscarf over her head and ran.

Triss opened the door and ushered them in.

"It's raining cats and dogs out there," Mrs. McCabe said, propping her umbrella in a corner by the door where a pool gathered on the linoleum rectangle that served as an entryway. "Do I smell dinner cooking?"

"Not exactly. I was running late and picked up Chinese food."

"I could eat the bark off a tree, I am so hungry," Mrs. McCabe said as she pulled her notebook out of her handbag. They gathered at the table and dished out the food, and Mrs. McCabe surprised them by using the chopsticks that had been included.

"Where did you learn to use chopsticks? You need to teach me," Triss said.

"I had to learn when Flynn and I went to Korea and had dinner with the president."

"The president of what?"

"Of South Korea."

When no one responded, Mrs. McCabe looked up to find the two young women staring at her. "What?" she said.

"Did you actually have dinner with the president of South Korea?"

Mrs. McCabe waved her chopsticks. "Oh, Flynn and I got around back in the day. Anyway, Everlove, why don't you tell Triss about what we found."

Everlove hesitantly described their trip to the library, but she spoke more confidently as she plowed on, telling Triss how Mrs. McCabe talked to a librarian who knew Haine, and how she recalled both the girl's name and the year she died. This helped them find the articles quickly—what there were, at least. She summed up what little information they had gleaned. "And the last one was about her funeral, and that was it. No more stories at all."

"Seriously? Nothing about an investigation or anything?"

"No. And I went slowly and even went back to look."

"That does seem a bit odd," Triss said. "Do you think they hushed it up?"

"That's what it looks like to me," Mrs. McCabe said.

Triss leaned back in her chair. "Even if they did," she said, "I don't understand how this will help me."

"There's no statute of limitations on murder," Mrs. McCabe said. "And when I think of that young woman . . . when she died, I was dancing the Charleston with Fred Astaire."

"Excuse me?" Triss asked, eyebrows raised.

"Flynn and I ran into him at a club in New York before he was famous. Years later, I said to Flynn, 'Isn't that the young man I danced with in New York?'"

"Mrs. McCabe, you need to write a book about your life," Everlove said.

"Maybe one day I will. Meanwhile, it just makes me mad that Haine may have had something to do with her death but got away scot-free. I'd love to get something on him."

"Me, too, but after fifty years, I don't think we'll find anything."

"I think it's still worth checking. This could lead to more questionable things. The other day, we had nothing. Now we have this and another person to see. Everlove, since you know Mr. Moon, could you go talk to him?"

"You seem to be on a roll. Maybe you should talk to him," Triss said.

"I think I need a day of rest. I'm not used to all this running around." She turned to Triss. "So that's settled—"

Everlove blinked. "It is?"

Mrs. McCabe plowed on. "And Triss, if you're not going to give the moolah back, perhaps it's time to give it to those who could use it."

Triss pushed her plate away and closed her eyes. "Ugh. I know you're right, but the thought of touching it makes me nauseous. Most of the time, I can pretend this didn't happen. But if it's sitting right in front of me . . ."

"I'll touch it for you. How much is it?" Mrs. McCabe said.

"I don't know. I didn't count it."

"Bring it out then, and let's get to counting."

"I hid it. I can't exactly get to it right now."

Everlove and Mrs. McCabe exchanged curious looks. "What do you mean you can't get to it?" Everlove asked.

"Well, I can. Just not tonight."

"I do hate to pressure you, but the end of the month will be here in no time," Mrs. McCabe said.

"I know," Triss groaned. "How did I create such a mess?"

"Because you're a girl with a good heart," Mrs. McCabe said, patting her hand. "And don't worry. We'll be with you every step of the way. Is that man still following you?"

"I still spot his truck sometimes. It's like he wants me to see him, too. I guess to intimidate me."

"Maybe. What about Mr. Haine? Does he act suspicious?"

"No, thank goodness. I don't think I could keep up the pretense if I thought he suspected something. This is the most nerve-wracking thing I've ever been through."

A knock sounded at the door, and the three women froze.

"Oh, God. What if it's him?" Triss asked, placing a hand over her heart.

Mrs. McCabe pushed herself up and straightened her dress. "I'll handle this."

"Are you sure?" Triss asked.

"If it's who you think it is, who better to answer the door than a little old lady? Who messes with them?"

Mrs. McCabe strode to the door, ready to do battle. In the few steps it took her to cross the living room, she belatedly remembered stories on the TV of little old ladies getting mugged. She should stop watching the news. Triss followed her but stayed to one side of the door, and Mrs. McCabe realized she had picked up a baseball bat very similar to the one she kept near her own door. Mrs. McCabe yanked open the door.

A young man stood on the porch. Even in the pouring rain with his face shadowed by his umbrella, Mrs. McCabe could tell he was not that Copper fellow. He tilted the umbrella back, and the light shone on a pleasant face with large, brown puppy-dog eyes.

"Um, hi?" he said, puzzled. "I was looking for Triss Littlefield?"

Before Mrs. McCabe responded, Triss peeked from around the door. "Jay!"

"You know this man? Or should I strong-arm him out of here?" Mrs. McCabe said. She pushed up one sleeve.

"He's my brother." Triss waved him in. "Come on in."

He closed his umbrella and peered at Mrs. McCabe. "Is this another roommate? Are you adding one a week?"

"No, this is my neighbor from across the street, Mrs. McCabe."

"Nice to meet you," Mrs. McCabe said.

"And you."

"We were just cleaning up after dinner, but there's some food left over. Would you like something?" Triss asked.

"I'm famished," Jay said.

"Chinese takeout good?"

"I think I would even eat your cooking at this point."

"I could just dump this on your head," Triss said, but placed the carton in front of him instead.

The four sat around the table as Jay ate.

"What do you do?" Mrs. McCabe asked Jay.

"Family business," he said.

"Because he's male, he gets to follow in footsteps my dainty little feet apparently can't fill," Triss said.

"Ah, so you're a lawyer," Mrs. McCabe said.

"Guilty." He lightly punched Triss in the arm. "You'll get there."

"Yeah, when I'm fifty."

He turned to Mrs. McCabe and Everlove. "She'd make an impressive attorney. Our grandfather is making a serious mistake not bringing her on board."

"Aw, Jay. What a nice thing to say," Triss said.

"I'm only saying it to pump you up in front of your friends. Also, it makes me look like a great big brother."

Jay stayed for a little while. He told Mrs. McCabe about his volunteer work at the community center, and, she noted, he spoke far more enthusiastically about that than about his job at his grandfather's law firm. When he left, Mrs. McCabe turned to Triss.

"He seems nice," Mrs. McCabe said.

"He is. But don't tell him I said that."

"Mum's the word. But back to the business at hand. The whole time he was here, I was wondering where you hid the money. Can't you at least tell us?"

"Fine," Triss said, sounding rather like a petulant child. "It's under the house. I buried it."

Everlove started laughing and immediately clapped her hand over her mouth.

"What?" Triss asked.

"I got a mental picture of you burying cash in the backyard. I wouldn't have thought you would know which was the business end of the shovel."

"I take offense at that," Triss said.

"I don't mean to offend you, but . . ." Everlove trailed off.

"It's not exactly brain surgery."

"No but picturing you in your nice clothes and perfect hair shoveling dirt is pretty funny."

"I do not have perfect hair!" Triss exclaimed.

Mrs. McCabe saved them from further argument. "So the reason we can't get it tonight is because it's raining?"

"That, and I am worried about Copper hanging around."

"That redneck scoundrel," Mrs. McCabe said. She pictured him lurking about. He couldn't spy on them from the neighbors' yards, but the winter woods behind Triss and Everlove's house wouldn't conceal a cat. And the trailer didn't have any underpinning, so anyone could see under it and into the backyard. He could park around the corner and at the right angle might be able to see. Although that would put him at the edge of the unfriendly territory known as Mr. Pritchard's yard. "Wait! Mr. Pritchard can help!"

"Excuse me?"

"Mr. Pritchard is a handyman."

"We're aware of that."

"We have him come over, dig the hole for us under the guise of fixing something, and voila! We have the money."

Triss stared at the older woman. "And how are we going to explain that he's digging up a wad of cash wrapped in aluminum foil buried in my backyard? Won't he be a bit curious?"

"That's the beauty of Mr. Pritchard. He doesn't want to know. But he'll help us because somewhere under that thorny shell is a tiny but generous heart. He won't ask questions. And he certainly won't tell anyone."

"I hope not," Triss said.

"I'll talk to him this week and get him to come over Saturday," Mrs. McCabe said, deciding the matter was settled. And that usually meant it was.

25
Triss

On Wednesday, the brisk winds of a cold front chased away the rain and rippled the surface of leaf-lined puddles. The temperature dropped twenty degrees. Triss had little to do at work that week. Because it was the middle of the month, no renters came into the office. Her only visitor was Copper, who breezed in on Friday afternoon, bearing the duffel bag and a knowing grin. He knocked on Haine's door, and Haine summoned him in, telling him to close the door. Which he did—almost. The latch did not hold, and the door remained ajar. Still on the lookout for information, Triss listened in. Weevil Carr was still behind on his payments, and Jenette Blazey had paid in full.

Haine took the duffel to the file room and came back out a few minutes later. He handed the duffel to Copper, and Copper left, giving Triss another skin-crawling nod.

As soon as the door closed behind him, she closed up the office, then stood in Haine's doorway. "Do you need anything else, Mr. Haine?"

"No, that will be all, Patricia."

After she turned, she rolled her eyes. Not even "Have a nice weekend" or "Thanks for typing that deposition." She slid into her coat, grabbed her pocketbook and the weekly deposit, and headed out the back door into the leaf-scented wind. She clutched her collar to her throat to hold onto what warmth she could.

A voice cut through the darkness, making her jump.

"Howdy."

The streetlamps cast just enough light for her to see Copper leaning against the front fender of her car, seemingly unbothered by the cold wind.

"I thought you left," she said. Uneasiness crawled down her spine. For once, she would welcome Mr. Haine's presence. She told herself if Copper had any information on her, he would have shared it with Mr. Haine already. He was fishing. So don't bite.

"Yeah, well," he drawled, peeling himself off the car. "I want a word with you."

"I really have to get home," Triss said, and reached for her door handle, but he stepped into her path.

"I won't keep you long," he said.

She made herself meet his steady gaze.

"What do you want?" she asked, jutting out her chin.

"I think you had something to do with the break-in a couple of weeks ago."

"Why would you think that?"

"My gut says so. And my gut's usually right. Mr. Haine don't agree. But I'm watching you. And I'll figure it out sooner or later."

The wind that tugged at Triss's coat hem had nothing to do with her blood turning to ice. "Do you know who my grandfather is?"

"Oh, I know. And I also know he cut you off. So maybe you're desperate."

She wondered how on earth he knew that but forced a laugh. "I like to earn my money the old-fashioned way. Now if you'll excuse me, I'll be on my way."

He stepped aside. "Be my guest," he said with a mocking bow. "Y'all have a good evening. I'll be seeing you."

Triss climbed into her car and slammed the door, grateful for the barrier between them. She was glad he couldn't see her shaking hands as she dug her keys out of her handbag and started her car. As she drove away, she glanced at her rearview mirror. Copper tipped his seed cap at her. Although she couldn't make out his features, she was sure he was still smirking.

The deputy assigned to follow her fell in behind her from his space on the street. At the bank, she parked under a light and sat, breathing deeply for a minute before she entered the building. Unlike two weeks ago, she was thankful for its brilliantly lit interior and Misti's incandescent smile.

"Hello, Miss Littlefield. How are you today?"

"I'm fine," she lied and slid the deposit across the counter.

"You have plans for Thanksgiving?" Misti asked.

"I haven't quite pinned that down yet," Triss said, with forced cheerfulness. She had never spent a holiday alone, but Thanksgiving might be her first.

"We're going to my parents' house. My husband doesn't have any family. Which is sad, don't you think? But luckily, my parents love him."

"That's good! It would be terrible if they didn't."

Misti counted the money, hit some keys on a keyboard, and printed out a receipt. "There you go! Have a nice weekend."

"You, too, Misti."

Triss had an urge to tell her that her cheerfulness made her feel better, but another customer was waiting. Maybe she would give her a card at Christmas or something.

Everlove was making dinner when she got home. "How about a spaghetti supper?" she asked as Triss closed the door.

"Sounds great," Triss said. She had tried to make her voice light, but it came out a bit squeaky.

Everlove noticed. "Everything all right?" she asked, turning to study Triss, holding aloft a metal ladle and oblivious to the sauce it dripped onto the stovetop.

"Yes. No. I don't know. I'm going to change out of these work clothes first, then we can talk."

How do criminals do this? Triss thought as she changed clothes. How could anyone live like this? She was a mess. She heard Everlove answer a knock at the front door, then Mrs. McCabe's voice rang out. She was getting to be quite a regular.

When Triss joined the two, she was surprised to find Mrs. McCabe making a salad.

"Hello, Triss. Thought I'd pop over to see how you both were doing."

"In the cold and dark?" Triss asked.

"You two are changing my routine," Mrs. McCabe answered.

Triss retrieved plates and cutlery and began setting the table.

"Did something happen at work today?" Everlove asked. "You seem a bit out of sorts."

"Something did happen." Triss set a plate. "Copper is really trying to find something on me."

"Oh, dear," Mrs. McCabe said.

"For some reason, he suspects I'm involved. Mr. Haine doesn't, and Copper admitted as much. But he told me he's going to be watching me. Thanks, Everlove," Triss said as Everlove placed a large bowl of spaghetti on the table. "And if he's watching, I can't get the money to the people who need it. I've done all this for nothing."

"Oh, pshaw!" Mrs. McCabe said. "I have an idea how to do that. We need a go-between to deliver the money."

"I might know someone who can help," Everlove said, slowly. "My friend Peach."

"Would she be willing?" Mrs. McCabe asked.

"I think so. And she'll keep this quiet. Triss, what do you think?"

"I'm wondering why we don't just take an ad out and tell the whole town."

"Oh, fiddlesticks," Mrs. McCabe said. "Everlove, can you call on your friend and ask if she'll help? Although we still have the problem of getting the cash to her."

"What do you mean? I can just visit her."

"I think that's a bit risky with this fellow snooping around. But maybe I can get Mrs. Fontaine to help. I give her the money, and Apple—"

"Peach," Everlove said.

"Apologies. Anyway, Peach can do her laundry at the laundromat when Mrs. Fontaine is working and pick up the envelopes from her. We could put it in envelopes, marked."

"There's one problem with that," Everlove interjected. "Peach can't do her laundry there."

"What do you mean?"

"It's the white laundromat."

"Oh, right. Good point." Mrs. McCabe said. Triss knew Peach could go there legally, but not without causing trouble.

"Peach can call on Mrs. Fontaine at her house," Everlove said.

"Excellent idea, Everlove," Mrs. McCabe said.

Triss thought about this. "So. We assemble payments each week as necessary, and Mrs. McCabe gives them to Mrs. Fontaine when she comes to clean. Then Peach will stop by Mrs. Fontaine's house and pick them up. It may not be weekly, by the way. Probably the first and last weeks of the month."

Mrs. McCabe clapped her hands. "This is the most fun I've had since we got Mr. Pritchard a dog. Or was it when I got Nick and Violet back together?"

"I'll get the envelopes," Everlove offered. "Triss gets the list. But first, we need to dig up the money."

Anxiety engulfed Triss once again. Mrs. McCabe noticed and patted Triss's hand. "Think about the people you're going to help. How else are they going to save their homes?"

The words sowed a seed in Triss, one that germinated and stuck its tender green head up into the turmoil of her mind. Her goal here was so short-term. What would happen to Haine's renters in the long run if they didn't stop Haine? She would be handing them another month or three or five, but her effort would merely be a stay of execution.

"We have to stop him," Triss said with sudden conviction.

"That's what I've been saying all along," Mrs. McCabe said.

"Yes, but that was to keep him from getting back at me. I want to make sure he doesn't keep evicting people he has no right to evict."

"Now you're talking," Mrs. McCabe said. "Everlove? Can you talk to Mr. Moon?"

"Yes," Everlove said.

Mrs. McCabe nodded. "And I will have Mr. Pritchard help us dig up the money."

"Ask him to bring his own shovel," Triss said.

"You don't have one? How did you bury it?"

"I used a cooking spoon."

"Goodness," Everlove said at the same time Mrs. McCabe murmured, "My word." Both women turned to stare at the ladle that rested in the pot of sauce.

"Oh, for Pete's sake. I bought a new one," Triss said.

Later, Triss thought about her situation into the wee hours. Her stomach still churned, but a sense of purpose now lay in the middle of the maelstrom, shining a beam of light on her path forward.

Maybe, just maybe, her good deeds would balance out her bad ones. She didn't know how, but for the first time, she let herself hope she—they—could figure it out.

26

Triss

Saturday, November 18, 1972

True to her word, Mrs. McCabe arrived the next morning with Mr. Pritchard in tow. He bore a shovel in one hand, a scratched metal toolbox in the other, and a look of confusion on his grizzled face.

Triss let them in. Mr. Pritchard tilted his head toward the elderly woman. "She said you needed help?" he asked, his voice gruff and rusty like an old pipe.

Triss glanced at Mrs. McCabe. "You didn't tell him?"

Mrs. McCabe smiled innocently. "It's your story to tell."

"Thanks," Triss said.

"You're welcome," Mrs. McCabe said sweetly, oblivious to Triss's sarcasm.

Mr. Pritchard swung his head from one to the other. He glanced at Everlove standing in the background, hoping she might provide answers, but she shrugged. "Can someone tell me what in Sam Hill is going on so I can carry on with my day?"

Triss took a deep breath. "I buried something under the house."

Mr. Pritchard cocked his head. "What's that?"

"I buried something, and I need help digging it up."

"If you buried it yourself, why can't you dig it up yourself?" he said slowly, as if talking to a not-very-bright child.

"It's a little complicated."

"Oh, for goodness' sakes," Mrs. McCabe said, stepping forward. "We're going to be here all day if y'all keep this up. Triss works for an evil, crooked man. She stole some of his crooked money. She buried it. We are going to use that money to save people from being evicted from their homes. She needs to dig it up. But that redneck that came knocking on our doors thinks she's involved in the theft and told her he'd be watching her. We thought that calling a handyman to help would be a good cover, in case said redneck is spying. And we also ask the handyman to keep this strictly confidential."

Mr. Pritchard blinked. Then blinked again. He started to say something. Stopped. Shook his head.

"Mr. Pritchard, I've always known you're a man of few words, but I've never seen you speechless," Mrs. McCabe said.

"And I've always known you to be a meddling old woman, but this takes the cake. How do you manage to be in the middle of everything?"

Mrs. McCabe shrugged. "Just lucky, I guess."

"So when you were in your backyard fixing your plumbing problems, you were really . . ." he said to Triss.

Triss grimaced. "Burying a bag of cash," she admitted.

"Jesus Christ in a getaway car."

"You don't have to get in the middle of all this," Triss said.

"Little late for that."

Triss's face turned hot, and she knew it must be red as a rose in June. Damn her Scottish heritage.

"I'm guessing this is why that son of a, er, gun came around the other day asking about you."

"Yes," Triss confessed.

"And when he broke in . . ."

"He might have been searching for the money."

Mr. Pritchard gazed at the ceiling for a long moment, then at Triss. "Let's get this over with."

Triss led the way into a little laundry room and out the back door into the weak sunshine of the late fall morning. She pointed to the recently disturbed earth behind the oil tank. Mr. Pritchard shoved the spade into the spot, its blade biting into the soil. He quickly unearthed the foil-wrapped package and scooped it up, brushing as much dirt off as he could. He handed it to Triss with a little shake of his head, without uttering a word. She stuck it under her coat.

Mr. Pritchard replaced the dirt, tamped it down, and turned to the women. "Anything else? Need a getaway car? A Gatling gun?"

Triss's blush had ebbed but now it seeped back. "No, we're good," she said.

"I'll see myself off," Mr. Pritchard said, nodding toward the end of the trailer.

"You sure we can't offer you some tea?" Mrs. McCabe asked.

"We? You live here now?" Mr. Pritchard said, his brows furrowing together.

"Well, no, but the girls and I are as thick as—" She stopped. "Oops. Maybe that's a poor analogy."

"Simile, you mean," Mr. Pritchard said as he picked up his toolbox and stalked away.

"Did he just say 'simile'?" Mrs. McCabe asked, watching him disappear around the corner.

"He did. And he's right. Thick as thieves would be a simile, not an analogy." Everlove stared at the space he had vacated.

"Well," Mrs. McCabe said.

"Well, indeed," Everlove said.

"He is a puzzle," Triss added.

"He is," Mrs. McCabe agreed. "He has a heart of gold, but it's buried as deep as King Tut in his tomb. You've got to go through a lot of rooms to reach it. And apparently, he has more knowledge stuffed into that great hairy head than I give him credit for."

Inside the house, Triss held the bundle over the trash can as she peeled away the dirty foil. Then she unwrapped the layer of plastic wrap and laid the money on the table as if the bills might bite her. "Well, there it is," she said.

Mrs. McCabe whistled, and Triss laughed because it didn't sound right coming from a little old lady. Plus, she felt slightly hysterical.

"That's a nice pile of cash," Mrs. McCabe said. "Can someone give me a piece of paper and a pencil?"

Everlove reached across the table for the notebook Triss had noticed she carried a lot. She tore out a sheet and handed it to Mrs. McCabe. "Can you make do with a pen?" she asked.

Mrs. McCabe took the proffered materials and got to work. She separated the bills into stacks of fives, tens, and twenties, and began counting. She stopped occasionally and jotted a number on the paper, and by the time she finished, she had a neat column of round figures to add up. Which she did quickly.

"$14,525," she announced.

Everlove and Triss had hovered over the older woman as she counted. Triss had been silently adding along with her and got the same figure. Her knees gave out, and she sat, hard, on a nearby chair.

"You okay, Triss?" Everlove asked.

"I had no idea it was that much, and somehow, the amount makes it worse. Like maybe Haine could excuse a few hundred. But fourteen thousand? That's a big chunk of change. This could help people for years."

"But you said there was even more in the safe, right?" Mrs. McCabe asked.

"Yes. A lot more."

"Greedy old skinflint," Mrs. McCabe said. "He could do some good in the world with that much money. Instead, he makes people as miserable as he must be inside." She had a steely glint in her eye. "We are doing this, Triss. We are going to right some wrongs. Tilt at windmills. Do some good. Everlove and I will back you all the way, right, Everlove?" Without waiting for an answer, Mrs. McCabe restacked the money and shoved it over to Triss. "You should probably hide it somewhere. Just in case."

Triss nodded. She stood, got the aluminum foil, pulled off a sheet, wrapped the money up, and stuck it in the freezer.

"The freezer? That's kind of brilliant," Mrs. McCabe said.

"I had an aunt who did that," Triss said. "She was nuttier than a fruitcake, but I am not so sure she and I don't have some things in common."

"You're not crazy," Mrs. McCabe said. "A little loopy, maybe. But not crazy."

"Thanks, Mrs. McCabe," Triss said. "That makes me feel a lot better."

27

Triss

Monday, November 20, 1972

Triss had trouble focusing on her work. Most of her brain was occupied with thoughts of who might need help in December. And the clock was ticking. While it was only the twentieth of November, the Thanksgiving holiday was this week, and that meant lost days.

Mr. Haine sat at his desk, oblivious to her turmoil and to her attempts at telepathy as she willed him to leave the office already so she could make a list of possible recipients. He had a hearing at eleven, but the preceding hours crawled by like a turtle with lead boots.

Finally, at ten forty-five, Mr. Haine stopped his work and strode to the door. All morning, she had surreptitiously studied his reactions, his demeanor, his tone of voice, and, so far, he seemed to be his usual brusque self. She noted nothing different about him. That was good. *Damn Copper. I can't let him get to me.*

Mr. Haine donned his hat and coat. "After the hearing, I have a lunch meeting. I'm not sure when I'll be back, but I'll come back to sign those letters." He nodded at the papers on her desk.

"Yes, sir."

He left without saying goodbye.

The phone rang, and she answered it, surprised to hear her grandfather's voice on the line. She didn't think he would ever call her here. Then again, she realized she had neglected to inform him she now had a telephone. *Oops.*

"I wanted to be sure you're coming to Thanksgiving dinner," he said, with no fanfare.

She closed her eyes. She had put off thinking about the upcoming holiday, even though it was only three days away. If she went, would they argue? If she stayed away, would their rift deepen? That he had called at all said something, didn't it? She breathed in courage and exhaled hope.

"I'll come, but on one condition."

A bristling silence followed her words. She imagined his left eyebrow shooting up.

"You are delivering conditions to an invitation for Thanksgiving dinner?" he asked.

"Yes, because I want a pleasant time with you."

"What is this condition?"

"We don't talk about my job or my plans. We just enjoy the day."

Another pause, and she wondered if he had hoped that talking over the bounty of a holiday meal would have persuaded her to abandon her ambitions.

"I can agree to that." Her shoulders sagged as they released a tension she didn't know she was holding. "Georgina will serve dinner at six sharp," he continued. "Cocktails at five thirty."

"I'll be there," she said.

She finished the last letter, feeling a little lighter. Perhaps they could get past this. With her mind on a possible reconciliation, she shuffled the sheaf of letters into a neat stack and took them to Haine's office. She placed them on his desk and slid some other papers to the side so the new pile would be front and center. But as she did, something caught her eye: a letter addressed to Mr. Haine at his house. Strange. In her couple of months here, she had never seen business correspondence sent to his home. She studied the letterhead: the letters BE sat in a circle of renderings of little houses.

Curious, she skimmed the body of the letter. She dealt with all the communications in the office, and she wondered why this one had gone to his house. Beldin Enterprises—the BE of the logo—was proposing to buy some land from Edenton Development Corporation. The latter was the name of Haine's property management company. A notation for enclosures appeared beneath the signature, so she lifted the letter and found a plat map. The writing on the streets was faint and blurry, so she leaned down to peer at it. She saw Oak Street, then Pine Drive—both were in Cumbee Creek. Underneath was another plat map. But none of the street names were familiar. Maybe another town? Then she noticed "Proposed" written at the top. The puzzle pieces slid into place, a coherent picture emerging from jagged shards. She lifted the two papers together and held them up to the light. The outer limits of both maps matched exactly. The streets lined up. But the lots in the second were bigger and the street names were different.

"That son of a biscuit," she said out loud as she realized what these papers meant. She placed them back on the side of the work surface and headed to the file room, grabbing the stack of filing as she sailed by her desk.

She set the papers on the center table and opened a cabinet drawer that held the eviction files. She quickly thumbed through them, checking street names. She closed her eyes. Almost all of them fell into the tract of land outlined in the plat map.

This was why he was so unforgiving about his late-paying tenants. Or those running a business out of their homes when they weren't zoned for it. Or if they had an additional person living with them. God forbid they should take in poor Grandma. He was trying to sell the land out from under them, without buying them out the way the development company had done for the new shopping center. But surely someone would notice the increase of empty houses in Cumbee Creek? But, she thought, who would care about a neighborhood of working-class Black people struggling to make ends meet? Who cared if they lived in that house or this house or anywhere, for that matter? As long as they didn't try moving into white neighborhoods.

She stopped herself from slamming the drawer. She wanted to kick the cabinet and kick Haine in his family jewels. How many people had been evicted since she had worked for him? How many homes and livelihoods lost? For the first time, she was glad she had taken the money. She was glad Mrs. McCabe was helping. And Everlove. Maybe together, they could outwit that greedy, grasping, money-grubbing, penny-pinching, miserly, miserable old man.

28

Everlove

Monday, November 20, 1972

While Triss was at work, Everlove called on Peach, thankful that Monday was one of her days off from her job taking care of an elderly white woman.

Everlove dreaded this visit. As with every other first since she ran away, she hated having to explain what she did. Hated waiting to see if she would be judged or excused. But Peach was her oldest, closest friend. And she had winked at Everlove at church. Now, Everlove studied her as she got two cans of soda out of the refrigerator. She was still the prettiest woman Everlove had ever seen, with her flawless skin and perfectly curving mouth. Hence her nickname. When she was small, people always said she was pretty as a peach. Having four children had transformed her girlish figure into more womanly curves that added to her appeal. And Everlove would be lying if she said she didn't occasionally experience squirming strands of jealousy. But Peach also possessed a bubbling personality that had its own gravitational pull. People could not resist her.

"Lawd, I cannot believe you ran away from the church thirty minutes before you were supposed to be walking down the aisle."

"Please don't rub it in. I feel bad enough already."

Peach drew her brows together. "Aw, don't feel bad." As Everlove started to object, Peach raised a hand. "Listen, I had four kids in six years. I dropped out of school. My man can't work because he hurt his back, and Lord willing, I hope that's gonna be better soon. But all that is hard, Evvie. It is damn hard. I go to bed exhausted and worrying. And I wake up exhausted and worrying. But I love that man. God help me, I still love his broken-ass self."

"You're saying I should have stuck through the tough times," Everlove said quietly.

"I'm saying you did the right thing. I'd have slit my own throat with a rusty razor blade if I didn't love my man and my children. They are a trial. But that's what carries you through. If you didn't love Rodney, what would happen if he got sick or lost his job? Because I may adore Robert, but there are times I resent like hell that he fell off that damn ladder. Sometimes he throws a shirt at the laundry basket and misses and walks off like it's nothing, and I want to bean him in the head."

Something large and seismic shifted inside Everlove as Peach's words plucked out the shapeless, nameless aversion Everlove had about the wedding and formed it into something she could identify: she liked Rodney, but she didn't love him. Not like that.

"Evvie? You in there?" Peach mimed knocking on Everlove's head.

"Yes. I am. Just thinking about what you said."

"You said you had something to ask me," Peach said, glancing at the clock. "And I don't want to rush you, but my mama's gonna bust through that door any minute with my kids, and all hell will break loose, so better get to it while you can be heard."

"I need a favor. You know how I told you I was living with a friend? Her name is Triss, and she works for Horace Haine."

Peach cocked her head. "Oh, I know her. Little short white girl with reddish hair. Takes in the rent payments?"

"That's her. It bothers her when people can't pay and Haine won't give them a few days to pull their rent together. Especially when they have a good reason." She didn't add *Like you*, but the words hung in the air. "Triss thought of a way to help those people. She has access to some money, and she wants to give it to people who are coming up short. But she also doesn't want Haine to find out, so she is worried about giving it out herself. That's where you come in."

Peach's eyebrows had inched up her forehead as Everlove talked.

"Why me? I mean, not that I mind helping, but why don't you do it?"

"Like I said, she wants to make sure Haine doesn't find out about this. And since I live with her, I'm too close to her."

"But if you're giving me the money …"

"We are going to give it to Mrs. Fontaine. She cleans for one of Triss's neighbors a couple of days a week."

"And she will give it to me?"

"Exactly."

"This is like a James Bond movie," Peach said, her eyes sparkling. Everlove thought she and Mrs. McCabe would get along like a house on fire.

"Also, please don't tell anyone what you're doing or where the money comes from," Everlove said.

"Mum's the word. But I do have a question."

"What's that?" Everlove asked, glancing at the clock.

"Why can't Haine find out? I mean, won't he be happy that people can pay their rent? It's money in his pocket."

"I can't tell you right now."

"Can you tell me later? Because I'm burning with curiosity."

"I can't promise anything, but I'll try." Everlove explained the details she, Mrs. McCabe, and Triss had worked out. "For now, all you have to do is call on Mrs. Fontaine."

"Fair enough. And then what?"

"We will put the money in individual envelopes and write the person's name on each one, and you deliver it." A light bulb flicked on in Everlove's head. "And we'll pay you for doing this." She mentally patted herself on the back for coming up with this idea.

"Why didn't you say that first? I'm all in."

The front door banged open, and a posse of children tumbled into the room, running over to Peach, clamoring for her attention, their voices echoing off the walls. Mrs. Johnson followed, carrying Isaiah, Peach's youngest. Peach was almost lost in the pile of her kids and their two cousins, including Sha'ree. Peach clapped her hands and said, "One at a time, please! Lord have mercy! Do we have to do this every day?"

"They're just excited to see their mama," Mrs. Johnson said. "Evvie, how are you doing?"

"I'm fine. And you?"

Mrs. Johnson shook her head. "Plumb wore out. Once I hand these kids to their mamas, I go home and collapse. Don't even watch the TV 'cause I don't want to hear another voice for the rest of the day." She turned to the children and grabbed one by the hand. "Come on, young'uns. Let your mama and Auntie Evvie talk."

Everlove stood. "I have to go anyway," she said.

"Don't let my kids scare you off, Evvie," Peach said with a grin.

"I'm not. But I do need to get back home." The last word fell out easily, and Everlove wondered when her brain had made the shift from thinking of it as Triss's house to hers.

"Wait. When should I visit Mrs. Fontaine?"

"Try Wednesday. I know that's probably a busy day with the holidays, but we are trying to help people before Thanksgiving."

"This is a cool thing y'all are doing."

"Let's hope it helps," Everlove said.

Everlove was writing in her journal that evening when Triss stormed into the house, slamming the door. Everlove jumped and dropped her pen.

"Good Lord. You scared the life out of me." As she picked her pen up off the floor, she saw Triss's face. Fear gripped her. "Uh oh. What happened? Haine didn't find out about . . ."

"No, nothing like that." Triss threw her handbag onto the table by the door and hung up her coat, then joined Everlove in the kitchen. Everlove pushed her pen and notebook to the side. "I found out why Haine is evicting people right and left and on the flimsiest of grounds. Think about the people I told you about. The ones who were coming in late. Where do they all live?"

Everlove ticked off the names in her head. Then frowned. "Most of them are in Cumbee Creek," she said.

"Exactly. And that son of a biscuit has apparently been talking to a company to sell that land for development. For a richer neighborhood."

"Ohhhh," Everlove said as awareness flooded through her. "That makes sense."

Triss leaned back in her chair and kicked her shoes off. "I actually had a moment where I was glad I stole the money."

"Just a moment?" Everlove asked.

"Maybe two moments," she said and shared a smile with Everlove. "Oh, and . . ." She crossed the room and pulled a slip of paper out of her purse. "I made a list. These are the people who I think will have trouble paying." She handed the paper to Everlove.

Everlove read through the names, and her heart contracted when she saw Peach's, even though she had expected it.

"I see Peach is on here. I hope you don't mind, but I told her we'd pay her to deliver the money."

"Mind? That's a great idea. You met with her today, right?"

"Yes. She's delighted to help." Everlove handed the list back to Triss.

"Shall we do it?" Triss said.

"Do what?"

"Figure out how much we are going to give to everyone."

"Yeah, I guess we should," Everlove said. "Some of them might be able to pull together their rent without our help."

"So? Is it so bad if we give them a little gift anyway?" Triss asked. "It's not like any of them are rolling in cash."

"You have a point."

"You're ready to do this?"

"I think seeing Peach convinced me this is the right thing to do. I don't know what Peach would do if she got evicted. Go live with her mother and brother in their two-bedroom house? With her four kids and her husband? I guess she could. And she could get back on her feet. Her husband is on the mend and taking on small jobs. But knowing Haine just wants to take people's homes so he can sell the land burns me up." Everlove took a deep breath. "Well, anyway. You don't need to hear my rant," she said.

"Actually, I do. I appreciate the perspective."

They sat at the table, and Everlove offered up what she knew about people's circumstances. Together, they estimated what they thought people might need.

"I think Mrs. Calvin would be okay with ten or fifteen dollars," Triss said. "She was only seven dollars short for this month." She paused. "Honestly? I'd like to give her more, but I am afraid of causing too much of a stir. We really need to keep this quiet."

"I hate to tell you this, but receiving anonymous gifts of money is going to cause a stir." When Triss winced, Everlove rushed on. "But I don't think this will get back to Haine. There isn't anyone I know who likes him."

"I hope you're right," Triss said.

Everlove continued to peruse the list. "I'm worried about Peter Powell. Everyone calls him Pie-Eyed Pete because he's always drunk. Any money you give him will end up in Weevil Carr's pocket instead of Mr. Haine's, although they're the same thing, I guess. But one gets him a bottle and the other gets him a roof."

"I'm familiar with Mr. Powell. Is there anyone who can pay his rent for him? I'd try to slip it in myself, but I am tempting fate enough as it is."

Everlove thought for a minute. "His sister might. Maybe Peach can give her his envelope. We can put a note in it, so she knows what it's for."

"I think they all need notes. First to explain what the money's for, and second to tell them that this is confidential. Do you think Peach can keep who we are a secret?"

Everlove gave a short bark of a laugh, thinking of how Peach kept her first pregnancy secret for months. As well as her relationship with Robert Singleton. Not even Everlove had known they were seeing each other so much. "Peach can definitely keep a secret," she said.

They finished their list, and Everlove realized she was ravenous. She and Triss cooked dinner together. After they ate, Triss took a shower, and Everlove returned to the poem she had been writing. She added some words, changed a few others, and was feeling satisfied when the phone rang.

She answered it, surprised to hear Leona's voice on the other end. She was the first family member to call Everlove. "I'm calling to invite you to Thanksgiving dinner."

Everlove figured she'd be spending the holiday alone. "I don't think I'll be welcome."

"I have permission from the queen herself."

"Seriously?"

"Serious as a heart attack."

"But this wasn't her idea, I'm sure."

"But she agreed, Evvie. It's a step."

Everlove had a vision of herself not going, of snubbing her mother's tiny gesture toward reconciliation. But that picture was followed closely by one of her sitting at home on Thanksgiving, wondering how angry her mother was. The thought made her shudder. "I guess I'll take my own step and be there."

"We'll see you at four then."

She replaced the handset into the cradle as Triss entered the room, hair damp and smelling of flowery shampoo. Everlove suppressed a shake of her head at how easy it was for Triss to wash her hair with hardly a thought.

"You want to watch *Laugh In*?" Triss asked.

"Sounds good to me."

Triss turned the TV on and moved the rabbit ears around until she got a decent picture. Then they sat and laughed at the antics of Dan Rowan and Dick Martin, Ruth Buzzi, and Johnny Brown. Everlove put aside her worries. For an hour, anyway.

29

Triss

Tuesday, November 21, 1972

Triss padded groggily into the kitchen, plugged the percolator in, and watched the liquid pulse tantalizingly in the glass knob on the lid. She stuck a slice of bread in the toaster, and by the time it popped up and she had slathered it with butter, the percolator had stopped. After pouring the steaming coffee into a cup, she carried it and her plate to the table. She nibbled the toast while waiting for the coffee to cool to a drinkable temperature.

As the morning mental fog started to dissipate, she began to ponder her to-do items for the day. Should she buy a bottle of wine or fruit basket for her grandfather's? A dessert? Did she, Everlove, and Mrs. McCabe have a good plan for distributing the money? Perhaps she should write it down and get a clear picture of their steps. She reached for Everlove's notebook and pen that lay nearby. She didn't think Everlove would mind if she tore a sheet out.

She uncapped the pen and opened the notebook, flipping the pages as she looked for a clean sheet. She noticed most of the pages weren't lists or paragraphs. She took a closer look at the last page with writing on it. It was—apparently—a poem. Some words were crossed out and others penned in, but it was still readable. Intrigued, she read it.

They say the world is darkest in that space
Before the dawn
When hope has ebbed, and life turns bleak and
We are left forlorn
Then we look to the gentle moon and
Tender silver stars
To find faith that kindness lives somewhere not too far

This gift is from a secret friend, an attempt
to light the way
To help you find a path through night into
The radiance of day
It isn't much, this quiet gleam of handheld starlight beams
A thread of hope that whispers gently
Not all is as it seems

When she finished the last line, Triss had two thoughts: one, she shouldn't have read it; and two, it was beautiful. She slid the notebook over, ashamed and embarrassed. Snooping at the office was one thing. Snooping on her roommate was quite another.

She was washing her cup when Everlove came in and headed straight for the percolator. A knock sounded at the door.

"Bet I know who that is," Everlove said.

"Good thing I made a full pot," Triss said as she dried her hands and strode to the door. "Mrs. McCabe! Fancy seeing you here."

"No one called me with an update, and I am dying to know what's going on. So spill the beans and pour the coffee. And don't mix those two up!"

Triss realized they had a lot to tell. They filled Mrs. McCabe in on Triss finding the plats and Everlove recruiting Peach.

"I'll buy some envelopes today," Everlove said when they had finished. "And we can get started tonight."

The idea both exhilarated Triss and appalled her. She felt like she was looking at a huge roller coaster she didn't know if she wanted to go on or not. What she really wanted, she realized, was for the ride to be over and to be safe and secure again.

"I'm ready!" Mrs. McCabe said. "By the way, I stopped at Violet's house. She's hosting Thanksgiving dinner for our little group of friends. I asked if you two could come. She said the more the merrier."

"That's nice," Everlove said. "But I'll be with my family."

"And I'm going to see my grandfather," Triss said.

"What time?" Mrs. McCabe asked.

"Six," Triss said.

"Four for me," said Everlove.

"No problem! You can do both. We're having our Thanksgiving feast at twelve. Stop by Violet's—she lives on the other side of me from Mr. Pritchard—for a little while. You don't have to eat until you explode."

"I don't know . . ." Triss started.

"Mrs. McCabe," Everlove said. "Don't count me in."

"And why ever not?" Mrs. McCabe asked.

"I'm not sure I would be welcome."

"Why wouldn't you be welcome?"

"Um, not everyone would be thrilled to have a Black person in their home."

"Poppycock. You've already met Mr. Pritchard, and he didn't seem to care if you were white, Black, or had polka dots. When I mentioned this to Violet, she loved the idea of inviting you. We'll see you at twelve. Why don't you bring some deviled eggs? Everlove, you can teach Triss how to make them. I need to get home. I have pies to bake. I'll be by tonight for our secret mission. I'll also let Violet know you'll be at her house on Thursday."

And she left.

Triss turned to Everlove. "How does she do that? We said no, but I think we're still going."

"I reckon we are."

Triss and Everlove were fixing dinner that evening when what had been a drizzle turned into a heavy rain that pounded on the metal roof of the trailer.

"Did I just hear knocking, or was it the wind?" Everlove said.

"I'm not sure, but I'll check," Triss said.

When Triss opened the door, Mrs. McCabe nearly knocked her over as she scrambled inside.

"Goodness. We may need to build an ark," Mrs. McCabe said.

Triss took her umbrella and coat and grabbed the afghan on the sofa and wrapped it around her. "That umbrella didn't seem to help! You're soaked. Here, kick your shoes off and have a seat. Dinner is almost ready."

Mrs. McCabe shuffled to the table in her stocking feet. They ate a simple dinner of pasta with mushroom sauce and green beans. Afterwards, they sat at the table with the cash, the envelopes, and the list.

"Everlove and I talked about including notes in the envelopes explaining what the money's for and how it should be kept confidential."

"Like 'This is for your rent, from a friend.' Something like that?" Mrs. McCabe said.

"Something like that," Triss said, but an idea formed. She turned to Everlove. "I have a confession, an apology, and an idea."

Everlove looked amused. "What now? Did you kidnap Mr. Haine? Are you holding him for ransom?"

Mrs. McCabe snorted. "Nobody would pay it."

Triss let their words wash over her. Everlove need not ever know she had peeked at her notebook. Yet Triss was trying to mend her ways, and honesty seemed the right way to do that. "Your notebook was open. Here on the table. I didn't mean to look at it." Everlove's levity evaporated. "And as soon as I read it, I closed it. I'm sorry."

To Triss's dismay, Everlove looked mortified. "You really shouldn't have," Everlove said, with more force than was usual for her.

"You're right. I was looking for a piece of paper, but your words caught my eye, and, Everlove, they drew me in. You're an excellent writer. But also, I was just thinking. Maybe we could use the poem in the envelopes."

Everlove shook her head. "I don't think so. It's not very good."

"You shouldn't sell yourself short. And the poem would be perfect for our . . . gifts. It's so hopeful."

"Nobody wants to read that stuff."

"Nonsense! Have you ever put your words out there?"

"No, but—"

"Give it a test run. Next time it won't be so difficult."

"What do you mean 'next time'?"

"I joined a debate club in college so I could improve my public speaking, and the first time, I was terrified. The second time, I was still terrified, but a little less so. It's hard to put yourself out there, but Everlove, you should try."

"I don't think—"

"Hello! Remember me?" Mrs. McCabe said, waving a hand. "Perhaps we need an unvarnished opinion. Such as mine."

"That's frightening," Everlove said.

"She might side with you and say we shouldn't use it," Triss said, but there was no way Mrs. McCabe could hate the poem. "Can she read it?"

Everlove kept shaking her head.

"Somewhere between the two of us," Triss said, "is a perfect balance of my impulsivity and your timidity."

"I'm not timid!"

"Prove it."

"You've been hanging around Mrs. McCabe too much."

"Hey! I resent that," Mrs. McCabe said. "Everlove, why don't you let me read it, and I will try not to like it."

"Fine," Everlove said. She retrieved the notebook from where it now rested on the coffee table. "Which one was it?" she asked.

"The one about the stars and moon."

Everlove opened it and handed it to Mrs. McCabe. Triss watched Mrs. McCabe intently, but Everlove fidgeted and averted her eyes. Triss reached over and squeezed her hand.

Mrs. McCabe looked up. "Darn it."

Triss's breath caught. Had she made a mistake in forcing this issue?

"I'm sorry, Everlove," she said. "I tried to not like it, but it's quite lovely. And it would be perfect for this."

Triss grinned. Everlove groaned. "Look at it this way, Everlove. It's anonymous. No one has to know you wrote this."

"Fine," Everlove said. "Use it. Y'all are relentless. And this proves I'm not timid."

Triss took the notebook. "Everlove, you have better handwriting than I do. Would you mind copying the poem for the envelopes? Mrs. McCabe and I can count the money." She sat back as a thought occurred to her. "We can't get these to people before Thanksgiving."

"Why not?" Everlove asked.

"Mrs. Fontaine won't be cleaning Mrs. McCabe's house on Thursday."

"She's offered to stop by in the morning to see if there's anything I need doing," Mrs. McCabe said. "I told her I was sure she would have her hands full with her own cooking. But she said her son was going to his in-laws' house on Thanksgiving, and she'd be celebrating with him and his family on Friday. So I invited her to Violet's."

"What did she say?" Everlove asked.

"She said yes, after some persuasion," Mrs. McCabe said. "But you helped."

"Me?"

"I told her you'd be there. A familiar face."

"I can't wait to meet her," Triss said. "Now, shall we get to work? These envelopes aren't going to stuff themselves."

As the three worked companionably at the little kitchen table, Triss allowed herself the hope that she would make it out of this okay. And help some people as well.

After they finished, Mrs. McCabe walked across to her house. Triss was glad to see the rain had slowed to a light mist. When she closed the door, she turned to Everlove.

"Would you like some wine?" Triss asked.

"Sure," Everlove said, and Triss winced as she heard the distance in Everlove's voice. She poured the garnet liquid into the usual jelly jars, and they flopped onto the sofa.

"Should we get a tree?" Triss asked.

"Might be a good idea."

"I think it would brighten up the place," Triss said. Everlove didn't respond as she swirled the wine in her glass. Triss inhaled and wished for some courage to smooth the roughness between them. "Listen, I honestly didn't mean to read your journal. It was early in the morning, and I was having coffee, and it was just there."

"I know," Everlove said. "It's fine. I shouldn't have left it open."

"Don't take blame for something that is mine to own. I shouldn't have read it. But maybe some good can come of this."

"What do you mean?"

"I think you should do something with your writing. Maybe you need a little push."

"And you're volunteering for the job?"

"Absolutely!" Triss gave a salute. "I would be your biggest cheerleader."

"You have nothing to cheer for. It's just babbling on paper."

"It is so much more than that," Triss said. "You could submit to magazines. Contests. I have big plans for you!"

30

Triss

Wednesday, November 22, 1972

On the day before Thanksgiving, Triss bustled about the office. She was more jittery than usual but didn't think it showed until Mr. Haine called her on it.

"Patricia, do you think you could stop flitting about like an overwrought bird?" he said when she brought him papers needing his signature.

"Yes, sir. I guess I'm excited," she said, as if it was the holiday and not the fact that she had started the process of distributing stolen money yesterday. Anxiety strummed through her like she was a plucked harp string.

They closed the office at noon, and relief flowed through Triss as Mr. Haine gave her a curt nod and eased himself into his funereal Cadillac DeVille. She didn't have to see him for the next four and a half days.

Triss drove to her house but was at loose ends waiting for Everlove to get home from work. She ate lunch. She tried to read, then gave it up and paced. She dusted. Swept the floor. Made a mental note that she should borrow a vacuum to clean the carpet. She lay on the sofa and stared at the moonscape of their popcorn ceiling and idly remembered the moon landing three years ago. Watching it with her brother, his girlfriend at the time, and her grandfather on a sweltering summer day. Her grandfather, up past his bedtime, spoke with unusual loquaciousness about the things he'd seen invented in his lifetime that were now commonplace to Triss and Jay: telephones, electricity, running water, automobiles, airplanes.

"Triss. Yoo-hoo. Triss." Someone was shaking her arm. She opened her eyes and saw Everlove, bemused, standing over her. She sat up, startled, groggy, wondering what time it was. Wondering what day it was.

"I must have fallen asleep," Triss said.

"I'll say."

"I meant to make dinner."

"It just so happens I have leftovers from the Thanksgiving sale today. Pre-made stuff, so we can just heat it." As Everlove heated the food, she set some eggs in a pot of water to boil them for the deviled eggs they had been commanded to bring.

After they ate, Everlove showed Triss how to peel the eggs and scoop out the powdery yolks to be mashed up with mayonnaise, vinegar, mustard, salt, and pepper. After plopping the mixture back into the egg halves, they sprinkled them with paprika.

"That was pretty easy," Triss said.

"Most cooking isn't terribly hard," Everlove said.

"But there are so many things I don't know. How long do you cook steak? When you make gravy, how much flour do you add? You never measure anything."

"Maybe some nights when we are both home, I can show you a few things."

"Sounds good," Triss said, and her words turned into a yawn. "I can't believe I fell asleep so hard."

"Relief at being away from your boss?"

"That could be. It'll be nice not to see him for the next four days. Although I have to spend time with my grandfather."

"And I have to face my mother." Everlove frowned.

"Twenty-four hours from now, our Thanksgiving dinners will be behind us. All of them." Triss grinned at Everlove.

Everlove groaned. "Think I can go to my parents' house early and skip out on the neighborhood one?"

"And leave me to face Mrs. McCabe alone? No way! We're in this together."

"I guess we are."

Triss liked the sound of that.

31

Everlove

Thursday, November 23 (Thanksgiving), 1972

At noon on Thanksgiving Day, Everlove and Triss stepped into a crisp breeze that smelled of cold earth and warm wood smoke, of rotting leaves and flourishing evergreens. Triss carried the plate of deviled eggs and Everlove closed the door behind them. The sun sparkled on the pine needles and on flecks of quartz in the pavement in the newly paved road. Everlove thought of Thanksgiving last year: dinner at her parents' and then Rodney's—this wasn't her first double-dinner holiday. At that get-together, she had imagined she'd be married by now, and the vision twisted her insides into a knot of anxiety. She had chalked that up to pre-wedding jitters, but she should have known a bride doesn't get nervous a year before the wedding and right after getting engaged. Her gut had been trying to tell her something, but she had squashed the little voice like an ant at a picnic. Now she had doubts about this get-together, but for different reasons. A Thanksgiving with a bunch of white people, almost all of them strangers. She had certainly steered her life into bizarre waters.

Triss seemed to sense her discomfort. "If you're uncomfortable, we can go at any time. Okay?"

Everlove nodded.

"We'll have a secret sign. Pull on your ear like Carol Burnett, and I'll make up an excuse," Triss said as they arrived at the house. Everlove couldn't help but smile at the idea.

Violet greeted them with her own wide smile. "Triss! Everlove! I'm so glad you came. Come in and meet everyone!"

They entered a living room splashed with color, a blue-and-green throw here, a red pillow there, all creating a bright, welcoming ambiance. A blonde woman sat on a sofa, and a little boy knelt on the floor at her feet, bent over a coffee table, intently building a Lincoln Log house. Arabella sprang up and bounced over to them.

"Hi, Miss Triss. Hi, Miss Everlove. It's nice to see you here!" Her beaming smile put Everlove at ease.

Violet introduced Caroline, Arabella's mother, who looked up and smiled and caressed the hair of the young boy at her feet. "This is Allen. Say hello, Allen." He gave them a quick wave but didn't look up.

Triss held up the plate. "We brought deviled eggs," she said.

A tall, handsome man with short-cropped dark hair—definitely from the air base, Everlove thought—leaned out of a doorway through which Everlove could see a counter mounded with food and dishes and cooking utensils.

He waved. "I'll take that. Thanks for bringing it, but you didn't have to."

"We were ordered to," she said.

"Ah. Mrs. McCabe, I'm guessing."

"You would be right."

"I'm Nick, by the way. Violet's fiancé and chief cook and bottle washer."

Before Everlove could answer, a zephyr of cold air swept through the room as Mrs. McCabe swung open the door. She carried a casserole dish that she thrust at Violet.

"Ah! Good. You're here," Mrs. McCabe said to Triss and Everlove. "Did you meet everyone?"

"Hi to you, too, Mrs. McCabe," Violet said.

Mrs. McCabe patted her hand. "I see you all the time." She scanned the room. "Where are Mr. Pritchard and Tommy?"

"They should be here soon," Violet said as she walked to the kitchen with the dish.

"And I assume Tommy's bringing Joanna?"

"Yep," Violet said with a smile. "They have become inseparable."

"Once they arrive, you'll have met the whole gang," Mrs. McCabe said to Triss and Everlove. "Except George, of course. George is Arabella's father, and he is on a tour somewhere called Goose Bay."

"Tour of duty," Violet said. "You make it sound as if he's on vacation."

"It's really, really cold there," Arabella added.

"I want to see a penguin!" Allen said, tearing his attention away from his creation, face bright with expectation.

"Silly!" Arabella told him. "Penguins are in the South Pole. Daddy's closer to the North Pole. And he's not even that close."

"Please have a seat," Violet said to Everlove and Triss, indicating chairs placed around the room for extra seating.

The door opened once more, and a young man holding hands with a girl about his age walked in, followed by Mr.

Pritchard. *His son?* Everlove wondered. She had not pictured him with a family.

"This is Mr. Pritchard," Violet said.

"We've met," Mr. Pritchard said, and Triss blushed.

"He helped hang a picture," Everlove said quickly. "In our living room."

If she had thought Mr. Pritchard would give them away, she needn't have worried. "This is Tommy. My apprentice. And his girlfriend, Joanna."

Who has apprentices these days? Everlove thought and imagined the two of them at a blacksmith's forge wearing leather aprons.

Tommy bobbed his head and mumbled something Everlove couldn't make out. It could have been anything from "Nice to meet you" to "You bet your bippy." He carried cans of soda into the kitchen, and Mr. Pritchard followed with a basket. "Biscuits," he grunted as he set the basket on the table.

Triss and Everlove sat, and Everlove tested the temperature of the room, the same way she checked a store when she walked in. But everyone had turned to Mrs. McCabe as she asked Tommy how he liked his new job. No one snuck sideways glances at her. She relaxed a little.

"I'm learning a lot about semitruck engines, so that's cool," Tommy said, ducking his head.

"Are you still working with Mr. Pritchard?" Caroline asked.

"Yeah, he still keeps me busy."

"You mean out of trouble," Mr. Pritchard said.

"I bet Tommy hasn't sniffed trouble since he moved in with you—what, three years ago?" Violet said.

"Never underestimate the trouble a teen boy can get into," Mr. Pritchard said.

"Um, Mr. P, I'm twenty-one now."

"Never underestimate the trouble a young man can get into," Mr. Pritchard amended, without missing a beat.

A knock sounded at the door, and Violet ushered in Mrs. Fontaine.

Mrs. McCabe patted a chair between her and Everlove. "Mrs. Fontaine, I saved you a seat. You know Violet, and I believe you know Everlove."

"Nice to see you all," Mrs. Fontaine said. She handed Violet a dish. "I brought a sweet potato casserole," she said.

"Oh, you didn't have to do that. But thank you," Violet said, and once again introduced everyone.

"May I do anything to help?" Mrs. Fontaine asked.

"You just sit right there and enjoy being waited on for once," Mrs. McCabe said. "Right, Violet?"

"That's right. Nick and I have everything almost ready."

Nick and Violet brought out appetizers, including the deviled eggs, which everyone proclaimed to be delicious.

Nick disappeared into the kitchen, turning down several offers of help as he went. "I have it all under control," he said.

Caroline shook her head. "I can never say that when I'm making a big meal for so many people."

"Me either," Violet said.

Caroline shared the latest news of her husband George and the cold weather he was already facing.

"Been there!" Nick called from the kitchen. "Brrrr! And sorry George can't be here for this, but dinner is served. Line up and help yourselves!"

They filed into the kitchen and scooped turkey, dressing, potatoes, and more onto their plates and carried them back into the living room.

"I hope you don't mind holding your plates on your laps," Violet said to Triss and Everlove.

"It's not a problem," Triss said.

"We eat like this all the time at my parents' house," Everlove said.

The food was delicious. Everlove had to force herself not to go back for seconds since she had another feast waiting for her later.

As they ate, Caroline asked what brought Triss and Everlove to the neighborhood. "Both of us were looking for fresh starts," Triss said. Mrs. McCabe, thankfully, kept mum.

"Violet, how are the wedding plans going?" Mrs. McCabe asked.

Everlove suppressed a wince at the still-tender subject and concentrated on the turkey and dressing on her plate.

"Funny you should ask," Violet said.

"Uh-oh," Caroline said. "I don't think anyone ever says that and then shares good news."

"I'm afraid you're right about that. The Bride's Boutique went out of business. Just poof! I went for a fitting last Saturday and found they've locked the doors with my wedding dress trapped inside."

"Oh no!" Caroline exclaimed. "That's terrible."

"I told her she could wear a potato sack, and she would still wow everyone," Nick said.

Violet jabbed him playfully in the ribs. "So you'll show up looking like Cary Grant in a tuxedo, and I'll look like Elly May Clampett with a rope belt. No thanks!"

"Surely there are other shops around," Caroline said. "And doesn't Bennett's have a bridal department?"

"Yes, but I didn't find anything I liked there the first time. Plus, I lost my money, and it's not quite in our budget to buy two wedding dresses."

Everlove thought of the irony that she possessed a ruined dress that no longer had a bride while here sat a bride who no longer had a dress. She wondered if Violet might . . . but no. She pushed the thought out of her head. No one wanted a dress from a failed wedding.

Everyone clucked in disappointment. "I am sure it will all work out somehow," Mrs. McCabe said.

"My mom can make one!" Arabella piped up from her perch on the sofa next to Caroline.

Violet shook her head. "She's far too busy for that."

Caroline shrugged. "I don't know. Perhaps if we go scouring secondhand shops, we can find something we can alter. My best friend in high school and I used to do that. We'd take a day dress and add tulle or flowers or seed pearls, and next thing you know, we had a prom gown."

"That's a thought. I guess I'll look around."

Arabella beamed. She turned to Mrs. Fontaine. "Mrs. Fontaine, do you have to use that cane all the time?"

"Arabella, don't put new guests on the spot like that," Caroline admonished.

"It's okay," Mrs. Fontaine said, smiling at the young girl. "I use it all the time."

"That's really cool," Arabella said, and Mrs. Fontaine raised her eyebrows. "I mean, if you're out walking and someone tries to mug you, you can whack them with your cane!"

Mrs. Fontaine chuckled. "I had never thought of that," she said.

"Arabella, I think you've been watching too much TV," Caroline said.

"I think it's from reading Nancy Drew," Arabella said. "You never know when you're going to run into a bad guy!"

Everlove couldn't help but smile, and that caught Arabella's eye.

"Miss Everlove!" Arabella exclaimed. "I've never heard of anyone with that name. Where did it come from?"

"It's kind of a long and boring story," Everlove said.

"I bet it's not boring! Please tell us!" Arabella pleaded.

With everyone's eyes on her, Everlove resisted the urge to squirm. Still, she couldn't resist Arabella's eager interest. "Okay. Here goes. Years ago, when my parents were expecting their first child, my father said he didn't care if it was a boy or a girl. So he wasn't disappointed when Leola was born. But when my mother was expecting again, Pop made no bones about wanting a baby boy. He strutted around town, talking about what he would do with his son, how he would teach him to fish and fix cars. But when the time came, another daughter appeared. That's my sister, Rosie. My father shrugged and said, 'Next time, we'll have our son.' But the next time came, and still no boy. My mother gave birth to Jasmine. And then baby Josephine was born—that's number four in case you lost count. A year and a half passed, and my mother is expecting child number five. My dad thought five would be his lucky number. But he learned his lesson and didn't strut around town this time, but all our friends and neighbors gave him a hard time. 'You having a boy this time, James?'" Here, Everlove made her voice deep and gruff. "'Hope you get that son, James!' My mother went into labor, and the midwife came. My mother was in labor all day.

Finally, just before midnight, I arrived in the world. My mother was laying in bed, exhausted, and my father came in. 'Avenia,' he said. 'That better be a boy you're holding.' My mother did not take too kindly to his attitude. She narrowed her eyes at him and said, 'It's a girl.' Her expression dared him to say something. But my father did not take the hint and said, 'What in the ever-loving'"—Everlove glanced at the two children in the room—"'heck are we going to do with another girl?' 'We will love her and raise her up like we are doing with our other girls, that's what,' my mother snapped. My father stomped out, and my mother turned to the midwife and told her when she filled out the birth certificate to put down Everlove as my name, so that he would always remember he should love me and my sisters no matter what. And that's how I got my name."

Arabella clapped her hands, and everyone else chuckled. "You were wrong, Miss Porter! That's a great story!"

The neighbors nodded their agreement.

"My dad had a law school friend who named his son Court," Triss said.

"I had an aunt who named her daughter Comfort because she was born very late in her mother's life, and her mother thought she would be a comfort to her in her old age. She turned out to be a wild child who wreaked havoc wherever she went," Violet said.

"I have a cousin who named her daughter Macy because she went into labor in Macy's," Mrs. Fontaine said, somewhat bashfully. From there, the neighbors threw out ideas for babies being named after where their mothers went into labor: Woolworth's Five and Dime, Taxi, Roadside. Soon they were laughing until they were wiping away tears. Everlove was happy she came. At least this Thanksgiving dinner would be remembered for its camaraderie and joy. She didn't expect that much at her next one.

After a little more chatter, Everlove realized she needed to head over to her parents' house. She rose and offered to help clean up, but Nick and Violet told her not to worry about it. She offered to give Mrs. Fontaine a ride home, which she accepted, and the two women left.

That evening, Everlove was back in her room, glad the family Thanksgiving dinner was over. She had been glad to have company on the drive, which had saved her from thinking too much about what was in front of her. Once she was home—or what used to be home—it had not been as bad as she feared. Her mother's silences had slid almost unnoticed into the spaces between the strident voices and lilting laughs of her siblings, their spouses, and their children. Everlove knew everyone was aware of the thread of tension that pulled taut between her mother and herself. But the other threads of conversations and jokes had filled the rooms and softened what otherwise might have been an unbearable thrum. But two things happened that she would treasure: Ruby had insisted on sitting next to her and chatted unceasingly about her life, and her father had hugged her when he walked her to her car. That he did it out of her mother's view didn't matter to Everlove. Neither he nor she wanted to poke that bear.

Now as she changed clothes, Everlove realized she was smiling. She had faced an uncomfortable situation, kept her head high, and felt better for it.

As she put away her clothes, she considered the wedding dress she had stuffed into the closet. She pulled it out and inspected it. There were a couple of tears in the skirt, but they were small, and some ornamentation could be sewn onto the material to disguise the damage. Same for the stain. Other than that, the gown was in good shape. It had long sleeves for winter, but they could easily be shortened for a late-spring wedding. Maybe she should at least offer it to Violet and let her decide.

She shook her head. It was probably a bad idea. She would be putting Violet on the spot. She pushed the dress back into the closet and closed the door.

But the notion nagged at her all night. In the morning, she woke with vague memories of dreams about dresses that talked and walked, like Dr. Seuss's pale-green pants with nobody inside them. After breakfast, Triss left to run errands. Everlove had an hour before she needed to be at work. Enough time to make a delivery.

She lay the dress on the bed and pulled her bedspread around it, gathering it in her arms as best she could. Walking over to a neighbor's with bed linens seemed a little less strange than walking over with a wedding dress. Barely.

The surrounding houses sat in post-holiday stillness. She walked briskly to Violet's house and knocked before she lost her nerve. But second guesses consumed her. This was stupid. No one would want her not-quite-used but still damaged wedding dress. She needed to go back to being the girl who did not act impulsively.

But Violet opened the door, and it was too late.

"Everlove! What a pleasant surprise," Violet said. "Would you like to come in?"

"Yes, thank you. I, uh, have something to show you."

"Can I get you something to drink?" Violet asked, her eyes flicking down to the yards of green fabric Everlove was carrying.

"No, thank you. I have to go to work soon." Everlove cleared her throat. "I was supposed to get married earlier this month, but I changed my mind at the last minute. So I have a gown." She laid the wrapped dress on Violet's sofa and pulled away the chenille spread, revealing the white satin and lace underneath. "It's got a few rips and stains, but I think it's fixable. And we're close enough in size that it could be altered to fit you. I know it might seem like a bad omen to wear a dress from a canceled wedding, but I had to at least offer. You can say no, and there'll be no hard feelings."

"Well, this is unexpected," Violet said. She ran her fingers over the fabric lightly. "It's beautiful."

"It was. I mean is."

"How much do you want for it?"

Everlove almost laughed. "I'm not selling it. I'm giving it to you. It's taking up space in my closet."

"Wow. Everlove, I don't know what to say. May I?" She gestured at the garment, and Everlove nodded. Violet held it up and turned it this way and that. "It really is very nice. And I do think this could be fixed."

"I guess it comes down to whether you're superstitious or not."

"You know, I don't think I am. It's just a secondhand dress." She cocked her head for a minute. "Heck, I'm a secondhand bride, so it actually seems kind of fitting."

Everlove couldn't hide her surprise. Violet smiled at her. "I'm a widow."

"But you're so young," Everlove blurted, then regretted the words. What a stupid thing to say.

"On the outside, maybe. Sometimes I feel older than Mrs. McCabe. Or used to. I'm better now. I didn't think I'd ever marry again, but here I am. And I guess if Nick can take a secondhand bride, I can wear a secondhand dress. I'd like to pay you for it, though."

"Please don't. It makes me happy to know it will be used." She studied Violet's face. "You don't have to take it."

"I think it's a great solution. It's going to save me time and money. Thank you for thinking of this."

Everlove made her goodbyes and rolled up her bedspread. *What do you know*, she thought as she walked back to her house. *That actually went well. Maybe my instincts aren't so bad after all.*

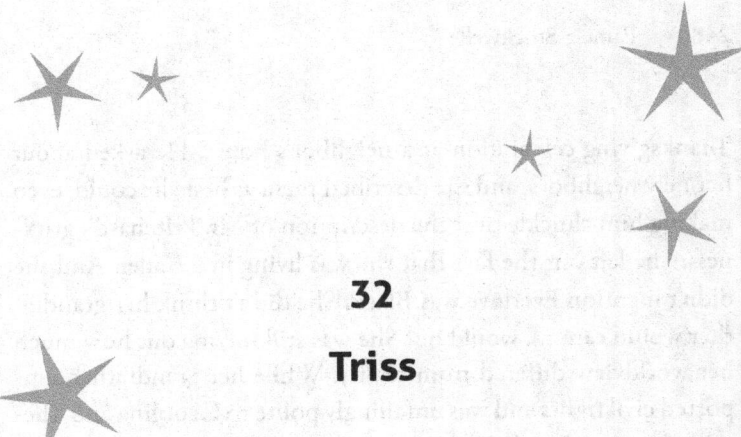

32

Triss

Thursday, November 23–Wednesday, December 6, 1972

As Triss sat in Violet's living room stabbing a piece of turkey, she realized she had thought of this street and her rented mobile home as temporary, a home away from home until her grandfather understood she was serious about her ambitions. But here, amongst her new neighbors, Triss thought she would be okay if she lived here for a while.

She enjoyed the food and the bantering of her neighbors. She hid her own small smile as she watched Mr. Pritchard almost crack his own. She saw Mrs. Fontaine slowly and subtly relax as Arabella moved her chair near hers and chatted with her. The room felt like a comfortable blanket—snug and warm.

She didn't think her second dinner would be as agreeable, but true to his word, her grandfather made no reference to where she was living, her job, or her desire to go to law school. Triss stuck with that script, although she did mention she had a roommate—he had raised his eyebrow ever so slightly—and that she had an earlier

Thanksgiving celebration at a neighbor's house. He asked about her new neighbors, and she described them as best she could, even making him chuckle over the description of Mr. Pritchard's gruffness. She left out the fact that she was living in a trailer. And she didn't mention Everlove was Black. She didn't think her grandfather would care . . . would he? She was still sorting out how much her worldview differed from reality. While her grandfather supported civil rights and was unfailingly polite to Georgina and Theodo, Triss wondered if he ever had a Black friend. Black colleague? If it hadn't been for the strain between them, she might have asked him about that. He could appear formal and forbidding, but she had never had a problem talking to him. But now was not the time.

Maybe one of these days, she and her grandfather could get back on the right track.

As November faded into December, the front door of Haine's office might as well have been a revolving one with the flurry of people paying their rent. Some brought checks. Most brought cash. And a few brought promises to make up a shortfall in the coming week. Triss took note of these, questioning them lightly about when they might be able to bring the balance, listening to their answers and reading their faces to see if they were certain or not.

Sprinkled in the steady stream of people were some Triss and her crew had already helped. Triss kept her face impassive. Like she had with the break-in, she repeated to herself that she knew nothing about anything. She worried someone would broadcast their small windfall, but, to her relief, no one said a word.

Copper dropped by every now and again and made pointed remarks about seeing Triss around. She occasionally spotted his red truck behind hers. But the fact that Mr. Haine did not seem suspicious made Copper easier to deal with. As did picturing him trussed up in duct tape. She tried not to let him bother her and instead carried on with both her jobs: the one where she worked for Mr. Haine and the one where she worked against him.

One day when Copper came in, he and Mr. Haine had their usual tête-à-tête, then Mr. Haine strode to the file room, the duffel dangling from his left hand. Triss had been working on the office ledger and was just finishing up. As she stuffed it back in her drawer, she saw Mr. Haine in her peripheral vision as he stopped in the middle of the room. He shook his head, placed the duffel on the table, and stalked back to his office.

"You can wait out back for me," Haine said to Copper. If Copper minded being so summarily dismissed, he didn't show it. He strolled by Triss and leaned toward her. "I'll be seeing you around, Miss Littlefield," he said with a wink.

Triss tried to smile pleasantly as if he were nothing to her, but he still made her stomach churn. She heard him leave through the back door as Mr. Haine emerged from his lair, holding a slip of yellow paper. He returned to the file room and opened the safe. He had changed the combination to the safe, and she guessed he had forgotten it and had to go back for it. A tiny, little thrill of satisfaction that she had inconvenienced him made her smile.

Triss heard the thud of the safe door closing, followed by the clunk of the bolts sliding into place. She could trace the sounds of Mr. Haine's footsteps clomping down the back hall and the back door creaking. Inaudible conversation drifted through the office. After a few minutes, Haine strode back through the lobby, empty-handed.

Well, not quite empty-handed. She glimpsed him opening his desk's center drawer and placing the little slip of yellow paper into it.

By Wednesday of that first full week of December, Triss brought home two new names, and she and Everlove made up envelopes for Mrs. McCabe to give to Mrs. Fontaine. By Friday, those two people had paid their rents in full. Mr. Haine did not look pleased.

Over the weekend, Triss and Everlove sat down to dinner.

"I think Haine suspects something is going on," Triss said.

"Already?" Everlove said, alarmed.

"I don't think he knows what. But the fact that most people are paying their rent might seem suspicious. I feel like I should leave some people out, but how on earth would I choose?" Triss shook her head and poked her fork into a pile of turnip greens. "I'm not sure I'm cut out for being an attorney and making ruthless decisions."

"I would think being a compassionate person would be a plus," Everlove said.

Triss grunted. "Maybe. But both Haine and my grandfather are quite capable of making hard decisions without emotion playing into it. And they are both successful at what they do."

"Successfully making money, you mean. But isn't there more to being an attorney than that?"

"I suppose." She pictured future Triss as she had always imagined her. Wearing smart clothes like Jackie O. Rushing around on important business. Commanding a courtroom. She had always pictured corporate law—something with high stakes and a high salary. Now she realized why: she wanted to show her grandfather she could be successful in a language he would comprehend, and that language was money. But would that make her happy? "I will say having to make ends meet for the first time in my life, I can understand the allure of the mighty dollar."

"I agree with you there. I definitely want a job that pays more than I make as a cashier."

A silence fell, a comfortable blanket that made no demands as both women contemplated their futures.

"What would you like to do?" Triss asked.

"I have no idea."

"What are you passionate about?"

Everlove let the question drift and dissolve before answering. "I don't know. Reading? Can I work as a professional reader?" She paused. "I would like a job where I could say 'This is what I do' and say it with pride. I know being a cashier isn't something to be ashamed of. And maybe it's not even in the job title. I want to do something that makes me look forward to going to work instead of counting down the hours until I'm done. I want to feel like I'm my own person. I want to be visible. I want to make a difference. Now, if I could just figure out what that would be."

"I think you would be a good writer," Triss said.

Everlove snorted. "How would that pay the rent?"

"Being a journalist maybe?"

"Who would hire a Black woman as a journalist?"

"Who would hire a white woman as an attorney? But to quote Bob Dylan, 'The times they are a'changin'. Now is our moment, Everlove. It's time we came out from beneath the rocks we've been placed under. Or off the pedestals we were put on. Whichever it is, both keep us from achieving our potential. I think of the women out there who never got to be what they wanted, and it crushes me. What would the world be like if we could add the contributions of women?"

"You sound like you've been reading *Ms.* magazine."

Triss turned to Everlove and raised her eyebrows. "I have, and how would you know?"

"I read it, too. Much to my parents' chagrin."

"Everlove! You're a feminist."

"I don't know about that." Everlove shifted in her seat.

"It's not a bad thing. Feminism is women wanting to have a fair shot at whatever they want to do. To be paid equally for the same work as men. What's wrong with that?"

"Nothing, I guess. But the world makes it such an uphill battle."

"That's why we need a sisterhood. Alone, we are pushed down. Together, we help each other up the hill, one hand to another." She held up her iced tea. "Here's my promise to you: I will give you a hand when you need it. And you can give me a hand when I do. I think we make a good team."

"Do you, now?" Everlove said but raised her glass and clinked it to Triss's.

"Don't you? Look at what we're accomplishing!"

"Listen to you change your tune."

Triss took a sip of her tea. "It felt good seeing those people coming in, heads held high instead of bowed down with worry. Which reminds me of what started this conversation. How do we stop Haine from being suspicious without allowing people to get kicked out of their homes?"

Everlove considered this. "I think we do what Mrs. McCabe suggested. Find something on him." She got up from the table.

"Where are you going?" Triss asked.

"To put my money where my mouth is." She retrieved the phone book from the living room, placed it on the table, and flipped through the pages. "I'm looking up Haskell Moon's address. I'll go see him after I get off work tomorrow."

33

Everlove

Thursday, December 7, 1972

Everlove hoped to have a more successful visit with Mr. Moon than she had with Mrs. Galliford. As she drove to his address, she tried to summon some self-confidence by picturing herself as Shirley Chisholm, who had run for president and lost, or Barbara Jordan, who had run for a seat in Congress and won. If they could face the bigots of the world, she could face one elderly Black man.

She pulled up in front of his house and was dismayed to find him sitting on his weathered wooden porch with a young man. Now they would both witness her scooting across her seat and then straightening her clothes. This was not a good start for the confident demeanor she wanted to project. Thank goodness she had worn slacks.

As she walked across his yard, she thought she detected wry amusement on the lined face of the older man and a smirk on the younger one. Well, so be it. She took in their appearances. Mr. Moon wore a thick-collared cardigan over a white shirt and suspenders. A well-worn fedora perched on his head, and he sat on an old kitchen chair, his hands planted on a cane between his legs. The young man sported a royal-blue shirt with a wide collar pulled out and resting on a gray leisure suit jacket. Two different generations and two divergent clothing styles.

"Mr. Moon?" she asked as she got to the bottom of the steps.

"That's me," the older man said, lifting his hat and plopping it on his head again. "You got a door on the other side of that there car?"

"Yes, sir, I do. It's dented and doesn't open."

He chuckled. "Good thing you have an alternative."

"Yes, it is. I'm Everlove Porter."

"Everlove Porter." He rolled the name in his mouth.

Before he said anything further, the younger man grinned and said, "Everlove the runaway bride."

She suppressed a wince and jutted her chin out—a Triss mannerism she seemed to have picked up. "Yes, that's me."

"You sure are the talk of the town," the young man said.

"I know."

"You were so quiet back in high school."

"I was also quiet when I ran away from my wedding." Everlove couldn't believe she said that. Her face heated up.

The young man threw back his head and laughed.

"Everlove, I take it you know my grandson. Matthias, is that any way to treat someone who comes a-calling?" Mr. Moon shook his head, then looked back at Everlove. "Don't mind my grandson. Kids nowadays got no manners. What brings you to my porch steps on this fine afternoon?" Mr. Moon asked.

"I was hoping you could answer a few questions."

"I got nothing but time but not a lot of answers. But you can try."

Everlove inhaled and shot a look at Matthias, who still seemed amused. But he stood and said, "Pops, I gotta split. I'll drop the groceries by later. Miss Everlove, pleasure to run into you." He started down the steps, then turned. "Listen, bring your car by, and I'll fix your door for you."

"My cousin's going to take care of it for me when I scrape up enough money."

"Reg? I work in the garage with him. Bring me something sweet, and I'll call it even."

He walked to his car, and she was glad because she didn't quite know what to make of his proposal. She turned back to Mr. Moon.

"The boy's pretty good at bodywork," he said. "You should sure enough take him up on that."

"It's a kind offer, but I'm sure he was joking."

"He meant it. But let's talk about what brings y'all here."

She inhaled deeply, hoping to take in courage as well as air. She went with the story Mrs. McCabe had concocted at the library. "I have a friend who is considering a business deal, but she's not sure she wants to do work with the person on the other end."

Mr. Moon cocked his head. "I'm thinking y'all came to the wrong porch."

"Maybe. But it concerns Mr. Haine, and I understand you used to work for him."

His eyes narrowed. "I sure did. But I don't know anything about his business. All I did was shine the man's shoes and keep his clothes in order."

"That was back in his college days, right?"

"Ayuh."

"You were working for him when Marjanne Sadler died?"

Haskell Moon leaned back in his chair as if her words pushed him there. He regarded her, his jaw flexing. "Well, now, I think sometimes what's in the past should stay right back there. You bring it into the present and you mix things up and have a right old mess on your hands."

"Don't you think what we learn from the past can keep us out of messes in the present?"

"I don't see how that would work in this case."

"Do you think it's right that girl died and didn't get justice?"

"No, I surely don't, but if I had a nickel for every time justice wasn't served, I'd be sitting on a mighty fine porch instead of this worn-out one."

"What if you could right an injustice now?"

"I'd like to think I'd do what I can."

"Then tell me what you know about Marjanne."

He studied Everlove, assessing her, taking her measure. She forced herself to wait patiently. "I got a feeling you ain't telling the entire truth here."

"There's more to the story, I'll admit. I can't tell you all of it, but I promise you, if you can tell me what you know, you're helping other people."

"Mr. Haine can be a nasty piece of business, especially to folks like us. It ain't wise to poke a bear if it ain't coming after you." He narrowed his eyes. "Or have you already poked him?"

"Maybe a nudge. But he's still sleeping."

"What exactly are y'all after here?"

"You ever hear the saying that information is power? Me and a couple of friends are trying to find out all we can about Mr. Haine. The more we know, the better equipped we will be for what we have to do."

"Which is what, exactly?"

"I can't tell you that. But our goal is to help some people who really need it."

"I feel like you're a'leading me into a hall of mirrors, and I don't know when I'm going to run smack into one."

"I promise I won't let you walk into a wall. No one has to know you're talking to me." Everlove wished she could be as persuasive as Mrs. McCabe. Maybe Mrs. McCabe could give her lessons.

"You're a-standing on my front porch, and right now you're the most famous person in Cumbee Creek and Willow Mills combined," Mr. Haskell said, tapping his cane on the floorboards.

Everlove closed her eyes. "Thanks for reminding me. I keep forgetting," she said, her voice as dry as parchment.

This made Mr. Moon chuckle. Then he looked thoughtful. "It ain't a pretty story," he said quietly. Sadly. "Dredging all that stuff up . . ." He shook his head. "Don't seem like a good idea."

"I can't say if it is or if it isn't," Everlove said. "But I have a strong feeling I am supposed to be asking these questions." The words rang true. Marjanne looked at her from the past, pushing her to do something. So here she was.

He heaved a sigh and settled himself into his chair. "I ain't told a living soul about that time." He stared at the sky above the house across the street as if he could see the events from that long-ago time play out on the cerulean expanse. "Mostly cause of fear of what Haine could do to me and my family. This is dangerous stuff.

I want you to know that right now. But I don't want to go to my grave thinking I was a coward my whole life. On the other hand, I also don't want to put you or anyone else in harm's way. So before I say another word—you sure you want to hear it? Cause what's said can't be unsaid."

"Mr. Moon, I'm very sure."

"All righty then," he said.

And he began to talk.

34

Haskell Moon

1921–1926

It was the summer of 19 and 21. I remember it cause I was none too sure I would come out of it in one piece. But I'm getting ahead of myself. Mr. Horace, he was a spoiled young fella. He never had to want for a thing that wasn't put right in front of him. His daddy wanted him to take over the family business, but it didn't seem like he would ever settle down to do it. He liked to go out, dancing and drinking and whatnot. Many a night he come home so drunk he could barely stand. It was during that time that his daddy made seeing to Mr. Horace my main job. When his friends dropped him off, or he drove himself home, I was the one that got him upstairs, undressed him best I could, got him into bed. I'd take his clothes to Liza, who did the laundry, and she would mend the tears and get out the stains, if she could. Old Mr. Haine, he was disgusted with his son and threatened him all day and all night, but it did not one bit of good. I had been there long enough to know that Mr. Horace couldn't do a thing to please Mr. Haine. He'd criticize Mr. Horace for every little thing even before he started stepping out. The way he dressed, how late he slept, how he didn't attend to his studies. His carousing only made it worse.

But then there come this one night when he got home and he was different. He was drunk, for sure, slurring his speech and whatnot and hardly able to put one foot in front of the other. But this night, he was jabbering about something. Worse, he was crying. But I helped him take his jacket off, and that's when I saw it. He had bloodstains on his shirt front and cuffs. I looked him over careful-like, thinking he must've fallen, but he looked just fine to me—no cuts or nothing.

Now this put me in a fix. I was supposed to take care of him, and if he was hurt and I didn't tend to it, I'd get in a heap of trouble, ya see. But I didn't see a mark on him. Just blood. I looked at his jacket and realized it also had blood on it I hadn't seen before. And on his trousers. So I stand there as he's sitting on the edge of the bed, and the gibberish he's talking starts to sink in. I realize he's a-saying "I didn't mean to do it" and "It was an accident." I tell you, my own blood run cold then, because when the white family has problems, you can be sure the Black folk that help 'em are gonna have problems, too. I went and roused Mr. Haine. He told me it better be life or death, me waking him up like that, and I says, "Sir, it might just be." That woke him right up, and he followed me to Mr. Horace's room. He'd fallen over on the bed. I had gotten his shirt off him and laid it on the chest at the end of his bed, and in the lamplight, Mr. Haine saw the bloodstains right away.

"Is he hurt?" he asks me.

"Not that I can tell, sir," I says.

Mr. Haine, he walked over and looked him over, turning him over to his other side, and we didn't see a scratch on him. Mr. Haine told me to set him up, and I did. He wasn't quite passed out yet, and he mumbled, and Mr. Haine slapped him across the face.

"Sober up," he said, and I remember a-thinking, 'Does he think he can just order a body to not be drunk anymore?' But a-course I don't say a thing. He turned to me, and he says, "That pitcher have water in it?" I nodded. "Bring it here." I still had one hand on Mr. Horace's arm to keep him from falling over. I let go, and he swayed a bit, head lolling around. I fetched the pitcher, and Mr. Haine told me to throw the water on his son. Well, now, a Black man don't just go doing things like that to a white one, you understand. I hesitated, and he grabbed the pitcher from me, all huffy, and I am thinking there ain't no way to win here. No sir. So he threw the water in his son's face. Mr. Horace, he yelled and spluttered and cursed, and his father stood over him, cold as the grave in winter.

"What have you gone and done?" he asks him.

"Father, I-I didn't do anything."

"Tell me what happened." You coulda taken each of his words and cut rope with it, his voice was so sharp and mean.

Mr. Horace ran his hands over his dripping hair. "There was an accident."

"Tell me every single thing. Now."

"It wasn't my fault."

"Just tell it before I whip your sorry ass to hell and back."

"There was a girl," Mr. Horace said, still slurring his words but sounding a little less drunk. "She's been going to parties with us for a few weeks now. And tonight . . . she and I ended up alone, and she, uh, sort of fell. I tried to kiss her, but she moved away. And I tried again, and I was holding her arm, but she jerked away and tripped. She fell. And she . . ." Mr. Horace mumbled this last bit.

His father leaned in close, eyes narrowed. "She what?"

"She hit her head." Mr. Horace closed his eyes and looked pained. And he went on, his voice barely louder than a whisper in that hot, dark room. "I think she's dead."

"You think she's dead?" his father says, as angry as I've ever seen him. Veins stood out on his head and neck, and I thought, Lord, that man is gonna have a fit right then and there.

"I couldn't feel a pulse," Mr. Horace said, "but I was—I don't know if I was doing it right. There was a lot of blood. And I didn't know what to do." He broke down in sobs right then. I can tell you I was wishing I was anywhere but in that there room, bearing witness to what was pouring outta that boy's mouth.

"So what did you do? Where is she?" his father asks.

"I-I put her in the river."

His father stands there, thrumming with rage. If anger could have turned into a living, breathing thing, it woulda been Old Mr. Haine that night. I stood as stock-still as any statue ever made, wishing I didn't even have to breathe and praying they'd forget I was there. I wanted to slip outta that there room, but I didn't dare try.

"What do you mean you put her in the river?"

"We were near the old mill, so I picked her up and I carried her to the bridge and dropped her in." He winced as if he was replaying the scene in his mind, which I reckon he was. Even I could imagine the sound she made, the splash of warm water in the quiet summer night. I shuddered.

His father swore and says, "I knew I should have stopped your carousing. I knew it was getting out of hand. Who was it, goddammit?"

"Just a girl from the mill village." He was sniffling now, face all wet from water and tears and snot.

"What was her name?"

"Marjanne something. I don't remember."

"Goddammit, goddammit, goddammit." Mr. Haine paced the room. He slapped his hand on Mr. Horace's desk, and Mr. Horace and I liked to jump all the way to heaven.

He turned to me. "Haskell!" he said.

"Yes sir," I say, thinking, 'Here it comes, and whatever it is, ain't no way going to be good for me.'

"I want you to throw away those clothes. Take them somewhere and get rid of them where no one will find them. Don't let anyone else see them, and if you breathe a word of this to a single living soul . . ."

I scrambled to gather the clothes and stuffed 'em in a duffel bag. I decided I would take them to the dump the next morning. I felt just a little bit of relief because I was getting away from the two of them, but it was only a tiny bit. I knew I would never get away from knowing what I knew, and from them knowing that I knew it. That's a dangerous place to be for Black folk.

The police came 'round the next day asking about the young lady. By then, father and son had hatched up a story. Mr. Horace said yes, she had been with the group the night before. He told the police the group left her at the speakeasy with a young fella with a Yankee accent who she said she knew. I heard Mr. Haine say he was a-going to talk to the other young people who were there that night. I learnt that one or two of them had talked to the police and the newspaper and told them the last they had seen of her was when she and Mr. Horace went for a walk. But after Mr. Haine's visit, they suddenly remembered they got the events all wrong, and she had left with the Yankee fella. After that, they all stuck to that story like moss on a rock. Mr. Haine also came to me and told me again I'd better keep my mouth shut. Which he didn't need to do. I didn't like to think what that would get me. No, sir. I don't like to think of that a-tall.

People later said Old Mr. Haine went to the sheriff and talked to him as well. About a week later, that poor girl's body was found downriver, and they said the cause of death was accidental. After that, you never heard another word about it.

Old Mr. Haine, he told Mr. Horace he wasn't cleaning up any more messes, that if he didn't straighten up and behave, Mr. Haine would kick him out of the house and cut the purse strings. Then Mr. Haine sent me and Mr. Horace to a kind of curing place for rich folk who have trouble with the bottle. Mr. Haine told Mr. Horace if he didn't come back sober and with the intention to stay that way, to not come home a-tall. Of course, I wondered what that would mean for me, but nobody bothered to clear that up. So me and him went off to this fine mansion all filled with gentlemen. And Lord, that first week was something awful. Mr. Horace got the shakes and fevers and chills. He spent half the day threatening to fire me and the other half trying to bribe me to get him out of there or sneak him a bottle. But after ten days or so, he started a-coming out of it. By the end of the month, he was looking less yellow and thin. On the thirty-first day, we headed home. I think him getting dried out shriveled something inside him because he became a hard man after that. Or maybe his soul went into the water with that poor girl. He never showed much compassion for anyone or anything, but after that summer, he showed nary a shred of it.

Mr. Haine watched his son like a hawk at first. Didn't trust him nohow. But I never saw Mr. Horace take another drink. He went back to his college in January and then went on to the law school. Mr. Haine himself only had the one college degree, not two, so you'd think he'd be proud of his son, getting further than he did. But he still didn't seem to think much of Mr. Horace's accomplishments. Money was the only thing he understood. After Mr. Horace came home for good, they had guests over to dinner, and one of 'em raised a glass and said, "Here's to Horace! Our newest attorney!" and everyone clinked their glasses all together and whatnot, and Mr. Haine barely lifted his and said, "Let's just see if he can translate that into profit."

I peeped over sideways-like at Mr. Horace, and he looked sad. I almost felt sorry for him. Any other man would be right proud of a son getting not one but two college degrees, but that wasn't good enough for Mr. Haine. No, sir.

I thought I was going to be tied up with those two for the rest of time, like a fly in a spiderweb. I used to have nightmares that one or the other of them would throw me in the river like that poor girl. I'd wake up thrashing, thinking I was drowning. Because I knew too much, you see. But I kept my mouth shut tighter than a duck's backside. I never said a word to nobody. I never even told my Saree, and we were married fifty-two years. I never heard another thing about that girl after that year. Not anywhere. So the lies, they grew like kudzu. They took over the truth. And after a while, you could only see the kudzu, not what was underneath.

And you began to think maybe that's all there ever was. I think that's how you live with lies like that. You start to believe 'em yourself, and the next thing you know, they're as real as you and me. I think as far as Mr. Horace was concerned, she was just a bad dream he had once and then put behind him. Yes, sirree.

35

Everlove

Thursday, December 7, 1972

Everlove came back to the present as Mr. Moon stopped talking, feeling like she had traveled in time. She tried to pair the image of the current Mr. Haine—a cold-hearted old man whose most distinct feature was a chin that slid into the wattle of his throat—with the youthful Horace, stepping out with the ladies and frequenting speakeasies and blind pigs. She gave the story some space to settle, letting the words drift to the porch, between the rough splinters, where they settled among grains of sand before she spoke.

"When did you finally stop working for him?"

"It was about five years later."

"What made you leave?"

"I was watching and waiting, trying to judge when they weren't looking at me like I might up and tell someone about what had happened. But before I reached that judgment, Mr. Horace got mixed up in his side business with Boden Carr and wanted me to get mixed up in it right along with him, like two pigs in a mudhole. I wanted nothing to do with it."

"Boden Carr?"

"He was a moonshiner. Used to run liquor 'round these parts. At the time, he was a tenant of Mr. Haine's. One day, he got thrown in jail after being caught with a wagon full of liquor. He didn't know who else to call, so he called Old Mr. Haine. Mr. Haine told Mr. Horace to go bail him out and tell him the cost would be added to his rent. He also told him to tell Mr. Carr to quit running moonshine. Mr. Horace did the first part, but not the second. Instead, he made him a deal. Said if he gave Mr. Horace a cut, he'd make sure he didn't get arrested again. And whatever he did, it worked. Boden Carr never got hauled off to jail again, and he ran liquor even more. Started off in town, then a little further out, like ripples in a pond. It wasn't long before he added other moonshiners, like it was a real business. Which I rightly reckon it was."

"From what I understand, Haine is still doing this."

"That's what I hear. Boden Carr is long gone. Hit by a train back in the '50s. Smashed a load of liquor along with his car. But his son took over after he passed. Every once in a while, Mr. Horace, he'd pull me away from my duties and ask me to deliver an envelope to Carr or the sheriff. And told me not to tell anyone. Including his father. Well, sir, I did not like that one little bit. If any one of 'em was caught, who do you think would be blamed? Not Mr. Horace and probably not Mr. Carr. No, sir. It would be the Black man. I knew I'd be handed over quick as a duck on a June bug. And jail would be the best thing that would happen. Decorating a tree the worst. So I was fixing to quit right before Mr. Haine and Mr. Horace had a big fight." He shook his head. "Mr. Haine found out what was a-going on and confronted Mr. Horace. Mr. Horace didn't bother to cover it up a-tall. Instead, he told him he was making a fortune, so his father should be proud. Mr. Haine said he was not proud of ill-gotten gains, and Mr. Horace says, 'You think paying mill workers in chits and forcing them to buy from your company store is all fine and upright? You're as much of a crook as I am. Or maybe you're just mad because your sheriff is as much in my pocket as he is in yours.' Mr. Haine backhanded him and told him to get out. Mr. Horace said gladly. It was about a month later I told Mr. Haine I had another job. I was shaking like a leaf because I knew me and him was thinking about that bad business from a few years before. But he looked at me for a right long minute and he said, 'You've always been trustworthy, Haskell. I expect you will remain that way. Good luck on your next endeavor.' The words sound right pleasant when I say 'em, but the way he said 'em, with his eyes squinting at me . . . I knew what he meant. That I could go, but I still better keep my mouth shut. So that ended my time with the Haines. I was glad to be shed of 'em. If I were to see one of 'em on the street, I'd turn and go the other way."

"Did they ever make up? I know the elder Mr. Haine still lives in the house near the old mill," Everlove asked.

"As far as I know, Mr. Horace never stepped foot in the house again. Mr. Haine sold the mill in the thirties, and I guess he did all right 'cause he's still a-holding on to that big old place."

"He must be ancient," Everlove said.

Mr. Moon shook his head. "'Bout near a hundred, I reckon. Some folks are too mean to die."

"I appreciate you telling me all this, especially since they're not good memories for you."

"I hope whatever you are getting into, you're gonna be careful because even old snakes can still take a bite outta you."

"We're being careful."

"And I surely don't see how this is going to help you."

"We are just trying to learn as much as we can," Everlove said, but she agreed with him. She didn't know how a fifty-year-old incident that may or may not have been a crime would help. She was not a detective or a lawyer, but even she knew there was no evidence that Haine had intentionally hurt that long-ago girl and never would be. If there ever had been any, it was long gone. But it burned her up that he could get away with disposing of a human being like she was garbage.

"I gotta admit, I'm a mite curious what this is about." Mr. Moon looked at her expectantly.

She was tempted to divulge Triss's secret. He had trusted her enough to tell his story, but Triss's story was not hers to share. "Maybe one day I can tell you. But I can't right now."

"You keep me in mind, then."

"I will, I promise." She hoped he didn't think that as a runaway bride, her promises were worth as much as two wagons in a one-horse town.

"I hope y'all can do something. Never had any hope before, but maybe now, with the world changing and young folk like you pushing for it, maybe things can be different."

Everlove? Pushing for change? He had her all wrong, but she didn't bother to point that out. "I have one more question. Do you remember the names of Mr. Horace's friends from way back then?"

He nodded his head slowly and flexed his hands around the cane they still rested on. "I remember more from when I was a young'un than I do about this here week. But I don't know what they're a-gonna tell you. Not a one spoke up fifty years ago."

"Maybe because it has been fifty years. Maybe somebody has regrets and would like to clear their conscience. If any of them are still around."

He nodded solemnly and rattled off two names. Everlove jotted them down. Then he added a third. Her head jerked up. "Are you serious? He was a friend of Haine's?"

"Indeed he was."

She snapped the book closed and rose stiffly to her feet. "Well, that is interesting. Is there anything else you can think of that might help?"

"I can't, but I wish you luck."

He leaned back and settled his cane in front of him. "There's a lot of people pressed down under that man's thumb. I wouldn't mind seeing a few get out."

"We'll see what we can do," she said.

He tipped his hat, and she gave a little bow before she walked to her car as the sun disappeared behind the trees and afternoon melted into evening.

36

Everlove

Thursday, December 7, 1972

Everlove got home before Triss. She began making dinner, but her mind was on everything she had learned that afternoon. She absently pulled leftover chicken out of the fridge and combined it with cream cheese, cream of mushroom soup, and a few other ingredients, making a quick casserole that would take longer in the oven than it had to put together. As she was slicing cucumbers for a salad, there was a knock at the door, and Mrs. McCabe peeked in.

"May I come in?"

"I think you already are."

"You're getting as sassy as Violet."

"Sassy? She's nice as she can be," Everlove said, thinking of when she gave her wedding dress to her.

"I didn't say she wasn't nice. A person can be both, you know. What are you making?" Mrs. McCabe said, peering at the counter where Everlove worked.

"A salad. Would you like to help?"

"Would I like to help, or will I help?" Mrs. McCabe said, but she cackled at her own joke. "What can I do?"

Everlove nodded at the head of lettuce she had rinsed and set on the towel. "You can tear that."

"So how did it go today?" Mrs. McCabe said as she washed her hands and got to work.

"It went well, I think. When Triss gets home, I'll tell you both what I learned."

"She better hurry up because I'm dying to hear what you found out. Also, I'm hungry and inviting myself to dinner. Also, I'm not getting any younger."

"I certainly hope thirty minutes won't see the end of you," Everlove said.

"That's what I mean! Sassy." Mrs. McCabe asked how things were with her family.

Everlove shrugged. "No real change. I'm still the talk of the town. And let me tell you, I never thought that would be me."

"One of these days, you'll fade back into obscurity, and you'll miss your moment of fame."

"I doubt that."

Dinner was almost ready by the time Triss got home. "Man, whatever you're cooking smells good," she said as she hung up her coat.

"Your timing is good as it's almost ready."

"Were you able to talk to Mr. Moon?"

"I was. Let's get dinner on the table, and I'll fill you in."

As Everlove retrieved the casserole from the oven, Mrs. McCabe put the salad on the table and Triss set out cutlery and plates. As they ate, Everlove related Mr. Moon's story: his description of

Mr. Haine as a young man, of his group of friends and how they frequented speakeasies all over the Midlands. And how one evening, he ended up alone with Marjanne, and she fell and hit her head and all that followed.

"Wow," Triss said. They had gotten through most of dinner during Everlove's monologue. "So . . . did he kill her, or was it an accident?"

"If it was the latter, everyone certainly worked hard to cover it up," Everlove said.

"I want to make sure I understand one thing," Mrs. McCabe said, her mouth a grim line. "Haine said he didn't know if he was checking her pulse accurately, but he threw her in the river anyway?"

They fell silent as they considered the ramifications of that. The thought that Marjanne might not have been dead had already occurred to Everlove, but it had been too horrible to dwell on.

"I guess that's why they had to cover it up," Triss said. "Did the newspapers say anything about an autopsy?"

"Not that we could find," Everlove said.

"I wonder if they did one. Did Mr. Moon say who the friends are?" Triss asked.

Everlove's stomach clenched. "He did," she said, swallowing hard.

"Are they still around?" Mrs. McCabe asked.

"Well . . ." Everlove cleared her throat. "One is. Triss, one of the friends who was there that night was Jeremiah Littlefield."

Triss blinked at her. "My grandfather? You're saying my grandfather was not only friends with Haine back then, but that he may have been with him the night that girl died?"

"That's what Mr. Moon told me."

Triss sat, dumbfounded. "But my grandfather has always despised Haine. When we argued, I applied for the job at Mr. Haine's office to spite him. I had no idea there was anything between them other than my grandfather not approving of his business practices." She looked at Everlove and Mrs. McCabe in turn. "So now what do we do?"

"We should probably talk to the friends," Mrs. McCabe said.

"Can we skip my grandfather for now? I need to think about this."

"Two of the other names were in one of the newspaper articles," Everlove said. "They are the ones who changed their stories. Maybe we should start with them anyway." Everlove fetched her notebook from the coffee table. "Those two are Ethel Baxley and Paul Sullivan. Louise Cowley is the only other person. They were a group of six, so with Haine, your grandfather, and poor Marjanne, that's all of them."

Triss considered the names. "I don't know Louise Cowley. Paul Sullivan is an accountant. He moved to Columbia about five years ago. I'm friends with one of his daughters. And Ethel Baxley is now Ethel Baxley-Picket. She's the grande dame of Edenton society. At one time or another, she's run the Methodist Church Ladies Auxiliary, the Junior League, and the Edenton Cotillion." She shook her head. "It's so hard to imagine my grandfather and Mrs. Baxley-Picket running around to speakeasies and stuff."

"You do realize we were all young once," Mrs. McCabe said.

Triss's cheeks turned pink.

Mrs. McCabe continued. "How about I start with Ethel? I used to be in the Junior League myself, so we'll have some common ground."

Triss stared at Mrs. McCabe, incredulous.

"Don't look so surprised," Mrs. McCabe said. "I've done a lot of things you can't even imagine."

"I'm just surprised Junior League is one of them," Triss said.

"What's so hard to believe about that?"

"You don't seem the, um, type . . ."

The corners of Mrs. McCabe's mouth twitched, and Triss swore the older woman was enjoying watching her squirm. "You're kind of a nonconformist," Triss added, happy she had dug her way out of that hole.

Mrs. McCabe beamed. "I did get asked to leave."

"What did you do?"

"They were raising money to put up a Confederate monument in downtown Charleston while right down the street, poor people were huddled in squalid shacks. I suggested that our funds might be better spent on living, breathing people, rather than on dead and moldering traitors. It didn't go over well."

"Ah, no, I guess it wouldn't have," Triss said.

"Not only was I asked to leave, but I suddenly found my foyer table quite bereft of invitations to anything else of a social or networking nature."

"They cut you off completely?" Triss asked.

"They did. But by then, I was married and had begun traveling the world with my new husband, so it was no great loss to me. In fact, it may have helped me. Set me free, so to speak. From the Junior League and some of the biddies in it."

"They can do some good work, you know."

"They can. So can I, without all the fuss and bother. Anyway, I'll find her address and call on her tomorrow. Captain McGarrett has nothing on me."

Everlove raised her eyebrows. "Who?"

"Captain McGarrett. On *Hawaii Five-O*."

"Oh."

"Too bad I don't have a sidekick so I could say, 'Book 'em, Danno.'"

Later that evening, Triss and Everlove sat on the sofa, feet propped on the battered coffee table. Triss had bought a small Christmas tree from a secondhand store, then raided her grandfather's stash of decorations, picking some she knew he wouldn't miss. Everlove had bought some lights and tinsel. Now their own little tree sat twinkling merrily in the corner of their living room.

"I can't stop thinking about that girl," Everlove said.

"Marjanne?"

"Yes. You didn't see her picture. She was pretty. Which sounds like I wouldn't care about her if she was plain. But there was something about her face . . . so full of life. And she was simply . . . erased."

"It's terribly sad," Triss said. "I wonder if anyone in her family is still around to remember her."

Everlove pondered this. Marjanne didn't even get an obituary, so they had seen no mention of her family except in the first article that said her parents had reported her missing. They might still be alive. And perhaps she had brothers and sisters. Nieces and nephews she had likely never met. And if she had, they would only remember the vague story of Aunt Marjanne who died so young, frozen in time in the sepia tones of an old photograph.

Everlove shook her head as if to shake off her melancholy thoughts. She didn't know why she was so caught up with her. She had heard plenty of tragic stories in her lifetime, some involving her own family members. But still. She couldn't stop thinking about the girl.

Hopefully, her fixation would fade as time went by. She certainly couldn't do anything about Marjanne now.

37

Mrs. McCabe

Thursday, December 12, 1972

Mrs. McCabe stood on the curb beside her green Chrysler Imperial and took in the well-maintained Foursquare house. The arches of its deep porch framed clusters of wicker furniture. Like the surrounding neighborhood, it had an understated elegance. The residents of Dunlaven community had gone from movers and shakers to retirees then back to the movers and shakers again. And one of those movers and shakers was Mrs. Baxley-Picket. When Mrs. McCabe had called her, the woman had said the holiday season was quite busy, but she had an opening on Thursday. If Mrs. McCabe couldn't meet then, she would have to wait until the new year. Mrs. McCabe said she would make it work. As if she had a busy social calendar she would have to rearrange.

A woman about ten years younger than Mrs. McCabe answered the door. Trim and attractive, she wore a twinset and skirt. Her jaw-length brown hair had been teased up into a bouffant, adding at least three inches to her height.

"Mrs. Baxley-Picket?" Mrs. McCabe asked.

"You must be Mrs. McCabe. Please come in. May I take your coat?"

Mrs. Baxley-Picket hung the proffered garment on a coat tree and led her guest into a small sitting room, populated with furniture Mrs. McCabe might have grown up with. Nostalgia washed over her, but she quickly shook off the unusual sentimentality about her girlhood, which had been filled with the appearance of riches but none of the actualities of it.

Mrs. Baxley-Picket gestured for her to sit, and Mrs. McCabe did, perching on the chair's edge, her back ramrod straight, ankles crossed, just like her mother had drilled into her over seventy years before. She remembered reading about a study in which a dog called Pavlov learned to drool at certain sounds. Or maybe the scientist was named Pavlov. Anyway, here she was, reverting to old behaviors because her fanny had encountered a brocade parlor chair. She defiantly scooted into the back cushion.

"I have tea and blueberry muffins if you'd like. Hot or iced, whichever you prefer."

Mrs. McCabe wanted to get right to the point, but she knew her part of the script. Besides, she was a trifle hungry. "I would love some iced tea and muffins."

A maid materialized at the entrance as if summoned by telepathy. Mrs. Baxley-Picket nodded at her, and she disappeared, reappearing moments later bearing a tray of refreshments arranged on wafer-thin china plates and crystal glasses. Mrs. McCabe wondered if the Pickets ever ate off aluminum TV dinner trays or allowed their lips to touch a plastic cup.

"You mentioned an old friend you were trying to locate, and you thought I could help?" Mrs. Baxley-Picket asked.

"That might have been a tiny white lie. I am thinking of doing some business with Mr. Haine"—the woman's spine stiffened ever so slightly, but her face remained impassive— "and I've heard some disturbing things about him."

"I'm sure I can't help you. I hardly know him."

"The things I'm referring to hark back to a time when I think you knew him better."

Now Mrs. Baxley-Picket's face had stiffened along with her spine.

"I don't think I can help you. I'm afraid you've wasted your time coming here."

"This muffin is so delightful; it makes it all worth it. But perhaps you can tell me a little about when you were friends with Mr. Haine."

"I was never friends with him," she asserted.

"But you had been known to go out socially with him."

Mrs. Baxley-Picket's eyes flicked to the staircase and back to Mrs. McCabe. "He was sometimes in the group I socialized with before I married."

Mrs. McCabe decided if she didn't get to the point, she'd be here all day as the two women politely circled one another.

"Mrs. Baxley-Picket, here's the situation. I've uncovered some unsavory information about Mr. Haine, and I want to learn the truth. I don't believe people should be able to get away with covering up a girl's death, even if fifty years have elapsed. Do you?"

Mrs. Baxley-Picket sucked in a tiny sip of air. "It was an accident," she said, her voice a low hiss.

"Was it, now? Then why did Haine and his father go to such lengths to cover it up?"

"I have no idea what you are talking about," she said. But her eyes slid away from Mrs. McCabe's gaze, and she concentrated on her tea.

"I think you do," Mrs. McCabe said. "And I think you feel bad for that poor girl."

Mrs. Baxley-Picket opened her mouth, and since Mrs. McCabe was sure more denials were going to pour out of it, she held up a hand. "I saw the newspaper articles. You knew Marjanne Sadler. What's more, your memory of the event changed between one article and the next. I wonder why."

Mrs. Baxley-Picket's eyes met hers, and Mrs. McCabe saw the same steeliness her mother's eyes had possessed when she pulled them—single-handedly—through the hard years. Here was a woman who would not bend easily. But neither did Mrs. McCabe.

"Marjanne had her whole life ahead of her," Mrs. McCabe said, shaking her head. "And it was tragically taken away. And while it may have been an accident, I have it on good authority that Horace Haine did not leave with you and Paul Sullivan."

Mrs. Baxley-Picket blanched. She sat for a long moment, then finally stood, smoothing her skirt. *I guess she's showing me the door.* Mrs. McCabe fished about for something else to say to persuade the other woman. "Wait right here," Mrs. Baxley-Picket said, surprising Mrs. McCabe.

Mrs. McCabe nibbled on her muffin and sipped her tea. Mrs. Baxley-Picket returned wearing a coat.

"Perhaps we could go for a walk."

Mrs. McCabe's days of scrambling and rushing were pretty much behind her, but she did the best she could lest Mrs. Baxley-Picket change her mind. She rose, thinking, *It's forty degrees and breezy, and my internal heater doesn't work anymore, but sure, let's take a walk.* She grabbed her own coat as they neared the front door.

"Do watch out for the sidewalks here as the tree roots have wrought havoc with them," Mrs. Baxley-Picket said.

They walked half a block before Mrs. Baxley-Picket spoke. "My husband is at home, and he doesn't like hearing about that summer, as it came out that although I was engaged to him, I was going out with a group that included several eligible young men. Now what is this good authority?"

"I'm not at liberty to reveal my sources." A little thrill ran up Mrs. McCabe's spine at those words. She should have been a reporter or an investigator. How terrible to find your calling when it's far too late to act upon it. "Why don't you just tell me the truth about that night?" Mrs. McCabe said.

"Why does this even matter? Why now, after all these years?" Mrs. Baxley-Picket stopped walking. They had arrived at a small park with benches and a playground. The sunlight flashed off the silver slide, and Mrs. McCabe stepped out of the blinding path of its reflected beam.

"He's evicting poor families so he can sell the property and make a fortune," Mrs. McCabe said. "And some friends and I are trying to stop him."

"While I admit that sounds contemptible, it is his property."

"Yes, it is. But when the new shopping center was built, the development company paid the families so they could find other places. Haine is not doing that. It's immoral."

"I agree, but how is dredging up something from fifty years ago going to help?"

Mrs. McCabe wasn't too sure herself, but she wasn't going to admit it. "I can't tell you all the details," she said. "But wouldn't you like to see justice done?"

Mrs. Baxley-Picket turned her gaze to the tall pines surrounding the small park.

"No one should be allowed to treat people the way he did. And still does," Mrs. McCabe said. If Mrs. Baxley-Picket was standing at the crossroads of honesty and secrecy, Mrs. McCabe hoped to nudge her in the right direction.

Mrs. Baxley-Picket sighed and studied a crack zigzagging through the pebbled sidewalk.

"Please, Mrs. Baxley-Picket. Tell me about it."

"Let's have a seat," Mrs. Baxley-Picket said.

They made their way to a wooden bench, walking through blades of sunlight that slashed through the tall pines. Mrs. McCabe was thankful for thick winter clothes that protected her from the cold and what looked like inevitable splinters.

"It was such a long time ago," Mrs. Baxley-Picket said. "I was twenty-one. It was my last summer in college and as an unmarried woman. Robert and I were to marry the following year. One day in late May, my friend Louise Cowley asked me to go out with her on a sort of double date—understanding I was only there to be a chaperone as Robert was getting his medical training. The four of us—me, Louise, Jeremiah Littlefield, and Paul Sullivan—went out, and next thing you know, it became a regular thing. We bumped into Horace one night at a blind pig. It turned out he knew where all the drinking spots were, so we began including him.

"I am sure you remember those years. The horrid war and the awful influenza were behind us. I think we were all a little giddy because we'd all made it through when so many others didn't. For a brief time, I was a party girl, going out with men—in a group, mind you. I didn't abandon all my principles, and I never forgot I was affianced. We drank, danced, flirted. All harmless fun. We'd pile into a car and drive, the summer air like velvet as it swept over us, the stars bright in the night sky." She trailed off, remembering.

"What was Horace Haine like back then?" Mrs. McCabe asked.

"He was somewhat disagreeable, frankly. A know-it-all. But he always knew where the drinking spots were, even when they moved, which is why I think Paul and Jeremiah put up with him. That and habit. We were all part of the same social circles. I always remember him drunk or heading there. He ran us off the road more than once, but with the insouciance of youth, we just laughed about it and kept climbing back into his car. We went on like that for some time. All of June. And it was late June, I believe—it was before Independence Day—when Horace brought a new young woman to our group. Marjanne Sadler. I must admit to being a bit jealous. She was quite beautiful. Incandescent. When Marjanne was present, all eyes were on her."

Mrs. Baxley-Picket took out a cigarette and a lighter from her coat pocket and fought with a breeze for a minute before she won and her cigarette flared. She inhaled deeply and blew the smoke away from Mrs. McCabe.

"She didn't know how magnetic she was. She was shy, but sometimes you could see these little bubbles of enthusiasm try to burst forth. As the summer wore in, I found out she was from the mill village but wanted desperately to leave it. Horace had met her at a bakery where she worked. Her first step, she told me, to escape the mill."

"Do you think they liked each other?"

Mrs. Baxley-Picket contemplated the question. "I think Horace did like her. I mean, most men did. I don't think Marjanne was attracted to him, but she might have seen him as a way out of her life into a different one. That makes her sound cold and heartless, but you know how it was in those days." She looked at Mrs. McCabe.

"I do indeed. I was expected to make a marriage to save what was left of our family name."

Mrs. Baxley-Picket nodded. "As the summer wore on, I wondered where this would all end, because Horace was never going to take it further than flirtation. To the Haines, money reigned supreme, but appearances were a close second. Horace's grandfather had been a carpetbagger who married a Confederate widow and changed his name to hers so he could live under the umbrella of her prestige. He had the money; she had the standing. But their children were like tarnished silver and were always trying to rub off the taint. They worked hard to do all the right things: join the right clubs, support the right charities, go into the right professions. Horace Senior wanted Horace Junior to pursue a law degree and go into politics. His father would have rather shot him than allow him to marry someone from his own mill village."

"How did it all end?"

"One night—it was August sixth—we drove to Columbia. There were six of us in two cars—Louise and I rode with Paul, and Marjanne and Jeremiah rode with Horace. It was oppressively hot. We went to a few speakeasies, but the crowds made the heat even more unbearable, so we drove back to Edenton, to a barn near the Supplejack River that was set up as a blind pig. We paid our fee to get in and took our drinks to the river. Our laughter and singing drowned out the frogs and insects. Walking in the night, under the stars, was magical. At one point, we passed through a clearing, and a lone palmetto tree stood near the water with the crescent moon rising behind it just so, and Paul joked, 'Look, everyone, our state flag!' We saluted it, and Paul broke into song."

Mrs. Baxley-Picket softly, wistfully sang the lyrics of the state song.

> *"Call on thy children of the hill*
> *Wake swamp and river, coast and rill*
> *Rouse all thy strength and all thy skill,*
> *Carolina! Carolina!"*

She paused and smiled. "Horace's voice was terrible, so everyone started teasing him. When the joking died off, Louise said she wasn't feeling well, so Jeremiah told her he'd take her home. The rest of us walked a little more, but my feet hurt, so I stopped to take my shoes off, and Marjanne and Horace kept going. Paul and I stood near the river and watched the scant moonlight glinting off the dark, smooth surface. We talked for a bit—long enough for Horace and Marjanne to move out of our view. We headed back to the barn, but it was winding down, and I realized it must be late. Jeremiah returned but was disappointed when I said I was tired, but he was always a gentleman. He said he would give us a ride home so we didn't have to wait for Horace and Marjanne. I figured she wouldn't mind. Paul left word with the bouncer so they'd know we'd left. And that is all I know." She shook her head.

"But you do know you and Paul were not with Horace, which is what the papers said."

Mrs. Baxley-Picket sighed. "Yes, I do know that."

"How did the papers get that wrong?"

"Jeremiah dropped me off, and I assume he dropped Paul off and went home. The next day, I was packing to return to school when the sheriff came by. I remember it scared my mother because she thought something had happened to my sister in Columbia, but they were there asking about Marjanne. No one had seen her since the night before. She never went home. I was baffled. I told them I had last seen her with Horace. They asked if she'd been drinking, and I said she had a couple of drinks. She might have been a little tipsy, but she was not completely inebriated. A newspaper reporter also came by, and I told him the same thing I told the sheriff." Mrs. Baxley-Picket stopped, picking at the cuff of her sleeve.

"What happened next?" Mrs. McCabe prompted.

"That evening, Mr. Haine—Horace's father—came to visit. After dinner, which was highly unusual. He asked to see me and enquired about what I had told the sheriff. And I told him. He said I must be misremembering—that Paul and I had stayed with Horace, and Marjanne had gone off on her own, that she had a friend she was meeting. And she probably had too much to drink. When I told him I remembered perfectly well, he said I might want to think again. That my recent behavior had been unseemly, and he said it would be a shame if my reputation were ruined. His implication was very much that he would be the one to ruin it."

"What did you think about this?"

"I was confused. I didn't think until much later that Horace must have had something to do with Marjanne's disappearance. I thought perhaps they had argued, or he made a pass at her that went too far. I thought maybe they didn't want word spreading that he was going out on the town with a mill girl. So when the sheriff came back, I told him I had misremembered, and I forgot we all left together and Marjanne had gone to meet with a friend. The sheriff didn't bat an eye at my changed story. And he never came around again. The next day the reporter came by, and I told him the account I'd told the sheriff. The second version. And it appeared in the paper when they identified her body, but nobody ever questioned the discrepancy. The paper said no foul play was suspected. But I had the chilling thought that something terrible had happened to her, and Horace had something to do with it. But what could I do? I had already told two different versions of that night. And the sheriff did not come around again. By then I was back at Columbia College. I wondered if I should say something, but I am ashamed to admit that I told myself that nothing I said would change the outcome."

"You couldn't have changed what happened to Marjanne, but perhaps it's not too late for justice to be done," Mrs. McCabe said. "Would you be willing to go on record with the right story? And why you changed it?"

Mrs. Baxley-Picket looked down at her lap. "I'd have to think about that."

"It would be a chance for you to set the record straight. Maybe to find out what happened to Marjanne."

Mrs. Baxley-Picket stared at the empty playground and the grand houses surrounding them, their staid fronts giving nothing away. Mrs. McCabe resisted the urge to poke her in the arm to hurry her response.

"What would she have become?" Mrs. Baxley-Picket said. "She wanted a better life. Who would have been her husband? Who would have been her children?" She met Mrs. McCabe's eyes. "It has weighed heavily on my soul for all these years. I'll tell the truth to whoever I need to tell it to."

38
Triss

Thursday, December 12–Monday, December 18, 1972

"We are really back at square one," Triss said.

Mrs. McCabe had dropped in for coffee to brief Triss and Everlove on her talk with Mrs. Baxley-Picket.

"I am afraid so," said Mrs. McCabe.

"Should you call on Paul Sullivan?" Everlove asked.

"I don't think it will do any good," Mrs. McCabe said. "It doesn't sound like we will ever truly know what happened to Marjanne."

"I think you're right. Nobody witnessed what took place between her and Haine, so all we have is his word about it." Triss rested her elbows on the kitchen table.

"Don't give up hope. We'll figure this out yet," Mrs. McCabe said.

"I hope so."

As December marched on, Triss did her Christmas shopping and felt a little thrill that she was using her own money. She was invited to a few parties, some of which she made an appearance at and some she didn't. She and Everlove spent several evenings watching Christmas specials like *Frosty the Snowman* and *Rudolph the Red-Nosed Reindeer*, eating Jiffy Pop popcorn and reminiscing about their past holidays. Sometimes, especially here in the middle of the month, Triss could almost forget she had ever done anything so terrible as to steal money from her boss. But she was still keeping an eye out. She had no idea what she thought she'd find, but she hoped for something. And soon.

A week before Christmas, Triss was stuffing envelopes when Copper swaggered in with the duffel. She continued folding letters with a fierce attention they did not merit as he carried the bag past her and into Haine's office. He gave the door a little shove as he passed it, ostensibly to close it, but the old door resisted.

Muted conversation leaked from the opening, punctuated by an occasional intelligible word. "Blazey ... promised ... better ..." Then a clear directive from Mr. Haine. "See that she does."

Haine carried the bag into the file room as usual. She was about to turn to her typewriter when she saw Mr. Haine pull something out of the safe. Curious, Triss opened the drawer that was to the right of her desk and rummaged through the files, watching Mr. Haine through the curtain of her hair. She plucked out a file and leafed through the papers, trying to see what he was doing. Was he writing something? Reading something? Without looking directly at him, she couldn't see clearly.

He abruptly replaced whatever it was in the safe, closed the door, and spun the dial. He looked directly at her as he turned, and her heart dropped into her shoes. She closed the file and opened the drawer and smiled brightly as he strode past. Brightly and innocently, she hoped. A minute later, Copper walked out with the duffel, pointing his index finger at Triss like a gun as he went by. Soon after he disappeared, Haine brought her a Dictaphone tape and told her he needed some letters typed as soon as possible.

Later that evening, Triss drove home alongside the twinkling lights of the Air Force base runway. She was weary of her adrenaline-filled life, always perched on the edge of panic. And in the long run, she was only supplying a bandage to a gaping wound. Maybe she should just return the money before she had a nervous breakdown. But she no longer had all of it. She imagined going to her grandfather and asking to borrow some money. Even if she lied to him about why she needed it, she shuddered at the interminable lectures she would have to endure about her spendthrift ways. For one deranged moment, she imagined telling him the truth but squelched that thought immediately. He already thought her flighty and undependable. What would he think if he knew she had broken the law?

But Peach. Mrs. Calvin. Mrs. Kettingham. Even Pie-Eyed Pete.

She needed a way to stop him, but how? She had nothing except the fifty-year-old questionable death of a young woman and not one iota of proof that Haine had done anything wrong. What about the kickbacks? Same story. What could she prove? That Copper came into the office with a duffel bag and Haine went to the safe. Yes, she had seen the money with her own eyes, but she could not say for certain where it came from. And who would she go to? The local sheriff? That man was more at home in Haine's pockets than Haine's keys.

Distracted, she almost missed her turn and had to take a hard left. Her handbag flew into the floor. She sighed. She needed to stop being so preoccupied with her predicament—at least while she was driving.

When she got home, she pulled the keys out of the ignition and walked around the car. Her bag had—naturally—landed upside down and spilled the contents all over the mat. She gathered the tumbled items and thrust them into her purse. She reached for the book she always carried to read at lunch, and an image shook itself free from the jumble of her mind: Haine going into the safe room, taking something out of the safe, and then reading or writing something.

Notebooks. He had notebooks in there. She now remembered seeing them sitting sideways, propped between the wall and the cash, but she had been so mesmerized by the pile of money she had paid them no mind. She slumped onto the seat. What an idiot she was.

He kept records. They had been right there the whole time.

39

Everlove

Monday, December 17, 1972

When her shift was over, Everlove stepped out of the store and into a night crackling with cold air. Under the streetlights, the pavement glittered as if the stars had fallen to the ground. She strode to her car at the end of the parking lot, ducking her head down against a wintry wind. Tomorrow, she intended to go Christmas shopping, and she mentally made a list of what she might buy for who. Should she put Triss on that list?

"I thought you and I might have a word."

Everlove jumped. A white man leaned against her dented fender. He was tall and lean and spoke with a drawling, gravelly voice.

She stopped several feet from him, and he peeled himself off the car, closing the distance between them. Everlove's heart pounded. She tried not to act nervous, but she couldn't stop herself from glancing around the empty lot. Yet what was the point? They both knew she was at his mercy, that no savior would step between a white man confronting a Black woman.

"Ain't no one around but me and you. I thought maybe you could tell me about your roommate."

Everlove tried to still her body's trembling. This must be the man Copper she had heard about. "What would you like to know?" Perhaps if she cooperated—or appeared to—he would go away.

"Like what's going on with the money from our office. You heard about that, right?"

"I know the office was broken into."

"I think she had something to do with it. We never had a break-in before, and she works there for a month and boom, some-one's breaking in. Plus she's been mighty jumpy ever since. Seems fishy, don't ya think?"

"Actually, I don't." Everlove swallowed. *How do I walk the line between making him think I'm helping but still keeping Triss's secret?* "Triss's grandfather is rich. Why would she need to steal money?"

"She ain't living with him anymore. So maybe she can't live in the fine style she was used to."

"She has a trust fund." Everlove didn't mention she wouldn't have access to it until she was twenty-five.

"She does, does she?"

"Her parents died. You don't think they made provisions for their kids?" She realized she was starting to sound argumentative. She turned down the temperature of her response and hated her-self and him for having to do it. "She doesn't even charge me for the whole half of the rent."

This information seemed to surprise him. "Huh," he grunted. "But maybe she has a boyfriend or something. Maybe she got in-volved with some bad people."

A car pulled into the parking lot, its headlights raking across Everlove, Copper, her car. Copper paid it no attention.

"The only people I know she has seen since I moved in are her family, our neighbors, and a few of her old friends—at a bridal party. So no boyfriend."

The car parked near the doors of the store, to Everlove's dismay. But why would they park out here where the employees had to park?

Copper caught her glance. "You hoping someone'll rescue you?" He chuckled. "I ain't going to hurt you. Gal like you ain't worth bothering about. But I'm keeping my eye on you, so if you hear or see anything, you best tell me. Got it?"

"Yes," Everlove mumbled, her voice shrinking in proportion to her soul.

He turned and ambled to a truck parked far enough away and so deep in the shadows she had not noticed it. She hurried to the other side of her car, climbed into the passenger seat, and scooted across, hating him, herself, the whole world.

Copper's truck pulled away, flashing red in the streetlight. Everlove started her car with shaking hands. She sat for a long moment, engine chugging and occasionally sputtering, until the fear melted into anger. She was done. She liked Triss, but this was too much. Too dangerous.

When she got home, she slammed her car door, but it did nothing to dispel the pent-up emotion churning inside her.

She found Triss curled on the sofa, wrapped in a blanket, immersed in a book. "Hey, Everlove. How was your day?"

"Not good, actually. And I need to talk to you about that."

Triss cocked her head and closed her book. "What's going on?"

Everlove took a deep breath. "I can't do this anymore. I understand what you're doing is helping people. But . . . this isn't good for me."

Triss frowned. "What do you mean?"

"That man Copper stopped me in the parking lot when I was leaving work."

Triss sat up. "What? Did he threaten you?"

"Not right out loud, but the implication was there. He still thinks you're involved somehow."

"Damn, Everlove. I'm really sorry I got you involved in this." Triss sank back into the sofa. "When I went off to college, I thought the world was getting better. The Civil Rights Act had been passed. Schools around here were finally desegregating. But then in my freshman year, the Orangeburg Massacre happened. I couldn't believe that three Black teenagers were killed, and the only person arrested was one of the Black organizers. Cleveland Sellers, wasn't it? And there was so little attention paid to it. I saw that while the surface may be a little shinier, underneath everything was still as rotten as it ever was. And I realized then that I can be disturbed by bigotry, but I can turn away from it and forget about it." She sighed. "I guess what I am trying to say is that I understand that you and I may stand side by side, but we aren't at all in the same place. And I am sorry Copper threatened you."

"I appreciate you saying that."

"So where do we go from here?"

"I think I'm going to move back home. I don't feel safe here."

"What if I can make it right?" Triss said. "Would you stay then?"

"I don't know," Everlove said. She was caught between the proverbial rock and a hard place. She didn't want to stay here and didn't want to go crawling home to her mother.

"Can you give me just a day or two to try to work this out?"

Everlove sighed. She didn't think Triss could fix this in forty-eight hours, but she would need time to pack up her stuff and ask her mother to take her back in. Despite everything, the thought made her sad.

40

Triss

Monday, December 18–Tuesday, December 19, 1972

Triss was once again struck by how different her path was from Everlove's. How could she make this right with her and keep Copper away? Her mind worked so hard on that problem that it wasn't until she climbed into bed that she remembered the books in Haine's safe. She wanted to talk to Everlove and Mrs. McCabe about them, but Everlove's problem had shoved everything else aside. It would have to wait until tomorrow night.

When she got home from work on Tuesday, Triss found Everlove and Mrs. McCabe in the kitchen. Everlove slid a casserole dish into the oven. Watching her, Triss realized that although they had only lived together for six weeks, this felt like the norm. And she liked it.

"How has work been?" Mrs. McCabe inquired.

"I'm glad you asked," Triss said and related what she had.

Mrs. McCabe clapped her hands. "That is good news!"

"Do you really think they are accounts of his illegal stuff?"

Everlove asked, drawing her eyebrows together. "Why would anyone keep records of that?"

"Plenty of crooked people keep records. The Nazis. Al Capone." Mrs. McCabe said. She tapped her lips with her index finger. "As a matter of fact, that's how they brought down Al Capone, and it was a woman who did it. What was her name? Dear me. I can only come up with the nickname some people called her: Prohibition Portia. Anyway, she was one of the first woman assistant attorney generals in the country. It was her brilliant idea to use income tax evasion to prosecute gangsters, although she didn't get much credit for it. If I wasn't afraid of snapping a bone, I'd dance a little jig. You need to get those ledgers, Triss!"

"Whoa, hold on there. I'm not stealing something again. One theft was bad enough."

"The universe is sending you a sign," Mrs. McCabe said. "Don't ever ignore the universe. You need to get back into that safe."

"Okay. Let's say for a minute I got back in. If he finds that the ledgers are missing, he'll go nuts. And I'm sure he will start suspecting me."

"Maybe you don't have to steal them," Everlove said.

"What do you mean?"

"Do you have a camera?"

"I do."

"Sneak it into the office and take pictures of the pages," Everlove said.

"Marvelous idea, Everlove," Mrs. McCabe said. "Just like in all the spy shows."

Triss ran the scenario over in her mind. She had the camera her grandfather had given her for high school graduation. She had her large Bohemian bag. She imagined herself in the file room, taking pictures of the ledgers, and Mr. Haine walking in. Despite the wave of nausea that washed over her at that thought, she had to admit it was better than anything she had come up with.

"That might work," Triss said, shaking off the pictures in her head.

"We still have the problem of you getting back into the safe," Mrs. McCabe said.

Triss drew in a breath as she remembered Haine returning to his desk for what was presumably the combination. "I may have the answer to that," she said and told them what she had seen. Admitting it felt like a commitment. She had no excuse now. "Also," she added, "he's out of the office starting Thursday until the beginning of the year." *In for a penny, in for a pound.*

"Triss, the universe is practically holding your hand and leading you," Mrs. McCabe said.

"Here's a question," Triss said. "Where would we get the film developed?" She imagined the developer at the Fotomat seeing the pages and doubted they would have any idea what they were. Then again, she had no idea what they were. Would it be in code? Or have actual names? They couldn't take the risk.

"What do you mean? Why not at—oh," Mrs. McCabe said, catching on.

A silence settled in the room as they pondered this new obstacle. Then Everlove cleared her throat. "I know someone in Willow Mills who owns a camera store," she said.

Triss wanted to say something about not getting Everlove more involved, but she didn't want to let Mrs. McCabe know about the talk they'd had the night before. Not yet, anyway. "Would he help us out?" Triss asked instead.

"Probably. I'll talk to him."

"Here's the plan," Mrs. McCabe said. "You sneak a camera in, take photos when you can, and get them to the developer. This is going to be a good week. I can feel it." She clapped her hands. "Mabel Willebrandt!"

Triss and Everlove both jumped. "Excuse me?" Triss asked.

"Mabel Willebrandt is the assistant attorney general I was talking about. Prohibition Portia."

"Why haven't I ever heard of her?" Triss asked.

"Because she was a woman, and we disappear when history gets written. My dear Flynn used to work for the Treasury Department and knew her. I might have been a little jealous. She was exactly my age, and Flynn talked of her with such admiration for her intelligence and dedication. I thought if things had been different, that could have been me. I mean, I had a brain. Just not the wherewithal. Which is why you two young ladies should do all you can to figure out your dreams and then follow them."

"That's all well and good, but I don't have the wherewithal either," Everlove said.

Mrs. McCabe reached out and took Everlove's hand. "Don't be a Negative Nelly, Everlove, my dear. You have three things I didn't have back in my day."

"And that would be?"

"First, more rights than I had; second, me; and third, Triss. We support you and believe in you. You know how many people supported me? Zilch. Well, Flynn might have, but it never occurred to him to send his bride off to college. My father died when

I was a teenager and my mother . . . she was a strong woman. Amazingly strong. But she was also a product of her times, and sending a girl to get a degree was not something she would have thought of."

"That sounds familiar," Triss said.

"And you," she said to Triss. "I know you're ambitious, but I also wonder if you're sabotaging yourself."

Triss leaned back indignantly. "What do you mean I'm sabotaging myself?"

"You seem to do things that take you away from your goal, not toward it."

"How could I have been farther than when my grandfather was putting his foot down? At least now I am independent."

"And spending all your energy assisting other people and getting out of the pickle you put yourself in." She held up her hand. "I'm not saying you're not doing good, but maybe you can help more people by pursuing your dream and being in a more influential position."

Triss opened her mouth, then closed it. She wanted to argue with Mrs. McCabe, but she heard the ring of truth in her words. Before she thought of what to say, Mrs. McCabe rubbed her hands together. "Well, this has worked up my appetite. Are we going to eat, or am I going to go home and heat up a TV dinner?"

As they ate, Mrs. McCabe talked about Christmas and her favorite decorations and how she had celebrated in the past. She did not seem to notice that Everlove and Triss were quieter than usual.

"That reminds me," she said. "You two are invited to Violet's this Saturday at five o'clock for a little Christmas get-together. No gifts, just bring a dish. How about Christmas cookies?"

Everlove and Triss grinned at each other.

"What?" Mrs. McCabe demanded.

"Nothing, Mrs. Dozer . . . I mean McCabe," Triss said.

"Oh, pshaw. I'm just being neighborly."

Triss patted Mrs. McCabe's hand. "I know. I'm just teasing. I can be there."

"I can, too," Everlove said, and Triss's heart lightened. Maybe if she took those photos and they turned out to be something she could use, Everlove would stay.

Still, after Mrs. McCabe left, the awkwardness returned. Triss wanted to say something but didn't know what. Instead, she and Everlove chatted about trivial things until they finally went to their rooms, murmuring excuses about early mornings and being tired.

Triss lay in bed fretting about everything: her job, her grandfather, her goals, the money. Everlove. And what Mrs. McCabe had said. Was she sabotaging herself? Was she throwing up more roadblocks between her and her future than her grandfather had? She swallowed hard at the thought.

But she also recalled what Mrs. McCabe had said about Mabel Willebrandt—a woman who had been an attorney fifty years ago. An effective attorney, working for the public good. And surely she had faced obstacles. Opposition. Ridicule, probably. And she still carried on.

Triss whispered to the dark, "If she could do it, I can do it, too," and drifted off to sleep.

41

Triss

Wednesday, December 20–Thursday, December 21, 1972

The next morning, Triss felt optimistic. They had a plan to get photos of the ledgers. And she had a new determination, thanks to Mabel Willebrandt.

Triss was having her toast and coffee when Everlove came into the kitchen.

"Everlove," Triss said, "can we talk about you moving out?"

"Sure," Everlove said, pouring coffee into a mug, then taking a seat at the table. The scrape of the chair and the clatter of the cup seemed overly loud in the silence that followed the initial volley of conversation.

"Look, I don't want—" Triss started.

"I've been thinking—" Everlove said at the same time. They laughed nervously.

"May I go first?" Triss said, hoping her words would sway Everlove. Everlove nodded, and Triss plowed on. "I want to apologize again. For involving you in my mess. For not understanding what that would mean for you."

"It's okay."

But Triss put up her hand. "No, it's not. I'm glad you talked to me. I thought I was pretty smart about the world. Turns out I'm not. I understand why you need to leave, but I'd like you to—" She fumbled for a better way to phrase her thoughts. "I wish you'd reconsider. I enjoy your company. I enjoy your friendship. I didn't realize how much it meant to me until you told me you wanted to move out."

"Want is not exactly the right word." Everlove's eyes slid away. "I just don't feel safe."

"I can understand that. But here's a plan B. Move out for now, and if you want to come back when things are better, your room will still be here."

"I appreciate that," Everlove said. "And I've been thinking maybe I could stay through the holidays. I'll keep an eye out for your coworker."

"And I will, too."

Before Triss left for work, she inserted a roll of film into her camera, wrapped it in a scarf, and stuffed it into her handbag. She hefted it, worried the weight and bulk of it would look suspicious. But then she doubted Mr. Haine spent much time thinking about her purse.

When she arrived at the office, Mr. Haine was at his desk and didn't glance up when she opened her usual drawer and eased the bag into it.

Haine left the office at half past eleven to attend a lunch meeting. As soon as she saw his car easing its way up the street, she took the camera—scarf and all—into the file room and hid it behind some closed case files.

Wednesday afternoon was a flurry of activity. Mr. Haine returned from his meeting and churned out work so he could take the next ten days off. Triss was to man the office Thursday and Friday, then close its doors until December twenty-eighth. With Mr. Haine out of the office, chances were she wouldn't see much of Sheridan or Copper. And rent payers came in at the end or the beginning of the month. Here in the middle of the month, right before Christmas, she didn't expect to see many people. She really would not have a better opportunity. Still, Triss was nervous as a squirrel.

On Thursday, Triss worked her way through the pile of Dictaphone tapes Haine had left for her. At midmorning, she strode into his office to collect the stack of signed correspondence he had left the evening before. But before she scooped them up, she eased open the center drawer. Inside lay extra Dictaphone belts and a couple of blank legal pads. She looked under these but found nothing. She opened the drawer on the right. Pens, pencils, paper clips, a stapler, and a staple remover were neatly organized in a small, compartmentalized tray. She was about to lift the tray when she spotted a tiny bit of yellow peeking out from under the edge of the stapler. Bingo! She eased the slip out and saw three numbers written on it: 84-67-23. Her heart hammered. She took her own paper out of her jacket pocket and jotted the numbers down, not wanting to take his cheat sheet with her but afraid to rely on her memory and have to come running back. She put the slip back, placing the stapler carefully on top and trying to leave the same amount of yellow showing as when she found it. She closed the drawer with shaking hands, then grabbed the letters, returned to her desk, and sat.

Dear Lord, she thought, *that was only step one.* She was a long way from done, but she was already a wreck. She breathed deeply a few times. In and out. In and out. Finally, she jutted out her chin, picked up her stack of filing, and marched into the file room. She opened the drawer where the first paper would go but did not file it. Instead, she placed it on top of the folders so that if anyone walked in, she could quickly grab it. She retrieved the camera from its hiding spot and turned to face the safe. *Here I go.*

She turned the dial, and the ratcheting clicks echoed through the office. When she had cycled through the three numbers, she put her hand on the T-handle and, with a deep breath, turned it. The solid thunk of the bolts retracting resounded through the room. Bundles of money lay inside, just like before. As did the books she had so stupidly disregarded. There were several, but she grabbed the one nearest the cash, hoping it would be the most current. She was right. The cover read January 1972. She opened it and saw columns of dates, initials, and dollar amounts. It did, indeed, appear to be a ledger. She flipped to the last pages that had writing to see the most recent entries. Then she laid it flat on the table, yanked the lens cap off the camera, and dropped it next to the book. She put her eye to the viewfinder and focused on the writing and snapped. She turned the page and repeated the process, working as quickly as she could. Focus, snap, turn. Focus, snap, turn. She had gotten to her fifteenth page when the sound of the back door opening nearly made her scream. Her heart went into overdrive. It was either Haine or one of his goons. Everyone else used the front door.

Heart banging away, she placed the camera back into the file drawer and slid the ledger into the safe, then eased the door closed.

"Be right there!" she called out as she turned the T-handle, hoping her voice would cover the sound of the bolts clicking home.

Triss grabbed a letter and fumbled through the files, but her trembling hands would not allow her to insert the sheet into the right place. She gave up and closed the drawer, letter in hand, just as a voice broke through the roar in her ears.

"Well, well, if it isn't Miss Patricia."

Copper stepped into the room, and she had a panicked moment when she feared he would wonder why she was pulling out a paper and not filing it. Then she remembered she did both. *Good Lord, my brain has seized up.* She gathered the other papers from the tabletop. "Can I help you?"

He stepped into the room toward her, and her heart lurched as she spotted the lens cap lying on the floor near her foot. In her haste, she must have knocked it off the table. She casually took a step to the side and put her foot on it.

"Just dropped by to see if Mr. Haine left any work for me." He looked around the room, and Triss slid the lens cap under the table, hoping the shadows thrown by the overhead light would conceal it.

"Not that I know of," she said. "If you will excuse me . . ."

"You okay? You're as jumpy as a cat on hot bricks."

"I just have a ton of work to do. So if you don't mind, I'll get back to it."

She stepped around him, heading to her desk, but then turned to face him. "I know you think I had something to do with the break-in. And it's one thing to harass me about it, but you need to back off my roommate. She doesn't need to get caught up in your crazy flights of fancy."

Copper didn't look intimidated. Instead, he looked amused. "And what if I don't?"

"My grandfather would not be happy to hear that a bully is bothering his granddaughter. Or her roommate."

Copper snorted. "I'm shaking in my boots now." But Triss thought his mouth had tightened. He glanced at his watch. "I have another place to be. Maybe I'll stop by another time," he said, pushing his hat brim up, "in case Mr. Haine calls in and has something for me to do." He tipped his cap at her. "Don't do anything I wouldn't do." He winked. She gritted her teeth.

She rolled a sheet of letterhead into her typewriter as she listened to his boots clomping down the hall. The back door opened and closed as she started typing a date. She struck the carriage return and continued with an address. She hit several wrong keys but continued working anyway. After ten minutes went by, she returned to the file room. She should probably take more pictures, but she didn't have it in her to do more right now. This would have to be enough. She picked up the lens cap and placed it on the camera. She cranked the remaining film into the canister, opened the camera door, and pulled out the roll. She pushed another roll into the chamber and fed it into the take-up spool. If for some reason the photos didn't come out, she would be ready for another try. But man, she hoped she wouldn't have to. She stuffed the camera into the drawer again. Everything seemed to be in order. At her desk, she made a quick call, attempting to banish all thoughts of crazy spy schemes before getting back to her work.

This had better succeed.

In the afternoon, Peach Singleton came in to pay her rent, although she still had more than ten days before the due date. She handed her cash to Triss, chattering the whole time about the weather, the price of milk and eggs, her son's upcoming birthday. Triss placed the receipt in Peach's outstretched hand—along with the film canister. Peach did not miss a beat. She kept talking as she dropped the canister into her purse and slid the receipt in her well-worn wallet.

"I better get to the rest of my errands. I'll see you next month."

"You have a nice day, Mrs. Singleton. And Merry Christmas."

42

Triss

Thursday, December 21–Friday, December 22, 1972

When Triss got home that evening, she collapsed onto the sofa next to Everlove.

"Everlove, I vow I will never, ever break the law again. I will think before I act. And if I survive this, I will do good for the rest of my life."

"Those are some mighty big promises. Wanna tell me what happened?"

"I got the photos. Or tried to. I hope they come out."

Everlove's eyes widened. She put her journal on the coffee table. "Really? You did it?"

"I did. I took about fifteen photos. And then Copper came in and almost caught me. I thought my heart was going to burst. I managed to hide everything, and as soon as Copper left, I called Peach to pick up the film."

"Could you tell anything from the ledger?"

"Not much. But there were a lot of entries for 'rent' and dollar amounts. He didn't list any names, only what I assume are initials. We'll have to figure out what they stand for. But . . . it looked promising."

"Lord, I hope so."

At work the next day, Triss did her usual filing and mail sorting as she waited anxiously for her lunch break so she could see the photos. Time slowed to a snail's pace. Finally, noon arrived, and she grabbed her purse and left for lunch. She walked to the library, trying to enjoy the mild day and copious sunshine, but she worried that the photographs would be blurry. Or blank. Lately, it seemed, she jumped from one worry right to another.

She spotted Mrs. McCabe and Everlove sitting on a bench. Triss's heart skipped a beat at the sight of the manila envelope in Everlove's hand.

"No problems?" Triss asked.

"Not a one," Everlove said. "Tucker mailed a set addressed to you to your grandfather's house like we asked. And here's the other set."

"Shall we have a look?" Mrs. McCabe said.

Everlove handed Triss the envelope. "You should be the one to open it."

Mrs. McCabe patted the space between her and Everlove. "Why don't you sit here so we can all see?"

Triss could not stop the trembling of her hands as she pinched the clasp, opened the flap, and slid the photographs out. The three women almost bumped heads as they leaned down to peer at the images captured by the camera.

At the top of the first page, written in Mr. Haine's careful, tight script, were the words "Cash Account 1972." Below that, columns ran down the page, headed Date, Payee/Payor, Description, Income, Expense, Still Owed.

12/1: W.C. Rent, +$300.00
12/1: J.B. Rent +$100.00
12/1: Q.D. Services -$25.00
12/1: H.A. Services -$25.00
12/1: C.C. Services -$25.00
12/1: S.R. Services -$15.00
12/8: W.C. Rent +$200.00
12/8: J.B. Rent +$75.00
12/8: Q.D. Services -$25.00
12/8: H.A. Services -$25.00
12/8: C.C. Services -$25.00
12/8: S.R. Services -$15.00

"That's an awful lot of rent, don't you think?" Everlove said.

"It is. And weekly?" Mrs. McCabe said.

Triss pointed to the initials Q.D. "The sheriff's name is Quincy Durant." She ran her finger down to SR and CC. "I bet this is Sheridan Rudd and Copper Cavanaugh. I think W.C. is Weevil Carr and J.B. is Jenette Blazey."

"Seems likely," Everlove agreed. She blew air through her lips in a silent whistle. "Who is H.A.?"

Triss mentally ran through names she had heard around the office. "Maybe Hap Adams. He's a deputy." She took a deep breath, hardly believing what she was seeing. "I think we have something here."

"Now what do we do?" Mrs. McCabe asked.

"I'm not sure. Perhaps we can brainstorm tonight. I've got to get back to work. Everlove, can you take the photos and hide them somewhere?"

"Want me to dig a hole out back?" Everlove said, arching an eyebrow.

"Very funny."

"Yes, I'll hide them."

Triss eased the photographs into the envelope and handed it to Everlove.

"See you at eight when I get off work," Everlove said.

That evening, Triss and Everlove discussed what they had found.

"Are you going to confront him?"

"I have another idea I want to explore," Triss said. "I want to do what's right. What Mrs. McCabe said the other day struck a chord . . . about me sabotaging myself."

"Maybe we're both doing that."

"I don't think you are. You stopped yourself from making a mistake. Me? I ran headlong into a huge one. But I need to right the wrong. I just need to figure out how." She paused. "When I was little, I thought adults knew everything. They always seemed so sure of themselves. Have I just not reached adulthood yet? Because I feel like I don't have anything figured out."

"I know what you mean," Everlove said. "I keep waiting for the confidence my mother has to kick in."

"What if it never does?" Triss said. "What if everyone simply acts like they know what they are doing?"

"I'm pretty sure my mother knows exactly what she's doing and why. Always."

"Could it be that you don't know her as well as you think?"

"I'm not sure if I feel better thinking that or believing she has all the answers."

"I hear that," Triss said.

"So, what's your idea?" Everlove asked.

"I have to check something first, but I will let you know as soon as I can."

43

Triss

Saturday, December 23, 1972

On Saturday morning, Triss drove to the community center. She strode into the building, and a wall of interwoven sounds greeted her: children's shouts and sneaker squeaks; the *whap, whap, whap* of a dribbling ball; the occasional voice of a man. That would be Jay, coaching his budding basketball players. Suddenly, it struck her that just a few years ago, the center had been segregated. She and Everlove, both intelligent young women striving to find their places in the world, would not have crossed paths here. Or at school. What a world they lived in, she thought. To keep people from something because of how much melanin they had.

She approached the entrance of the basketball court and spotted Jay helping a young boy set up for a free throw. He didn't make it, but Jay caught the ball a girl tossed back to him and gave it to the boy. After some instruction on how to place his feet and tip his hand, the boy tried again. It bounced off the rim. A miss, but much closer. The boy beamed.

"Mr. Jay! There's a lady over there!" a girl shouted.

Jay turned and spotted her. He grinned. "That's no lady. That's my sister."

He walked over to her, and she punched him in the arm.

"What brings you here?"

"I thought I'd take my big brother to breakfast."

"Run out of food at home? Is Everlove away?"

Triss put her hands on her hips. "Can't a girl just want to spend time with her brother?"

"I guess a girl could, but I think this girl has an ulterior motive." Jay raised his eyebrow, a trait he'd inherited from their grandfather.

"I'm going to ignore that. When will you be free?"

"About twenty more minutes."

"Do you mind if I wait and watch?"

"Not at all."

Triss sat in the bleachers and watched as Jay coached the kids. The girls and boys listened to him intently, eager for his attention and praise, which he gave out freely and patiently. Where did he get that? She certainly didn't think they were traits they shared.

After he said goodbye to the last child, she drove them to a restaurant well-known for its plethora of pancakes and unlimited cups of coffee.

"What's up, Triss?" Jay asked, serious for once.

"It's not anything specific. I just feel . . . unsettled."

"I have never known you to be settled, so what's different now?" he said.

"Okay, more unsettled than usual." She told him about Everlove being accosted by a white man—leaving out why—and of their subsequent conversation. "I learned some things in college about how the world treats Black people. But now . . . I feel like I'm learning it all over again."

Jay nodded. "Most of the kids who come to the community center are Black," he said. "Sometimes I talk to their parents. And while I think things have improved, I also think a lot of things have stayed the same. I see parents who can't get a better job because of their skin color. Not that they tell me that, but when you know someone with a college degree who can't get a job as a bank teller, although the bank has a sign that tellers are needed, you put two and two together. So they have to work two jobs. And they can't be at home as much, and the kids don't receive the help and encouragement they need. Then they don't do as well in school. Then they can't land a better job. It's an endless cycle. They can't move into the better neighborhoods. They can't get bank loans."

"But how can this happen when these things are illegal?" Triss asked.

"No one is coming right out and saying, 'I'm not selling you this house because you're Black.' It's more subtle, so it's harder to fight."

Triss sighed. "This is so depressing."

They ate in silence for a few minutes, then Triss said, "I thought I was this hip white person who wasn't a bigot. But that's not enough, is it? It's passive. I want to be active. I want to help the world change, but I have to accept my place in it first."

"What do you mean?"

"It's like all along, I thought just being a good person and not using racial slurs was enough. I don't discriminate against anyone. So I'm good, right? But I'm not changing anything that way. I'm just sitting on the sidelines while the world continues to beat up on Black people. But hey, I'm not doing that, so I'm good."

"What are you going to do about that?"

"I'm not sure yet. I'm still mulling this over." She regarded him across the rim of her coffee cup. "You are at least doing something by volunteering at the community center."

"Want to join me?"

Triss snorted. "Not as a coach. Got anything else?"

"Actually, I've been thinking about starting some craft classes. Nothing fancy."

Triss had been joking when she asked if Jay had anything else. But she remembered when she and her friends would get together and tie-dye shirts or paint rocks. She could see herself doing that. "I hate to admit you had a good idea, but that actually sounds fun and like something I could do."

Jay grinned. "I am full of great ideas. That would be cool. I'll talk to the committee and pitch it to them. If they don't have to pay for anything, I'm sure they'll back it. Maybe we can get some businesses to contribute supplies."

"That would be a start for me in my new quest to do something instead of sitting on the sidelines."

"Any other life crises I can help solve?"

"I do have a question for you," Triss said and got to the real reason she had called on her big brother. "If I wanted to tell someone about some illegal activities, but not the local sheriff, who would I tell? FBI?"

Both of Jay's eyebrows shot up now. "Care to explain?"

"Not really."

Jay pursed his lips. "I need a little more information to answer the question. What kind of activities?"

Triss sighed. "Kickbacks from Weevil Carr, perhaps."

"Gambling or bootlegging?"

"Both?"

"Is this about Haine?"

"Ask me no questions, and I'll tell you no lies."

He frowned. "Fine. If it were me, I would take it to the South Carolina Investigative Department."

"SCID?"

"Yep."

"Why not the FBI?"

"They are notoriously slow. Methodical, but slow. I think your best bet would be SCID. Also, SCID was established to enforce alcohol laws after Prohibition ended, so that's their thing."

"Ah," Triss said.

"I have a connection there. He and I worked together on a case when I was doing my internship in Columbia. He's a good guy, and he knows his stuff. You have something to write on? I'll give you his name." Triss reached in her purse for a small notebook and handed it to Jay. He turned to the last page and jotted down a name.

"Thanks, Jay." Triss leaned back against the booth.

Their check came, and Jay paid it. They walked to the car. "Thanks for being there for me," Triss said.

Jay put his finger on her chest then up to her nose, the way he used to when she was little, asking her what was on her shirt. He no longer did it as a trick, but the gesture had become his way of showing affection. "That's what handsome big brothers are for."

"I wouldn't know about that, but it's nice to have a not hideously ugly big brother. I'll call your friend after the holidays."

As Triss drove him back to the community center, she said, "Sometimes I wonder how different my life would be if Mom and Dad hadn't died."

"I've wondered that, too."

"I'm not sure your life would be any different, but maybe mine would be."

"How so?"

"I wouldn't have had the argument with Grandfather. I would have Mom and Dad's support. Or at least Mom's."

"In what?"

"Going to law school. She always told me to stretch my wings."

Jay snorted. "Yeah, as long as you stretched them within her little box of rules."

"What do you mean?"

"Triss, you were a lot younger when they died, so maybe you don't remember. Mom was a stickler for the conventions. She wanted Dad to run for office, and she would have been the perfect senator's wife. Or even a first lady. She would have stood beside him with her immaculate hair and strand of pearls and supported him. But she would never have had a career. And I don't think she would have wanted you to have one."

All the air left Triss's body. She felt sucker punched. "But wait. You mean she was like Grandfather? Believing a woman's place is in the home?"

"Honestly, I think Grandfather is far more liberal than she was. I think he has tried to raise us the way they—she—would have wanted."

Triss pulled in front of the community center. Jay reached over and gave her hand a squeeze. "Gotta run. Please be careful with that business we talked about." He opened the door and was gone, leaving Triss feeling like her entire life had been erased and rewritten.

That night, Triss lay in bed as memories that had not visited her in eleven years played out on the popcorn ceiling. Her mother, remonstrating her about her posture. Showing her how to cross her legs at the ankles. How to talk softly. Telling her she needed to rein in her impulsivity, that a husband would not appreciate it.

How had she not remembered all this before? She thought of the long-ago trip to the art store and her mother helping her pick out a painting so they could create a room where she could spread her wings. What had her mother meant if not to pursue an education and become an independent woman? Had she only intended a launch into Edenton society?

She reexamined other memories, like when her mother took her to the family doctor because Triss had a stomachache. The doctor did not believe Triss was sick because she kept spinning in the doctor's chair and playing with the examining table and jars on the counter. She giggled when he touched her abdomen. He had talked to her mother like she was a worrisome dog with a nervous disposition. Her mother had narrowed her eyes and told him it would be in his best interest to not misdiagnose a child. And it turned out Triss had appendicitis.

Another time, her mother took the family car to the shop, something their yardman, Theodo, usually did, but his wife was having a baby that day. The mechanic approached Triss's mother where she waited, perched on the Naugahyde and chrome chairs, legs crossed at the ankles. He started to explain that she needed new tires. She objected, but he insisted, telling her a "little lady such as herself didn't know much about cars." She told him in no uncertain terms that she might not know much about cars, but she knew a swindler when she saw one. Triss had gaped as her mother stood and spoke in her quiet but forceful voice—the same one she used when Triss got into trouble—her tone like downy feathers hiding razored claws.

As Triss inspected every scrap she could gather from the musty attic of her past, she found no example of a feminist bent. Simply a mother and wife putting her delicate, high-heeled foot down when she needed to.

In a sixty-second conversation, her whole world had turned upside down. Nothing had really changed. But yet, everything had.

44

Everlove

December 1972

At five o'clock, Triss and Everlove walked across the road in the growing darkness. Their neighbors' cheerful Christmas lights contrasted with the gloom. Everlove glanced back appreciatively at her and Triss's little porch with its inexpertly draped strands. It might look a little crooked, but it warmed her to see them.

She looked from the lights to the tent of shimmering stars over her head and realized the strange calmness she felt was . . . contentment. She liked living here. She liked Triss. The neighbors. And mostly, her independence. The idea of her future still unsettled her, but instead of fearing it, she almost looked forward to it.

They arrived at Mrs. McCabe's, who answered the door promptly and ushered them in, closing the door against the cold.

"The party is at Violet's," Mrs. McCabe said.

"We know. We came by a little early hoping to catch you," Triss said.

Mrs. McCabe eyed the cheery package Everlove was carrying. "What is this?"

"It's for you," Everlove said. "From Triss and me."

"For me? You got a present for me?" Everlove felt a flutter of pleasure as Mrs. McCabe's face lit up with joy. "You didn't have to do this! I don't have anything for you two." She looked stricken.

"Don't worry," Triss said. "We just wanted to show our appreciation for how . . . friendly you've been."

"That is very thoughtful. Can I open it now?"

"Of course!" Everlove said.

Mrs. McCabe tore the wrapping off and turned the box over in her hands. "A telephone! But I already have one."

"That phone is older than I am," Triss said.

"It probably is," Mrs. McCabe said. "But it works well. I don't even know how to use this new-fangled thing."

"It's easy. It has buttons instead of a dial. Look." Triss pulled the powder-blue phone out of the box. "You just press them. It's faster. It also has better sound quality. We got it because you are such a forward-thinking person." Everlove suppressed a smile at Triss's unabashed attempt to manipulate Mrs. McCabe, using a technique right out of Mrs. McCabe's handbook.

But Mrs. McCabe looked pleased. "I am, aren't I? It is kind of pretty," she said, taking it from Triss and pressing a button. "I guess I could give it a try."

They left the phone on the kitchen table and walked to Violet's house. Triss and Everlove stayed for a few hours, eating hors d'oeuvres and drinking punch. Near the end, Arabella urged Violet to play some Christmas music so they could sing carols. Violet placed Nat King Cole's album *The Christmas Song* on her stereo turntable, and most of the guests joined in. Except Mr. Pritchard and Tommy. And Joanna, who seemed too shy to sing. Arabella skipped over to Mr. Pritchard. "Are you going to sing this year?" she asked amidst decking of halls.

"Nope."

"Are you sure? It'll make you feel happy inside."

"I am happy inside," he said, scowling.

She laughed at him. "Silly," she said and skipped back to her mother and joined in the fa-la-las.

"Violet," Mrs. McCabe said. "I've been meaning to ask how the wedding dress situation is coming along."

Everlove's ears perked up.

"Caroline and I are working on it," Violet said. "That's all I will say. But it's going well."

Everlove would love to know if they were using her dress or not. But she thought they had likely found a different dress. Maybe new, maybe secondhand. She tried to tell herself she had been doing a kindness, but she still felt foolish for pawning off her damaged wedding gown on poor Violet.

"I don't understand how they could just lock the doors," Caroline said. "Couldn't they give the brides their dresses, at least?"

"Probably not," said Triss. "The store will have to pay their creditors first."

"Triss, you sound like a lawyer." Mrs. McCabe grinned at her.

"It's still not right. People—even businesspeople—should do the right thing. Maybe not doing the right thing is what got them into trouble to begin with," Caroline said.

"I'm sure it wouldn't have been easy to face a bunch of angry brides," Violet interjected.

"Who said doing the right thing is supposed to be easy?" Mr. Pritchard said.

When the two women returned home and hung up their coats, Triss put her hand on Everlove's arm.

"Before you head off to bed, I need to talk to you about a few things."

Everlove nodded. "Go ahead."

"Let's have a seat." Triss sat on the loveseat while Everlove settled herself on the sofa. Triss cleared her throat. "First, I talked to my brother. I didn't tell him specifics about what's going on, but I mentioned possible kickbacks from bootlegging and gambling. And I asked him if I had information about that, who would I take it to. He told me the South Carolina Investigative Department would be the best place to go. And there are two advantages: they work faster, and he knows someone there."

"Oh, wow. Did he know you were talking about Haine?"

"He asked, and I declined to comment."

"Are you going take his advice?"

"Yes, I am. I wasn't too sure until tonight, but what Caroline and Mr. Pritchard said about doing the right thing helped me decide. I think it's best I pass this off to someone else. Someone who can do something." She paused. "I also talked to my brother about what I've learned about myself lately. I wanted to talk it out with someone before I talked to you. Kind of get it straight in my head." Triss looked down at her lap. "Look. I have a lot of faults. But I didn't think one was kind of being a bigot by blindness. I thought

I had my eyes opened to a lot of things in college. But I've come to realize I still have blind spots. That not being a bigot isn't the same thing as standing up against bigotry. So sometimes, I have not been as sensitive as I could have been or said the right things, and I want you to know I realize that, and I want to try harder."

"I appreciate that, Triss. And maybe I should talk to you more about how I feel."

"I would like it if you would. So, with all that said, and with me turning my information over to SCID, would you consider staying?"

"You know nothing is going to happen overnight, right?"

"Yeah, I know."

Everlove stood. "I'll give all this some thought though, okay? For now, I'm tuckered out."

"Oh, I almost forgot! I have something for you," Triss said.

"I do, too."

They both ducked into their rooms, and Everlove reemerged carrying a slim, flat parcel wrapped in festive Santa paper. Triss held something that looked very similar, but with Christmas tree gift wrap.

They agreed to open their gifts simultaneously, and the sound of tearing paper filled the trailer, followed by oohs and aahs.

"Oh, I love this," Triss said at the same time Everlove said, "This is beautiful."

Triss had gotten Everlove a leather-bound notebook with a loop at the edge of the front cover to hold a pen and an attached red ribbon to mark her place in it. Everlove had given Triss a leather portfolio with a large pocket for papers and two smaller ones for business cards.

"It seems we were thinking alike," Everlove said.

"It does. Thank you so much. I expect you to put that to good use." Triss nodded at the notebook.

"Ha! You sound like Mrs. McCabe," Everlove replied.

"Oh, dear," Triss said.

45

Everlove

Tuesday, December 26, 1972

Everlove spent a fairly pleasant Christmas Day with her family. Her mother had given her the usual useful gifts she always gave, so there was that. But Avenia had also found out Everlove was living with a white girl in a white neighborhood.

"Nothing good has ever happened to this family when they mix with white people," Avenia said. "You've gone from a little crazy to a lot crazy, and I hope you come to your senses before something awful happens."

Everlove endured the lecture. Her mother was not wrong. But Everlove liked Triss and she liked her independence. She had to forge her own path in the world, and that meant interacting with white people. But maybe she could find a way to advance the cause of equality. Do her part to make the world a better place. She didn't know what that was, but she had a feeling she would find it. It was the most confident she had ever felt about her future. And maybe that was a sign she was on the right path.

The day after Christmas, she had just grabbed her pocketbook to head out the door for work when someone knocked on the door. She opened it, expecting to find Mrs. McCabe, but instead found Matthias Moon.

"What on earth . . ." she started.

"Just call me Santa Claus," he said, grinning.

"Now why would I do that?"

"Because I'm here to give you a gift."

She narrowed her eyes. He held up his hands. "Just hear me out. We got a wrecked Rambler in at the shop that we're using for spare parts. I can change out your door with the one from it."

"I don't have time right now." In truth, she didn't have the money right now, but she didn't want to tell him that.

"I'm offering my services as mechanic and chauffeur. For free."

She shook her head. "Uh, uh. No way."

He put his hand to his chest. "You don't trust me?"

"No, as I matter of fact, I don't."

"You can check my references with Reg. He'll tell you I'm a fine and upstanding citizen."

"Maybe he will, but that still doesn't tell me why on earth you want to fix my car for free."

He gave her a lazy grin that she bet he thought was charming. "Because I'm trying to get on your good side."

"Why?"

"Lord, girl, do I have to spell it out?"

"I think you do."

"I like you."

"You what?" Everlove could not have heard him right.

He leaned down a little, eyes locked on hers. "I like you. I thought you were cute back when we were in school. I would have asked you out a while ago, but you've been with Rodney since God wore knee pants. But now you're not with him. So here I am."

Everlove shook her head and stepped into the space between him and the door. She twisted her key in the lock and turned to face him.

"So how about it? I'll fix your car door, and you can repay me by going out to dinner?"

She took her time picking out her car key from the ring in her hand. Then she looked at him. "I appreciate the offer, but I'll take care of my own car repairs when I can. And Rodney and I just broke up."

He ducked his head in agreement. "That's why I like you. Strong, independent, and smart. So how about we do this . . . I'll be your friend for now. Maybe have a coffee and a chat. I'm willing to wait for a good thing."

She snorted and pushed past him. "I've got to go to work, and I don't have time to stand here arguing with a crazy man."

As she headed to her car, she fervently wished she could open her door and get in with dignity instead of sliding across the seat. Especially since he turned to watch her with that cocky grin. Which irritated her no end.

When she situated herself in front of the steering wheel, he got into his car and drove away.

She shook her head in annoyance. But wondered why she had a smile on her face.

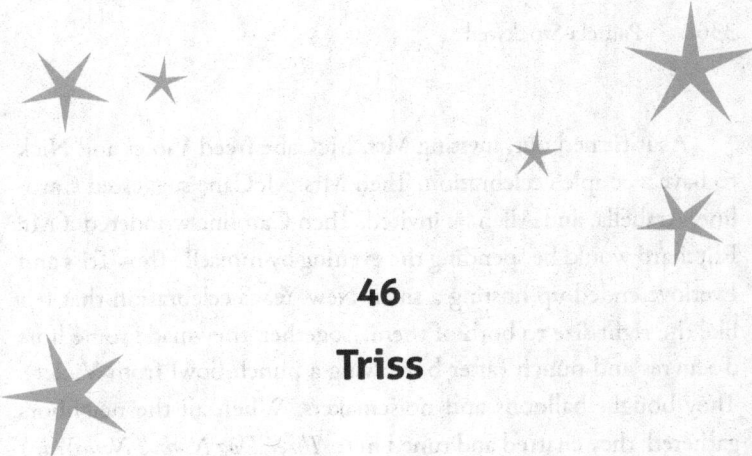

46

Triss

During her family's Christmas celebration, Triss thought the tension between her grandfather and her seemed less fraught. Maybe it came from her new perspective on her mother's view of life. Or maybe both of them were getting used to the new normal.

She worked Thursday and Friday, and then it would be New Year's Eve. Triss's friend's family always threw a huge New Year's Eve party, but the idea of getting all dressed up and hanging out with her old gang did not appeal to her. When she asked Everlove what her plans were, she said most of her friends were married now and had kids, and now did family-centered celebrations.

"Sounds like we are both between worlds," Triss said. "How about we just stay home? I read that Dick Clark is going to host a New Year's Eve show."

"I could do that," Everlove said.

"Do you think Mrs. McCabe will be busy? I would hate to see her spend it alone."

As it turned out, inviting Mrs. McCabe freed Violet and Nick to have a couple's celebration. Then Mrs. McCabe suggested Caroline, Arabella, and Allen be invited. Then Caroline wondered if Mr. Pritchard would be spending the evening by himself. Thus Triss and Everlove ended up hosting a small New Year's celebration that felt like the right size to both of them. Together, they made some hors d'oeuvres and punch (after borrowing a punch bowl from Violet). They bought balloons and noisemakers. When all the neighbors gathered, they chatted and tuned in to *Three Dog Night's New Year's Rockin' Eve*. Triss caught Mrs. McCabe tapping her foot to the music.

"Mrs. McCabe, are you a rock and roll fan?"

Mrs. McCabe snorted. "You kids think you invented rock and roll, but I'll have you know I was dancing to it when you were still in diapers," she said. "I remember the first time I heard it like it was yesterday. Flynn and I had gone to Memphis and went to a club where Jackie Brenston and his Delta Cats were playing. That was three years before Elvis came out with 'That's All Right.'"

"Mrs. McCabe, you should write a book about your life," Arabella said.

"I should."

"I'm sure it would be a bestseller," Caroline said.

Mr. Pritchard looked at the ceiling and seemed to be mouthing a prayer.

All in all, Triss had quite a nice evening. And while she was still worried about what was going to happen, she felt at peace with her decision to turn her information over to SCID.

★

On Tuesday, Triss came out of her room, ready for work, and found Mrs. McCabe sitting in the kitchen with Everlove.

"Are you still going through with this?" Mrs. McCabe asked. Triss had told her about her plans on New Year's Day.

"Yes, I am."

"I'm going with you," Mrs. McCabe announced.

"You don't have to. I got myself into this mess, and I'll get myself out."

"You might need moral support," Mrs. McCabe said. "What time are we going?"

"I'm telling Mr. Haine I have a doctor's appointment, so I plan to leave at eleven."

"Just so happens I'm free. How about you, Everlove? Would you like to join us?"

"That's okay, Mrs. McCabe," Triss interjected. "We don't need a whole platoon going in there."

"I say the more the merrier."

Everlove considered this, then said slowly, "I think I will."

"Really?" Triss said.

"I have the day off, and I wouldn't mind hearing what SCID has to say."

A surge of gratitude filled Triss's heart. She didn't realize she wanted company until they offered. "Looks like we have a date." She paused. "I find it ironic that I'm asking my boss for time off so I can turn him in to law enforcement."

Triss may have found it ironic while still at home, but in the office, when she told Haine she had a doctor's appointment that afternoon, she found it nerve-wracking. Haine, however, did not bat an eye except to say perhaps she could work through her lunch hour the next day to make up for her time off. *Miser*, she thought.

The trio met at the house and were headed out the door when Triss remembered something. "Everlove! The photos!"

Everlove crossed the living room and lifted the Van Gogh reprint off the wall. The envelope was taped to the back.

"Clever," Mrs. McCabe said approvingly.

Triss drove them to Columbia under a gleaming January sun that had her thinking of crocuses and daffodils and new beginnings. But beginnings could be unfamiliar and uncomfortable as well as hopeful.

"What if I'm wrong about all this?" she asked her companions as she parked in front of the white-washed building with its rows of narrow windows. They reminded Triss of arrow slits in castle walls.

"Oh, pshaw," Mrs. McCabe said. "You're not wrong. We all know what he's into."

"And when you turn everything over to the SCID, you can quit worrying about it," Everlove added. "It'll be out of your hands."

"But what if he retaliates in some way?"

"With SCID watching? That would be foolish, and I don't get the impression he's foolish," Mrs. McCabe said. "Now stop dillydallying. I'm going, and I'm not waiting for you two lollygaggers." Mrs. McCabe opened her door and swung one leg out, scooted toward the door, swung the other leg out, and scooted some more. By the time she was standing, both Everlove and Triss had walked around the car and were standing next to Mrs. McCabe's door, waiting.

"Show-offs," Mrs. McCabe mumbled.

They strode up a wide walkway lined by rustling palmetto trees. Triss hesitated at the glass door, but Mrs. McCabe gripped her arm and propelled her forward into a carpeted lobby. She was surprisingly strong for a little old lady. The three women approached a desk where a dark-haired woman clacked away at a typewriter. She glanced up as they came in, looking at Everlove, then Triss, then Mrs. McCabe, furrowing her brow as if trying to make sense of them.

"We'd like to see Alex Donahue, please," Triss said.

"And what is this in regard to?"

"Um, it's confidential. I have information about a crime."

"I need to tell Agent Donahue what this is about."

Triss opened her mouth to answer, but Mrs. McCabe leaned over and whispered, "We've got the name of a bad guy to turn in, see? A big fish. But if too many people hear about what we're doing, word might get back, and he'll destroy evidence."

"I'm still supposed to ask."

"And you did," Mrs. McCabe said. "So now you can call Agent Donahue with a clear conscience."

The woman narrowed her eyes and huffed. She picked up a phone, hit a button, and said, "Agent Donahue, there are some . . . women here who believe"—she stressed the word—"they have information about a crime. They asked for you specifically." Pause. "No, I tried, but they won't tell me." Pause. "I need a name," she said in an I-told-you-so tone.

"Patricia Littlefield," Mrs. McCabe said. *Perhaps she could handle the whole thing,* thought Triss. *I'll go sit in the car.*

The woman repeated the name into the phone and hung up. "He'll be out shortly," she told them curtly and turned back to her typewriter.

They sat on a chrome and vinyl sofa with flat, square cushions that were even more uncomfortable than they appeared.

"What was with the James Cagney impression?" Triss asked.

"I wanted to get in the spirit of things," Mrs. McCabe said. "Be glad I didn't call her a dirty rat."

"I think we're the rats here," Triss said.

As they waited, she remembered the night she confessed to them. She recalled thinking it was easier to tell them because they weren't part of her real life. But somehow, they had become her friends, and she was glad. She remembered what Arabella had said: "When you share your problems with friends, you cut them in half." She took their hands and gave them a little squeeze. Everlove raised her eyebrows, but Mrs. McCabe smiled.

Fifteen minutes ticked by, each one chipping away at her determination. She could still leave. Flee through the glass doors and to her car. Just when she didn't think she could take any more, a man materialized in front of them, startling them with his sudden, silent appearance. Everything about him was linear and sharp, from the razor-edge crease in his pants to the keen fold of his collar to the undeviating part in his brown hair.

He glanced at each of them with no expression, his eyes finally landing on Triss. "Patricia Littlefield?"

Triss stood. "That's me. Good guess."

He didn't crack a smile. "I'm Agent Donahue."

"Yes, thank you for seeing us."

"Follow me."

The women followed him down the echoing expanse of a wide, white corridor. He led them into a small conference room and gestured at the chairs. He was not chatty. And it seemed to be catching, because Mrs. McCabe, who usually was chatty, might as well have taken a vow of silence.

Agent Donohue indicated three chairs with torn vinyl seats lined up haphazardly on one side of a scratched table. On the tabletop sat an overflowing ashtray that filled the room with the acrid ghosts of old cigarettes. The walls were bare and white, their only ornamentation an occasional scuff mark and one deep dent that made Triss wonder what had happened. As the ladies sat, Agent Donahue settled himself in the chair across the table from them. He clasped his hands and rested them in front of him. "Tell me what brings you here." His voice was even, measured, and strangely calming.

He trained his gaze on Triss, his gray eyes as sharp as the rest of him.

"I work for an attorney in Edenton, and I recently discovered he's taking kickbacks from a moonshiner." Triss waited for a reaction but got none, only a continuation of his steady, intent gaze. She cleared her throat. "And in addition to running liquor, the moonshiner runs a gambling den out of his barn. And there's also a, um . . ." She stumbled over how to describe Mrs. Blazey's line of work. ". . . a madam who makes payments to him. And he pays local law enforcement to look the other way."

He took a pen and a small notebook from his coat pocket. "Does this attorney have a name?"

"Horace Haine."

He scribbled on a page. "Do you know the name of the moonshiner? And the madam?"

"Weevil—I mean Weaver Carr. His nickname is Weevil. And Jenette Blazey."

She couldn't tell if he thought the accusations incongruous or credible. She cast about for more to tell him, then remembered the manila envelope in her bag. "I have these."

She opened the clasp, pulled out the photos, and handed them to Donahue. He scanned the pictures, one after another, his face perfectly composed. Was he impressed, bored, curious? Did he think she was a crackpot, a vengeful employee, or someone who was on to something? He placed the prints on the table and met her eyes, still giving nothing away.

"What am I looking at?"

"I'm Mr. Haine's secretary, receptionist, and bookkeeper. He has some law clients, and he owns a bunch of houses that he rents out. I take in all the payments from both and keep the office ledgers. I write out checks for his signature for repairs, office supplies, utilities—all his expenses, and I record those in the ledger as well. He also has a petty cash box for small purchases. That is also meticulously accounted for. He has two other employees besides me, and I write out their paychecks and mine. But I discovered this second ledger that he keeps in a safe next to a rather substantial amount of cash. These initials"—she stabbed at the two sets—"match the names of his other two employees, but the payments noted are different from the checks I have written."

"What are the names of these two other employees?" Agent Donahue asked.

She ticked them off. "Copper Cavanaugh and Sheridan Rudd."

"Is Copper his real name?"

"His real name is William."

"Anything else you can tell me?"

She described the duffel bag scenes she had witnessed. And some things she had overheard. "I have also heard Haine tell Copper to take money to the sheriff. And I once saw him hand Copper the money."

He made a note, then his eyes traveled from Mrs. McCabe to Everlove. "And your friends here? Do they have any knowledge of this?"

"No. They're here for moral support," Triss said.

"Maybe you can tell us what you plan to do with the information Miss Littlefield has provided you," Mrs. McCabe said.

"We will look into it."

"Does that mean you'll look into it as you throw it into File Thirteen? Or you will look into it and open an investigation?"

"I'm not at liberty to say. And I would appreciate it if you would not say anything about this to anyone outside of this room. Is there anything else?"

"No, that's it," Triss said.

Agent Donahue reached into his shirt pocket and slid a business card across the table. "Thank you for coming in, Miss Littlefield. Here's my name and contact information. Where can I reach you if I have more questions?"

She gave him her number, which he jotted in his notebook. Mrs. McCabe cleared her throat. He glanced up at her, raising his eyebrows, which was the first expression to cross his face since he had introduced himself.

"May I have one as well?" she asked.

He pulled out another card and handed it to her, then gave Everlove a questioning glance. Everlove shook her head. "I'm good," she said.

He stood, and the women rose with him. They followed behind him as he led them to the lobby. Mrs. McCabe attempted small talk. "Lovely weather we are having for January, isn't it?"

"Yes," Agent Donahue said. They reached the front door, and he held it open for them. "Thank you for coming. Have a nice day."

As they walked toward the car, Triss said, "I don't know what I was expecting, but I feel oddly let down."

"He had quite the poker face, didn't he?" Everlove said.

"He did. But he was also rather handsome, don't you think?" Mrs. McCabe said.

"He wasn't too bad," Triss said. "But so serious."

Mrs. McCabe moved on to another topic. "And I am seriously hungry. Ratting out Mr. Haine to the feds worked up my appetite. Anyone else?"

"You know he's a state agent, not a federal one, right?"

"Potayto, potahto. I know a little hamburger place that's right on the way home . . ."

They stopped at a little unprepossessing building on the outskirts of Columbia. The interior was no more impressive than the outside, but the juicy burgers and hot, crisp fries were delicious.

"What now?" Everlove asked.

"Good question. I have no idea. I hoped the agent would give us some hint of what might happen next," Triss said.

"We wait. These things take time," Mrs. McCabe said. "We just have to be patient."

"Patience is not my strong suit," Triss said.

"Now would be a good time to practice it."

"You sound like my grandfather."

"We old folks are wiser than you young folks give us credit for."

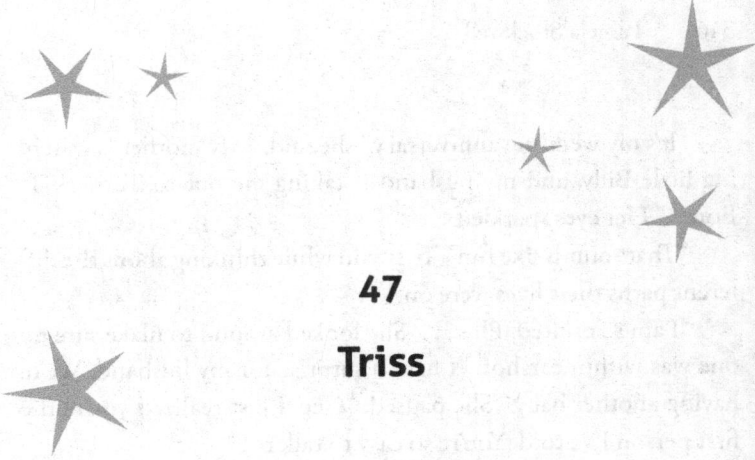

47

Triss

Wednesday, January 3, 1973–Saturday, January 6, 1973

Because the meeting with the SCID agent had not given Triss any hint as to what was going to happen, she was able to go back to work without too much anxiety. But while that was at bay, her dislike of Haine had built up to enormous proportions, and she couldn't wait to quit. This time, though, she was determined not to do her usual rushing in. She went to work every day but combed the help wanted ads at night. And on Friday, when Haine left earlier than she did, she stuck a few items in her handbag to take home: a jar of hand cream, a lipstick, her stenography manual. Doing that little bit gave her a sense that there was light at the end of the proverbial tunnel. Afterwards, she went about her evening routine, then grabbed the weekly deposit and locked up.

She waved to the deputy who still followed her, and he raised a hand in acknowledgement. At the bank, Misti beckoned her over, more bubbly than usual.

"It's my wedding anniversary," she said. "My mother is watching little Billy, and my husband is taking me out to Turner's T-Bones." Her eyes sparkled.

"That sounds like fun," Triss said while thinking about the different paths their lives were on.

"I am so excited. Plus . . ." She looked around to make sure no one was within earshot. "I have a surprise for my husband. We're having another baby." She paused. "Gee, I just realized you're the first person I've told. You're so easy to talk to!"

"I'm flattered. And congratulations," Triss said. "I hope you have a wonderful evening."

"Thank you!" She leaned forward. "And definitely don't mention it here, or they'll fire me. I want to work as long as I can."

"Mum's the word," Triss said. An easy promise, as who would she tell?

She exited the bank and walked next door to the five-and-dime to pick up a few necessities, and as she did, she pondered that even in 1973, women were still afraid of being fired for getting pregnant. It made her want to burn her bra along with the protesters at the Miss USA pageant a few years back. She couldn't deny there'd been progress, but it was more like hairline fractures rather than earth-shattering change. She grabbed the items she needed and got in line. The woman in front of her was arguing about an item that was supposed to be on sale, but the clerk had rung it up for the regular price. Triss repressed the urge to tap her foot. The issue was finally resolved, and the customer walked away ten cents richer.

Triss made her purchases, left the store, and headed to her car in the bank parking lot, but immediately stopped, heart pounding.

Copper's truck was parked near hers. Damn it. When would he leave her alone?

She resumed walking, trying to keep her pace steady and her breathing slow. She turned at the sound of the door opening. Relief swept through her as Misti stepped outside, throwing a cheerful goodbye over her shoulder to the manager who let her out. She spotted Triss. "Hi again!"

"Hello. You'll have to tell me all about your evening the next time I see you," Triss said, more to keep Misti near her than because she was that invested in the anniversary celebration. Misti stayed in step with her as they neared Triss's car.

"Oh, I will," Misti said. "And you must meet my husband!"

"Sure. I'd like that."

Misti walked up to Copper, who had stepped out of the truck. She threaded her arm through his. Triss suppressed a gasp, blinking as Copper gave Misti a peck on the cheek. Triss was nonplussed. As she fumbled for a socially acceptable reaction, Misti said, "Honey, this is my favorite customer, Triss. Triss, this is my husband, Billy."

His eyes had widened, but other than that, he kept his surprise in check. She hoped her face was as unreadable as his because she was confounded. Copper was Misti's husband? Before she could think of anything to say, Copper thrust out his hand. "Pleased to meet you. Any friend of Misti's is a friend of mine."

Even as her brain struggled to make sense of this new development, her mother's training took over. "Pleased to meet you, too," she said, because what else could she say? "I understand you two have plans, so I will let you go. Y'all have a good evening," she said.

Was she imagining things, or did he shoot her a grateful glance as he escorted Misti to the passenger side of the truck?

Triss got into her own car and sat, stupefied. Billy. Billy was Copper and Copper was Misti's husband and Copper was William Cavanaugh who's name she wrote on checks on paydays. Did Misti not know where he worked? All this time, as Triss made the deposits with checks made out to Horace Haine or to Edenton Development Corporation, Misti had never said, "Oh, you must work with my husband." Odd.

Everlove was working, so when Triss got home, she heated some leftover soup, navigating on autopilot as she kept turning the situation over in her mind. Billy. Copper. Misti. How on earth could someone as sweet as Misti marry someone as sleazy as Copper? She considered what she knew about Misti and her family. Little Billy's recent bout of croup, the time he got into the Vaseline jar and smeared it all over himself and the crib and the wall. About her husband Billy who sometimes brought her flowers. Triss was surprised at how much she had gleaned from five-minute conversations every Friday. Except who Misti's husband actually was.

She washed her dishes and scribbled a note for Everlove, telling her she was turning in early. She read for a while, or tried to. The sound of Everlove returning home jolted Triss. She had dozed off, her book abandoned on her stomach. She set aside the book, turned out the light, and slept fitfully. And during one of her wakeful moments, she sat straight up as she realized that Misti and little Billy—and the little Cavanaugh growing in Misti's womb—might be swept up in the investigation she had possibly initiated.

Her mother's words came back to her, and they still rang true. She still hadn't learned to fix the wrongs in the world without making things worse.

When Triss woke the next morning, Everlove was already gone. Everlove had told her she had almost enough money to repair the door on her car, and she was determined to have it fixed sooner rather than later, so she was working like a fiend these days. Triss puttered around the house and pondered what to do about Copper and his family. *Dammit. Just when I think I'm really and truly doing the right thing, I find out I am, as usual, making a huge mess.*

Close to noon, a knock sounded at her door, and the object of her worry stood on her porch. Copper himself, in the flesh. And suddenly, he was not a villain, but a man, still unlikable, but with a family and insecurities and secrets and possibly a good trait or two.

"Can I help you?" Triss asked.

"Yeah." He nodded at the interior of her house. "Mind if I come in?"

She shrugged and opened the door wider. "I think you know your way around." She didn't invite him to sit, but waited, arms crossed.

"Misti doesn't know where I work," he said, sweeping his hat off his head. "She hates Mr. Haine. Well, as much as Misti can hate anyone. He evicted her cousin's family right before I met her. I was doin' odd jobs for Haine then, but not what I do now. And once I got to know her, I couldn't tell her."

"But you still took a job where you evict people?"

"As long as they ain't white, ain't no skin off my teeth," he said.

"They're people," Triss hissed, wanting to choke him.

"Shoulda known you're one of those."

"One of those what?"

"Never mind. Anyway, Misti thinks I work in a warehouse. Which I do. I do jobs for Haine when I am not working there. I'm puttin' aside what I make from him so Misti and me never leave our boy the way . . . well, I aim to make sure he's taken care of."

"But I write out your paychecks. How could Misti not know?"

"I have a separate account at another bank, so I don't have to tell her I'm working for him."

Triss considered this. Thought of what was about to happen. Thought of Misti's happy face and deep dimples. The look of love when she gazed up at Copper. The picture of little Billy displayed at Misti's station, with his dimples and cheeky grin. Copper saying evicting Black people was okay.

She sighed. She would toss Copper to the wolves in a heartbeat. But she couldn't do that to Misti and her growing family.

"I have something to tell you, and I'm only telling you because of Misti," she said.

Copper raised his eyebrows.

"The SCID may be investigating Haine."

Copper's eyes narrowed. "What?" he spit the word. He was all venom now.

Triss swallowed, trying not to look intimidated. "SCID may be looking into his business dealings with Carr and others."

"Is that why you took this job? To rat him out?"

"No, actually. But they've talked to me. And I'm sure they'll be around to talk to you soon." She was stretching the truth so far that she was afraid it might snap.

"Shit." Copper rubbed his chin. "Shit."

"If I were you, I'd disentangle myself as fast as I could."

They both jumped as someone pounded on the door. Triss opened the door to find a scowling Mr. Pritchard.

"Want me to get rid of that scum?" He inclined his head toward Copper.

"Actually, no. Not this time. And I'm pretty sure this is the last time he'll be dropping by."

Copper nodded. "It will be. Nice to see you again. Without duct tape." Triss could see how he used his swagger as a cover. He was shaken by what she had told him, but he wasn't about to let Mr. Pritchard see that.

"I had something more memorable in mind for this time," Mr. Pritchard said. "You sure you're good?" he asked Triss.

"I'm sure," she said.

"All righty then. I'll be going." He furrowed his brow. "And you better be, too," he said to Copper.

"I was just leaving."

Mr. Pritchard turned to go, and Copper was about to follow him when Triss put a hand out and touched his arm, then recoiled as if she had tapped a . . . well, a copperhead. "You should contact a lawyer," she said. *Oh, the irony of it all.*

Copper bobbed his head and his hat on it. "I knew you were more trouble than a bag of wet cats," he said. "Knew it all along." He adjusted the bill of his cap as he walked out.

48

Everlove

Saturday, January 6–Friday, February 9, 1973

That night, Everlove and Triss sat on the sofa, sipping wine.

"So something happened last night and today," Triss said, and she told Everlove about Copper being Misti's husband and how he had come to talk to her and she'd let him know there might be an investigation. "I think he'll be too preoccupied with his own problems to worry about what happened to Haine's money."

"Aren't you worried he'll tell Haine?"

"Not really. I think he'll be more worried about what happens to him and his family. His wife is the sweetest person on the planet. I worry about what will happen to her and the kids. I told him to get a lawyer. Best-case scenario is he tells what he knows about Haine's activities and gets a reduced sentence for his part in them."

"If he does that," Everlove said, "SCID will have to investigate."

"In light of all this, how do you feel about staying here?"

"Considering I have yet to gather up the courage to face my mother, I'd say pretty good."

"Really?" Triss asked, sitting up and grinning. "That would be great!" She tapped Everlove's glass. "Here's to being roommates for a while longer."

They fell silent for a bit, and then Everlove spoke up. "It's a shame we couldn't find any proof about what happened to Marjanne."

"Yeah, I agree. What do you think happened to her?" Triss asked. "Do you think he killed her, or do you think it was an accident and they covered it up?"

"I'm leaning toward an accident," Everlove said. "I can't stop thinking about her." She still saw the dark eyes, so full of life despite being captured in murky newspaper ink.

"I can understand that. It doesn't seem fair her life was cut short. And it doesn't seem fair she was basically erased."

Everlove agreed, but she also knew there were thousands of people like Marjanne who left barely a ripple in the ocean of life. Her ancestors, for example. Slaves who were sold away from their families, leaving only memories that faded with time. They were born, they breathed, they died and were most likely buried in unmarked graves, their lives coming and going like ethers.

"Why don't you write about her?" Triss's words shattered Everlove's reverie. "You like writing, and you obviously have a knack for it."

"I don't think so. There's more to writing about someone than putting words on paper."

"Did you write term papers in high school?"

"Sure, but—"

"Then you have some idea of how to research. You interview a couple of people—Mrs. Baxley-Picket, for starters."

"I doubt she would talk to me," Everlove objected.

"Mrs. McCabe and I will help."

"But if I don't do it on my own . . ." Everlove said.

"No one does anything in a vacuum. My grandfather is part of a whole network of attorneys. They often help each other. Mrs. McCabe and I can be your network."

"But what would I even do with it?"

"Take it to Columbia and present it to the newspaper or the monthly magazine."

"I don't have any credentials."

Triss shrugged. "You won't ever have any if you don't try to get some. What have you got to lose?"

Later, it occurred to Everlove exactly what she had to lose: the nebulous dream she didn't let herself think too hard about. If she tried to get her writing published and failed, her hope would evaporate like mist on a summer morning. But she remembered what Mrs. McCabe said: *Not being successful a few times isn't failing*. Giving up is failing. And what good is a dream if you don't work toward fulfilling it?

She also wondered if she got the story published whether her mother would be proud of her. Would it break down the wall between them?

She pushed the thought away. She was investing too much into one article that wasn't an article yet.

Still, the idea nagged at her. What if she wrote it? What was the worst that could happen? That it didn't get published? Only a handful of people would ever have to know.

Like always, she was overthinking.

Maybe it was time to change.

As the three women waited to see if anything would come from their visit to SCID, Everlove tentatively began researching the short life and tragic death of Marjanne Sadler. Mrs. McCabe smoothed the way for her to interview Mrs. Baxley-Picket. Everlove bought a new outfit to look as professional as possible, wishing she could change her skin color as easily as a blouse. But if Mrs. Baxley-Picket was not keen on talking to a Black woman, she did not show it. Instead, she seemed intent on unburdening herself of the secret she had carried for fifty years.

Everlove did not have the same luck with Paul Sullivan, at least not at first. She couldn't tell if it was because she sounded Black on the phone or because he simply didn't want to talk about the past. But she told him she had interviewed Mrs. Baxley-Picket and was proceeding with the story, and that his name would be mentioned, so if he wanted to share his point of view, now was the time. She surprised herself with her persuasiveness. He asked where it would be published, and she hedged, telling him she wasn't at liberty to say. He accepted this and agreed to talk to her. The interview was quick and to the point and she was on and off his porch—he had not invited her in—so fast, her seat didn't have time to get warm. His recollection matched Mrs. Baxley-Picket's in all essential details.

Next on the list was Triss's grandfather. Triss, with some trepidation, called him and persuaded him to talk to Everlove.

When Everlove drove up to Triss's grandfather's house, her mouth dropped open. The house, with its wide veranda, black shutters, and bold Ionic columns, loomed over the circular driveway. Triss came from this? Everlove knew her grandfather was wealthy, but this . . . whew. She reminded herself that no matter how grand the house was, the people inside were just as buffeted by misfortune and misunderstanding as any other family. But it was hard to believe.

She rang the bell. A tall, slender woman answered the door.

"Hi. I, uh, I'm here to speak with Mr. Littlefield. I have an appointment."

"Of course. Please come in."

As Everlove stepped into the titanic entryway, a voice echoed down a set of stairs that rose in an elegant curve to the second floor.

"Miss Porter. Right on time."

Everlove stopped herself from gawking at the scale of everything: the rooms that branched off the main hall, the staircase with its carved banister, the Oriental rug under her feet. She thought her parents' entire house would fit into the parlor to her right.

Mr. Littlefield led her into a study stuffed with books and leather. He bade her to sit in one of the two club chairs as he settled into the other one. He was tall, lean, had a strong jaw—much like Triss's—and under thick white eyebrows sat brown eyes that were surprisingly kind in his otherwise stern face.

"My granddaughter tells me you want to ask me about the night Marjanne Sadler disappeared," he said, appraising her.

"Yes, I'm writing an article about it."

"Why now?"

"I stumbled upon her story, and I think she deserves to be heard in spite of all these years."

He nodded.

"Can you tell me about that night?" Everlove asked.

And he did. His story meshed with Mrs. Baxley-Picket's. With Mr. Sullivan's. He didn't remember the singing of the state song, though he acknowledged with a slight smile it sounded plausible.

"I understand the group split up at that point. What happened then?"

"Louise was not feeling well, and I offered to drive her home. The rest stayed there."

"Were Horace and Marjanne there with the others when you left?"

"Not where we could see them, but I figured they had wandered ahead."

"And when you came back?"

"The night was over, apparently. I got back, and Ethel and Paul were ready to go. If nothing else had happened, it would have been a weak ending to a pleasant summer. Unfortunately, it turned out to be a tragic ending."

"Were you concerned about leaving Horace and Marjanne?"

"Not at all. We'd been palling around together all summer."

"So you didn't worry about the impropriety? Or her safety?"

"I'm afraid I didn't. Horace did not come across as the kind of person who would compromise her honor. To my younger self, anyway. I've since learned people can surprise you in both good and bad ways."

"What do you think did happen?"

"I won't sully the waters by making assumptions I can't support."

"But there does appear to have been a cover-up."

He glanced up at the ceiling. "Ah, the changing stories of Ethel and Paul. That doesn't confirm or negate it being an accident. But people back then made more of reputations than they do today. A tarnished one could break someone."

"You and Horace didn't remain friends after that night. Why is that?"

"Horace and I were not birds of a feather, despite our similar backgrounds and social standing. We look at the world differently. Then and now."

She asked a few more questions, then closed her notebook.

"I do appreciate you taking the time to talk to me, Mr. Littlefield."

"It was no trouble at all." He stood. "I wish you luck with the article. My granddaughter spoke quite highly of you. If I can put in a word somewhere, let me know. I am not without influence in the publishing world."

"Thank you. I'll keep that in mind."

Everlove stood on the bottom step of the library, gathering her courage. On her last visit, she had felt distinct hostility from Eunice, the reference librarian. But the other librarian, Mary, had seemed friendly enough. She would start there. She might have to recruit Mrs. McCabe or Triss to ask for microfilm if it came to that.

She found Mary checking out a stack of books for an older woman. Everlove waited patiently until she was done, then approached her.

"Hi. I don't know if you remember, but I came in a couple of months ago with an older lady . . ."

"I do remember. She was asking about that poor Marjanne Sadler."

"That's right. I was wondering if you had any records from the mill from the early 1900s."

"That's a question for the reference librarian. She's right over there."

"Here's the thing. I don't think she'd be willing to help me. Is there anyone else?"

"Nonsense! Peggy would be happy to help."

"Peggy?" Everlove asked. She glanced at the reference desk and saw a young woman sorting books, and she was definitely not Louise. Everlove's heart lifted. "Where's Eunice?"

"She doesn't work on Wednesdays and Saturdays."

Good to know, Everlove thought. "Thank you."

Mary was right. Peggy was happy to help. She brought out the microfilm canister, and as she set it up for Everlove, she said, "We are very fortunate to have these. When the mill was sold, the new owners didn't want the old records, so they gave them to the library. They sat moldering in boxes for a while. Then about ten years ago, a group of college students worked all summer to photograph them to preserve them. This even has a table of contents."

The table of contents was a godsend. There were categories for financial records, disputes, strikes, and what Everlove sought: employment records. She found six Sadlers, and, to her surprise, one was Marjanne. She had worked there from 1914 until 1919. Everlove knew from the newspaper article that Jared Sadler was her father. Going by the dates of employment, she guessed Edna was probably Marjanne's mother. There was also an Elmer, Virgil, and Lloyd. All the other Sadlers except Marjanne left their employment at the mill in 1921.

She thanked Peggy as she returned the film.

Once Everlove had names to track down, she headed to the section of the library that held phone books from Edenton and surrounding towns. She remembered what Mary had said about the family moving away in a Tin Lizzie. She had a hunch they didn't move far—they probably had roots in the area. And just to make sure she didn't overlook the obvious, she checked Edenton first. There were twelve Sadlers listed, though none matched the names she had jotted down. She added those names and phone numbers to her list as possible leads but checked other phone books, hoping for a direct hit. And sure enough, she found Elmer and Virgil in Columbia.

She called Elmer first, and he agreed to talk to her, so she drove to Columbia on her day off. The surprise on his face when he opened the door was unmistakable. But in case she misunderstood it, he voiced it.

"You're the one writing an article on Marjanne? I didn't expect a Black gal."

She mustered all the confidence she could. "I am. I'm Everlove Porter. Thank you for agreeing to see me.

He stepped outside, letting the screen door bang shut. "I reckon we'll talk out here," he said.

They settled in some old creaking chairs, and Everlove asked him what he remembered about the night Marjanne disappeared. "I remember my ma being real upset that Sunday when she saw Marjanne hadn't slept in her bed. Marjanne had never stayed out before. Ma went to the sheriff, but he didn't want to do anything on account of Marjanne was nineteen, but Ma put up a fuss, so they asked around. They found who she'd been with and asked them about her. I don't remember much, honestly. But I remember when they found her. Ma fainted and took to her bed for days. Pa didn't think it was an accident, and he went down to the sheriff's office and lit into him about it. I'd followed Pa, and I saw him yelling at the sheriff, and he threw a punch at him, and so the sheriff threw him in a cell to cool off. I ran home and told Ma, and she and me both hightailed it back there. The sheriff brought us and Daddy into a little old room where Mr. Haine himself stood. He shook Pa's hand and said, 'I am terribly sorry this happened. Such a dreadful accident. But I want to help you out. Your family's been working in my mill for a couple of generations, isn't that right?' Pa said, 'Yessir, that's right.' 'Well, I take care of my people. I'm going to give you a car and a little money, and you can start new somewhere else. Somewhere you won't always be reminded of your tragic loss. And I'll pay for Marjanne's funeral.'"

"What did you think about that?"

Elmer shrugged. "Mr. Haine owned the mill and pretty much owned us. We had a company store debt, and he forgave that too. My daddy was sad about Marjanne, but I'm pretty sure he knew there wasn't nothing he could do about it." He paused for a moment. "I do remember one more thing. Mr. Haine, he told Pa that it would be best not to tell people about this, because then they'd come asking for things."

"And what do you think about it now?"

Elmer looked off into the distance. "I reckon his son was responsible for Marjanne's so-called accident and that's why he wanted us gone. He thought money would make up for it. Maybe it did in his books. It didn't in ours, but what could we do?"

"What's one thing you remember about Marjanne?"

Elmer smiled. "Her laugh. I can barely picture her face or hear her voice. But I remember she had this laugh that made you want to laugh right along with her. She was a good sister."

"Thank you for talking to me."

"Will you let me know where I can read this when it comes out?"

Everlove sucked in her breath since she didn't even know *if* it would come out. "I certainly will," she said, wondering if she should cross her fingers behind her back.

At home, Everlove spread out her notes and began writing. Sometime later, Triss walked in, and Everlove shook her head to bring herself into the present. She had been in the space she loved when she wrote her poetry—a creative trance where she was out of body and out of time.

"Sorry to interrupt," Triss said. "You look like you were really concentrating."

"I was, but I need a break, so it's good."

"Are you working on the article, by any chance?"

"I am."

"And..."

"You know what? I think it's going pretty well."

Triss grinned. "I knew you could do this." She glanced at the table and the scattered pages. "Do you need a typewriter?"

"Yeah, I was going to ask around and see if someone had one I could borrow."

"We have one. I'll get it tomorrow. No one is using it right now."

"Thanks, Triss."

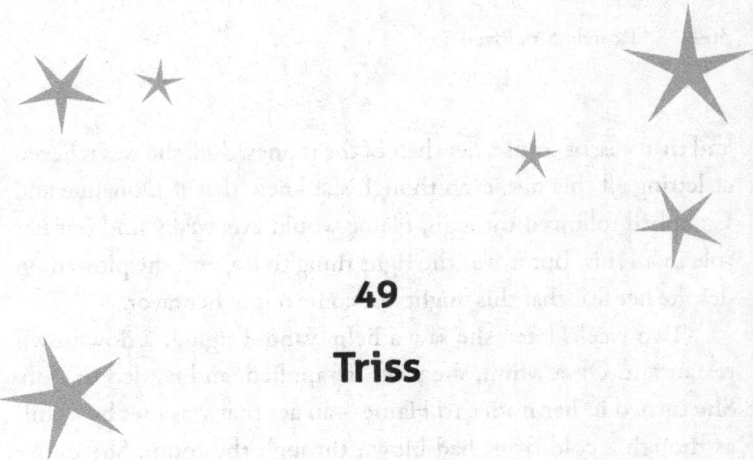

49

Triss

Monday, January 15–Wednesday, March 6, 1973

On the evening of Monday, January 15, Agent Donahue called Triss at home and asked if she could come in to make a formal statement. They set a time, and as Triss dropped the handset into the cradle, she knew she would have to resign soon. Not quite yet, but she doubted she would be there for more than one more rent cycle.

She took Wednesday morning off and drove to Columbia alone. Mrs. McCabe offered to go with her, but this was something Triss needed to do on her own. She met with Donahue and another agent named Lester Campbell. Campbell was older than Donahue by a good twenty years and looked like he hadn't trusted anything since he was in short pants. And as they questioned her, his skepticism did not dissipate.

Triss told them everything she knew. Why she had gone to work for Haine. When she began to suspect he was involved in something illegal. What she had seen and when. She only held one thing back, and that was, of course, her theft of the money. Still, she was relieved at letting all this out, even though she knew that if Donahue and Campbell followed through, Haine would eventually find out her role in all this. But it was the right thing to do, and she plowed on despite her fear that this might not come out in her favor.

Two weeks later, she saw a help wanted sign at a downtown restaurant. On a whim, she went in, applied, and landed the job. She turned in her notice to Haine—an act that was met by a chill as though a cold front had blown through the room. She didn't think for a minute it sprang from anything more than the inconvenience she was causing him.

At the end of February, she went to her mailbox to get the newspaper. She casually glanced at the headline, and her feet stopped moving.

Law Office Raided!
The law office of prominent Edenton attorney Horace Haine was raided—

The words blurred, and Triss's legs nearly gave out. She ran into the house and almost trampled Everlove, who was coming out of her bedroom.

"Whoa! What's wrong?" Everlove said.

Instead of answering, Triss held up the paper. Her hands shook so much that Everlove had to take it to read the words.

"Oh my," Everlove said. "Oh my goodness."

They both collapsed on the sofa and read the short piece.

The law office of prominent Edenton attorney Horace Haine was raided on Tuesday, February 27, by a dozen officers from the South Carolina Investigative Department. Officials declined to comment on the nature of the raid, and Mr. Haine was not taken into custody.

The article had little other new information except the officers had taken out scores of boxes. It went on to talk about Haine's accomplishments but no word on the nature of the raid.

"I can't believe this is actually happening," Triss said.

"Are you worried?" Everlove asked.

"I can't say I'm not. But I'm also glad. I really wasn't sure if this would lead to anything. But this is huge."

The next day, another article about Haine ran and mentioned an informant who had "turned state's evidence."

"Is this you or Copper?" Everlove asked.

Triss stared at the words. "I think it must be Copper. Turning state's evidence means admitting guilt and testifying against someone else."

"Wow. So he did that to protect his family like you hoped."

"I reckon he did." Relief and dismay tangled themselves up in Triss's heart. Relief that Copper was doing what he could for Misti and his kids, and dismay that he put them in this position. That she had helped put them in this position.

News of the raid spread through the state, and other newspapers and news channels picked up the story. Some tracked Triss down and tried to question her, but she no-commented them all.

Talk about it was everywhere. Apparently there are few things more titillating than a glimpse of the dirty laundry of a powerful white man.

Still, the wheels of justice may as well have been square given how quickly they turned. But turn they did. And while the investigation of Horace Haine and his associates proceeded slowly, the repercussions did not. Haine's law business dried up. Jay heard—his ear pressed tightly to the grapevine—that the development company that had been interested in Cumbee Creek backed out and found an alternative property northeast of Columbia. Triss hoped they would use more ethical means to obtain the land.

At her new job, the work was hard but the tips were generous. One day, after working the lunch shift, she came home and lay on her bed, propping her feet on the wall to ease their throbbing. Her phone rang, and she groaned. She didn't want to talk to anybody. What she wanted was a nap. But she answered it anyway, surprised to hear her grandfather's voice on the line. She had told him she had quit working for Haine but didn't say why or that there might be an investigation. Now, his voice came across the line inviting her to dinner, and she was sure he wanted to ask what she knew about the investigation and Haine's crooked business dealings.

At the appointed hour, she stood on the veranda, hand on the doorknob, summoning courage to face him. She had taken on Horace Haine, so she should be able to handle her grandfather. And what else could he do? He'd already kicked her out and cut her off. There was nothing left except . . . blackballing her from the legal community for all time. Fine. She'd manage this without him. She'd move to another state if she had to.

She had dressed carefully, choosing an outfit that was both modern and modest—a nearly impossible feat these days. Jay was out, so it was just Grandfather and her and the very large elephant in the room. Grandfather always insisted they not discuss business over dinner and certainly didn't allow uncomfortable family discussions. They talked of books read and movies seen while Triss squirmed, wishing he'd just question her and get it over with.

After dinner, Triss followed Grandfather's tall, unyielding back into the parlor. He offered her a sherry, and she accepted, glad for a little liquid courage.

"Have a seat, Patricia."

She perched on the edge of a mint-green sofa and crossed her ankles. Her mother would have been proud.

Grandfather cleared his throat. "You know I have not approved of your . . . decisions during the last year or so." She resolutely kept herself from looking away. "I believed what you were doing was unbefitting a daughter of the Littlefield house. We have never been a family where women had to work. And law can be a very dirty business."

Despite her best intentions to not let him irk her, her anger rose like mercury on a hot day.

He put his hand up as she opened her mouth. "Allow me to finish." She closed her mouth. She would listen to him, and then she would have her say.

"But that was my thinking in the past. Now, you have shown me I may have held a narrow view of the world."

Triss blinked at him, resisting the urge to tilt her head and hit her ear to dislodge whatever it was that was causing her to mishear him.

"Perhaps ladies—women," he continued, "can work outside the home. I've done a bit of reading since you moved out. What I am seeing is women moving into newsrooms. Into courtrooms. Into boardrooms. I still don't think the majority of females are suited for that sort of environment. But I will consider that perhaps you might be one who is."

It was the most tentative of turnarounds, full of obfuscations and switchbacks, but . . . he had yielded a small strip of his staunchly held territory. She never would have dreamt he could concede even that tiny piece of ground. She hoped it was enough land to begin building a bridge.

"I don't know what to say," Triss said, wishing she could live up to his newfound faith in her abilities with some profound words. But all she came up with was: "What changed your mind?"

"I have it on good authority that a certain witness may be related to me."

Triss swallowed. "I, uh—"

He raised his eyebrow at her. She stopped talking, still fumbling for how to explain the recent events. "Many of us in the legal community have abhorred Horace Haine's business practices," her grandfather continued. "We knew what he was up to, but no one lifted a hand to restrict or censure him. I will grant you there are many who didn't want to stop him as his profits often helped them. When you went to work for him, I was afraid you would end up sullied by his sordid dealings. I never once imagined you would be the one to bring him to a standstill."

Deep inside her, a bud of pride erupted, bloomed, and glowed, as bright as any blossom in full summer.

"I did have help."

"No one does anything of consequence without the aid of others. It's the quality of the people they attract that matters." She wondered what he would say if she told him the people she attracted were a bossy elderly lady and a shy Black woman. He drank the last of his brandy and set the glass on the table. "I used to call your father Don Quixote. It was meant as an insult, I'm afraid. One I hoped would snap him out of his desire to help others at the expense of the family fortune." He gazed at a portrait of one of their ancestors looming over the fireplace. "And then he died, and what was my fortune worth then? I would have given it all to have him back and all the derisive, divisive words we exchanged erased." He returned his attention to Triss. "You and I are more alike than either of us would care to admit," he said, a gentle smile turning up the corners of his mouth. "You are driven. Stubborn. And apparently so am I. But your kind heart comes from your father. Perhaps you can teach an old dog new tricks."

Triss cast about for something to say in the face of his unexpected—and unprecedented—humility. "Thank you, Grandfather," she said. Her eyes stung, and it wasn't from the alcohol.

Her grandfather walked to the bar. He held up the bottle of sherry, but she shook her head. She didn't need alcohol loosening the tentative hold she had on her emotions. He cleared his throat again and squared his shoulders as he poured himself another brandy.

"Perhaps you could move back in," he said, taking a sip from his glass.

She imagined moving back into her room. Her soft bed. Meals made by Georgina. The warm security that had always enveloped her here, even after the horrible accident. No more palmetto bugs. But . . . no more Everlove? Or Mrs. McCabe? Of course, she could visit them. But Everlove needed a roommate. And living in her little trailer had given her a sense of pride and accomplishment. She realized she wanted to hold on to that feeling. That *I-did-this* feeling.

"Grandfather, I appreciate the offer. But I think I'd like to stay in my little place."

He turned to her. Did she imagine an almost imperceptive sagging of his face, his shoulders? He was aging. The knowledge pulled at her heart, and she almost changed her mind. She rose and walked over to him, placing her hand in his arm. "It isn't because I don't love you or that I'm still angry. But I have a roommate I don't want to leave hanging. And also—mostly—it's because living on my own makes me feel . . . strong. I like the independence. Not just being able to come and go without checking with someone. But . . ." She groped for the right words.

He placed his hand over hers, pressing it into his forearm. He smiled down at her, the lines around his mouth and eyes softening. "I understand. I don't know if I ever told you about how my father and I did not get along. He wanted to control every aspect of my life. Even tried to marry me off to a colleague's daughter as if we were European royalty strengthening our alliances." He guided her back to her seat. "Perhaps I'm more like him than I ever wanted to be," he said as he sat. He placed his drink on the table and leaned back into the wingback chair. "Do you think it's too late for an old man to change his stripes?"

"I don't think you have much to change. All I ask is for you to understand I can do anything a man can. I'm smart. I enjoy researching and reading and listening to people's problems. I truly think I would make an excellent attorney."

"You don't have to ask any longer. I have seen what you are capable of."

"That's the only stripe you need to change."

50

Everlove

Monday, February 26, 1973–Wednesday, March 13, 1973

On a gray and chilly Monday morning, Everlove drove to Mr. Moon's house. She knocked on the worn wooden door and waited. She heard a chair scrape and steps shuffling, and the door creaked open. "Well, Miss Porter. What brings you to my humble home on this fine morning?"

"Fine?" Everlove asked, looking over her shoulder at the unwavering gray sky.

"Every day I'm still drawing breath is a fine one."

Everlove nodded. That was not such a bad view of the world. "I'm sure you've heard the news about Mr. Haine."

"Ayuh. This have anything to do with your last visit to me?"

"It does."

"Well, you are full of surprises. But the business he's in trouble with ain't got nothing to do with me or the time I worked for him."

"No, but a friend of mine was trying to find out anything she could, so we were asking all around. And I've decided to write an article about Marjanne. I wanted to talk to you again, but this time as a real interview."

Mr. Moon shook his head in wonder. "And there's yet another surprise coming from you." He opened the door wider. "Come on in and I'll make some coffee."

Everlove finished her article. She read it over and over. She read it out loud when Triss wasn't home. She knew she should have someone look at it for errors, but she didn't have the courage to let anyone else see it. Summoning every ounce of bravery she could possibly gather, she drove to Columbia on her day off for an appointment she had made with the editor of *The Palmetto Pulse*. When the secretary said he was ready to see her, she walked—nerves skittering like mice—into his small, brimming office. She made her pitch, her words quavering and stumbling through a cloud of cigarette smoke and ink fumes. She knew she was floundering, but there was nothing for it but to plow on and get it over with.

"Horace Haine, you say?" the editor said, showing the first flicker of interest since she entered the office.

"Yes. There's quite a question about his role in the story." She tried to explain that the article was about Marjanne more than Horace, but the editor held out his hand. "I'll give it a quick read."

Her fingers tightened on the pages as she realized part of getting published was releasing your work into the world. She felt like she was exposing her soul. And what if people didn't like it? What if they scoffed? And what if this man, so casually holding out his hand, lost the piece? She should have used carbons. But she still had her earlier drafts, typed out on Triss's typewriter. She swallowed hard and released her grip. He told her he'd get back to her but did not provide a time frame.

The next evening, after dinner, Triss was cleaning up and Everlove went to her room and changed into her flannel pajamas. She had just tied her headscarf in place when the phone rang. She didn't hear Triss answer it, so she went to the living room and grabbed the handset.

"Hello?"

"Is this Miss Porter?"

Everlove recognized the brusque, gravelly voice of the editor. "Speaking," she said, heart pounding.

"This is Mac at *The Palmetto Pulse*. Your piece is good," he said. "I'm running it in the next issue. I pay twenty-five dollars a story. You think of a good idea, run it by me. Your writing is solid."

He hung up, and Everlove let out a whoop and did a little happy dance around the living room. Triss came running down the hallway.

"Everything okay?"

"More than okay," Everlove said, grinning. "I wrote the article about Marjanne, and the editor at *The Palmetto Pulse* just called and told me he's going to run it in the next issue!"

Triss screamed and hugged her until Everlove had to wave her hands to signal she couldn't breathe.

"This is fantastic news, Everlove!" Triss said, clasping her hands and squealing like a toddler on Christmas morning. "I am so happy for you!"

"Thanks, but don't get too excited until it's out. These things can still get bumped by bigger news."

Triss snorted. "What bigger news could there be than Horace Haine being investigated? Your timing is perfect."

"Yeah, I suppose so. But I don't guess that will ever happen again."

"You never know!" Triss said.

Later that night when she lay in bed, Everlove sank into her pillow, thinking how amazing it was that someone was paying her for her writing.

Two weeks later, Everlove checked the mailbox, raking out a pile of envelopes and a *TV Guide* before spotting the glossy cover of a magazine. Her magazine. Her heart leaped in her chest. She shuffled the other mail underneath. She savored the weight of the periodical in her hand, the reality of it. Her article was inside. Her words on paper for all to see. She managed to restrain an urge to dance, but she could not suppress her grin.

She tossed the bills on the table by the door as Triss came out of her room, pulling her hair into a ponytail.

"Oh, you got the mail." She shuffled through the pile. Everlove cleared her throat, still smiling broadly. She held up the magazine.

"The magazine is here! Let's see it!"

Everlove sat on the sofa and laid the publication on her lap as Triss eased into the spot next to her. She opened the cover, flipped past a couple of ads, then stopped at the contents page. She ran her finger down the list of articles, and there it was. "The Short and Tragic Life of Marjanne Sadler" by Everlove Porter.

"Oh my word!"

Triss squealed and squeezed her arm. "I knew all along you could do this!"

They scanned the article, which included photos of Marjanne and the river where she had died. Everlove had laid out the facts but drew no conclusions, leaving it to the reader to decide what had happened. She gazed with wonder at her words in crisp type on the glossy magazine page.

The next day, Everlove bought several copies of *The Palmetto Pulse* and drove to her parents' house, arriving right before dinner.

"Everlove. What on earth are you doing here in the middle of the week?" her mother said. Avenia had thawed toward her, but frost still clung to the edges of her words.

"I want to show you something," Everlove said. She placed the magazine on the kitchen counter and flipped it open to the place she had bookmarked with a slip of notebook paper. Her mother glanced at Marjanne's picture and the type sailing across the page.

"What is this?" she asked, puzzled. "Is this someone we know?"

"The author is," Everlove said.

"The auth—oh! Everlove. You wrote this? You got your name in a magazine? Well, I'll be," her mother said. Avenia strode over to the back door and called through the screen, "James! Come in here. I got something you need to see!"

"I'm in the middle of fixing this car, Venia."

"Just come in here now. It'll only take a minute." Her voice had changed to her don't-mess-with-me voice. James came clumping in, wiping his hands on a rag so greasy, Everlove thought he was probably making his hands worse.

Everlove didn't think she'd ever had a greater moment than the one in which her parents stood oohing and aahing over her article. Over the next few weeks, Everlove's sisters told her that their mother went around the neighborhood practically browbeating everyone she met into buying a copy of *The Palmetto Pulse* or, if they couldn't scrape up the fifty cents, finding someone to borrow it from. She would not, for love or money, give up her copy.

Several days after that, Everlove drove to Alpha Auto Shop. Matthias was placing tape around the window of a car. He spotted her through the bay door.

He straightened up, appraising her as she closed the passenger-side door for what she hoped was the last time.

"Well, well. If it isn't Author Everlove."

She blushed, hoping he couldn't tell. But that sure had a better ring to it than Everleave. "Hello, Matthias."

"You here to get that fixed?" he asked, nodding at her car.

"I am."

"I'll take your key. You got a ride home?"

"I was going to walk downtown and meet my roommate when she gets off work."

"How about I drive you?"

"Shouldn't you be fixing my car?" Everlove offered him a little smile and realized she was flirting with him.

"Yeah, but a man needs a break every now and again. And maybe a bite to eat." He raised his eyebrows questioningly.

Why not, Everlove thought. The wedding was months ago. If anyone saw them, it would start tongues wagging for sure, but she was going to have to do this one day or another. "Maybe a tiny bite," she said. "A tiny, casual bite."

"Yes, ma'am."

He shouted back to someone in the garage that he'd be right back, that he was taking his break.

They walked down the street together, and Everlove wondered if she would ever lose the self-consciousness she had gained from being the talk of the town. But she knew Rodney had begun seeing Lynette Keeler, exactly as Mrs. Johnson had foreseen. And it seemed right that he started dating someone before she did. But now, perhaps it was her turn.

They split a barbecue sandwich at the stand across the way from the shop, sitting outside in the warm sunshine. According to the calendar, it was not yet spring, but the sun didn't seem to know that. As Everlove and Matthias chatted, she found she enjoyed his company. Matthias had a better sense of humor than Rodney. Guilt pinged her conscience at the thought, but Rodney could be so serious. Matthias asked her questions about herself: did she enjoy writing, how did she come across that story, what made her want to write it. Her answers were yes, that's a tale for another day, and she thought no one should be erased like Marjanne had been.

He was silent at that, then gave her a sidelong look as if unsure how she would take what he was about to say. "You know how many of our people have been erased?"

She nodded. "Countless. And in the back of my mind, I have this idea of finding some of those stories and telling them. I am not sure how yet, but I'll be looking for a way." She couldn't believe she told him that. She hadn't even told Triss.

He gave her his lopsided grin. She was suddenly reminded of that first night in Triss's trailer when she made a joke about her wedding regalia, and they had laughed and Everlove had a sense of happiness in spite of everything. That's how she felt now. She liked this new skill of appreciating where she was and when was. She needed more practice at it, but she was determined to get better.

51

Mrs. McCabe

Saturday, June 16, 1973

Mrs. McCabe sat in her pew, more dressed up than she'd been in fifteen years. The music had started, and Nick stood at the front of the church, looking like the cat's pajamas in his dress blues. Arabella's father George, home from Goose Bay, stood beside him along with Nick's old roommate, Harry Cisse, and a few of Nick's cousins and friends. They had New York accents as thick as molasses, though she knew they could say the same about her Southern one.

The music changed to the processional, and Mrs. McCabe—along with Everlove and Triss, who sat on either side of her—stood and turned as Allen, the four-year-old ring bearer, high-stepped down the aisle in a way that made Mrs. McCabe think he'd watched *The Music Man* one too many times. When he joined his father at the altar without incident, he loudly exclaimed, "I did it, Daddy!" George put a finger to his lips but gave him a wink.

The bridesmaids came next. Mrs. McCabe had been touched when Violet asked her to be one, but she told her she didn't think her knees would hold her up for the whole ceremony. Violet asked if she would at least read a verse for her, and Mrs. McCabe readily agreed. Bought a new dress and all. So instead of Mrs. McCabe, Arabella and her young, nimble knees walked up the aisle as the first bridesmaid. She had lost her baby softness, and her long, pale-blue dress disguised her coltish legs with their scabs and mosquito bites. She reminded Mrs. McCabe of herself as a girl, always climbing trees and riding her bike. Arabella caught her eye, and her face lit up in a way that swelled Mrs. McCabe's old heart. The girl gave her a tiny wave with one hand, a gesture almost hidden by the bouquet she held. Mrs. McCabe gave her a tiny wave back.

Caroline came next, along with a few other women Mrs. Mc-Cabe didn't know.

And then came the bride.

Violet marched down the aisle like a woman who knew what she wanted and wasn't afraid to go after it. Her short-sleeved dress glowed white, and the light glinted off little chiffon butterflies in different pastel hues that adorned the skirt and trailed up the bodice and over one shoulder. It was, she had to admit, a clever design, thought up by Caroline. Mrs. McCabe noticed Triss turning to Everlove and raising her eyebrows, and Everlove shrugged, but grinned. What was all that about? She'd ask them later. She didn't know why a simple white wedding dress wouldn't suffice, but young people these days had their own ideas about things. Violet's father—a bear of a man whose eyes shimmered with moisture—kissed her on her forehead and handed her off to Nick, who beamed at his bride.

Mrs. McCabe spied Mr. Pritchard further down their pew, and he gave her a curt nod. He stood stiff as a mannequin in his decades-old suit. That it was practically vintage was a positive thing, as she couldn't imagine him in what passed for suits these days, with collars like buzzard wings and colors that made your head swim. She squinted slightly, wondering if he also was a little damp around the eyes. Tommy and Joanna sat beside him. They turned to each other and smiled, and Mrs. McCabe supposed there would be another wedding soon enough.

The ceremony started. Mrs. McCabe remembered her own wedding and those of her children, both of whom had died too young. If the world were a nicer, fairer place, she would be watching her own granddaughter get married. But she pushed the useless thoughts away. She could mourn them—for the millionth time—later. And if the world had taken away her family, it had at least given her a new one. And not just Violet and Arabella and Mr. Pritchard and all the rest, but also Everlove and Triss. She reached out and squeezed their hands, and out of the corner of her eye, she saw them give her surprised looks, but she stared straight ahead at Nick, who was gazing at his bride with adoration so visible and tangible it could break your heart into a million pieces and then sew it back together. Violet radiated happiness. She who had such an early tragic loss had found love again. The world was, indeed, unfair and cruel, but sometimes it handed out gifts. You just didn't always recognize them at first.

The reception was held at a nearby hotel. Everlove, Triss, and Mrs. McCabe were joined at their table by Caroline, George, Arabella, and Baby Allen. She supposed she would call him Baby Allen for as long as she had breath in her body, though she tried not to say it in front of him. Mostly. A babysitter came to whisk him away, and he started to cry about missing all the fun, but Caroline explained that he could eat his ice cream first if he went, and he wouldn't have to sit and behave at the table with all the grown-ups. He glanced around at all the people sitting sedately in their seats. No one was running around. No one was kicking balls or playing hide-and-seek. He stuck his chubby hand in the babysitter's and turned his back on the boredom. Caroline sank into her chair, relieved.

Mrs. McCabe smiled as Mr. Pritchard, Tommy, Joanna, and Harry bent to greet her with hugs and cheek kisses before taking their seats. No one would know from looking at them that just over three years ago, she barely knew them. *This is what comes of not giving up*, she thought.

At first, talk revolved around the wedding—how beautiful the bride was, how handsome the groom. *The two of them resemble models in a wedding magazine*, Mrs. McCabe thought as she observed them at the head table, laughing and chatting as people congratulated them.

But before long, the talk turned to the investigation of Horace Haine. Harry, who had been stationed at a base in Illinois and had flown in for the wedding, asked for details. "Why didn't something this exciting happen when I lived here?" he asked.

"Our house fire wasn't exciting enough?" George asked.

"That was not the kind of excitement I meant. I rather like the kind you can watch from afar. So lay it on me."

Mrs. McCabe jumped in to explain: a greedy local power broker who was getting kickbacks from illegal gambling, prostitution, and moonshine outfits was finally being investigated.

Harry whistled. "Wow. Who knew that was going on here in this sleepy little burg. So what happened? How did he get caught?"

"An informant, apparently," Mrs. McCabe said, emanating innocence.

Harry's eyebrows climbed up his forehead. "This just gets better and better."

"Triss, you worked for him," Caroline said. "Did you have any idea this was going on?"

"I had a vague idea, but how do you prove vague ideas?" Triss said with a shrug. *She must have practiced that*, Mrs. McCabe thought. "The one thing I know is that the longer I was there, the less I liked him and what he was doing with his tenants. That's why I quit."

"What happens next?" Tommy asked. Bless his heart. At twenty-one, he probably thought himself an adult, but to Mrs. McCabe, he was still a shy, skinny kid. Twenty-one was like a shiny new penny—hardly any wear and tear at all.

"From what my brother told me, there will be a trial, unless he agrees to plead guilty," Triss said. "And somehow I don't see him doing that."

"How about we talk about something more pleasant?" Mrs. McCabe suggested. "Triss has some news about her brother, don't you, Triss?"

"I do. Jay was hired to run the community center."

"Really? I thought he was a lawyer," Caroline said.

"He was. But when they finally decided to hire a full-time director, they asked him. He jumped at the offer. He loves that place far more than he likes practicing law."

"I'm surprised they can afford it. They've always struggled financially," George said.

"I read in the paper that someone donated a nice sum of money to the center, but it was contingent on hiring a director," Caroline said.

Mr. Pritchard harrumphed, and Mrs. McCabe gave him a light kick under the table. Although perhaps it wasn't as light as she thought because he yelped. All eyes turned to him, and he waved their attention away. "Cramp," he said.

"Will he keep practicing law?" Caroline asked.

"Not for now. He says the place needs a lot of work and he has a lot of ideas," Triss said, then looked around the table. "He can always use more volunteers."

"What does the community center do, exactly?" Harry asked.

"It's a safe place for kids to hang out, but also to learn. They have different seasonal sports. Right now, it's baseball and softball."

"Ruby is not happy," Everlove said. "She loves her basketball."

"I bet Jay would let her come play on the courts whenever she wants to," Triss said. "He wants to start some classes like macrame, cooking, woodworking. Stuff like that."

"Woodworking?" Mrs. McCabe said. She turned to Mr. Pritchard and Tommy.

"Nope," Mr. Pritchard said. "Don't even look at me."

"Perhaps I'm looking at Tommy." Tommy's eyes widened like a rabbit caught in the crosshairs. "Okay, I'm looking at both of you. What a fantastic team you would make. Between the two of you, you could complete a whole sentence." Mr. Pritchard scowled. "But more importantly, you'd be helping some young person find a skill that might help them." Mrs. McCabe wanted to add "Like you did with Tommy," but she didn't want to embarrass either one of them. She knew everyone thought she said whatever she wanted, and they were kind of right, but she did sometimes hold her tongue.

Triss leaned toward Mr. Pritchard and Tommy. "I think that's a marvelous idea. And you might as well just say yes. You know how this is going to turn out."

Mrs. McCabe suppressed a smile. Only the three of them—she, Triss, and Everlove—knew where the community center's windfall had come from. Triss seemed lighter and happier now that she had relieved herself of the burden of all that cash. And relieved herself of the burden of Mr. Haine. She would still have to testify at his trial, but the media had turned its attention to Copper when he was named as the key informant.

Mrs. McCabe's gaze turned to Everlove, who was talking to Caroline about recipes. She had blossomed after her article had been published. She held her head higher and spoke up with more self-confidence. How lucky those two women were to be young at this time. They had so many more opportunities than she had at their age. Mrs. McCabe sighed about what might have been. Then shook herself out of her funk. What's done is done. And her life had not been a bad one. She had married Flynn. Had her two beautiful children. Got to travel. She would keep an eye on Triss and Everlove and make sure they found some balance. But now that she had helped them, Mrs. McCabe needed something new to occupy her. She glanced around the table, considering the possibilities. Tommy was doing well and now had Joanna. But what about Mr. Pritchard? Maybe Mr. Pritchard could use some companionship. He might be lonely. Now that would be a tough nut to crack.

Mr. Pritchard caught her looking at him and scowled. She smiled beatifically. He shook his head, as if he knew she were up to something. *He's not wrong*, she thought.

52

Triss

April–August 1973

Before Triss had quit working at Haine's law office, she had surreptitiously made a list of tenants and their addresses. Once she quit, she continued to give cash to Mrs. McCabe, who gave it to Mrs. Fontaine, who gave it to Peach, who passed it onto the tenants. She still did not want an immediate link between her and the payments and still did not like the idea of sending cash in the mail. But she wasn't as nervous as she had been before.

In April, she drove to a Columbia bank where no one would know her and took out two cashier's checks: the larger one was made out to the Edenton Community Center, and the smaller one was made out to Misti Cavanaugh. She wanted to make sure Misti could take care of her family in the coming months when Copper would be unable to work. Whether he would spend some time in jail or not remained to be seen. She had no idea what kind of deal he might have worked out.

Then August came with its melting heat.

Triss stepped into a darkened chamber, and the frigid air conditioning chilled the damp edges of her hair and turned the sweat trickling down her back to ice. But she barely noticed. She settled herself in the second row of a medium-sized auditorium. She was here. Finally, she was sitting in her first law class with eighty other hopeful young law students. Only two others were women. She heard snickering, saw some elbowing, and she leveled her gaze at the instigators. She wanted to let them know right off that they did not intimidate her in the least. Their eyes skittered away. She hid a smile.

She had earned her place here. And if she had started a year ago, she would not have had this confidence, this strength. She thought of all that had happened in the last year—moving out on her own, helping people who no one else seemed to care about, facing up to her mistakes, and taking a stand against Haine in a way that mattered. And having Everlove and Mrs. McCabe bolstering her when she faltered. All of this had poured molten steel into her spine and hardened it into something indefatigable. The road in front of her was paved with hard work. She would get tired. She would make mistakes. But she would persevere.

She had reached for the stars, and while she wasn't there, she was on her way.

Dearest Reader,

If you enjoyed *The Tender Silver Stars,* I hope you will take a moment to review it online: on Goodreads, Amazon, BookBub—wherever it is convenient for you. It doesn't have to be long. Even just a rating helps. Reviews and ratings are so important for struggling writers, so any help you can give would be greatly appreciated.

Thank you for going on my journey with me.

Author's Note

Horace Haine Junior began his criminal activities during Prohibition, but he was able to carry on after its repeal because taxes on liquor were so high. Not only was there a federal tax, but South Carolina had one of the highest tax rates in the country. Illegal distilling and distribution of liquor was profitable, and the struggle between moonshiners and law enforcement continued well after the repeal of the Eighteenth Amendment. Even when South Carolina passed a law allowing people to open microdistilleries, not everyone wanted to go legal. As late as October 2019, a still was found in Charleston County and destroyed.

In the novel, Haine and his group went to speakeasies and blind pigs. Both were establishments where one could get a drink during Prohibition. Speakeasies were usually higher class and might offer food and entertainment. Customers were encouraged to keep their voices low—in other words, to "speak easy." Blind pigs were lower class, and the owners would charge a fee to see an attraction of some sort—such as a blind pig or tiger—and the guest would get a "complimentary" drink. This enabled them to bypass the law against selling alcohol.

The Orangeburg Massacre Everlove alludes to is a real historic but little-known event. During a protest to desegregate a bowling alley, Samuel Hammond Jr. (18), Henry Smith (18), and Delano Middleton (17) were killed. Delano was a high school student and was not protesting that night. He had stopped on his way home from basketball practice to visit his mother who worked as a maid on the campus of South Carolina State College (now University). He was shot seven times. Nearly thirty more people were injured—many of them shot in the back. You can also count a fourth victim: the unborn child of Louise Kelly Cawley (27), who was beaten during the protest and miscarried the following week. This tragic event received none of the attention Kent State received two years later, when four white students were killed. Even though I grew up in South Carolina, I never heard of the event until I was well into adulthood.

Mabel Willebrandt, whom Mrs. McCabe talked about, was a real person and was the second woman to hold the position of U.S. Assistant Attorney General from 1921 to 1929. She was only the second woman to hold that position and was the highest-ranking woman in the federal government at the time. And as Mrs. McCabe said, she was indeed the person responsible for finally putting Al Capone in jail. If you'd like to read more, Jerry Summers wrote an excellent article about her on chattanoogan.com ("Al Capone's Female Nemesis—Mabel Walker Willebrandt."). Ms. Willebrandt made for an excellent role model for Triss.

Acknowledgments

Having one novel under my belt, I was determined to keep track of who offered advice, assistance, and support for this second book, but sometimes I got carried away with the writing and neglected to make immediate notes. So, to anyone I have left out, please forgive my poor memory. I apologize for any oversights.

Thank you to my critique partners: Priya Gill, Stephanie Claypool, Marina DelVecchio, Mikaela Huntzinger, Beth Brookhart Pandol, Shana Wilson, Deb Atwood, Ann Menke, and Janet Roberts. With your help, I was better able to flesh out scenes, develop characters, and work out plot issues—all of which helped make The Tender Silver Stars a better book than it might have been otherwise.

Thanks also to Gabi Coatsworth and Beth Sulzberg, who read an early draft of the novel and gave me early feedback.

Although I lived through 1972, my memory was sometimes a bit foggy, so I turned to some of my South Carolina friends for help. I want to thank Harry Little and Margaret Edwards, whom I have known since elementary school, for filling in some of the details from that time. Raymond Morgan also was a big help, especially when it came to the car references. Rachelle Barrineau rounds out this awesome group. I appreciate all of you!

As I finished my penultimate edit, my wonderful mother-in-law, Margaret Smyres Stockwell, passed away. At the celebration of her well-lived life, her grandson Kevin Wilcox told the anecdote about my mother-in-law dining with the president of South Korea. This was such an excellent story I gave it to Mrs. McCabe. So, thanks, Kevin, for telling it, and thanks, Micah, for bringing him into the family. And thanks, Margaret, for being one of my biggest fans and the best of in-laws.

Thank you to my brother-in-law, Chris, from whom I first heard the word "outlaw" to refer to in-laws, when they are just a little outside of a family discussion. Which is no slam on my in-laws, who are wonderful people and have wrapped me in love since I joined them.

Thank you to my publisher Shannon Ishizaki and her wonderful staff, especially my fantastic editor, Lauren Blue, and talented graphic designer, Jayden Shambeau. I was delighted to work with all of you and was so glad you took on my second novel.

And where would I be without my fabulous Write Inmates? Thanks to the butt-in-chair time, the unwavering support, the cheerleading, and the camaraderie of being in the same boat, I have managed to publish two books, a few poems, and an essay or two. You guys are always an inspiration.

Dad, you have been my constant star throughout my life. Thank you for being there for me and always having my back.

I can't leave out my sister Cindy and my mom Gail, who left this world too soon but who I always carry in my heart. I still miss you both so much.

And speaking of stars, my children, Kiana, Connor, Kyra, are the guiding stars of my life. I always knew that being a parent meant also being a teacher, but I had no idea it also meant being a student. I'm not always the fastest learner, but thanks for patiently instructing me.

Finally, thank you to my husband, Rich, who is my North Star: you always give me direction, guidance, and support. Thank you for reading everything I write and for always supporting me.

1970s
Themed Recipes!

HOLIDAY PUNCH

Ingredients:
- *1 (12-ounce) can frozen lemonade concentrate, thawed*
- *1 (12-ounce) can frozen orange juice concentrate*
- *1 (12-ounce) can frozen pineapple juice concentrate*
- *3 liters lemon-lime flavored soda*
- *1 orange, sliced*
- *1 (8-ounce) jar maraschino cherries*

Directions:
Combine the fruit concentrates in a large bowl or pitcher.
Mash the concentrate.
Stir in lemon-lime soda.
Pour mixture over ice in large punch bowl. Add orange slices
and cherries. *(To make this a really fun party punch, you can add a
750 milliliter bottle of whiskey or vodka!)*

CHICKEN AND RICE CASSEROLE

Ingredients:
- 4 cups cooked chopped chicken
- 2 (10.5-ounce) cans cream of chicken soup
- 1 (10.5-ounce) can cream of mushroom soup
- ½ teaspoon onion powder
- ¼ teaspoon garlic powder
- ¼ teaspoon pepper
- 1 cup water
- 1 cup milk
- 2 cups instant rice, uncooked
- 1 sleeve Ritz crackers, coarsely crushed
- 4 tablespoons butter, melted

Directions:
Preheat oven to 400°F. Lightly spray a 9×13-inch pan with cooking spray. Set aside.

Remove skin from rotisserie chicken and discard. Remove chicken meat from bones and chop.

In a large bowl, combine chopped chicken, cream of chicken soup, cream of mushroom soup, onion powder, garlic powder, pepper, water, milk, and instant rice. Pour into prepared pan.

In a separate bowl, stir together Ritz cracker crumbs and melted butter. Sprinkle over top of casserole.

Bake uncovered for 40 to 50 minutes.

DEVILED EGGS

Ingredients:
- 1 dozen eggs
- ½ cup mayonnaise
- 2 teaspoons white vinegar
- 2 teaspoons yellow mustard
- ¼ teaspoon salt
- Black pepper to taste
- Paprika, for garnish

Directions:

Place eggs in a single layer in a saucepan and cover with at least an inch of water. Heat on high until water begins to boil, then cover, turn the heat to low, and cook for 1 minute.

Remove from heat and leave covered for 14 minutes, then rinse under cold water for 1 minute.

Crack egg shells and carefully peel under cool running water. Gently dry with paper towels. Slice the eggs in half lengthwise, removing yolks to a medium bowl, and placing the whites on a serving platter.

Mash the yolks into a fine crumble using a fork. Add mayonnaise, vinegar, mustard, salt, and pepper, and mix well. Evenly disperse heaping teaspoons of the yolk mixture into the egg whites. For a fancier look, use a piping bag fitted with a star tip to add the yolk mixture to the egg white halves. Sprinkle with paprika and serve. (For easy-to-peel eggs, buy a week in advance and allow them to age in the refrigerator for 5-7 days.)

CHEESY CHICKEN AND RICE CASSEROLE

Ingredients:
- 4 tablespoons butter
- ¼ cup flour
- 2 cups shredded cooked chicken breast
- ½ tablespoon fresh minced garlic
- Salt and pepper to taste
- 2½ cups chicken broth
- 1 tablespoon olive oil
- 4 cups cooked rice
- 10.5-ounce can condensed cream of chicken soup
- ½ cup milk
- ½ cup sour cream
- 3½ cups shredded cheddar cheese, separated

Directions:

Preheat oven to 350°F. Heat butter in a large pot over medium heat until melted. Whisk in flour and cook for 1 minute. Add the chicken broth a little at a time and whisk to blend. Add the garlic, salt, and pepper and simmer until sauce is thickened.

Reduce heat to medium low and add 2 cups of cheese. Stir until melted. Turn off the heat and add the cooked chicken, cream of chicken soup, milk, sour cream, optional seasonings.

Pour into a greased 9x13 casserole dish and top with remaining cheese. Cover and bake for 25 minutes. (To add some crunch, you can melt 2 tablespoons of butter and mix with 1 cup of crumbled Ritz crackers. Add the topping to the casserole and bake uncovered for 10 additional minutes.)

PIGS IN A BLANKET

Ingredients:
- 2 (8-ounce) cans refrigerated crescent rolls
- 48 cocktail-size smoked link sausages or hot dogs (from two 14-oz packages)

Directions:

Heat oven to 375°F. Unroll both cans of the dough; separate into 16 triangles. Cut each triangle lengthwise into 3 narrow triangles.

Place sausage on shortest side of each triangle. Roll up each, starting at shortest side of triangle and rolling to opposite point; place point side down on 2 ungreased cookie sheets.

Bake 12 to 15 minutes or until golden brown, switching position of cookie sheets halfway through baking. Immediately remove from cookie sheet. Serve warm.

PIMENTO CHEESE DIP

Ingredients:
- 2 cups shredded extra-sharp cheddar cheese
- 8 ounces cream cheese, softened
- ½ cup mayonnaise
- 1 (4-ounce) jar diced pimento, drained
- ¼ teaspoon garlic powder
- ¼ teaspoon ground cayenne pepper (optional)
- Salt and pepper to taste

Directions:
Place all ingredients in a bowl and mix well. Can be served with cut vegetables or crackers or made into a sandwich.

AMBROSIA SALAD

Ingredients:
- 8-ounce container Cool Whip
- ½ cup sour cream
- 10-ounce can mandarin oranges
- 15-ounce can pineapple tidbits
- 16-ounce jar maraschino cherries
- 1 cup mini marshmallows

Directions:
Fold together the Cool Whip and sour cream in a large bowl. Fold in the oranges, pineapple, cherries, and marshmallows. Cover bowl and let chill in the refrigerator for at least 1 hour.

Award-winning author Pamela Stockwell was born in Texas and raised in South Carolina. In between, she lived in the Philippines and, along with her big sister, became fluent in Tagalog name-calling. She abandoned her foreign language studies at age five but went on to earn a BA in journalism from the University of South Carolina. She lives with her husband in central New Jersey. She is a member of the Princeton Writers Group and Women's Fiction Writers Association. Her writing has appeared in several anthologies and online literary magazines. Her first novel, *A Boundless Place*, was published in 2021 and has won several awards.